SKYEYES

Hope is the thing with feathers
That perches in the soul,
And sings the tune without the words,
And never stops at all,

And sweetest in the gale is heard;
And sore must be the storm
That could abash the little bird
That kept so many warm.

I've heard it in the chillest land,
And on the strangest sea;
Yet, never, in extremity,
It asked a crumb of me.

Emily Dickinson
Part One: Life
XXXII

Earthset Press
2560 East Sunset Road, Suite 116
Las Vegas, NV 89120-3517

Publisher's Cataloging-in-publication Data

Es, Edward
    Skyeyes / Edward Es
    p. cm.
    LCCN: 2003105387

    1. Fathers and sons--Fiction. 2. Space flight--
Fiction. 3. Healing--religious aspects--Fiction.
4. Prayer--Fiction. 5. Science fiction. 6. Religious

PS3605.S723S59 2003   813′.6

03 04 05 06 10 9 8 7 6 5 4 3 2 1

SKYEYES

Edward Es

Earthset Press
www.SkyeyesNovel.com

Preface

John Gardner, a foremost authority on the art of fiction, made great issue of an author's responsibility to create what he termed "the fictional dream". This mandate implores the author to reverently maintain that dream, keeping the business of writing transparent. The reader, then, continues uninterrupted in the noble endeavor of entering the dream of fiction, a ghostly character suspended in a stream of consciousness the author has gathered from the rich landscape of his universe, fashioned into a tale that transports the author equally as it does the reader.

The extent to which the reader enters the dream is a function of her or his willingness to suspend disbelief, preconception, and preoccupation, and in doing so be transported across the threshold to the characters, places, and circumstances in that wonderful land of "once upon a time".

We encourage our children to read for many reasons, none less important than any other. Through books of all kinds, and specially through fiction, they learn to view the fabric and texture of life through magic eyes, eyes that depart the world of everyday life and view the splendor of human emotion, triumph, pain, and courage through the untainted prism of imagination.

This author humbly thanks you, whoever you are, for turning the first page of this story, and further entreats you to put on those magic eyes, build a nest, curl up, and enter the dream of. Skyeyes. We honor ourselves when we swing open the gates to the kingdom of legend and story, and there allow ourselves to be brand new, to be transformed, to meet new people, endear them to ourselves, and most of all, participate in their travails, their watersheds, their discoveries, and ultimately, their reconciliation and rebirth.

I, your fellow traveler through this dream, join you.

Edward Es

For the three stars
in my heaven,

Melody,
Noël,
and Dustin

And for Tom
Peace be with you, brother...
I'll see you in Forever Land

Et Itur Ad Astra

One wish, two, I have for you,
Wish number three is just for me.
Wish number four for my friends next door,
Wishes left over when you need some more.

I was eight years old when I died.

Most of all I remember the colors. It wasn't like they said. It wasn't a white light. It was all around; the colors were inside me and I could feel them.

There was music, too. It came from the colors and sounded like them, and I could see what the music was saying.

He told me to sit next to a bright little river that had the music and the colors in it, swirling around and falling over stones I could see through. I remember the water in the river sounded like where the music was coming from.

It was all green grass, bright emerald green like the green came out of it, green like that ring Mama wore, only brighter. Brighter even than the time I looked through it at the Sun and it hurt my eyes. I didn't see any sun or light, other than what came from him.

There was a nice warm wind that went all through me. It didn't come from anywhere, or go anywhere, but where it was inside me. When he talked to me, the wind came from him, and all the colors and the music were saying what he said.

I asked him if he was going to tell me a story, and he told me to tell him one instead, so I thought about my life and it was all there like it just happened. I didn't have to say anything. It was there already, all the people in it, and everything that was, and it made me happy. That's when he told me that there weren't really any stories at all, but there were the people who told them. It was the telling that happened, not what was told. Then I understood.

Angel's Landing

Against The Wind

CHAPTER ONE

If God Were A Child

I dreamed a dream two nights ago
That swept across my soul.
It took me hours to fall asleep,
Afraid, alone, and cold.

But when I did I found myself
Adrift on angry seas,
Inside the pea-green boat I knew
From Nonsense poetry.

The night was cruel and dark, no Moon
Above to light my way.
I only saw when visions froze,
As lightning flashed like day.

Mountain waves were breaking high,
White burning crests of foam
That sprayed on me a salty fear,
A taste I've grown to know.

The clouds above rolled thick and deep;
They rained on me the tears
I'd cried so hard in bed that night,
With no one there to hear.

Bolts of blinding pain, they struck
The places where I hurt.
Thunder shouted rumbling words
Of death, and shoveled dirt.

That's when I felt a shadow cross
My heart from overhead.
Something with wings I could not see
Cast shades of hope or dread.

I wondered then, from in this dream,
From under sad, forsaken skies:
Were God a child, a child like me,
What ear would hear his Holy cry?

If He were on this wooden arc
Of sorrow, floating hopeless seas,
In all this universe, what heart
Would grant His prayer, would heed His plea?

Daybreak on an overcast morning approaches as if the world were hesitating to reappear. Above, the Sun rises, spraying dawn colors across a soft undercast. That great celestial drama, the grand illusion of stars vanishing behind a veil of vibrant blue, continues in silent, spinning wonder, unnoticed under the damp gray sky.

The Cardona building, painted earth-browns over cement block, lends a pale hint of warmth to an otherwise dark, cold, San Fernando Valley morning. Louis Cardona's Mercedes 500 rolls into its reserved spot in the empty parking lot. He steps from the car and walks toward his machine shop's side entrance when he notices someone with his head lowered in the trash dumpster near the alley. Louis moves over cautiously, trying not to alarm him, typical of his gentle manner.

"Can I help you with something?"

The stranger in the dumpster straightens up, banging his head on the heavy rusted lid he's holding up with one arm. Marshall Thomas Holmes would not look his age but for the toll of grievous times.

"Tom. What are you doing?" Louis asks, his cobalt-blue eyes empowered by thick black hair. Louis' compact Colombian stature carries the build of an amateur weight lifter.

"I thought I saw titanium down there," Tom says, brushing off his bluejeans and straightening the red flannel shirt. He too is solid, strong, but not as muscle bound as Louis.

"I've got that part ready," Louis says. Tom's hair, a little too long for a forty-one-year-old, stands on end from hanging in the dumpster. He finger-combs it as Louis leads him toward the shop entrance, unlocks the metal door and smiles, watching Tom enter ahead of him. Amusement turns to concern when he spots an unfamiliar car parked silently across the street. Louis stares, unable to make out figures through the tinted windows, darkened further by the gray of the morning. He hesitates, tempted to investigate, but thinks better of it and continues in.

Tom and Louis weave their way between unnaturally still lathes and mills to the inspection room which Louis unlocks. He enters, but Tom stops to look around the shop he once worked in, lifetimes ago when he lost his job. Cardona Manufacturing has doubled as an employment agency for nearly every relative, friend, or relative's friend that needed work or a green card. Tom remembers the smell of metal and oil, the droning of electric motors and grinding wheels screeching burrs from parts of turbine engines and fighter jets.

For years he walked through the shop as the owner's son-in-law, the workers looking upon him as a favored class, married to the boss' daughter. Then he was one of them, among them when misfortune fell. Memories flood in: the time he met Louis and his daughter at the flight school, spotting for each other at the gym, the marriage. All landmarks of a life gaining momentum, then falling into that swirling wormhole of sorrow. And out the other end is now, the twisted, otherworld where everyone is a caricature, distorted, including himself; mirrored images of what should be, or never will be. A cruel, elongated dimension that never ends.

Tom walks out among the iron monoliths, standing at attention to grind out parts for things more complicated than they, controlled by remote computers waiting to drive them to a drilling, turning frenzy. They stand there, industrial green, shining and cold, over-lit by bank after bank of fluorescent lights.

Unexpectedly, he encounters a young dark-skinned boy pushing a nubbed broom across the battleship-gray concrete floor. The boy stops and looks slowly up at him. Tom stares into his face, round, nearly a circle, browned by generations of sun, eyes as bright as the smile beneath. Suddenly the shop melts away and the boy stands in a Mayan jungle, noble, dressed in loincloth and adorned with necklaces of teeth and bone. He shines, a prince of some ancient nation, beaming his people's wisdom and glory from generations of generations. He holds in his hand a scepter studded with crudely cut jewels, the head a gold god grimacing at those who would worship him. The boy smiles wider and gestures toward the sky with his other hand. Then, in a flash of light, he stands where he started, the scepter once again a broom. The boy looks down and quietly pushes the broom as Tom turns away, jolted and confused again.

Louis opens a cabinet and removes a cardboard box, sets the box on the granite inspection table, and lifts out a heavy, complicated mechanism, machine tooled and hand assembled. Tom, disoriented, pushes the inspection room door open and Louis looks up, but restrains any reaction as he hands him the part. Tom inspects it superficially, placing it back on the table.

"Any problems?" Tom asks.

"We milled the channels twelve-thousandths, like the Doctor said, but we had to install a new valve-axle bushing. I haven't even run the cycles on it. What's the rush?"

Tom shifts with the question. "We've got a... situation. We're running out of time."

Louis digests the lack of information. "Somebody called here yesterday asking questions. They wouldn't say who they were, but they wanted to know what kind of business I was doing with you."

"What'd you tell them?"

"I told them you gave me a print and I built a part. What else could I say? When are you going to tell me what this is all about?"

Tom puts his arm around Louis' neck. "You'll find out soon enough. Besides, if I told you—"

"I know, I know. You're not doing anything crazy are you? Do I need a lawyer?" Louis asks, half joking.

Tom puts the part back in the box and wedges it under his arm. "You don't know enough to be in trouble. Sam's got everything covered, trust me. Now, come on. I've got someone out there who wants to see you."

Louis lights up. "Did you bring that boy with you?"

Tom and Louis walk to the cab of a twenty-six foot U-Rent truck. Tom opens the driver door and trades the box for a short-haired cat, striped at crossing angles with brown, black, and red strata, all clashing against a preposterous splat of orange that covers one eye and slants across half his nose, as if he'd been shot in the face with a paintball. "Let me squeeze this boy," Louis says, pursing his lips in anticipation as he grabs Zion.

Tom pulls them to the back of the truck and rolls the payload bay door up a few feet while Louis squeezes the unwilling cat. Louis squints in, astonished once his eyes adjust.

"Oh, my gosh. Did you build that?"

"With a little help from my friends," Tom says with a muted glint of pride.

Tom closes the bay door and latches it as a weighted silence descends. Louis struggles for words. "Sonora is upset. She misses you." Tom glances up to the nonexistent sky, it's gray reflecting his lack of response. "She doesn't understand why you have to shut us out. Francine never calls either. Does it have to end like this?"

Tom's evasive gaze crystallizes toward him. "End? Is there an end to it, Louis? By all means, somebody please end it so I can make it to the next minute."

Louis transfers Zion back to Tom, trying to temper his welling anger. "What happened to the 'Legacy of Dreams?'" Louis chokes out as Tom walks to the cab and puts Zion back in, then turns. Louis sees that look in his eyes, the one that was gone for a while.

"Don't start with the pulpit poetry, Louis. It sounded in-spiring when everyone was crying in their tissues and the sun was pouring through the stained glass. It's so easy to rationalize it, tie perfect sentiments around everything. Dot all the pathetic little i's and cross all the horrible little t's. That way everybody gets to walk out with a wrapped-up answer to it, like some twisted party favor after the wake. Just put it up on the mantle and look at it, and think you feel better every time the pain starts to throb from somewhere you didn't even know existed."

"Stop that right now," Louis flares back.

"You see? That's why I don't come around. Apologize to your wife for me, but I don't have any 'Legacy of Dreams' to rest my head on at night. It's best this way."

Louis walks up to him, stopping a foot away, and Tom braces. "We love you, Tom, but listen to me. You dishonor him with this. You shame yourself with it."

Louis' breath strikes his face. "Well then, that's the legacy I'm left with. Shame and dishonor. But I tell you what, that's one legacy I'll keep alive because the whole world, heaven and hell, were shamed and dishonored the day he was taken away. That's my place in it all right now."

Tom picks up a rock from the sidewalk, examining it as if its hardness made some point. "What came after 'Legacy of Dreams'? Wasn't it 'Shining Light of Hope'?" Louis looks down, unable to respond. "No thanks. I'm done with the poetry. If it makes you feel better, I'm happy for you. Me, I'm down to the basics. The simple stuff. Grief. Anger. As long as I'm here, it makes me feel like I'm still fighting."

Louis looks at him looking at the rock. "Fighting for what?"

Tom sidearms the rock across the street. They watch as it pings off a railroad tie and ricochets straight up, then wait for it to drop down the other side of the rail bed, but somehow it doesn't, seeming to disappear into the overcast. Tom slaps his hands clean. "Does it matter?" Louis turns away. Tom looks in the same direction. Nowhere.

"His favorite color was silver," Tom recalls from somewhere

far away, some distant, shimmering vision. Louis dabs his eye as he looks back at Tom, who remains fixed. "I never asked him why." Tom takes a breath, then sighs out, one of many such breaths that expel pain only to inhale it back in again. "Most kids, you know, they say red, or blue, something in the rainbow."

Louis softens in the memory. "That was like him. Always special like that."

"I never asked him why!" Tom looks away, fighting back another wave of anguish as Louis lays a hand on his arm.

Tom gets in the truck and drives off while Louis watches, his day already crippled with sorrow. After he reenters the building, the unmarked car rolls into the parking lot.

Tom drives southbound on the Golden State Freeway with Zion on his lap. He fixates on an exit sign on the opposite side of the freeway, turning nearly all the way around to see: Buena Vista Blvd. He turns forward as pain fills his eyes and the past echoes in his heart.

Spattering rain on the windshield and the drone of wipers sound distant, muffled as Tom passes the Buena Vista Blvd. exit. He turns a glazed look toward the silhouette of a woman next to him. She stares out the window.

Tom drifts across a lane, an irate horn startling him back to the present as Zion looks up.

The Justice department in Washington D.C. stands stalwartly like most government buildings, an intimidating edifice of granite, pillars, and high bronze-green doors presented by a run of marble steps. The morning's dusting of snow softens the sharp edges of the severe structure. A plain black car pulls up and from it emerge two men in gray suits. Norbert "Bud" Meyerkamp, an angry-looking, moderately overweight man pushing the limits of middle age, is a high level FBI operative. His patient younger partner, Sidney Knowles, follows a step and a half behind carrying a thick briefcase. Bud stops unexpectedly at the base of the steps, causing Sid to bump him forward.

Bud's reluctance to mount the first step betrays his distaste of climbing upward toward the very authority implied by the task. Not that he's generally contrary to the pillars of justice. After all, he considers himself, of late, to be holding them up entirely on his own. It's just that in this particular matter, the effects of the system have grated against his efforts, and he'd rather not have to actually look at the pillars themselves in his ascent to a certain argument. His breath fogs in the cold morning air as he bolsters what little patience he has left and continues upward, oblivious in his mood to the bump.

Sid and Bud barge through the imposing mahogany doors guarding the offices of the Attorney General, and Bud falls with a thump into a leather armchair, watching Sid approach the receptionist's desk. Karla is her name, a handsome woman several years his senior and a veteran to the Capitol. A ballet of glances precedes their exchange from which Bud looks away in annoyance, preferring to examine the silver studs cluttering the chair than witness Sid's indiscretions. Before Sid can speak, she says, "I'll tell the Attorney General you're here."

Sid nods and sits next to Bud who, without hesitation, blurts out, "And tell him to keep the chair warming under an hour. I've got a few other behinds to kiss today." Karla pretends not to hear as she answers her bleeping phone, speaking softly enough so Bud can't hear, though he's obviously trying. She hangs up and addresses Sid. "He'll see you now."

Bud mumbles, "L. I. B., M. R. ducks."

Karla, always annoyed by Bud's presence, snaps, "Excuse me?"

Sid intervenes. "Thank you very much." Another glance exchanges behind Bud's back when they walk past the desk, and Karla's eyes remain fixed on Sid as he enters through the double doors.

Patrick Herlihy has, as one of his achievements, the distinction of being the youngest Attorney General to ever hold that office. He also had the good fortune to be a law student of Jonathan Stamp, now the President and his mentor. He stands at a tall window, looking across the snow covered lawn while his two guests stand silently at his desk, then takes a strategic breath.

"Ah. Sid and Bud." He turns around with a crooked Irish smile, a smile that angles more at the aspect of Bud clashing against the traditional decor, the smell of books, the tocking of a mantle clock. A badly dressed gargoyle, he muses. "Don't you guys make wine coolers or something?"

Bud is not amused. "Did you read the file on Holmes?"

Herlihy keeps rolling. "Really, one of you should change your name if you're going to hang around together. Sidney and, what the heck is Bud short for? Budman?"

"Norbert, sir," Bud forces.

Herlihy tries his best to keep the dark cloud Bud brought with him from drifting in his direction. He looks just above Bud's head, nearly certain he saw a small flash of lightning, and Bud darts his eyes up, wondering what Herlihy is looking at. "Norbert? Sidney and Norbert. Now you sound like a men's store. That just won't do."

Bud rarely shows this much restraint, reluctantly knowing his place for the moment. "With all due respect, the *folder*."

Equally reluctantly, Herlihy gives in to the smoldering insistence, looking at Sid for sympathy, though Sid's blank stare delivers little. "All right, all right. Take it easy." He takes another breath. "Right. The folder." Herlihy looks around his folder-covered desk, picks up one the size of a phone book, and wags it at them. "Is this coming out in paperback any time soon?"

Bud jumps right in. "This guy's got more going on than a one-legged paper hanger."

Herlihy shakes his head. "Uh-huh. The one legged man is in the ass kicking contest, Meyerkamp. It's the one-*armed* man that hangs wallpaper." Bud stares back. "Anyway, give me a quick profile of this thing. Refresh my memory." He turns to Sid. "Better yet, you do it. If we keep the four-letter words out, we'll save time."

Bud curses under his breath while Sid pulls another file out of his briefcase. "Marshall Thomas Holmes, born in Seattle, educated at MIT, finished Harvard Law School in twenty-six months. Initial fortune came from his invention of new technology for encrypting digital streaming in satellite transponders, quadrupling their capabilities. He owns an airline, a cruise ship line, cable channels, communications network, including satellite transponder systems, and millions in hotels and travel related ventures. Principal residence, 15,000 plus acres near Rockville, Utah, with a large business on the property. Estimated net worth over eleven billion, and we think he's got as much sheltered where we can't find it."

"Look, I know who Tom Holmes is. What's the basis of this petition for a warrant?"

Sid closes the folder. "Mr. Holmes has a history of unstable behavior since the loss of his eight-year-old son and the attempted suicide of his ex-wife, Francine. Besides risking his life trying to rewrite the Guinness Book of Records, he's stayed one step ahead of the slammer thanks to a legal firm which he supports wholly."

"So what?"

"Psychological profile indicates trauma induced neuroses—"

Bud explodes. "Listen, Herlihy, this guy's got some blades missing in the windmills of his mind. If you'd found the time to read the book on him, you'd know we've been tailing him for almost a year now and he's up to something big. Possibly dangerous."

"I read your book on him. You're talking about those purchases from NASA junkyards. I see nothing here to warrant a raid on his property. You know how powerful he is. You pull a questionable search and get nothing, we'll be in court for years."

Bud locks eyes with him and clenches a fist, the one hanging by his side. "The sonofabitch is building a rocket, damnit!"

Herlihy looks down at his desk. He shuffles papers around, then picks up a pencil, holding it up, looking it over with one eye. "A rocket."

"A rocket," Bud insists. "What the hell else do you think he's doing with all that hardware? He's got a so-called bakery out there that's surrounded like Fort Knox, and our sats picked up an infrared event that was a test fire as sure as the Pope is... whatever he is."

Herlihy looks to Sid. "You know very well that was reported as a gas explosion with no consequence."

"By his own fire department," Bud retorts.

Sid avoids the Attorney General's glance by walking over to the same window. Herlihy taps his desk with the pencil eraser. "As for the hardware, he's got kids crawling all over old Atlas boosters in a park out there. He donated millions to children's charities for that rusting space junk. Sounds like a good citizen to me."

Bud walks over to him and stands much too close. In a pressurized half-whisper, he hisses, "Don't you think I know all that? For godssake, man, do you really believe it?"

Herlihy leans into him. "Look, Meyerkamp, I'm telling you I see no grounds to let you go rolling in there. The FBI's flown off half-cocked and made monkeys' uncles out of enough administrations for the next century. Until you come in here with something more concrete than 'the sonofabitch is building a rocket,' you'll get no help from me."

Bud arches his back, then walks toward the door, stopping to pivot around. "I'm warning you. I'll take this to the President. This is national security."

"You go right ahead, but Jonathan knows Tom better than I do. In fact, he owes a piece of his election to Tom Holmes."

Sid returns his presence to the room by walking over to the door and opening it, creating an escape path for Bud, who declares, "Mark my words. If this fruitcake blasts off, I'm going to enjoy seeing you fry. In fact I'll be there to flip you over 'til you're brown on both sides." Bud walks out as Herlihy turns to Sid, who makes an apologetic face, then follows, closing the door.

As Bud storms across the anteroom, Sid in trail, Herlihy opens his door, exclaiming, "And boys..." They stop, pirouetting like a pair of music box clowns. "Do something about those names."

Bud raises a finger in response, but curls it back. He turns away to leave and runs into someone entering, blowing by without apology, followed by Sid who is at best able to keep up.

Bud vaults down the steps toward the car three at a time, boiling. "*Damn* him!"

When they reach the car they find a parking ticket under the wiper, which Bud summarily wads up and throws on the ground. He looks up at Sid, exasperated as Sid picks up the ticket. Bud opens the driver door, but pauses before entering. "By the way. Not a good idea to be rogering secretaries."

"Rogering? But, how'd you—"

"Wouldn't you be a little disappointed if I didn't? That's my job, to know things, isn't it?"

"I guess so, —"

"Listen, I'm just trying to give you some advice. It's hard enough to kiss one ass, much less having to kiss another one to get at it. Get my point, *Sidney*?"

"Got it, *Norbert*!"

Sid gets in the car as Bud fights back a smile.

The truck pulls into the parking lot of Villa Scalabrini, a single-story convalescent home nested into a residential area of deep lots and horse properties. Tom climbs down from the cab, and Zion, hanging from his arm, squirms loose and hits the ground running, stopping in a flower bed. Tom scratches the palm of his hand and after a few rushed licks, Zion runs under a bush.

Tom walks up the cement steps to a patio that spreads left before the glass doors. It's sheltered on three sides by tall hedges, broken every six feet by trellises of blossomed white jasmine, their airy fragrance surprising visitors as they come and go. In the middle of the patio there's a stone fountain, still figures of a farmer pouring water into the bucket of an adoring granddaughter. She looks up at him, smiling a pretty marble smile, and the shadow of grandfather's straw hat cuts across her alabaster arms. Tom stares, unable to join the carved smiles.

Tom enters the lobby and walks down an antiseptic corridor made bearable by children's finger-paint drawings pinned to the walls. He continues into the Sunroom, a greenhouse enclosure filled with plants, flowers, and potted ficus trees. Seniors shuffle about, some in walkers or wheelchairs, others under their own reduced power. Sitting in a wheelchair in the corner looking out is Nonna, Tom's grandmother. When Tom sees her, he walks over.

"Hiya, sweetheart," he says in his best Bogart.

Nonna sits motionless, staring intently at the courtyard outside, an old lioness locked onto her prey. "Not just now, dear, I'm busy," she says, barely moving her lips.

Tom bends down and rests his chin on the top of her head, scanning to see what she's watching. "Don't you ever get tired of sitting in this corner?"

"Not with a view like this." Suddenly flustered, she sighs, "Phooey. He's gone. That gardener's got a nice pair of biscuits. Can't be a day over sixty. Oh well, come give us a hug."

Tom bends down and administers the hug from behind, turning it to a form of affectionate restraint. "I want you to do something for me."

"No."

"Come on. I haven't even asked yet."

Nonna struggles loose from the embrace by turning her wheelchair toward Tom, looking at him with loving reproach. "You ask me this every time you come. No, I won't come live with you, I like it here. All these old farts running around make me feel younger, and besides, you built this place for me. How can I possibly leave?"

"For your information, Nonna dearest, I wasn't going to ask you that this time."

"Oh, really? What's the matter then? Down to a few million? Need to dip into my cookie jar?"

He wheels her out of the room as she strains for a last glimpse of the gardener, ignoring Tom's persistent campaign. "Listen you, you're going on this cruise and I won't take no for an answer."

"A cruise," she scoffs. "Any kind of sea at all and I'd be a duck in a shooting gallery in this thing."

"Oh, come on. You'll be the terror of the poop deck."

Nonna swashes her cane ahead of their accelerating journey. "Make way for the sea hag on wheels! I don't think so." Tom pushes her down the hallway a little too fast, prompting a nurse to frown as they speed by.

Tom continues. "I've got a whole deck blocked off, and guess what? You can bring as many of these 'old farts' as you like. If it's biscuits you're so into, you'll see more of all shapes and ages prancing around than you ever imagined, or fantasized, or whatever it is you do in that gray think-tank of yours."

This finally gets her attention as she looks toward him, keeping a cat's eye on their flight path. "You've got a point there." As they turn into the lobby, Tom nearly runs over Arem, a rumpled old man in a striped terry-robe sitting in a wheelchair, forlornly holding a football. His eyes light up when he sees Tom.

"Hey, Tommy! Split left on three!"

Tom crouches to quarterback position. "Hut, hut. Hut!"

Arem flips him the ball and with all the agility of a ninety-year-old, pumps his chair down the corridor, then turns his head around, coasting perfectly straight. Tom fires a tight spiral to his outstretched arms and the nurse grabs a wall rail, ducking as the pass flies by. Arem turns ahead, brakes the best he can, and rolls through open double doors into the kitchen. The nurse, running toward the faint crash of pots and pans, blurts out, "Mr. Holmes! Honestly!"

Tom skids the wheelchair to a halt after free-rolling through the automatic door onto the terrace. Nonna looks up in feigned annoyance as Zion hops on her lap and she rhythmically whacks his raised behind. "Is Isabel going?"

Tom looks up at the breaking overcast. "Yes, she is. She's going to headline."

"Is that voluntary, or did you 'ask' her, too?" He looks away, inspecting a fingernail. "I see. Well, in that case, count me in."

Tom bends over and kisses her cheek. "Good girl. Call Janet and give her a list." Nonna looks up at him, squinting at the Sun breaking through behind his head. "I love you," Tom whispers. "Take care of yourself."

Nonna grabs his shirtsleeve as he tries to walk away. "You've never been able to hide anything from me. Now what's going on?"

Tom takes the cat from her lap. "Gotta run."

He walks toward the parking lot, leaving Nonna unanswered and unnerved. In a far corner of the expansive lawn between the parking lot and the home, a young man overzealously rakes leaves onto a pile already peaked to capacity. Walter, born with Down's syndrome, spots Tom and drops the rake, running full speed.

"Mr. Holmes! Mr. Holmes!" he yells, throwing his arms around Tom's waist.

Tom rubs the cat in his face. "Hey, Walter! How's the greatest leaf-raker in the world?"

"Good! Good! I raked this whole front here!" he brags, letting go of the hug.

"I see that. Atta boy, Walter," Tom says, grinning. "Listen, how would you like to go on a big ship way out in the ocean?"

"A big ship? By myself?"

Tom pokes his arm. "No, no. With Nonna, and lots of other people. You can go swimming and play with kids. And you can bring some friends from your school."

Walter wags his tail. "Really? Will you be there?"

Tom starts to reply, then stops. "I tell you what. Maybe later... I'll come out of the sky and surprise you." He ruffles Walter's hair. "Now, you go tell Nonna I said you could go with your friends."

Walter runs off. "Nonna!"

Tom watches, then turns away. As he walks up to the truck and throws Zion in, he hears the faint sound of two voices intertwining in harmony, echoing, fading, and rising again. He looks toward the Scalabrini Chapel, a faithful replica of an old New England stone church, closes the truck door, and walks in that direction.

The thick, carved-timber doors creak open as Tom enters and comes upon two vocalists rehearsing a classical duet from an arched choir loft behind the sanctuary. Walking quietly down the aisle, he looks around the church, observing parish helpers on ladders taking down Christmas decorations. Every sound echoes musically in the patient silence while Tom sits in the front pew and blankly watches altar boys dismantle a life-size nativity that decorated the sanctuary, reverently packing the objects in boxes. He turns to the deep red and blue robed figures poised in the stained-glass turrets of the stone walls, each with a hand raised toward heaven.

It's still raining hard. Red flashing lights pulse ahead as the car approaches, slowing as if commanded by their presence. Through the glittering downpour, a booth takes form and from it steps a Mexican border official dressed in full yellow slicker, advancing like some plastic creature. He shines his flashlight into the car, causing the woman on the passenger side to wince and look away. She is blond, 31, her pretty features contorted by heartache and by rain flowing down the windshield, projected onto her face by the flashlight of another guard. The official shines the light into the back seat and the woman and Tom turn to look back, then at each other, desperation reflected in each other's eyes.

Desperation remains in Tom's eyes as he stares at the altar boys. One of them picks up the figure of the Christ child and carefully puts it into a carton, stopping to look down at it. He motions the sign of the cross, then closes the carton. A wave of pity breaks through him and he turns around to see Tom staring at the carton. Looking further into Tom's eyes, he sees a man of sorrows.

The truck roars down a city street bordering Mile Square Park and turns onto a dirt road, rumbling through ruts into the parking lot of a miniature airstrip and grinding to a dusty halt beside a candy-apple Corvette. Matt Clifton, Tom's lifelong friend and most ardent critic, leans against it and watches as Tom gets down from the cab with Zion on his shoulder. Matt, tall and heavily mustached, ambles toward him, pushing his rodeo-worn Stetson further back.

"Nice of you to show," Matt drawls.

Zion jumps to the hood of the truck as Tom surveys the area. A five-year-old boy watches his father fuel a bright orange radio-controlled biplane, a task the boy could easily have done himself. Tom gazes skyward, shielding his eyes from the morning Sun as a tenth-scale Spitfire, red smoke trailing, performs a power climb straight up to a hammerhead stall, then looks back at Matt's half scowl. "Sorry. Had to stop for kerosene."

From around the back of the truck appears a county sheriff, startling both of them. He walks up slowly, carrying the burden of a long career of doughnuts and coffee, gazing up at nothing in particular. He doesn't look at them, but directs his address to Tom as if throwing his voice.

"Morning, son." The sheriff creaks a half smile, half grimace.

"Morning, sir," Tom replies with a glance toward Matt.

The sheriff looks at Zion. "You boys flyin' today?"

Tom still looks at Matt, who raises an eyebrow. "Yes, we are, officer. Is there a problem?"

The sheriff finally looks both of them over. "Well, I hope not. Just keep it high. Had some fools out here this weekend trying to knock over beer cans. One of 'em hit the dirt and threw a prop. Nearly put a kid's eye out."

"We don't go for any of that stuff. I promise, we'll keep it plenty high," Tom says with a hidden grin.

Matt starts a laugh until the sheriff glances pointedly at him and stops chewing his gum. The sheriff looks back skyward and resumes the chew. "All right, then. You boys have a good one."

Matt replies, "And you too, Sheriff." The sheriff looks them both over again, looks at the cat, then walks around the truck and out of sight. A moment later his cruiser pulls away in a plume of dust.

"Where are they when you really need 'em?" Matt sneers.

"Probably chasin' you. Let's get this show on the road. Where's Sam?"

Sam's deep voice jolts both of them. "Nyaaa, what's up, docs?"

Sam Brown, three hundred pounds of Afro-American attorney, had been observing the interrogation from the other side of the truck. Much of what was once solid offensive lineman has succumbed to gravity. Matt, easily annonyed, complains, "Jesus, Sam, how the devil can somebody big as you move around so quiet?"

"That's what the quarterbacks used to ask."

Only Matt could get away with, "Yeah, well, I'm surprised you can even live on land."

"Why I oughta…" Sam says, raising a mock fist.

Under different circumstances Tom would be amused. "OK girls, let's go," he says, motioning to the back of the truck. Sam throws a lemon drop at Matt hard enough to be surprised when Matt catches it and puts it in his mouth. Tom pulls a ramp from the back of the truck and all three walk up, disappearing into the bay. They emerge, under considerable strain, carrying the brushed aluminum fuselage of a 747-400 scale replica, detailed with a blue stripe down the length and a tan tail with a large "H" on it. Painted in script under the cockpit window is "Noah 3".

Sweat drips off Sam's face, evidence of the effort required to assemble the Noah 3, and Matt sucks a finger, the victim of bolting on a wing. The aircraft is thirteen feet long, twelve feet wide, standing three and a half feet at the tail. Sam pours the last drop of kerosene into the fueling point on the right wing as Tom slides a black box into the opened cockpit. Matt stands beside him, eyeing the gathering crowd of gawking enthusiasts. Tom wipes his hands with a red rag. "All right, 'Before Start'."

Matt takes a folded checklist from his back pocket and squints to read it.

"Want to try the glasses for once?" asks Sam.

Matt looks up at him, still squinting. "That would mean I'd have to get a better look at you, now, wouldn't it?" He returns to the checklist and after a few experimentations with arm distance, clears his throat.

"Battery power."

Tom responds as he looks in the cockpit. "On."

"Avionics."

"On, checked."

"Navigation."

"Programmed, set auto."

"Start sequence and pressure."

"Selected and…" He looks at Matt. "How about turning the valve, Chief?"

Matt reaches down to an air bottle attached to the tail cone by a hose and turns the valve. A hiss of air moves the crowd a step back. "Sorry."

Tom looks back into the cockpit. "Pressure's up." He turns to Sam. "You ready?"

Sam power-walks away. "Aye, aye, Cap'n."

Tom looks around, wiping the sweat from his brow. "OK. 'Start Check'. Read it all."

Matt walks backward. "Parking brake, beacon, fuel pumps and start valves."

When Tom reaches in the cockpit, red beacons on the top and bottom flash in unison with white wingtip strobes, and the whine of miniature fuel pumps starts the crowd murmuring. "Set, on, on and," flipping the last switch, "open."

Tom hurries away as the high-pitched scream of small turbines brings everyone's hands to their ears. From the truck cab, he takes a metal briefcase and opens it on the hood. Matt stares at it like a dog staring at a clock while Tom enters commands on a keyboard, whispering, "N two, lightoff. N one." He turns to Matt. "Looks good. Pull the chocks and the bottle."

Matt has to shout. "Man, you're crazy! You pull the damn chocks!" Tom stares him down. "Hell, fire. I swear." Matt crouches down unnecessarily and, in that position, waddles his way to the front of the aircraft. He gets down on one knee and with a nervous finger, hooks the rope tying the two chocks together, jerks them from the nose wheel, then runs hunched over to the tail and disconnects the air bottle.

Tom moves a joystick and advances small thrust levers as the Noah 3 moves forward and turns toward the end of the runway, the crowd standing aghast. When it finally stops in position, Tom shouts at Sam. "Go for it!" Sam slumps into the Vette and punches buttons on his cellphone, sweat running down his face.

The radar room at SoCal Approach is like any other facility of its kind: a low-lit bunker, silent but for the disconnected voices of men at glowing screens. An air traffic controller sits at his terminal, staring intently and speaking to no one in the room. The phone near him buzzes and he answers, looks around, speaks under his breath, then hangs up.

Sam sticks his arm out of the Vette with a thumbs-up and Tom applies takeoff power, the resulting engine scream reaching such a pitch that the observers crouch down, one falling backward. Because of its size, the Noah 3 looks deceptively slow rolling down the runway. A dust storm blasts behind as it accelerates and rotates, climbing sharply into the air. One of the gawking spectators runs over to Tom, a look of awe and terror on his face. "Good God! Are those really jet engines?"

"Just the inboards. Four would rip the wings off," Tom replies.

"No way!" is the response as the gawk turns skyward.

Tom turns back to Matt and Sam. "We're outta here." He slams the briefcase shut and he and Matt climb into the truck as Sam fishtails off in the Vette. The truck strains a leaning, lumbering U-turn, rattling off in an explosion of dirt. The gawker looks back up, scanning to find the aircraft as it makes a high, sweeping turn overhead and climbs off into the peaceful light-blue morning sky. When it disappears, a soft mist of quiet settles back. He looks over at a friend, who looks back. "Are you thinkin' what I'm thinkin'?"

"No landing."

"Not here, anyway."

They both look back up. "How's that possible?" he says, sticking his hands in his pockets.

"You think we should call anybody about it?"

"What for? Did you recognize that guy, anyway? He seemed familiar, like on TV or something."

"Yeah."

The general aviation ramp at Orange County Airport is unusually slow. Row after row of lonely aircraft sit anchored by tie-downs, sadly tethered to the Earth. Standing in ready, however, in front of the Executive Air Terminal, is the Noah 4, a Citation One business jet painted the same scheme as its now airborne counterpart. Eddie, Tom's pilot, sits on the steps of the open cabin door reading a magazine, a mild sea breeze flapping the pages. He sees Tom, Matt, and Sam walking toward him, Tom carrying the suitcase and Matt holding the box Tom picked up from Cardona, while

Zion follows a few feet behind until Tom stops and scratches his palm, sending him to a nearby bush. Tom continues toward the Citation and after a few moments, Zion reappears, running full speed. As they approach, Eddie pulls the chocks from the right landing gear and, after the four enter, follows, pulling the door behind.

Tom straps himself into the Captain's seat and throws switches while Eddie pulls out the laminated checklist and fans himself with it. Tom sees him out of the corner of his eye, pretending not to notice. When he's done, he grabs the checklist, puts it vertically between his hands and closes his eyes. "'Before Start' check complete. Satisfied?"

Eddie grabs the checklist back. "Yeah, right. You know, the pages of this thing are stuck together."

Tom respects the friendly challenge. "I tell you what. If we're about to crash, you read me the 'Before Kissing Your Butt Goodbye' checklist."

"You know it's guys like you that—"

"Overpay guys like you to be a twerp. How about a taxi clearance?"

Eddie calls ground control as the second engine spools up and Sam sticks his big head between them with a glass in his hand.

They both reach for it, but Eddie defers. "Taxi Two-Six Right, hold short of the Left," Eddie says. Sam hands him the other drink he'd already made for him and knocks his headset off. "Shoot, man. For a token Negro lawyer, you think you're pretty hot," he says, replacing the headset.

Sam frowns. "Oh, really? What's the difference between a step 'n' fetchit token-white pimple-faced copilot like you and a duck?"

"I'm sure you're going to tell me."

"A duck can fly." Eddie looks out the window as Tom high-fives Sam.

The SoCal controller stares at the screen, picks up his target and says to himself, "Thar she blows." He transmits, "National

7235, turn thirty degrees left for traffic at one o'clock, one mile, climbing through eleven point five."

This radio call freezes the Captain and First Officer of the National Airlines Boeing 757, catching the Captain in mid-bite of a ham and cheese croissant.

A 757 cockpit is a comfortable place, spacious and colored in light browns as were most of the later generation jets, the choice of color a departure from the gray interiors of traditional airliners. Someone in human ergonomics decided it would be more soothing, conducive to a balanced work environment. None of this tempers the anxiety of an abrupt turn to avoid unexpected traffic at close range. A wide-eyed flight attendant sits in the jumpseat, stopped in the course of an identical croissant.

The First Officer disconnects the autopilot and rudely banks the airplane to the left, exclaiming to his Captain as he looks for the traffic, "Good grief! One mile? What's going on here?"

The Captain triggers the control wheel transmit switch, declaring with a mouthful to the controller, "We don't see the traffic. Isn't that a little close?"

The TCAS annunciator flashes on the instrument panel, followed by the loud and unnerving announcement, *Traffic! Traffic!* "What was that?" the flight attendant asks, wide-eyed.

The copilot answers while craning his scan outside. "Airliners are required to have a TCAS system. It's 'Tombstone Technology', the business of safety after disaster, in this case after two mid-airs here in Southern California." He points to computer-generated symbols on an electronic display in front of him. "It shows all the aircraft around us and gives commands to avoid a conflict."

Descend! Descend now! the black box demands. This time everyone's wide-eyed.

Noah 3 climbs serenely skyward at a steep angle. In the distance, National 7235 banks away in a descent.

Back in the National cockpit, the controller's voice finally dispels the tension. "Traffic no longer a factor. Cleared direct

Dagget," this followed by the TCAS report, *Clear of Conflict.*

The First Officer reengages the autopilot and enters the direct command into the flight management computer as his Captain responds to the controller, "Roger. Don't know how we could have missed that one." The two pilots look at each other, then back in that direction. The Captain takes off his glasses and furiously cleans them with his tie.

The Citation pulls into position on Orange County's runway 26 Right and stops. Through the cockpit window, down the runway, the shimmer of rising air sets in motion an otherwise still landscape. Tom stares as Zion jumps onto his lap, causing Eddie to shake his head. Over the radio the tower controller's voice declares, "Citation One-One-Hotel, cleared for takeoff. At the shoreline turn right, heading three-three-zero."

Tom stands in front of a dilapidated house, isolated on a Mexican beach, paint peeling off crude cement block. He watches an ambulance drive away in the distance, a rising vortex of dust twisting in the shimmering heat.

Eddie looks at Tom. "Ground control to Major Tom. Anybody home?"

Tom, jarred back, barely answers. "What?"

"Cleared for takeoff? Right at the shoreline?"

Tom abruptly advances the thrust levers, the rude acceleration spilling Eddie's drink. He looks down at his Coke-soaked tie. "Jeesus!"

Matt's voice exclaims from the cabin, "Whoa, Nellie."

Noah 4 rotates and lurches into the air.

Inside L.A. Center in Palmdale, California, the atmosphere is that of eternal night, dim lighting offset by the cool glow of radar screen after radar screen. Controllers gaze fixedly into their depths, appearing to talk to themselves though each word they speak radiates through hundreds of miles of airspace, striking a myriad of huge, roaring jetliners reduced to blips and creeping digital encryptions. Except for one not-so-huge jetliner hiding behind its otherwise normal blip.

Steve works the airspace below 24,000 feet. The controller next to him, Sherry, taps him on the shoulder. "Steve, when you've got a second, take a look at this."

Steve stares at his screen. "Go ahead."

Sherry looks at him and his lack of interest. "I've got a target here at three-four-zero, unidentified. The thing's squawking 1111, doing two hundred thirty-five knots."

Steve unsuccessfully tries to be funny. "Three-four-zero? He must think he's on the Pacific composite," he says, glancing over at her screen, not long enough to focus on anything there.

"Oh really? No kidding, you dink. I'm calling a super," she says, as irritated as she is unamused.

"Maybe it's just a bad encoder. He's probably down at thirty-four hundred."

Sherry picks up her phone. "We'll let Harold figure it out."

Noah 3 cruises at 34,000 feet, gleaming in the sun, a pair of tiny contrails crystallizing behind.

Harold stands over Sherry, frowning. He looks over at Steve, frowning deeper. "What's the matter, Steve? Didn't this thing come through your airspace?"

Steve, beads of sweat forming along his receding hairline, feels Harold's shadow on his back. "Yeah, well, I saw it, but I thought it was just a bad encoder."

Harold looks at Sherry, absorbing her raised eyebrow into his already bloating anger. "Horsefeathers, Steve! You know better than that!"

The controller on the other side of Steve interrupts, an obvious eavesdropper to the engagement. "Here's one comin' into your sector, Steve. VFR target at seventeen-five, doing three hundred twenty knots toward Utah. Not talkin' to anybody. Sound familiar?"

Harold's wheels are turning and beginning to smoke. Steve glances at him, then glares at Sherry, at this point feeling like a piece of curling cheese in a betrayal sandwich. Harold barks, "That's that Holmes guy." He turns to Sherry. "You got anybody near this other... target?"

"It's about to go under TranStar 100. Christ, I hope the altitude's right. Even so, it'll be a conflict if we don't turn him."

"See if they can get an eyeball on it." Harold is relishing this closing maneuver on Steve, some unresolved conflict.

Sherry focuses back on her screen. "TranStar 100, we have an unidentified target crossing at your twelve o'clock, two miles, indicating flight level three-four-zero. See if you can get a visual on it."

TranStar 100 is an MD 80, this interior light green, a precursor to the Boeing-brown philosophy. The Captain and First Officer look at each other, then both strain their eyes outward as the Captain banks the aircraft left, responding through a hand mic. "We'll give it a try." He turns to the First Officer. "You see anything?"

"I think I see something. It looks pretty far away though, no two miles." He pulls binoculars from his flightbag, scans, then locks on, hitting the push-to-talk switch. "Yeah, there it is. It's a 747. Looks funny, though. Must be at least ten miles from the size of it. But then again…"

Sherry presses her earpiece, looking up to Harold as she responds to the TranStar pilot. "747? It indicates less than a mile." She listens again, and reports to Harold while looking at Steve. "He says it's either a 747 ten miles away, or a ten-foot 747, one mile away."

Harold looks at Steve, then back at Sherry, then at Steve. "Weren't you supposed to be working Sherry's sector today?"

Crumbling, Steve confesses, "Yes, I was. We traded shifts, but she decided to come in anyway," glaring at her, "without telling me."

Harold turns to Sherry. "Where's that darn thing look like it's going?"

"Utah."

Harold grows darker, pointing at Steve's face. "Vectorfort, I want you in my office at the end of this shift." He turns back to Sherry. "Track that little UFO as far as you can and give me an event report." As Harold storms away, Sherry gloats quietly. Steve shakes an imaginary, tightly clenched fist at her.

Noah 4's interior is small by any standard. For Sam, however, it's more a matter of wearing the jet than sitting in it. Fortunately, Tom had a seat made especially for him. Sam concentrates on a video of Looney Tune classics, sucking a Tootsie Pop, Matt drinks a beer, and Tom has a newspaper in front of his face, the flying duties left to Eddie. He punches the newspaper and throws it down.

"I swear to God, I don't know where they come up with this lunacy."

Matt belches. Sam cocks one eye at Tom, then returns to his cartoon. "Now what?" Matt asks.

Tom picks up the paper. "Look at this. Some pervert was caught in front of a school for hearing impaired kids talking filth in sign language, and now he's in court with some lawyer who's got the judge tied up in knots trying to decide whether or not signing can be 'constitutionally considered obscene language.' The whole world's out on a sick coffee break."

Matt gets up, as far as the height of the cabin will allow, his hat squashing down on his head as it presses against the ceiling. "Well, you know what they say. There is no gravity," belching again, "the Earth sucks." As Matt walks toward the lav, Sam looks at Tom, who stares grimly out the window.

"Hey, man, loosen up a little. I can't remember the last time I saw you smile like you were happy. The few times you do smile it looks like... more like an upside-down frown. Look," pointing to the TV, "it's Red Ryder, your favorite."

Tom looks at the screen, then away. Sam musters up a fair impression of Red Ryder. "Duh, look at me horsy, I'm a ridin' side saddle, yeah." No response. "Come on, Tom. Have some fun. Good, clean, stupid fun."

Tom's gaze continues into the minus forty-six degree air outside. "When I was a kid, every time I was about to have fun, like the most fun I'd ever had, something inside me would stop it. It was like there was only so much happiness doled out to each person when they were born, and if you used it up too fast, there'd only be sadness left. Part of me was always afraid I'd use up my happiness."

Sam caves into the darkening conversation. "You still believe that?"

Tom stares deeper into nothing. "I don't think so."

"Why's that?"

He turns toward Sam, though the gaze remains unfocused. "I keep waiting for the sadness to run out." He turns back out the window. "But there's no end to it."

Sam closes his eyes, searching. "Maybe you were right. Maybe you'll use all the sadness up. Then there'll be nothin' but good times ahead."

Tom looks back at him, the helplessness in his eyes telling his friend he finds little hope in the theory. Tom turns back to the window, staring once more into the past.

From inside the car, scenes of a Tijuana ghetto pass by through the churning dust of the streets. The travail of the poor struggling through another day is not evident on their faces, as they know no different. Though pain and suffering are often their own analgesic, this is not so for Tom and his wife, Francine, who holds their listless son in her arms. His name was Noah, a blond boy of eight, wounded by a blood transfusion at birth. The traffic, not so much of automobiles but of people and animals, makes the going slow. At last, the car pulls in front of a building that looks in comparison to its lurid surroundings like a temple, masked with white-washed cinder block. "Clinica Popular de Tijuana" is barely legible in faded letters over the entrance. This, cruelly enough, is an outpost on the fringes of hope, a pitiful and far-off place to grasp for what few impossible odds those at home will not offer. They crawl from the car, which melds away into the street with its adornment of dirt. On Francine's face rests the look of lifelessness that's left when even despair has run its course and departed.

The persistent buzz of the airphone breaks the droning silence. Sam picks it up. "Yeah, Doc. Hold on." He extends the phone to Tom. "It's for you." No response. "Tom? Hey, brother."

"Who is it?"

"It's the Doc."

Tom forces himself. "Thanks." He takes the phone as if it weighed a hundred pounds. "Yeah vul, mein Doctor."

Dr. Werner Kirshner has been compared to Einstein both in appearance and intellect. As one's surroundings often take on one's character, his office is in disarray, due mostly to an overabundance of technical material. Kirshner addresses the speakerphone in his Polish accent. "Tommy, my boy. Did you forget about me? I've been waiting for your call."

Tom's voice carries his mood. "I'm sorry. I've been... never mind. Have you got a fix on her?"

"Yes. Position is one hundred fifty miles south southwest of Mormon Mesa, ETA 1933. Will you be here in time?"

"We're right on schedule. I got the valve from Louis. Did you get a delivery from Abex?"

Kirshner hesitates. "Listen, Thomas. It's not such a good idea to talk. Things are getting difficult here."

Static silence. "What's the matter?" asks Tom.

"We'll discuss it when you get here. Just... be careful."

"Sure. OK." He looks troubled as he hands the phone to Sam, who takes it without looking. Tom watches Sam's eyebrow rise in reaction.

"What?" asks Sam.

Tom cracks his neck, always making Sam cringe. "I think I hear footsteps."

Eddie sticks his head in the cockpit doorway. "We gotta start down. You want to do this?"

Tom gets up and leans into the cockpit, but sees Zion curled up on the Captain's seat. "No, you two go ahead."

Eddie pulls the thrust levers back to idle, looking over at the cat who turns up to him with a peaceful blink. "Well, I guess it's just you and me."

The anteroom to the Oval Office is intimidating, even more so in the silence that rests between clacks of an antique grandfather clock. Activity out in the hallway is faint, overshadowed by the ponderous quiet of waiting. The smell of heavy drapes, the austerity of raised striped-velvet wallpaper, the rhythmic ticking, each accentuate every fretting moment.

Counterpoint to this ticking is the tapping of a pencil, played by Margaret, the President's secretary, who focuses on a document on her desk. Bud sits too close to Sid on a sort of bench, a settee, nearly in formation posture with him, reminding Margaret of two overgrown boys waiting for the principal to call them in. All of this is about as much as Bud can take as Margaret imperceptibly peers over her glasses in distant disapproval. Standing next to the coffee station, pouring sugar into a mug of coffee, is a seductive woman in her early thirties with dark hair and sleek brown eyes.

An intercom buzzer shoots through Bud's nerves and Margaret answers her line from the Oval Office. "Yes, Mr. President. It's Meyerkamp and his assistant. He said it's a matter of national security, only five minutes… Yes, I tried that, but he's a little insistent… Very well, I'll tell him."

She hangs up the phone and turns to Sid. "The President says if you can wait until after he meets with the Ambassador from Italy, he'll see you."

Sid replies, "That'll be just fine."

Bud, in his blunt and persistently unsuccessful manner, has been giving the woman at the coffee station the eye. He motions to her, thinking she must be a secretary. "Could I get a cup of black?"

She nods, then, smiling, pours him a cup and hands it to him. Margaret addresses her. "The President will see you now, Miss

Larotta." Miss Larotta walks toward the Oval Office door, graciously rocking her hips. The door opens and two Presidential arms reach out for a warm embrace. Miss Larotta leans into a kiss on the cheek and, doing so, lifts one foot off the carpet. Bud and Sid watch breathlessly as she slips in, closing the door behind her.

Sid gasps, "Holy smoke. She's the ambassador?"

"I always did like Italian food," Bud says, frowning. Sid's briefcase beeps and the sound of a miniature printer buzzes like a two-pound bumblebee. "Do we *have* to drag that damn thing around with us everywhere?" Bud complains as he looks at the briefcase.

Sid considers part of his duties for the Bureau to keep Bud respectfully irritated. "New director's policy. He's high tech."

"Why don't we just hang signs around our necks sayin' we're feds?" Sid opens the briefcase and Bud winces at the even louder sound of the tiny printer grinding away. After a moment it stops and Sid tears off a small sheet, handing it to Bud, who tries to read it at various distances from his face, then gives it back. "That's just great. What they need is little agents," gesturing with his thumb and forefinger, "this big to read the blasted things."

Agent Knowles reads the dispatch. "It's from Western. Something about the FAA reporting an aircraft heading in the direction of Utah."

"Why'd they send it here?"

"Seems coincidental with our boy Holmes going in the same direction at the same time. Some crazy stuff about an object of 'unknown type and size.'"

Bud's irritation meter moves through yellow and up into the red. "Well, what the *hell* is that freak up to now? Just might nudge this super yuppie toward our point of view."

The Holmes private airstrip was scratched out of a gently sloping plateau on a remote corner of the estate. Tom purchased thousands of acres southeast of Rockville, Utah, some of which belonged to the remnants of a Paiute tribe whose bloodlines ran up through fading generations to reach Francine, and thus his son.

This he had done during the period when it seemed like owning anything and everything that touched his boy's life felt in some way like a muddled revenge against that lost life.

The cliffs of Zion Canyon rise up in the distance, layered in hues of off-whites and yellows, illuminated by a noon Sun filtered through rippled cirrus. Two pinpoint shimmering lights in the western sky transform into the Citation as it lands and taxis directly into a hangar, the only structure on the private airport. The engines whine down, the doors unfold, and Tom emerges carrying the briefcase, handing it to a ramp boy as he walks outside in a hurry.

He approaches a cart stacked with pieces of electronic gear and hooks on an earpiece and mic. "Hey, Doc, you copy?"

After a moment of static, the Doctor responds. "Go ahead."

"I show seven DME and autocoupled. You concur?"

"I do. Are you coming down here? I need to talk to you."

"Give me a couple of hours. I'll be there"

Kirshner's tone tightens, his mood accentuated by the phase shift in the transmission. "We need to talk."

Sam and Matt walk up behind Tom. "How we doin'?" Matt asks, as if he cared.

"A few more minutes."

"Tell you what," Matt says, shaking his head, "sell that thing, I'll put it down on a small ranch. Make it a big ranch." Sam, more in touch with Tom's moods than Matt, glares at him while Matt ignores the *drop it* look in his eyes. "Like they say, he who dies with the most toys…" Sam hangs his head in disbelief as Tom looks into Matt's eyes. Matt starts to apologize, but Tom reads his regret and turns away. Sam shoves him and yells silently at the top of his lungs as Matt steps backward, stops, then walks away kicking dirt.

Sam searches for words. "Hey, I don't know what—"

"Don't worry about it. It's my problem, not his." He looks down the runway. "Did you draw up the papers I asked?"

"They should be ready by morning. You want to tell me what this is all about?" Tom pushes a switch on his panel, feigning distraction, and a light appears on the horizon. "As if I didn't know.

You're really going through with this, aren't you?" Tom continues with his remote control. "It's impressive, the way you maintain cover on all this, but you've got to realize one thing. There's a grapevine of people who care about you. We all bend the rules to make sure you're all right."

Tom turns slowly to meet Sam's eyes. Though most of his urges to reach out remain prisoner, a rare moment of vulnerability flickers in his gaze. He's grateful for his friend's concern, yet unable to respond. "I need you on the outside. To take care of things. The less you know, the better off you are."

"Sounds like a line from a B movie."

"You got something against B movies?"

"I love B movies."

Tom lands the Noah 3 with a few strokes of a joystick, watching it flare inches above the ground and touch down with tiny puffs of blue smoke from sixteen miniature aircraft tires. He taxis the model toward them and as it moves swiftly past, Sam watches, then turns back.

"It's just too damn hard to figure you. Most people, when they spin around in life, we all spin around sometimes, they just... come to a stop. You, you just keep spinning faster, you keep feedin' it. It's a waste, Tom. It's not what he would've wanted." Tom revolves toward him with a burning stare that turns inward. "I'm sorry. I shouldn't have," Sam says as Tom looks away again.

Tom sinks farther in. "You think I'm not overwhelmed by what he would have wanted? It's everywhere. It's in the wind, it's in the sky. It's in everything I see, and feel, and hear. It's deafening, trust me."

Sam looks up, trying to dispel the wrenching emotion. The pain he feels for his friend always revives his own loss; Sam was Noah's godfather. "Look, I wouldn't even begin to say I know how you feel. Even if I did, what good would it do? The whole world's deafened by the sound of suffering."

Tom has his back to him and Sam walks up and covers Tom's ears. "But let me tell you something. There's another sound, even louder. It drowns out everything else. It's sweet music, Tommy."

Sam turns him around, holding him at arm's length. "It's the song of victory." Sam presses. "Can't you hear it? Isn't that Noah singin' it right now?"

It startles Tom to hear his boy's name, the sound of it alone a razor-sharp dagger. He looks up at the big man's face, closes the briefcase, and the two walk silently toward the hangar.

As Tom and Sam approach, Eddie connects a scale-size radio-controlled tug to the tow bar already hooked to Noah 3's nose wheel. Matt watches as Eddie opens the cockpit hatch and retrieves the black box, handing it to Tom. With the hatch shut, the Noah 3 is slowly tugged into the hangar, dwarfed by a Boeing 727 sitting spotlessly with its landing gear doors open. Tom turns to Sam. "You goin' running with me?"

"Is that a rhetorical question?" Sam asks, cringing. Tom's smile answers. "Well then, I guess I'm goin' running with you."

"Good. Tomorrow morning, usual place." He pats Sam on the back and walks away. Sam turns to Matt for sympathy, but Matt responds by clutching his chest, then laughs as he follows Tom.

Bud paces, locomotive puffing on a cigar in the hallway outside the anteroom. The doors open behind him and he turns to encounter Miss Larotta standing, staring at him, her long brown hair cascading across bare shoulders. She hands him her empty coffee mug, walks provocatively to a drinking fountain and bends over with precise aim, taking a long, long drink. After straightening up, Miss Larotta walks away without a look back, leaving Bud to commence throwing his cigar butt on the ground until he remembers where he is. He finds an ashtray on an 18th century dropleaf table before entering the anteroom.

Sid stands as Bud glares at Margaret in expectation. "The President will see you now," she says, starting to rise, but Bud bolts ahead and enters on his own.

President Stamp, like his former law student Herlihy, is the youngest man in history to hold his office. He looks up as Bud lurches in, then stops, his gross entrance stunted by the place itself.

Sid walks respectfully up to the desk as Jonathan stands. Tall and strikingly handsome, he's certainly a match for Bud despite their age difference and long relationship. He shakes Sid's hand.

"Mr. President," says Sid.

The President nods, then shakes Bud's hand. Wasting no time, Bud slams another thick folder on the desk. "I'm here about Holmes."

"I know. I just talked to Herlihy."

Bud is hardly surprised. "News travels fast around here."

"Especially bad news. Do you realize this is only the second time in my administration I've let somebody in here without an appointment?"

Sid cringes and Bud starts to work up an apology, but it sticks in his throat. "How's your dad, by the way?"

Stamp looks at the folder. "He's about the same, thank you. Been getting around. Just not himself, though. He asked about you the other day."

"I feel bad I haven't been by. I've meant to—"

"That's not what he asked about. He wanted to know if you were giving me any trouble lately." Stamp looks at Sid, then at Bud. "I said no. You're not going to make a liar out of me, are you?"

"I'm not here to make trouble for you."

"He said to keep an eye on you."

"Funny, last time I saw him he said the same about you. He said, 'Watch Jonathan for me. Sometimes he doesn't let his right hand know what his left hand's doing.'"

Stamp looks at his right hand, top and bottom. "You want to tell me what's on your mind?"

Bud taps the folder. "It's your buddy, Holmes. I'm sure Herlihy filled you in."

"My *buddy*?" the President asks with a sharp glance toward Sid, who rubs his eyes as Bud halfheartedly realizes he's being a little too familiar. The President resumes his attempt at patience. "I've known Tom since MIT, and he's been instrumental in my campaigns. I think I might resent the implication."

Meyerkamp wobbles. "I'm sorry, Sir. It's just that I've got serious evidence here that—"

"'The sonofabitch is building a rocket.' I heard. You're serious?"

Bud pulls a photo from the folder. "Look at this, right here." He taps the picture hard. "There's a canyon on his property and he's got some kind of huge... thing over it. Won't let anybody near it. Besides, look at all this."

Stamp looks at the photograph as if it were blank. "Where'd you get this? Certainly isn't LandSat. This is high altitude reconnaissance."

Bud looks at Sid and everywhere but the President's eyes. "It's from an... a preexisting file."

"Really? Then it must be pretty old. How do you consider it relevant?"

Bud thumps his fist on the desk. "Listen, I need to do a low pass and see what's really there, but it's under restricted airspace and 'coincidentally' the Colonel in charge won't let me through. I don't understand what's going on here. Everybody and his grandmother's out to protect this guy."

Stamp stares at the fist so inappropriately resting on the platform from which the free world operates. "Tom built a children's wing on the base hospital. Is it any wonder Colonel Halloran is a little reluctant to let a bunch of FBI through his airspace?" Again he looks at Sid, then Bud. "What do you want from me?"

"I want to go in there and take a look."

"If Herlihy says there's not enough to go on, then I defer to his judgment."

Bud abandons all pretense of respect. "All right then, I'm sure there's enough room in the pan for both of you. Him, I don't mind seeing fry. You, I feel sorry for. I'll be sure to tell your dad it's not your left and right hands he should be worried about. It's the First Cheeks. You're liable to be parading them around if you sweep this thing under your... Oval Carpet. For chrissake, you play golf with him, and now he's Peter Pan and you're Wendy."

Sid steps between them, facing Bud. "I think you're going

too far this time, Bud. I don't want to be associated with this kind of talk in this kind of place."

Bud throws Sid a raging glance, but before he can say anything, the President pulls Sid aside. "This guy throws a nice block. You're lucky to have him. Chapter one, paragraph one. 'Get to know your enemy. Become one with him.' Start showing a little empathy for Tom Holmes. You'll not only get more cooperation from us, you might also do a better job."

Bud pauses. "Maybe you're right. But I could say the same about you. What makes all of you think he's not capable of this? I can understand how *he* might be blinded by his pain. But why are you?"

Stamp catches his breath. "I tell you what. I'll get the Colonel to let you fly over. Check back here in a few days. This is only because I'm concerned about Tom."

Bud strikes quickly, a black, shark-eye look. "Tomorrow. I want to fly over tomorrow." The President looks up at the ceiling, scratching his neck under his chin. Bud keeps pushing. "I have reason to believe there's no time to waste, judging from his latest movements."

President Stamp exercises his authority to give in. "Very well, tomorrow. But make *sure* you check with the Attorney General or me before you take any other steps. Am I clear?"

"Thank you, Sir. Mr. President."

"Oh, please. I'd love to dance, but you already stomped on my foot. Now get out of here." The President shoos them away with his hand, winking at Sid. Bud heads for the door, but before they exit he throws the small printout on the floor.

"By the way, take a look at this. Peter Pan might be up for an FAA violation."

Stamp eyes the paper at his feet as Bud walks out, leaving Sid to tidy up his behavior again. Sid picks up the printout and hands it to the President, then tries to thank him, quickly dismissed by another shoo of the hand.

In the hall outside the anteroom, Sid finds Bud waiting with his arms folded, a piercing stare worth a thousand four-letter words.

Bud knows enough to respect him for what he said, though he'd never tell him, gesturing for Sid to walk ahead. Sid complies, looking back as Bud remarks, "You know, speaking of cheeks, you've got a pretty decent pair. I suppose I shouldn't kick 'em." Sid stops and Bud walks by him.

President Stamp mulls over the predicament, takes the phone in his hand, puts it down, and takes it again. "Margaret, put a call through to Colonel Halloran at Nellis."

He hangs up the phone as hesitantly as he picked it up.

It's a cold canyon day in Zion National Park, the wind whistling through skeleton trees long since stripped of foliage by an early winter. Patches of snow on the ground, starkly white against the red canyon sand, pulsate as cloud shadows move across. An autumn leaf swirls in a small eddy in the Virgin River, continuing on to another as it moves downstream. Tom, crouching on a rock, watches.

He sees Zion on a boulder some ten yards upstream in attack position, wiggling his butt. Tom looks at his eyes, follows the focused stare, and spies a field mouse darting between rocks across the river. Though the river is only twelve feet wide at that point, it's certainly beyond the leap of any cat, proving the show of hunting skill to be just that. Tom moves to get a better angle, a rare smile surfacing until a diamondback rattler strikes from behind a rock so fiercely that the mouse is wedged in its jaw from the sheer momentum. Zion jumps straight up and out of his fur, landing on the side of the rock and slipping one leg into the water before he regains his balance and streaks toward the bushes. Tom falls backward, hitting his tailbone hard enough to cause a biting discomfort. As mad as he is startled, he bolts up and rubs his hands, blurting out, "Damnit!" He brushes off his pants, then looks up and sees the snake still there, waiting, the mouse either dead or paralyzed. It makes eye contact with Tom, sizzles its rattles, and withdraws behind the rock. Tom stares, then looks away. Then he stares again and, realizing he'd been holding his breath, exhales, walking backward. Finally, he turns, breaking into a jog toward his Hummer parked up on the road. Zion darts past him.

An eagle glides high above the river, her mouse now the property of another. She tilts her head, watching Tom's vehicle speed down a dirt road flanked by a block wall. The Hummer makes an abrupt left turn into a guard gate and a barrier arm raises as the eagle continues upriver.

Tom skids across parking spaces in front of an imposing corrugated-aluminum structure that houses, evidenced by the ten-foot high logo on the side: Marshall's Bread- "There's Nothing Like It". Tom slides down from the driver's seat, cat hanging from one arm, carrying the box from Cardona under the other. He kicks the car door so hard it comes open again and, paying no mind, shoulders through a small door cut into the receiving bay doors.

Tom crosses the expansive warehouse floor, empty but for a pile of pallets stacked in the corner near a lonely forklift. Offices on the far side look out to the warehouse through a long bank of curtained windows.

Dr. Kirshner peers through half-closed curtains and sees Tom walking toward the offices. He quickly puts out the cigarette he was smoking and shoves the ashtray into a drawer, then picks up a can of scented spray, covering his smoke tracks as he fans the air. He ends up throwing the can in the drawer with the ashtray, just in time as Tom explodes through the door. The Doctor sits a little too casually on a desk while Tom looks around and Zion sniffs the air.

"Smells like a lemon grove's on fire."

He drops Zion onto the desk, prompting Kirshner to pull a handkerchief from his back pocket and sneeze heartily into it, over-rubbing his nose. "That darn cat." The Doctor sneezes again, eyeing Zion as he paws at the secret drawer. "Why do you bring this cat here when you know it makes me sick?"

"As far as I know, Doc, no one ever got emphysema, cancer, or heart disease from a cat."

Kirshner ignores the lecture and takes the box from Tom, pulling out the valve. He turns it over and looks into it with the eyepiece that lives around his neck. "Excellent work. Louis has outdone himself. With any luck, we should have this in and running in a week."

"I want it in tonight."

Kirshner dribbles out a nervous laugh. "Tonight? That's impossible. Why, everyone's gone home, and even so—" The Doctor knows this look all too well. He puts the box down. "Is something wrong?"

"Suppose you tell me."

Kirshner walks to the window and looks out. "We've got trouble. All of a sudden, people are asking questions, wanting to come on the property."

"People?"

"FBI, although they won't admit it. I'm sure it was FBI that stopped me at the market."

"At the market?"

"They're everywhere, Thomas. This one walked up to me right in front of the bananas. He said he knew what was going on. That I'd be smart if I quit before it was too late."

"And?"

"I put down my bananas and swore I'd never eat one again." Tom laughs as Kirshner reels around. "This is no laughing matter."

"How soon can we go?"

The Doctor parts the curtains again to look at nothing. He turns back to Tom, hoping he's not hearing what he's hearing. "When we started this project, you told me you'd never take chances. You said in the end, we would probably never go."

"I lied. When can we go?"

"I just don't think—" Tom repeats the look. There's always been an unspoken understanding between them, loyalty born of similar experiences with darkness.

"Werner, I'd threaten you, but since you once told Hitler to goosestep to hell, I doubt it would do any good. You've known all along I was serious."

The Doctor's response sounds childlike in its resignation. "Two weeks at the earliest. If I start with this valve tomorrow, run some tests, maybe two weeks."

"When's the next window?"

"You can't be serious. I don't know. I..." It's no use fighting. He drags himself to a computer terminal where Zion sits on top of the monitor, tail dangling in front of the screen. Kirshner sneezes again, scaring the cat across the room, and impatiently pulls up a graphics program: spheres with tracks arcing to and from one another.

"Well," trying not to be heard, "there's one tomorrow." Speaking with contorted enthusiasm, he says, "Here's one in eighteen days."

Tom grabs Zion by the midsection, walks across the office, and opens the door. He turns and declares, "Put the valve in tonight. Skip the tests, and put everybody on alert." Kirshner is too stunned to retort as Tom pulls the door closed behind his exit. He peers through the curtains as Tom disappears through the door at the other end of the warehouse floor, sneezes one last time, and slams the curtains closed.

The Holmes mansion is a daunting structure, extracted from the same matter as the spectacular cliffs that surround it. The colors, textures, and substance of the land were coalesced into a dwelling which, though dwarfed by the majesty of Zion Canyon, holds its own compared to Tom's Hummer, looking like a toy car as it approaches up the switchback driveway that scales the butte upon which the home was built.

Towers jut up in no particular symmetry, giving the impression of a village built upon itself. Irregular levels suggest it was erected on a hillside, as was the custom of the Anasasi that settled the canyon thousands of years before, though it rests on level ground. Tom has erected a palace, a monument to the previous inhabitants of the fifteen thousand acres he calls home.

A setting Sun sprays shadows up the canyon, those from distant cliffs cast subtly, feather-like. The house, instead, casts a severe pattern, a shadow like crooked teeth across the curving river-bed below. Tom parks the dust-covered Hummer a few feet from the front door, a full story of roughly carved cedar, and walks toward it. Zion bounds ahead and enters before him through a cat door cut into one of the door panels.

The foyer alone is as large and elegant as a New Mexican townhome. Skylights in ceilings of staggered heights send shafts of light cutting across walls of delicate pink plaster and antique Navajo wall hangings. Tom stops to look in a mirror, straightening his hair and brushing dirt off his pants onto the red Saltillo floor. Hanging next to the mirror is a chrome-framed poster, a caricature in sparse black ink strokes of a woman seated at a piano, her long hair covering one eye. In bold, cursive print underneath: Isabel Flore- A Sampling of Bach- Lincoln Center- January 11. Tom stares at her.

Rosalee, his housekeeper and surrogate mother, a full-blooded Paiute of sixty-six, hurries in carrying Zion in her arms. "Mr. Tom! Where have you been? We expected you hours ago," she exclaims as Tom hugs her, sensing her agitation.

"Rosalee, when I see your beautiful face, 'I feel the stars shining on my back.'"

"You speak the words of my father," Rosalee says with a mild blush. Tom finds rest in her embrace, finally holding her at arm's length. "Isabel, she has been waiting. I don't think I've ever seen her so upset." Tom's brief smile falls. "Is there trouble?" Rosalee asks.

"Where is she?"

"In the Cantina." Tom kisses her forehead and walks away. She watches him with a look of pity and fear, sensing what she knows nothing about.

A portion of the Holmes mansion was built around a miniature butte, surrounded on all sides of an inaccessible courtyard by glass, looking into various rooms, and they looking upon it.

The Cantina, one such room, is just large enough to hold a compact but complete bar, two stools, and two small tables; a cocktail lounge compressed into a walk-in closet, illuminated only by light reflected off the minibutte. Silhouetted, facing outward, is a woman with waist length ebony-black hair. Isabel Flore holds a smoldering cigarette in one hand, a glass of wine in the other. Tom walks in and stops when he sees her, noticing a suitcase by her feet. He also notices the cigarette.

"I thought you quit for good this time."

She responds without turning. "I never quit. You 'suggested' I stop. There's a difference."

"What about the conversation we had? The one about your health?"

"Well, you know what they say…" Isabel, a stunning beauty from the hill country of Spain, turns around. "It's not the years in your life, it's the life in your years." Thirty-six, as sensuous as she is angry, Isabel has loved Tom deeply for several turbulent years, even at the distance he kept her. What stilted intimacy he's been able to find, emotional or otherwise, he has found in her. Isabel's devotion and concern for him have been matched only by the frustration of not seeing them through.

"I thought that was what we were talking about. Life," he says.

She barely looks around for an ashtray and ends up putting the cigarette out in her wine. "I have a theory about smokers. We secretly like putting our lives in danger. That way it seems like we have some kind of control. If we stop, we live longer. Make sense?" No answer. She looks into his eyes. "You should understand that."

"Let's not argue. Not today."

"I see. Are you in charge of arguing now? You seem to be running everything else around here." She pulls a wad of paper from her pocket and throws it at him, holding tears at bay. "What about this? Since when am I *informed* by my agent that I'm booked on one of your cruises? Are you suddenly my manager?"

"Isabel, I didn't mean to—"

Isabel shouts, starting to cry. "You can't order me around like some... ingenue!" She grabs her cane, propped against the window, and attempts to storm out. Born with a clubfoot, her furious limping exclaims the tantrum of sorrow. Tom stops her, pulls her to him, and she drops her cane in an outburst of tears, embracing him. "Please don't do it! Please don't!" She looks up at him with begging eyes. "You of all people. You know what it's like to lose someone you love." He can't respond. "You're everything in the world to me. Doesn't that mean anything to you?" Still no answer. "Do you know how empty it feels to know you can't even give someone a reason to live?"

Tom closes his eyes. "Isabel, don't you know? I could never have made it this far without you."

He rocks her and feels compelled to tell her what she wants to hear, but doesn't believe. "I'll come aboard somewhere. I'll surprise you. Would you like that?"

"Yes, Tommy," she doubts, looking into his eyes. "That would be nice." She picks up the suitcase and walks toward the door.

"Here, let me help you," Tom says.

"No. I've got it."

She starts to walk away, then turns around to take one last look, starting to say something, then not. She lingers, lowers her head, and walks out. Tom stands wooden.

The Holmes property encompasses a vast landscape, some of it cliff and canyon at the outskirts of the Zion formations. Tributaries feeding the Virgin River have gouged smaller canyons. In one such gorge, two FBI agents make their way downstream, crawling over boulders and through vegetation, dwarfed on both sides by dark, red and black vertical walls.

Though the river that crafted the gorge is not wide, it moves swiftly, making steady work against the crumbling sandstone of its banks. This leaves little area for passage as the men, having clawed their way up a large rock, slide down the other side, landing knee-deep in water. They splash out and stop for gulps of breath. Both are in their late forties, outfitted for the mission, but not in shape for it. One wears a green and the other a red rafting vest, the most obvious evidence of recently and poorly chosen gear for the mission.

The smaller of them, wearing the green vest, looks up at the setting Sun, placed in the narrow wedge of sky above. The other opens a topographical map. "It should be right around the bend if I'm reading this right." He points ahead to a sharp change in direction of the gorge to the left; so sharp, in fact, that they appear to be facing a wall. As their eyes accustom to the darkness of the narrowing, they realize there's an unnatural shadow resting against the face of that rock wall. It's modeled, as if filtered through something, but has linear edges and unlikely to be caused by anything the river made.

They look at each other, then the larger man looks back upriver. "Don't canyons... widen out when you go downstream?"

"Not this one, I guess," the other responds, looking downriver. "Well, let's go. I think we're onto something."

They manage their way around a bushy tree, wading waist deep to do so. As they climb back onto the bank and bend over, slapping water off their pants, they're struck still by a low-pitched and ominous voice.

"Are you boys... lost?"

They straighten up slowly, simultaneously reaching behind their backs. Towering before them is Mr. Bullard, a huge, burled man with a wiry foot-long beard, dressed in a security officer's uniform three sizes too small. Were he not so foreboding, they'd be tempted to laugh, a temptation seasoned by the double-barreled shotgun he lays dangerously across his belly. The other striking oddity is that there's not a speck of dirt on him.

"I'd keep my hands out front if I were you."

They obey slowly. "What the *hell* are you doing here?" blurts out one agent.

"Now isn't that a question I should be asking you?"

They're startled again, this time by movement across the river of another person, also uniformed, but half the size. The gun, though, is identical, and more directly pointed at them.

"We, uh, we're lost all right, aren't we?" the other agent says.

"That's right. We're lost. You boys wouldn't mind taking us out of here, would you?" his partner says, pointing downstream toward the bend.

Mr. Bullard points upstream. "First rule of thumb when you're lost: go back where you came from. I think it's pretty obvious, with the river and all."

"Listen, mister, I said we're lost," says the agent with the red vest. "What good would it do to go back? We're trying to make it to... Roundtree."

"*Roundtree?*" thunders Bullard. He looks up at the sky and the shriek of a hawk echoes off the canyon walls. "This here river don't go nowhere near Roundtree." He glares through one at the other. "I don't know where you all started, but I can tell you one thing. This river only goes one way. Whatever your story is, I don't want to hear it. Now, move on back upriver."

"Hold on a minute. What right have you got to—"

Mr. Bullard cocks his trigger, silencing him. The giant of a man motions his head back without taking his eyes off them. They look over him at a land survey flag. "This here's private property, and I'm tellin' you right now, without a doubt, you ain't crossin' it."

Powerless without a warrant, they capitulate, walking backward into the water. "What's your name? And... who do you work for?" demands the one with the green vest.

"My name's Bullard. Mr. John Bullard. And who I work for's none of your *friggin'* business." They wade away and hear the uncocking of the shotgun as they leave.

Bullard watches them disappear, then pulls a walkie-talkie from his belt and calls into it. "Blockhead, Blockhead, this is River Rat, do you copy? Over."

The stables are a half-mile from the main house at the edge of a plateau that overlooks a meadow through which the Virgin winds in broad bends, disappearing occasionally beneath groves of winter-barren cottonwoods and Bigtooth Maples. Tom built the stable with the horses in mind, a thatched hut with the walls hinged up, leaving the structure supported by timbers on four corners. In this mode it's a peaceful shelter from the Sun during the day, allowing the canyon breeze to sweep through in the evening. The horses are happy, living outdoors, yet pampered by those who care for them.

Tom saddles Cirrus with the help of Billy, his stableboy. Cirrus is a Medicine Hat Paint. Mostly white, he has a few dark spots about him, the most distinctive a brown cap covering the top of his head and ears. So striking is this marking that venerable tribes of ages past named it a Medicine Hat, and considered it a talisman, bringing good fortune to its master and driving away evil spirits. Cirrus has the other characteristic of many Medicine Hats: nearly human blue eyes.

Billy is Rosalee's grandson and last living male descendant of her brother, Sunman Whitewater. Sunman was the reigning chief of the local Paiutes, a noble and long-standing tribe that flourished for generations, this particular band claiming mixed blood with the ancient Anasasi. Though Billy is the chief now by right, his tribe has been scattered, and thus his reign. All those who know say he has the spirit of a chief, and love and respect him, and therefore their ancestors through him. Billy is only fourteen, Tom's only brush with childhood since Noah.

The Sun has set, bringing the afternoon outflow from the canyon. Flurries of red dust whip up, rousing the horses against their reins, and canyon colors approach misty gray, preparing for the darkening sky. Tom strokes Cirrus's neck. "I don't know how you do it, Billy. Nobody makes a coat come out like this."

"My people believe that a man and his horse share a soul. This horse looks for you when you're not here, and his eyes shine when you ride him. It's no wonder his coat is so bright."

Tom stops to look at Billy. He's always felt a sense of awe toward the boy. No manner of lavish gifts would he accept from Tom, saying that his journey would be long and he must travel light. He did accept, at Rosalee's insistence, a trust for his education. She has always kept Billy's searching spirit in line with his keen intellect, as brilliant in school as he is wise. Tom takes a handful of oats and feeds them to his horse. "If only I had the blood of your people. Your strength and courage."

"Chief Sunman thought of you like a son, Mr. Holmes. Blood flows from the heart, and he said yours was a Paiute heart."

"No matter what came upon him, he stood tall. Even when he rode away for the last time." Tom looks at the oats in his hand and takes out one grain. "I'm like a seed. There's nothing smaller than I am."

Billy helps Tom throw a saddlebag over the horse, then fastens a hand-woven basket to the back of the saddle as Tom fills the bag with supplies. "Many times in a man's life he must ride into the wind, times when he is overcome by all around him. The sky weighs heavy and the Earth pushes up. He finds his pony and rides into the wind, and the Father of Winds speaks to him. The taller he stands, the harder the ride. But he always returns wiser, until he rides for the last time. And then the wind is the strongest, but he rides through it and comes out to the other side where there is only calmness and peace."

Tom looks out across the folds of red land. "That time the Chief rode off, the last time, he knew. He knew it was his last ride." Tom mounts Cirrus as Billy picks up Zion and puts him in the basket.

"I can see in your eyes, Mr. Holmes, that you are standing against the wind. You should know our beliefs say that before a warrior does this, he must face one enemy and make peace with him. The enemy may be a great warrior, or it may be an enemy within himself. And with that enemy, he must trade something, something hardest for each to give away. Only then will the wind speak." Tom grabs the reins, making Cirrus prance in place, then gazes into Billy's awaiting stare.

"You say you feel small," Billy says, leading Cirrus away from the shelter toward the edge of the plateau. Stars begin to glitter in the canyon breeze as he looks toward the north and, using his hand spread wide at arm's length, measures across faint constellations. "Look up here, Mr. Holmes. You see, just above the top star in that triangle?"

Tom takes a moment to locate the star. "OK, I see it. The star, I mean."

Go up one hand, and if you look hard, you'll see a small blur, like a feather."

"I think I see it."

"There's a galaxy next to it, MCG 6-30-15. It's a hundred thirty million light years away, too faint to see. Not a big one, really. Nothing special about it... except there's a black hole in the center. So far they think it's swallowed about a hundred million stars." Tom looks at Billy, not sure why he's ever amazed by what the boy says.

Billy continues. "There's a theory that in the end, a black hole collapses all that matter to the size of a subatomic particle. The force of gravity approaches infinity. In fact, it's said that all the matter in the universe," he picks up a rock, "was smaller than this. Before the light."

"I don't get it," Tom says as he takes the rock and looks at it, overcome with a flooding sensation.

Billy lays his hand on Tom's leg and cinches the saddle tighter. "Small is not what it appears to be, Mr. Holmes. Each great elm was once a seed, and all other living things, too. Before a man's spirit can grow, he must break away all that he has become in this world, down to the seed of his soul, and be watered with the Tears of God. Stand tall and ride. You will either return stronger, or you will ride through it." Tom stills as the young man's words filter through. He pulls Billy to him, stroking his head with affection and gratitude, then rides away.

Fading pink and orange contrails fan across the darkening blue-black sky above a pair of headlights barreling down a deserted stretch of highway, not far from Rockville. The truck is a double tanker, apparently in a hurry. Crudely stenciled on the side of the truck is: MOO JUICE- GRADE A MILK, FRESH FROM THE FARM. Two more headlights drift into the passing lane as a hand reaches out and places a spinning red light on the roof above.

Inside the truck cab, the driver and his partner, modern day cowboys of the road riding diesel rigs as if they were on the open range, look at the red light flashing on each other's faces. The driver, Jake, tightens on the steering wheel. "Where the *hell* did he come from?"

"I told you you was goin' too fast," says his partner, Henry.

"Sonofa... He must've had his lights off."

The unmarked car pulls ahead and forces them to a shuddering stop. Two plainclothes officers exit the car and walk toward the cab, each reaching into his jacket. Henry gnashes, "God dang. We're in trouble now. I get a bad feeling about this. You know damn well we were s'posed to do this in two rigs. Five miles apart, that's what they told us."

"Look, when Tom Holmes' people say jump, we don't even ask how high. Your rig was down and besides, we're gettin' paid for two. What're you bitchin' about?" They watch the men approach. "They don't even look like cops. How do we know they're not hijackers?"

"Now who in the world is going to hijack a truckload of milk? Only I wish it really *was* milk. No, they're not cops. They's worse." One of the officers pounds on the driver's door while wagging a badge, motioning them to come out. Jake and Henry climb down from the cab.

"Special Agent Bodine. This is Agent Watson. We're federal marshals. Can we see your load manifest, please?"

Jake plays dumb. "Marshals? What in tarnation is the problem? I didn't think we was goin' *that* fast. Do you have a warrant or something?"

Watson chimes in. "We don't need a warrant, now give us

the manifest."

Henry reluctantly retrieves a clipboard from the cab, handing it to Bodine who looks it over quickly, then hands it to Watson. "Taking this 'milk' to Holmes Breads are you?"

Henry camouflages his fear with unconvincing anger. "That's right. What's the problem?"

The marshals alternate responses, like raptors circling. "We'd like to see this 'milk'. You boys come on back here and spill some on the road for us."

Jake's voice vibrates with a frequency of panic. "Now look here, you can't make us—"

"Listen to me, cowboy. Can you spell, 'national security'? Can you use it in a sentence?" Watson snaps.

Jake clenches his fists and puffs his chest. "What the hell is *that* supposed to mean?" he snarls through gritted teeth, spitting in the agent's face.

"It means I got a license in my pocket with a picture of your ass on it. Now move!"

Jake starts to lean toward him, but Henry intervenes. "It's no use." He leads them to the center of the truck, between tanks, where there's a large valve through which milk would be pumped. He opens the valve and nothing comes out.

"You see, we're plum out of any milk. This is an empty run."

The marshals look at each other, then focus back. "I don't think so. We could tell by the way this truck was riding it's full of something," says Watson. They walk up and down the length of the truck until one notices two other valves, one on each tank, each a shade of red. "Now what might these be for?" Henry and Jake look at each other, backing up.

"I really don't know. Now can't we just be on our way?" Henry asks, backing up faster.

"How about if we find out?"

As the marshals each reach for a valve, Jake and Henry yell while running from the truck, "Don't! Don't open those!" The marshals move away from the valves.

* * *

Tom and Cirrus plod across a dry riverbed just outside Springdale. Streetlights burn orange in the distance and the faint sound of activity rises and falls with the breeze. Above, a thickening sky of stars sparkles behind swiftly moving clouds and Tom looks up, sensing the approach of weather. He turns and surveys his surroundings while he pulls a silver flask from his coat, takes a slug, and shudders as it goes down. He wipes his mouth with his sleeve, his attention focusing on the lights ahead. Billy's words float through. He must face an enemy... must make peace with one enemy. Tom puts the flask back in his pocket and starts Cirrus trotting with a whip of the reins.

Highway 9, also Springdale's main street, sits quietly on the outskirts of town until Tom and his horse clatter up from the dry bed below. He rides ahead, then stops, taking the flask out again. After looking at it, he changes his mind, puts it back, and continues down the street.

Cirrus stops in front of the Noah House and Tom dismounts. The building is in darkness but for a faint, moving glow through the front glass doors and a floodlight shining on the statue in front. He walks with leaden feet toward the statue and stops. Before him stands the bronze figure of a boy with his hand outstretched toward the sky, and balanced on top of his pointing finger is a chrome butterfly. Above, as if the pointing boy knew, the cloud cover has broken, revealing a bright patch of stars. Tom stares, swallows the lump in his throat, and walks toward the front door. Before pulling the door open, he reads the arched gold-leaf lettering over the top: IT'S A BEAUTIFUL DAY. Tom built the House in memory of his son, but has never set foot inside.

He enters and stops. There's no activity, though children's voices drift down the hallway. To the right he sees a small girl standing solemnly in front of a glass case recessed into the wall, before it a cherry-wood table. And in front of her, through the glass, is a painted scene of an ocean with moonlight reflecting across the water. On the table in front of the painting is a forest of candles, flickering as if in rhythm to some silent hymn. Tom breathes in the melancholy odor of scented flames and braces as the hallway walls shift with the candlelight.

Behind the candle forest is a photograph of a boy and a glossy brass plaque near it bearing the name "Bobby Wolford". Bobby smiles as he holds a shiny red fire engine, a gift for his fourth birthday, his last birthday, a loving parent's hand on his shoulder. This was a creation of the children themselves, who, when the first of them died, wanted to burn a candle in memory, and so it became a tradition. These children, facing death so courageously, had shown that through the loss of one of them, there was hope for the rest. To them, this little shrine was a statement that they could face anything. Bobby Wolford had been the last to pass, and his candles were lit.

The girl stares into the flames, then continues down the hall. Tom approaches the glass case and, searching for strength, looks in. Pinned around the ocean picture are many smiling little faces.

A nurse appears, walking briskly around a corner. She stops when she sees Tom, at first surprised by the mere presence of a stranger, then laying a hand over her heart when she realizes who he is. Following close behind is Roberta, a Guatemalan girl all of seventeen. Though practically a child herself, she raised her many brothers and sisters with little help from her father after her mother died. That caring spirit and affiliation with hardship drew her to this work.

"Oh, my goodness. Mr. Holmes. I... I'm shocked to see you here." She extends her hand. "Nurse Crumb." Tom takes it and she feels the sweat of his palm, withdrawing quickly. "And this is Roberta. She takes care of the children."

Roberta's accent complements her ancestral features. "Pleased to meet you, sir."

Nurse Crumb grabs Roberta's arm and flusters. "This is Mr. Holmes! He's the man who gave us this wonderful place!" She turns back toward Tom, focusing on his pale stare. "Are you all right, Mr. Holmes?"

Tom, aware of his emotional state, tries to reassure Nurse

Crumb, though within, the battle rages. "I'm fine, really. Just a little... I'd like to see the children. If that's permitted."

"Why, of course. Of course. They were just getting ready for bed. Come with me." Nurse Crumb leads him down the hall, motioning Roberta to follow.

The Starbridge is the sleeping quarters for the patients. It's a circular activity room with the children's individual cubicles opening into it. Designed to look like the flight deck of a spaceship, with pilot stations doubling as desks and futuristic conduits running along walls and ceilings, it gives the children of Noah House a special world, removed from their tribulations.

There are fifteen children, some playing, some sitting quietly, in various degrees of health. A few look perfectly normal, most look ill, the remainder have ravaged hair and gaunt faces. Nurse Crumb opens the double swinging doors that lead in, but Tom stops, frozen by what he's been avoiding since he built the House. It takes only moments for the children to realize there's someone watching. They turn and look.

"Children, we have a very special visitor. This is—" Tom touches her shoulder, arresting the introduction.

Jason, the oldest boy, steps forward. "You're Mr. Holmes, aren't you?"

Tom draws a difficult breath. "Yes, son, I am."

Jason takes Tom by the arm and leads him to a round table as the children gather. Nurse Crumb slips into an office that overlooks the Starbridge and initiates a phone call.

"This girl over here is my best friend. Her name is—"

"Melody. I know," Tom says.

Melody Baxter sits in a wheelchair, permanently bent over at the waist, her head resting sideways on a pillow. She turns her wheelchair to look at Tom.

"You know my name?"

"Sure I do. And that's Bridget over there, and Joshua. There's Sara, Stephanie, Jose, Maria, Jessica, Dusty, Robert, Shane, Raji. Let me see, Sonya, and... where's Angela?"

Maria, a frail little thing with pigtails as long as she is, responds. "She went potty."

"Oh. You see, when each new kid comes here, they give me your picture and tell me about you. I know all about you."

Bridget is bald, her head partly covered with a backwards ball cap. "I can't believe you know all of us. Because we've never met you. Why don't you come over and see us sometimes?"

Tom, convicted, replies, "Well, it's because I've had a hard time with a lot of things. And I've felt very sorry for myself. So, I was scared to come here."

Sonya clomps forward in her leg braces. "Is it because of Noah?"

It touches him they know. "That's right."

Melody rolls closer with laborious but persistent effort. She must position herself for each address, deprived of the ability to glance. "Could you tell us about him? All we know is what his favorite song was, that he died when he was eight, and that he wanted to be an astronaut and go to the Moon. That's why you made this place like a spaceship."

Tom's eyes close at the collision of pain from the mere mention of his son, and the pitiful state of the sweet girl asking.

"Sure, I'll tell you about him."

Sam and Matt sit on opposite poles of a never-ending modular couch, fidgeting. The Holmes living room is sunken a few feet and protrudes out over one end of the bluff, giving the impression a great ship came to rest in a sea of red sand. Uninterrupted glass presents a sweeping view of the pale-blue canyon narrowing in the distance. Sam gets up for the second time in the last minute and walks toward the glass, looking into the night.

"I wish he wouldn't go riding off like this. Did you try to call again?"

Matt snaps, "I told you, man. He's got to have the phone turned off. What's the big deal? He'll turn up. He always does."

"He needs to know about those two maroons we found on the river. I don't like what's going on. Besides, Doc's got his panties in a wad. Says he has to talk to him tonight."

"Well, stop the world, I wanna get off. Doc's got his panties in a wad. Doc's *always* got his panties in a wad. About this big." Matt mocks with his fingers, as if holding a BB. Sam doesn't even turn around.

"You know as well as I do Tom's not in the best state of mind."

"He just needs to go out and get lost for a while. Maybe he'll feel better."

The phone rings across the room, turning them around. After two rings Rosalee enters the room, drying her hands with a dish towel, and answers. Though they can't hear her words, Sam and Matt look at each other, sensing a tone of surprise, then back at her as she hangs up and walks toward them. Rosalee stops.

"It's about Mr. Holmes. He's at the children's house."

Sam is shocked. "The *Noah* House?"

Matt frowns and looks sideways at Sam. "I thought he's never gone in there."

"He hasn't." Sam turns back toward Rosalee. "What's he doing? Is he all right?"

"The nurse said he looked pale. To tell you the truth, I'm worried."

Sam reaches for his leather coat lying on the sofa back. "I don't like the feel of this. I'm going down there."

Matt stops him. "Whoa, big fella. I've seen Tom like this before. He knows I hang out at Wiley's across the street. I'll just say I spotted his horse and thought I'd nose in. Any objection?"

Matt looks at both of them and Rosalee nods. As Matt walks away, she exclaims, "Call us!"

"And tell him about Doc!" Sam adds, as if Matt were listening. Matt disappears, and after a moment of silence, the front door slams so hard they both flinch, even though he does it every time.

Wiley's is Springdale's most popular, and only, sports bar, though called a "club" thanks to local drinking laws. Matt's filthy old truck pulls up in a cloud of dust, some of which it brought on its own. He clangs the truck door shut, stops to snicker at a life-size cardboard figure of Khomeini with a sign hung around his neck reading "Sponsor", then walks across the street where he sees Cirrus standing alone. Alone, that is, except for one cat sitting on the saddle. He stops to stroke the horse's mane, scoops up Zion, and walks through the front doors of Noah House.

Matt saunters bowlegged down the hallway and stops to look at the candle forest, wondering what it is until he hears the sound of children laughing. He continues toward the sound and reaches the double doors to the Starbridge. He peers through the small windows, drawing back in disbelief, hesitates, then walks through like a cowboy barging into a saloon, pushing both doors open at once. There he finds the children sitting around Tom, who notices Matt's entrance. For a moment Tom tones down, but then smiles when Matt does. Zion leaps out of Matt's arms and hops into Maria's lap, she as surprised as the cat is comfortable.

Tom senses he's been there awhile. "Well, kids, it's late, and I bet you should already be asleep."

Jason lights up. "You know what? I think the kids would like to sing Noah's song for you. It's kind of our theme song around here."

Tom imperceptibly panics. "Oh, I don't think—"

"Please? Please?" they beg.

Tom looks at Matt and gets a thumbs-up. "I think that would be very special."

Tom watches the children run for instruments: maracas, tambourines, and a guitar that Jason straps on. Roberta, blushing, takes a dulcimer and sits with the rest. After checking with the others, she starts. Bridget sings lead, and the crowd accompanies.

> They say when the Sun shines down it's a beautiful day.
> They say when the Sun shines down it's a beautiful day.
> They say when the Sun shines down it's a beautiful day.
> Oh, oh, oh, oh,
> It's a beautiful day.
> It's a day to sing, sing to the beat.

It's a day to dance, ooh and tap your feet.
It's a day, for everyone,
Oh, oh, oh, it's a day of beautiful Sun.

They say when the Sun shines down, it's a beautiful day.
They say when the Sun shines down, it's a beautiful day.
They say when the Sun shines down, it's a beautiful day.
Oh, oh, oh, oh,
It's a beautiful day.

It's a day to laugh, laugh out loud.
It's a day to smile, and blow away a cloud.
It's a day, to clap your hands.
It's a day, to hear the band.

They say when the Sun shines, down it's a beautiful day.
They say when the Sun shines, down it's a beautiful day.
They say when the Sun shines, down it's a beautiful day.
Oh, oh, oh, oh,
It's a beautiful day.
Oh, oh, oh, oh,
It's a beautiful day.

When they finish, they generate a round of well-deserved applause, which of course Tom, and even Matt join as Tom rises to leave. He walks over to Melody and bends down, placing his hand on her back. She reaches out and touches his arm. "Thank you, Mr. Holmes. Thank you for everything."

Sara, a little black girl who hasn't spoken all night, surprises her friends. "Will you come see us again?"

Tom struggles to keep the smile. "Maybe. Maybe I will." Maria runs up and hugs his leg. He strokes her hair, and she smiles as she steps back. "You take care."

Tom walks out and Matt looks at the children, picks up Zion like deadweight, winks at them, and departs. They stand, watching the doors swing back and forth to a close.

Tom explodes through the front doors, followed by Matt. "Slow up there, mister. You forgot something." Tom stops, staring straight ahead, and Matt turns him around, sobering when he sees his face. "Oh boy. You look like you could use a beer."

"I think I'll just ride off. I'll be all right," Tom says, shivering.

Matt shakes his head. "Now, now, Thomas. I'm not givin' back this here pussycat until you say you'll have a beer with me."

"Some other time, Matt. I'm not in the mood."

Matt puts his hand around Zion's neck. "Which is it? A cold one, or seventy-five cents worth of fiddle strings?"

Getting no reaction, he persists. "Look here. Your 'mood' lately makes me think you and Uncle Ayatollah over there should be pen-pals. You two have a lot in common. You both got the same damn look on your faces all the time." Tom keeps his head down, but rolls his eyes up to meet Matt's. "I had to throw a short field tackle to stop Mother Sam from coming down here and cluckin' and flappin' his wings around you like an ol' barnyard hen. Now the least you can do is walk over there with me. Besides, I get the idea this might be our last chance. For a while." Tom capitulates with a poor excuse for a smile. "All right, good." Matt drags him across the street and before entering Wiley's, puts Zion down. "You go 'round back there. Wiley'll give you some nice calf fries or somethin'."

Wiley's is packed with some fifty regulars at the bar or tables, the close quarters making the small crowd seem bigger. There's an active pool table in back and a jukebox plays Garth Brook's *Low Places* a little too loud. Tom and Matt enter, Matt smiling, Tom squinting through the smoke. The smell of cigarettes, beer, and a stale bar pulls Tom into an old world, one as foreign as the present. At first they go unnoticed, but when enough see who it is, all but the music subsides as eyes turn toward the door. Tom stops, but Matt forges ahead.

"Hey, Phil, Ronny, fellas. How goes it?"

After an eternal second or two, a smattering of *Hey Matts* and even a couple of *Hiya Toms* rise back to chatter, though the tone remains subdued. Tom is as uncomfortable as they, for different reasons. Many think he's been unfriendly, aloof, or both, having not come around much anymore. Some feel uneasy around him, just knowing the tragedy he suffered, while others are in awe of him. And then there are those just plain jealous of his wealth. Nevertheless, as they sit at the bar, several passersby pat Tom on the back. Wiley walks up and plants a beer in front of Matt.

"Tom Holmes. I was beginning to think you'd opened your own joint down the road."

Tom's disquiet stirs his smoldering mood. "I've just been... busy."

"Hey, I've still got a case of Kalik in the cooler. Wouldn't give it to anyone but you. Want one?"

"Sure, Wiley. That'd be great."

Wiley reaches into the cooler and comes up with a dusty bottle that he wipes with a mangy bar rag. He pops open the beer and thumps it onto the bar. Tom takes a slug as Matt forces the mood upward. "Kalik. Ha! Remember the week we were stuck in Nassau? Hurricane Hortense wasn't it?"

Tom resurrects the smile. "Yeah, something like that."

"Yes sirree. Two days in a storm cellar. Just you, me, and a wall of Kalik kegs. 'Takes a Kalikin' and keeps on tickin.' I think it was you that came up with that."

Tom squeezes out a chuckle. Across the room, a woman laughs out loud as someone at her table knocks over a drink. She's just shrill enough to summon Tom's attention and he glances over, trying to focus through the confusion as she's handed a beer by the waitress. Tom turns back, frowning, and Matt notices, but he's determined.

"I think that was the time we rescued that poor native girl from those Russian sailors." The same woman bursts out again, causing Tom to turn immediately. She's obviously drunk and more than slightly uncouth, even to the point of grating against Matt, though he continues the disintegrating attempt to salvage a few moments of normalcy. He grabs Tom's arm and pulls him around. As Tom turns away, she stands up with her beer in her hand.

"Remember how 'grateful' she was?" Matt strains, buckling under the force of Tom's gathering storm. These words echo in the distant regions of Tom's being, unintelligible and unimportant compared to what his subconscious picks up from the corner of his eye. She's at least seven months pregnant, and a rage is ignited in the deepest part of him, a rage that's become common ground for his tortured existence. He bolts off his stool and charges toward her. It all happens so fast, Matt can barely react. "What the… Hey! Tom!"

She's still laughing and slobbering, unaware that Tom is standing three feet away, glaring at her as the chatter and noise come to a tittering halt. Finally, she can't help but turn her attention to the silhouette casting a black, disapproving shadow upon her.

Tom seethes, "Do you have *any* idea what you're doing? Or do you even think at all?"

She looks around, laughing and bleary-eyed. "Excuse me?"

Tom snatches the beer from her hand, spraying it in her face. "HEY!" she shouts as she rubs the sting of alcohol from her left eye.

Her husband halfheartedly grabs his arm. "Now just wait a second, there."

Tom breaks his grip with a swift arm fling, never taking his eyes off the woman, then splashes the beer all over her pregnant belly. "Why not try it like this? Maybe it'll get there faster."

She throws her chair back, hitting the cowboy next to her in the leg. "Why, you *bastard!* Who the *hell* do you think you are?"

She takes a wild swing, but Tom catches her hand as the husband really makes a start. Matt pulls his way through the crowd, pushing the husband back and holding him at bay with an outstretched arm. "Take it easy, Barney. Nobody's going to hurt your wife."

Matt peels Tom's hand off her wrist, which she withdraws, rubbing it with the other hand. "Come on. Let's get out of here."

Tom turns to the husband. "And you? You're the husband? You trying to defend her 'honor'?"

Barney looks down as she leers around, expecting some-one to come to her rescue. Most look away. "What's the matter with all of you? Afraid to stand up to the great Tom Holmes?" She turns to Tom. "Well, let me tell *you* something. You may own most of this town, but you don't own me. And you sure as *hell* don't own this baby."

Matt grabs Tom's arm and strains to pull him. Tom never unlocks his stare. "I guess I don't." He leans forward, six inches from her nose, and with red contempt spewing from his eyes, fires back, "But neither do you."

Matt pulls him overcenter with a grunt and drags him off as far as the bar where Tom shakes himself loose from Matt's grip. Matt grabs him again, but Tom slaps his arm away and holds up his hand in surrender.

"I'm OK. I'll be all right."

"Oh yeah? That's what you said ten minutes ago."

Tom notices Wiley standing at the end of the bar, one eye twitching. Pinned to the wall next to him is the poster warning of the effects of alcohol on pregnancy. Tom walks over, rips it off the wall, and throws it at Wiley. "Try printing this on some toilet paper and put it in the can where it'll do some good."

Tom stares him in the eye, then charges out, nearly knock-ing the door off its hinges. "You don't come around here for months, then you show up and cause a ruckus!" he shouts at Tom's back, the words lodging crossways in his throat. Wiley looks at Matt, who tips his hat.

"We'll stop by again when we can spend more time," Matt says, his concocted grin fading as he walks backward toward the door.

Tom stands in the middle of the street, steaming in the cold night air, his hands in his pockets when Matt explodes out, another test of Wiley's door as it recoils off the wall on its way to rattling shut. He walks furiously in all directions, his breath com-ing out in short, angry puffs. The wind gusts around them, spin-ning snow across the pavement, and Matt, truly beside himself, flails his arms.

"I don't know what the *devil* gave me the notion I could take you in there and just have a couple a beers and some meaningless conversation." He paces, fueling his anger by the motion of it. "But no. You got to walk in there and take the whole world on your shoulders again like goddamn Mr. Atlas."

Tom looks straight up toward the night sky, taking deeper breaths to calm himself. "Hold the world up? You've got to be kidding. Try... falling off the edge."

"You know, I thought *I* owned the title in finding trouble. But I give up my crown to *you*. You not only find trouble, but if it's not there, you conjure it up out of thin air!" Tom looks back down, expecting and deserving to take this round from Matt, who points at the Noah House.

"Take for instance, your little visit over there. Now why? Tell me why you had to do that to yourself. Especially now. You're a tickin' bomb, for chrissake. What's the matter? Your fuse wasn't burning fast enough?"

Tom whips around. "I had to face the enemy."

Matt reflects back confusion, clouded with skepticism. "Face the enemy?"

"That's right." He looks at the Noah House. "But he wasn't there."

Matt rubs his eyes. "I see. That's just great. So then you went right across the street here and made another one, or two, or three."

Now Tom starts the pacing. Matt rides the swell, his efforts to dispel it losing ground. "You know what the term in scripture is for being pregnant?" Tom says. "It's being 'great with child'. Did she look to you like she was 'great with child'?" Tom walks a few yards down the center of the street toward the darkness, winding up tighter. "Isn't this 'lovely' world hard enough to drag yourself through without your own mother reaching into her womb and trying to get at you during what should be the safest part of your life?"

Tom shakes a terrifying gesture with his arm and closed

fist. Matt can barely speak. "Good God, Tom. You paint some pretty nice scenes for yourself."

"Nice, huh? That's how I go through life. It's like a bad movie, one horrible scene after another. And you know what? I can't walk out. Somebody's holding my eyes open, and I have to watch it all, and none of it makes any sense. Look at this." He stands in the street, pointing to each side with his arms outstretched. "Two struggles for life on either side of the street. One before birth, one after."

"Who ever said any of it has to make sense?"

"You know when the wheels really started coming off for me? Remember Jessica McClure, the little girl who fell down the well?"

"Who doesn't?"

"The whole world came to her rescue. Everybody was hanging on the edge of their seats at the six o'clock news, and so they should have been. I was on my knees along with everyone else. And bless her heart, she made it." Tom fights back tears. "But you know what else was on the six o'clock news that night? Halfway across the country in a dirty, filthy building in New York City, a little girl was tied to a chair, beaten until she was brain dead by a drug addict father who walked out the door to find a fix." Tom turns to Matt, his eyes glazed over. "Where was the whole world for her? Who was on their knees for her?"

Matt is speechless. "Don't you see?" Tom begs.

Silence.

Matt gathers up a response. "Like I said, where's it written it has to make any sense?" He walks up, nose-to-nose. "You know who the guy is that it all makes 'sense' to? The one who has it all figured out? He's the one down in some jungle someplace that poisons himself and takes nine hundred people with him. And you know what? You know what, Tom? He has *no* trouble at all findin' people to go with him. Because if *they* don't have it all figured out themselves, they figure *he* does."

This time Matt walks to the center of the street and, holding his arms up, turns a complete circle. "Look around, Tom. Does this look like *A Wonderful Life* to you? Does this look like Bedford Falls?" He walks back up to Tom. "Do you think you're George Bailey, and everything is *supposed* to come out OK in the end?" Tom looks into Matt's eyes. "Every time a bell rings, pal, it doesn't mean an angel gets her wings."

Tom softens. "You sure about that?"

"When I was a kid, my daddy'd come home most every night, and he'd ask me questions 'til he found a reason to slap me around. There was always a good enough reason, just like clockwork. And guess what? It got to where while he was beatin' on me, it felt good. Know why? Because I figured it just couldn't possibly get any worse than this." This time Tom is hearing, and listening.

"I think that's the way people should look at life when they step in a pile of it." Matt puts his arm around Tom, trying to get a rise out of him, with little success. He's close though. "You know what my philosophy of life is?"

"I'm afraid to ask," he says, facing down.

"When I die, make damn sure they bury me face down." Tom looks up at him. "That way the whole world can kiss my ass."

Tom can't help but give a head shaking smile. "That's a hell of a philosophy, Matt."

"Isn't it? Makes a lot of 'sense', don't it?"

Tom blinks a couple of times. "You really know how to cheer a guy up."

Matt pushes Tom toward his horse. "Go on. Ride off into them canyons. There must be some poor critter out there you can pick a fight with." Tom mounts his horse, but not before surprising Matt with a swift but strong bear hug, Matt's uneasiness with affection heightened by a sense of farewell. Tom rides off into the enveloping night as Matt shudders quietly from a chill of sorrow that passes through him.

Towering cliffs become but jagged black edges around the dark horizon as the widening canyon follows the Virgin River downstream. They strike sharp contrast to a sky so thick with stars that star shadows, cast by clouds as they drift by, offer welcome relief to the eye. There's a small hill in the middle of this vast openness to the top of which climb a horse and rider, silhouetted by the bright night sky. A full Moon is about to rise, heralded by a ghostly radiance that shimmers and pulses through the cold air. Then the edge breaks, a searing white wedge between cliff and heavens.

Horse and rider are cast against the stars, watching the rising Moon, a flattened, wobbling ball, crushed by the atmosphere. Tom stands in the stirrups, tilting his head back as a gust whips him.

A fading campfire sparks and crackles as Tom, bedded down, pokes at it with a stick, trying to keep it alive. Occasionally a wisp of snow whirls by and the wind carrying it cuts through the sleeping bag. Tom sings softly, under his breath,

> Soap soap soap
> On a little Lucy Lucy,
> Makes for a very clean girl.

He drops the stick and rolls over on his back, propping on his elbows to look up. The Moon hid behind a billowing cloud as it broke the horizon, its piercing brightness spraying a fluorescent edge around the darkening thunderhead.

> Soup soup soup
> And a stack of soda crackers,
> Makes for a very fine meal.

Exhausted from a long and trying day, Tom lays his head down and quiets. Then, falling asleep,

> And sun sun sun,
> Early in the mornin',
> Makes for a very bright world.

Tom closes his eyes and drifts away. From his shoes upward, a sharp edge of moonlight advances as the cloud moves onward. When it cuts across his face, he squints from the threshold of an approaching dream, then falls into deeper sleep.

Overhead, a blinding full Moon overtakes the sky.

The Pulpit

Facing The Enemy

CHAPTER TWO

I looked straight up, before my eyes
The tempest parted wide!
I pointed to the patch of stars,
Each one, a beacon, bright.

I wished and wished upon those stars
That I could sail to them,
And then I knew the answer lay
Within my favorite poem.

"Hope is the thing with feathers,"
Emily said to me.
She taught me in my secret soul
That anything could be.

Just then an eagle white as light
Descended from the stars;
Her beating wings spoke words to me,
Her eyes were crimson fire.

"The wind you fear shall lift us up,"
She beat as she flew by.
"The lightning flash that blinded you
Will truly light our way."

She landed softly in my boat
And spread one perfect wing,
A downy sail to catch the wind,
Emily's feathered thing.

"Hold on!" The wing sang as it took
The storm into its fold,
Then lifted us up to the stars,
Away from nightmares' hold.

This One whose hand from dust did form
Me like I was His very own,
Is He a child who wishes on
The stars He spun from Heaven's throne?

Does He love Emily like me?
Does His imagination run
To feathered wings that, beating, speak
Of faith when all our hope is gone?

Deep night at the Tijuana beach house. Waves lap in the darkness, foam-fans patterning in the light of a waning Moon, a Moon over a different time. There are no other houses for a mile either way; an isolated strand, pushed up against a vast sea of despair.

A yellow porch light glows through the open bedroom window, bringing with it soothing sounds of waves and the healing scent of warm saltwater. A gentle but steady sea breeze billows tattered sheers from the window, reminding Tom, sitting up in bed while Francine sleeps restlessly, of the wooden sailboat he had when he was nine years old. As the sheers dance quietly in and out of the light, he drifts away to the shelter of old and comforting memories.

This respite is shattered by the chilling scream of a boy in a bedroom down the hall. The child is begging.

"No! No! Don't let them do it!"

Tom bolts out of bed as his wife groans and turns over.

Noah's room, with shades drawn, is darker, but the dim light from a lamp in the form of an angel praying falls upon the desperate boy. Noah is sitting up, rocking fore and aft, clutching a pillow, crying. His features are not visible, but the tears running down his cheeks are.

"Don't let them! Don't!" Tom runs in and embraces his son, holding him close and rocking with him. "Daddy! Daddy! Don't let them!"

"Shhh. Shhh. It's all right, scooter. Daddy's here now."

Noah's gaunt fear looks up at his father. He panics, searching the room. "Theo? Theo! Where's Theo?"

Tom finds Theo, a hug-worn bear on the floor by the bed, and gives him to Noah. Clutching Theo tight, Noah looks around again, worried and crying. "The Book! The Book!"

"Which book, Noah? Which one?"

"The Sazi Book, Daddy! Daddy get it!"

Tom looks around and finds a large, handmade, age-old book on the nightstand next to the angel lamp and gives it to Noah, who collects it with the bear and falls into his father, rocking with him again. The sobbing quiets to soft whimpers and little gasps for breath.

"Don't let them. Please? Daddy?"

"What is it, son? Don't let them what?"

"Don't let them put me under the ground."

When Tom realizes what his boy said, his heart is pierced, run through with a sword of impossible pain. How can such a small boy accept what he cannot? Tom's eyes squeeze shut as he takes this blow, and when they open again, the room is a blurred kaleidoscope of agony. In a futile gesture, he says, "Noah, honey, you're not going to—"

"Daddy, promise me you won't let them! Promise me!"

It's no use. Tom bites his lip, barely able to speak. "I promise. I promise I won't let them."

"I can just be in my room. Me... and, and Theo. And the Book. OK?"

"OK. I promise."

Tom rocks with him harder, no longer able to hold back the tears. Resting his head on the little shoulder, he cries, "I promise I won't let them."

* * *

Tom tosses, rolling back and forth in the throes of a nightmare. A thin dusting of night snowfall covers him and the ground, strangely lit rose-pink from the hues of a spreading twilight sky. Zion struggles his way out of the sleeping bag and darts a few feet away, looking back.

Tom moans. "I promise I won't let them. I promise."

He springs to a sitting position, eyes still shut tight. There's never any manageable wakening from this dream, one he's forced to relive with cruel regularity. The Sun's molten edge breaks the horizon, forcing Tom to squint and turn his head. He peels his eyes open only to be blinded until he holds his hand up, looking around at familiar surroundings, trying to shake off the wounds of another bad night. He looks down at the snow around him and runs his hand through it, smearing his face.

As he wipes his eyes, the sight of animal tracks in a perfect circle around his sleeping bag halts him. Tom looks closer, realizing they're cat prints, too large to be Zion's. He nearly falls over extricating himself from the sleeping bag and jumps out of the circle, looking back at it, then away. He takes a second look and starts collecting his gear.

The Sun is also rising above a Mexican jungle, but less obviously and one hour further along. There's a clearing in the jungle a few yards from a remote dirt road, five miles south of Zihuatanejo, a village on the northern curve of the bay of the same name. A mini RV is parked in the clearing with a plain white cargo trailer hitched to the bumper. The trailer is taller than it is long or wide, void of any markings and spotless, in sharp contrast to the vehicle that towed it there. All is quiet until a cellphone bleeps inside the RV.

Alberto is awakened by the phone resting in its charger a few feet away. He gropes, knocking it onto his head.

"Que lastima!" he complains as he fumbles for the phone, strains to see the buttons, then pushes one. "Bueno?... Oh, hello." He sits up to attention. "Yes, Doctor. I'm fine. No, no, I was almost awake."

Kirshner stares at a screen displaying data in scroll movements. It's the only illumination in the room, casting a rolling glow on his exhausted face. "Alberto, you are to proceed with Phase Three at 1530 Zulu. That is 0930 A.M. your time. Do you copy?"

Alberto's voice falters over the speaker phone. "You mean, 1530, today?"

"Affirmative."

"But, I thought—"

"I'm sorry, my friend, there's no time to explain. 1530 today."

Alberto turns to look at a clock. Puzzled, he responds, "Yes sir, I understand." He stares at the phone, then presses the disconnect button. He looks at the clock again and falls out of his cramped bunk, knocking over the bottle of Tequila left on the floor. Still dressed from the night before, he body-irons the rumpled Guns 'n Roses T-shirt with his hands, then tries to flatten his cockatiel night-hair in a small cracked mirror. "Aye, mommi," Alberto laments.

Sam occupies one of the Holmes three guest quarters, each secluded from the other by the fact they were carved out as elegant caves into three separate faces of the butte upon which the main house sits, only the individual glass walls opening to the outside. They connect to the main house through converging tunnels, but also have outside access by a path leading down from the narrow terrace in front of the glass.

Sam lays sprawled upside down on the bed, flat on his back, his arms over his head, his feet propped up on the headboard. The phone rings in the other room and he's instantly walking through the door, still asleep, one eye half-open. The Looney Tune boxers fit him figuratively, if not actually. "YEAH! Yeah, I'm coming!" he bellows, sleep-talking.

He partially wakens, opening the door to the terrace. As the ringing continues, he realizes it's the phone and turns, looking around to find it in its usual place, hanging on the wall. Sam lumbers over, giving the impression he does indeed have a hard time moving on land, and snatches the phone from its cradle. "What!" Sam looks around as the world begins taking shape for him again. "Doc? What the heck time is it, anyway?... Right now? What's the matter?"

He scratches his behind. "All right, all right, I'll be there. You talk to Tom?... OK. Bye." Sam slams the phone into the holder and it promptly bounces out. The second time he's a little more precise. "Sufferin' *succotash!*"

Morning mist still hugs the valley floor, but up on the bluff the air is clear and fresh. Cirrus poses majestically at the edge as Tom looks over a sweeping view of his land, breathing in the smell of wet dirt. He pulls a cellphone from his saddlebag, dismounts, walks over to a large flat rock and sits on it. After thinking and rethinking, he presses in a number. Clicks and buzzes precede the ringing tone.

Seated on a couch, staring outward through a picture window at waves crashing on a speckled granite sea wall, is the figure, from behind, of a poised blond woman. On the West Coast, the first light of day has crept in, forcing a barely perceptible distinction between the gray overcast and the insipid ocean, a distinction she cares little about. Even at this early hour she's perfectly dressed, coffee in one hand, a cigarette in the other. Only from a reflection in the glass is her featureless face visible, partly in shadow, without expression. On an end table a foot or so from her, a designer phone rings softly. She sets the coffee down, removes an earring, and answers.

"Hello?" she almost whispers.

Francine Whitewater-Holmes never remarried. Nor did she return to life. Tom turned the torment outward and built an empire, using his pain as the engine. Francine collapsed inward and retreated to the house at Pismo Beach. She has found no answers and, for that matter, asks no more questions. There's a point at which even self-pity brings no comfort and the only thing left to do is let go of the tiller and drift. Francine spends endless days watching those waves, at times crashing on the rocks behind the force of a storm, at others rising and falling over them with the tide. In either case, they mean the same. The relentless erosion and tearing down of once solid matter. After a long silence, a distant voice.

"Francine?"

She straightens up. "Tommy? Is that you?" she asks as if she'd imagined it.

"Yeah, it's me. How've you been?"

She hesitates to answer. "Oh, you know. I have my bad days, then I have my worse days."

"I refer to mine as bad 'moments'. Only because each one is so long, I've lost track of day or night."

Francine drags the cigarette. "It's too bad one of us didn't pull out of this. Might've been able to reach in and pull the other with."

"You mean there's a way out?"

She puts the cigarette out in a pink shell. "Why did you call? Is something wrong?"

Tom dodges the question, looking out across the Virgin River valley that used to be their home. "Guess where I am."

Francine's voice phase shifts through the cellphone, an unnatural sound. "You're sitting on Old Flat Rock."

"How did you know?" Tom asks, barely surprised.

"You promised me you'd always think of me there."

"But I think of you often."

"Not enough to call."

He nods. "You know, at times like this, I look out and wonder what happened to us."

"Yeah, I thought misery was supposed to love company."

"It's a lie. Misery loves misery. There's no room for company."

Francine walks out onto the balcony with the phone. Morning light reveals her features. A pleasant, round face that carries her few extra pounds well, short blond hair elegantly behind one ear, and sorrowful blue eyes.

"I guess we blamed each other," she says.

"Or ourselves. What's the difference?"

"Have you tried blaming God yet? It works for a while. Then it just hurts more."

"No. I tried, but I haven't found him. Must be hiding. Probably ashamed."

This brings a long silence. Francine wipes a tear from her eye. "Is there anything I can do for you?"

Tom stands. "No, I just needed to hear your voice."

She tries to cheer up a little. "Next time try to keep it under a decade. It's good to hear your voice, too. It helps."

"Goodbye, then."

Francine sits on the top step of the sun-bleached stairs leading to the sand and pauses to watch an egret fly past, stroking the air in rhythm with her heartbeat. "Take care of yourself." She hangs up and returns her gaze out toward the sea, knowing something's not quite right. But since nothing really is, it just blends in.

Tom turns the phone off and looks down.

Alberto has unhitched the trailer and removed three sides, leaving only the one that hides the payload from view. He looks up at it, vaults onto a corner, pulls a latch, and the panel falls outward revealing a nine foot, perfect scale reproduction of an early U.S. launch vehicle, polished metal, stripes, and all. It most closely resembles the Titan that carried Gemini into space, and has at its pinnacle a black section looking suspiciously like a capsule. Alberto's seen it before but is still astounded, taking a moment to marvel.

Kirshner, looking every bit like he's been up all night, paces the warehouse office, occasionally looking out the curtains. At last he sees someone walking across the expansive floor and opens the door. Leaning half out, he motions furiously with his arm. Sam strides into the office, puffing and exasperated.

"For crying out loud, Doctor K.," he says, catching his breath, "what in tarnation is this about?"

"Come in! Come in!" Kirshner yells in a whisper, looking to see if anyone followed. He closes and locks the door. "I couldn't find Tom on the phone all night."

Sam looks confused. "I'll be seeing him in about an hour. Unfortunately."

A look of pity comes over the Doctor. "The running business?" Sam rolls his eyes up. "I'm so sorry."

Sam waves it off. "Is there a problem?"

"You bet there's a problem. Tom wants to go."

"Go. Up?" Sam points to the ceiling and Kirshner affirms with a sad head shake. "He kept me away from this whole thing to protect me. I've just been hoping something happens to stop it."

"He wants to go. Now."

Sam looks at him in disbelief, then at his watch. "You mean... *now?*"

"He said a couple of days. I'm not sure if he's serious. I'm very afraid he might be."

Sam turns, holding his head. "Oh, Jesus." He whips back. "Can he go? I mean, is this thing real?"

Kirshner walks to the curtains and looks out. "He's pushing this too fast. We still have tests to run. Systems to check. But, I'm afraid to say, yes. It would be even more dangerous doing it so quickly, but it could be done."

Sam paces in short, frantic laps. "Well, we just have to stop him. You're in charge of this thing. Pull the plug!"

"As much as I'd like to, I can't. He has trusted me for seven years on this project. It's not even a question of the money he spent. I cannot stop it now. Don't you see?"

"Then, I'll do it. I'll just... drag him off. I'll beat the crap out of him. He'll thank me later."

Kirshner shakes his head. "We have no right to stop him from doing anything, short of killing himself." This statement hangs between them as its implication locks their stare. "There is one possibility. Come with me."

Kirshner leads Sam to a door across the room and pulls it open, revealing a dark, wide stairway turning down to the left. Sam assumed it was just a closet, although it was always locked now that he thinks about it. He sticks his head through the doorway and looks, realizing it leads to a hidden basement, then turns toward the Doctor with an accusing glance. Kirshner ducks under the glance and proceeds down into the dark. Sam follows, feeling his way down the handrails.

At the bottom of the stairs, Kirshner flips a wall switch, turning the cavern into a fluorescent-lighted bunker. It's just that, a block wall room with no windows. Along each wall are racks of computer monitors, TV screens, communication gear, and end-to-end banks of electronic equipment.

Sam's mouth draws open in astonishment. "Oh, my. I know what this is. This is a control room." The Doctor nods. "I guess I just never wanted to believe it was really happening. I mean I *knew* it was happening, but—"

Kirshner interrupts by rushing over to a central rack and throwing power switches, causing banks of colored status lights to blink on around the room, fans to turn, and computer screens to self test.

Alberto pumps a hydraulic stand at a corner of the trailer bed turned launch pad. He checks a leveling gauge, then adjusts the stand at the opposite corner. The platform now solidly planted, he consults a manual, opens an electronics panel on the rocket, and pushes buttons on a keypad. A digital display responds with running codes, changing to a clock that begins counting up from 1521:55. Alberto walks with dispatch to his RV and drives it a hundred yards down the dirt road where he gets out, places the vehicle between himself and the rocket, and stands to watch.

The Doctor monitors a screen with a similar clock, reading 1526:22 and counting. Below it, computer fields display: Telemetry, Dynamic Pressure, Downrange, and Trajectory. On another screen is a graphic representation of the Western Hemisphere. Sam's nerves arc out in the form of misdirected anger. "Are you going to tell me what's going on or do I have to strangle it out of you?"

"The authorities are closing in." Kirshner walks over to a rack housing a tape deck with twelve-inch silver reels of half-inch tape and turns it on. The tape reels move in jerks, recording data. He continues, watching the tape. "I feel guilty admitting this, but lately I've hoped we all get caught and thrown in jail."

"That could be arranged."

Kirshner turns toward Sam. "I told Tom in the beginning that I wouldn't go ahead until we fired a probe. We at least need reliable telemetry before I agree to launch."

Sam cocks his head. "A probe?"

"It's a smaller version, like a toy really. But it has many of the same systems. If the law is as close as I think it is, this little rocket may be all they need to walk in and shut us down."

"And?"

"And, for this reason, I'm sure Tom would not want to go ahead with the probe. But, I tried to talk to him last night and he wasn't available."

"Ah. I see. What's he going to say when he finds out?"

Kirshner can look boyishly clever by raising one of his bushy eyebrows. "If we're lucky, he'll fire me."

Sam looks around. "So, where is it? Light that sucker off."

"In Mexico."

It's Sam's turn to lift an eyebrow. "Mexico?"

Alberto fidgets behind his RV until a sparking sound draws his attention to the rocket, making him duck and peer around the corner of the RV. Puffs of white smoke drop from the propulsion nozzles followed by a harmless blue flame that quickly erupts into a cannon of orange and white gas. The first sounds are similar to the crack of a lightning strike, but quickly give way to a ground rumbling, body vibrating, low frequency wave. Within moments, the entire assembly is hidden in a pulsating cloud. Alberto takes momentary refuge, but can't resist and steps into the clearing. The support arm folds away and from the top of the rolling, billowing, expanding cloud appears a black tip, then, foot by foot, the remainder of the rocket. By this time the calamitous roar has brought Alberto's hands to his ears.

The rocket picks up speed exponentially and becomes but a burning spot of white light. Alberto realizes there's no more need to cover his ears and lets his arms down. At the launch pad the smoke is finally thinning, though still rotating in curls back toward the trailer. Alberto observes the platform sitting charred but intact, jumps in the RV, and roars off.

He rumbles and jolts across rutted jungle roads, branches beating at the windshield, and skids to a halt in a small clearing. Alberto gets out and walks to, then along a path that curves through heavy vegetation, ducks under a tree limb, and straightens up to a view of peaceful Zihuatanejo Bay. It looks as it usually does, except for the rocket cutting through the sky, laying a thin contrail shadow across a cruise ship anchored squarely in the middle. The ship has a plain "H" on the smokestack, and next to the smokestack a satellite dish tracks the rocket as it streaks toward the stratosphere.

Ixtapa's beach resorts string along the Pacific shore over the hill from Zihuatanejo Bay, towering quietly over the sand, casting long shadows. The first distant, unnerving shock waves of the launch drift across the beach, populated at such an early hour by die-hard sun tanners or all-night club refugees. A few scattered wanderers turn in unison toward the sound and as they look east, see a spitting ball of white light popping in and out of otherwise sleepy morning cumulus, leaving behind a billowing plume announced by a crackling, guttural buzz. Fear grips a few and they dart for cover. The rest, standing in groups, watch as this object, appearing more and more like an aluminum arrow on fire, screams skyward. All duck at the sudden thunder of a sonic boom and in growing numbers leave the beach, while others drift out of hotels to find out what's going on.

Kirshner and Sam lean over a computer screen, staring, when the Doctor yells out, "By God, Samuel! We've done it!"

Sam grabs his arm. "We have? What? What have we done?"

Kirshner points to the screen. "Here, look. Telemetry is working beautifully. Downrange sixty-four kilometers, altitude forty-four, velocity two thousand meters per second. Thirty seconds until separation."

Sam tightens a fist. "Separation? Separation of what?"

"First stage, man! First stage!" the Doctor retorts, almost rude in his excitement. He walks to another screen, types on a keyboard, and something appears on a television monitor that Sam views with confounded interest. It's a computer generated, cartoon-like image, the perspective a few yards in front of a rocket, looking upon it and the shrinking coastline of Mexico below. Though it seems real enough, the video game aspect makes it all the more peculiar. Sam looks at the Doctor as if he might be slightly off his rocker.

"Watch," says Kirshner.

Alberto squints through binoculars. The rocket appears now only as a point of light, wobbling with his unsteady hands. The light flares and the first stage separates, drifting down. "Santa Maria," is all he can say.

Separation is depicted in the control room through computer generation as the booster stage, after a flash of explosive fasteners, tumbles away and the second stage ignites, throwing a momentary flame, then a shock cone. Kirshner's face is lit up from the screen and from within. His voice shakes with excitement as he looks at Sam but doesn't really see him. "This has never been done. Multistage on a vehicle this size with full telemetry. Remarkable, I must say."

Sam taps his lips with a forefinger. "Let me get this straight. We, you, just launched a rocket from Mexico. Do you think anyone will notice?"

Kirshner looks naughty. "Oh, I suspect we've rung a few bells."

* * *

Inside Mexico City Center, a controller stares with suspicion at his radar screen, motioning to a supervisor. "Oscar, venga rapido. Que diablo es esto?"

The supervisor applies a forehead-wrinkled stare, then breathes, "Que demonio." This followed by a puzzled, "Pero va mui despacio."

The controller motions horizontally with his hand. "Si, pero," then motioning vertically, "en *esta* manera va mui veloz!"

The supervisor looks at him, not liking the theory.

A moderately high Mexican military figure, garnished by an overcrowded chest of ribbons, frowns as he listens to the phone. He grumbles and slams the receiver down. Staring straight ahead, grumble turns to cursing as he rises and marches out, as much marching as his extra fifty pounds will allow.

Sam shakes his head in wonder. "There's one thing you haven't told me yet. Where's this thing going?"

Kirshner saddens. "I'm sorry to say it will self destruct in a few moments. It will have traveled to a height of 141 kilometers and velocity of 13,700 kilometers per hour. In effect, a suborbital plane. We could have achieved an orbit, mind you, and considered it at one time. However, the purpose of this mission was telemetry, and the consequences of an 'unannounced' orbit would be too... complicated."

Kirshner turns toward the monitor and as they watch, the cartoon rocket explodes in a swirling arcade pattern. The two look at each other.

Alberto observes a barely visible puff of orange smoke until the whopping of rapidly approaching helicopters makes him drop the binoculars, revealing two military-green gunships nearly upon him. He ducks and runs hunched over into the jungle as they chuff overhead toward the launch site.

The Mexican military officer is on the receiving end of terse and loud words from his superior, a General, dwarfing him in both size and regalia. This General is obviously not pleased, taking it out on his bearer of bad news, the conversation taking place over the persistent buzz of an ignored intercom call. A flustered and worried secretary bursts in the room, silencing them both.

"General! En el telephono, esta el Comandante del Pentagon!"

The General freezes. "Pentagon? De'l America?" She gives him a look that curls his tail between his legs as he reaches for the phone.

Tom, crouched down, digs at something in the dirt with a stick while his horse munches on a bush. Cirrus stops and looks around, flicking ears, then looks upward. Tom picks up a whining sound and also looks up to see a small jet passing overhead, cruising unnaturally slow with the flaps partially down, low but in level flight. He stands, watching it continue out of sight, and looks at the horse who looks back, neither seeming comfortable with it. Tom appears to shrug it off, then walks over to the saddlebag and pulls out the phone.

Eddie, dressed in coveralls, is half visible as he performs routine maintenance on the landing gear of N111HC, the Boeing 727. His cellphone rings and he ducks out from the wheel well, walking under the wing to answer. "Hello?"

"Eddie, it's Tom. How are you?"

"Hey, boss, I'm fine. Where are you? I suppose you know everybody's been trying to find you, Doc especially."

"I know. Never mind that. Are you about done with the A-check?"

"About an hour left. Why?" Eddie asks, checking the landing gear strut extension with his pocket ruler.

"I've set something up, last minute, and I need you to fly out to Long Beach today. Can you pull that off?"

"I guess. What's this all about?"

"Just call the Noah House, they'll fill you in."

"Whatever you say."

"Thanks, Eddie. You've never let me down. And, thank you for that, for everything."

Eddie pauses. "Don't mention it. Hey, man, are you OK?"

"Listen, have you noticed anything unusual this morning?"

"Well, I went to wake up Sammy at eight and he wasn't sawin' his big ol' logs. In fact, he wasn't even there."

"That is unusual. But I meant, up. In the sky."

Eddie walks out from under the wing, looking up and around. "No. Why?"

"Oh, nothing I guess. Gotta go. And thanks again."

Tom disconnects and looks up.

Eddie holds the phone away and looks at it, then back up.

Facing straight on, 111HC appears to frown, as do all 727's. A caravan of children streams toward it from the side, some jumping for joy, others pushed in wheelchairs. The occupants of Noah House are departing on an unscheduled, and undreamed of, holiday.

The flight crew, Eddie as Captain, Craig as copilot, sit dutifully in their positions, level at 39,000 feet when a paper airplane flies through the open cockpit door, noses up and stalls out, landing on the throttle quadrant. Craig and Eddie look at it, then toward the door.

Angela, a curly-haired girl of four, dressed in a rainbow tutu with red tights, stands innocently at the cockpit door with her hands clenched in front of her. Behind her, the cabin is a madhouse, pillows flying and hysterical kids everywhere. The pilots look at each other, then Craig picks up the paper airplane and darts it over her head into the cabin. She bursts out a giggle and runs. One more look at each other and they resume their positions forward.

The town of Springdale rests peacefully at the entrance to

Zion National Park, seeming smaller than it is by virtue of the gran-
deur looming all around. It's an odd concoction of 50's motels,
tasteful cedar lodges, flickering neon, and carved stone facades. A
grandfather rocks in front of the Bumbleberry Inn, patiently watching as his grandson, sporting an Indian feather headband and carrying a toy tomahawk, circles around his chair, tethering him to it
with kite string. Tom crosses in front of them, jogging, wearing
earphones and a cassette player clipped to his running shorts. He's
not wearing a shirt, his upper body glistening with perspiration.
It's a brisk morning, so he's been at it for a while.

Moments later Sam appears, riding a bicycle. Because of
his size, he looks like a circus bear in a sweat suit riding a unicycle.
Zion sits in the wicker handlebar basket looking about as happy as
Sam, who peddles under great strain. The sight of this stops the
grandfather's rocking as they watch Sam labor by, and the boy
throws his tomahawk, bouncing it off Sam's back, something Sam
doesn't notice in light of his great hardship.

Tom sails effortlessly by the Park Ranger's booth and the
Ranger, wearing a jacket with a fur collar, calls out with a smile,
"Morning, Thomas!" Tom doesn't hear but raises a hand in saluta-
tion. Sam follows shortly after, grinding away, looking like he's
ready to give out. "Morning, Sam!" Sam looks back, glaring at the
smiling Ranger.

Farther down Highway 9, looking straight on, Tom gives
the illusion of pulling Sam behind him. At this point Sam is wobbling side-to-side just trying to stay up, like a gyro about ready to
tumble. As the two approach the curve in the highway that begins
the steep climb up the switchbacks to the tunnel, Sam quits, nearly
falling off his bike. Zion leaps out and turns back to look. "No
way," Sam coughs as he gulps for air.

Tom doesn't hear and keeps right on going while Sam gives
him a good riddance wave off, lets the bike drop to the ground and
plops down next to it. He unsnaps a water bottle from the bike
frame and squirts it in his face, looking up into the Sun and squinting. Zion sits a few feet away watching with catlike caution until
Sam squirts the bottle at him, sending him trotting off behind his

master.

Sam lays in the dirt, snoring, when Tom and Zion zoom by running downhill, rousting him into consciousness. It's the second time in one day he's been wakened against his will and when he realizes where he is, grabs a handful of dirt and throws it at them. "Tarnation! Out of one bad dream into another." Still not quite all there, he picks up the bike and tries to get going, almost falling off the other side. Finally he's back on and slowly builds speed, unaware or uninterested that shifting a couple of gears would help.

As Tom approaches the junction to the Narrows, Sam roars by with the momentum of a freight train and passes the junction, heading toward Springdale like a barn horse. This was wishful thinking, however, as Tom takes the turn. Sam cranes around and, seeing this, comes to a skidding halt, lowering his head in frustration.

Angel's Landing, a towering wedge of rock 1,500 feet high, is in the branch of Zion Canyon where the cliffs come closer and closer, leading to the Narrows where they eventually merge. From the top, the three are barely recognizable down on the road that follows the Virgin River in a tight loop around the Landing. Tom is well ahead with Zion a distant second and Sam far behind, reduced to walking the bike beside him.

A small park decorates the trailhead to the Narrows. Tom jogs through and continues down a paved path into the converging gorge, the canyon at this point a crack in the Earth. Vegetation is thick and every sound echoes off the wet, sheer faces on both sides. Zion appears, but is uncomfortable with continuing and jumps on a picnic table, licking and stretching his neck to see where Tom went. Finally Sam appears again, once more riding, gets off, and rests the bike against the table. He picks up the cat and scratches his neck as he looks over at the Pulpit, a pillar of rock that seems to have grown out of the ground, framed in the distance by a monumental cliff and its thin, misting waterfall.

Tom ducks under lowering tree limbs and zigzags along an ever-decreasing trail, occasionally climbing over a small mound or hopping across rocks to the other side of the river. He pulls a bush aside, slips into a clearing, and walks up a slope into a hollow in the rock wall, then sits on a flat spot and rests his forehead on his knees, catching his breath.

The sound of the Virgin River is loud compared to its size, omnidirectional and amplified by the towering walls. He looks straight up and contemplates the irregular cliff, angles and pockets where every few hundred years a wedge dislodges and crashes down in an explosion of shattering sandstone, an insignificant splinter in the evolution of the Narrows. Suddenly a red monarch flaps past his face and the sound of a small boy's voice sends a chill up his spine.

"Father? Where are you?" cries the lost voice.

Through the bushes, he sees the flickering image of a blond boy from behind. Tom stands slowly.

The figure of a man appears and takes the boy's hand. "I'm right here, son." As the father leads the child away, Tom sits down, tilts his head back and closes his eyes. When he opens them, he sees the converging rims high above, an apex jutting from the bottom of a chasm. Perfectly placed in a slice of pale-blue sky is a full, daytime Moon.

The commotion of frenzied travelers underneath acres of metal canopy that cover the cruise ship embarking area takes on the atmosphere of an open-air market. Moveable dividers organize stages of processing, each guiding a group of anxious cruisers through a checkpoint. Framed by the canopy at the pier's edge is a portion of a ship, visible only as a wall of stark-white riveted iron, dotted with portholes.

At the far end of this embarking area a crowd has gathered, posturing to see over a five-foot barrier, further guarded by a line of security officers. A wide banner flaps in the breeze behind and over them, attached to the edge of the canopy near the ship. It displays in bright colors, "FIRST ANNUAL HOLMES LINE MYSTERY CRUISE- *BON VOYAGE!*" Next to it hangs a vertical banner, a reproduction of Isabel's poster, titled: Special Appearances by Isabel Flore, Marcy Marxer, and Cathy Fink.

A stretch limo arrives and Isabel steps out, bathed in a flurry of reporters' strobes and greeted by a burst of applause, returned by as gracious a smile as her mood allows.

Nonna sits in her wheelchair at the edge of the pier smoking, drinking coffee from a paper cup, and looking down at the water. She sees Isabel, waves, and Isabel breaks the conversation she was having with a ship's officer, walking toward her as if she were an oasis. She hugs Nonna tightly, then holds her at arm's length.

"Oh, Nonna, I'm so glad to see you." The look of joyous relief turns to loving disapproval when she sees the cigarette. "Shame on you!" Isabel takes it from her and throws it over the pier's edge. Nonna watches it all the way down to the water, reaches into her purse, and pulls out the pack.

"Litterbug." She removes another for herself and offers one to Isabel, who sighs and accepts. Nonna lights both, then they each drag and exhale at the same time. Nonna picks a stray piece of tobacco from her lip. "Have you figured any of this out yet?"

Isabel tries not to lie. "I stopped trying a lifetime ago."

These two have taken shelter in each other since they met. Both share a deep love for Tom, as well as the disappointment at its meager effect upon his plight. Besides that, however, they are two grand women who, despite their age difference, share a commonality in spirit. The loneliness that accompanies a life of bittersweet memories forms a bond between them they find in no one else. Nonna knows Isabel is hiding something and silently accepts her reason for doing so, remarking, "I've felt something like this coming." She looks up at the ship. "Must he always be so... dramatic?"

"He's just using mirrors. I suppose Tom thinks all this will distract us."

"What, so he can... 'steal away' unnoticed?" She looks away. "He needn't bother trying to spare us. Maybe he should just get it over with, bless his heart."

Isabel's voice shakes. "How can you say that?"

"He's no good at suffering. Does it all wrong. Once when he was a little boy, about five or so, his Daddy came home drunk, like always. Belted the poor kid for leaving his trike in the driveway. Actually broke his nose. You know what Tommy did? He opened his piggy bank, took every cent he had, and ran out and bought the bastard a bottle of Chivas. The old man'd never seen liquor that good."

"How could a little boy buy liquor like that?"

"Oh, he always had Tommy run out to get his booze. Didn't matter in a small town like that." Nonna puts her barely smoked cigarette out in her paper cup. "Like I said, he's no good at it. Better off leaving it to those of us that are."

Isabel looks at her cigarette, then also puts it in the cup. A commotion near the boarding ramp turns them around to see Eddie showing the security guards his ID. "It's OK, officer, he's with us," Isabel shouts.

The officer lifts up a chain, letting Eddie through. He walks up, disheveled, his hair flying in various directions, one side of his collar sticking up. Eddie points out his army of misfits already fraying the nerves of the children's cruise director. "Mr. Holmes said you'd keep an eye on them. Good luck."

President Stamp sits alone, contentedly eating a Happy Meal cheeseburger, napkin stuffed in his collar. He pulls out this week's toy, a plastic order of French fries which, after some deliberation, transforms into a car. He places it with certain contentment next to the rest of the collection on his desk near the photo of his wife and two small daughters. This simple recess in the day of a world leader is interrupted by the buzz of the intercom. He pushes the button. "This better be important."

"It's General Whitley's aide. He says the General wants you to take a look at something."

Stamp pulls the napkin from his collar. "Send him in."

Enter a decorated young Marine, Sergeant White, who salutes smartly. "Mr. President. Sir."

Jonathan motions him forward with a wave of the napkin, wiping his mouth. "At ease, Mark. What have you got?"

The Sergeant marches up to the desk and carefully lays a short stack of photos next to the Happy Meal box, eyeing it with calculated curiosity. He spots the five figures of plastic food, wrestles off a barely perceptible smile, then assumes the angular at ease position, staring straight ahead.

Jonathan watches the drill and grins as he resumes chewing. "You have children, Sergeant White?"

"Sir, yes Sir. Two, Sir."

"Do they collect these figures?"

"Sir, yes Sir."

Jonathan fixes on this chiseled figure of a Marine, always amazed by the display. "Well, are they missing any?"

White pauses. "Sir... Yes, they are."

"Darn it, Mark, will you look at me when you talk? Which ones? What are they missing?"

The Sergeant, with great effort, adjusts his gaze downward to meet his President's. "The McNugget... character, Sir. We seem unable to get the Nugget character." He can look at the President only so long, then returns to form, focusing one hundred meters out the Oval Office window.

"I hate it when they try to pawn off their oversupply on you, then you miss the next one. Don't you?"

Sergeant White almost smiles again. "I know what you mean. It seems, unfair. Sir."

Jonathan opens a desk drawer, rustles around, and comes up with a Nugget character, placing it directly in front of the Sergeant. "Here, you can have this. I 'procured' a few extra during the shortage. I love how I can do things like that."

White shifts his gaze four times from his focal point outside to the figure before him, finally locking on it. He picks it up, returning to position.

"Thank you, Sir. Very much."

Jonathan shakes his head. "Very well, Mark. That'll be all."

Sergeant White clicks to attention, pirouettes toward the door, and exits. Jonathan looks down at the photos, then pushes the intercom button. "Margaret, get Herlihy on the phone."

Margaret watches the Sergeant come through the door. He sticks the gift in his pocket and smiles as he looks at her. She points to a shelf near her desk where he sees her own Presidentially mandated collection.

Taco Bill is Springdale's only fast food restaurant, taken over from an abandoned chain outlet that was designed slightly off the franchise blueprint to blend with the canyon. Next to it sits a deserted gas station and looking markedly out of place stands Cirrus, tied to a drinking fountain. He eyes a suspicious looking car parked across the street, then noses down and manages to get a drink from the fountain. Tom appears from around the corner on the last yards of his run and slows to a fast walk with his hands on his hips.

Sam follows shortly looking as if he's about to collapse— or if he doesn't, the bike will—and gets off in one fluid motion, letting it crash to the ground. Drenched in sweat, he stops only long enough to glare at Tom, then walks tight circles, catching some breath of his own.

Tom enters, followed by Sam, and stands at the counter. There to greet him is Joseph, a young Moqui boy. "Hello, Mr. Holmes. What can I get for you?"

"Joseph. Water for me, hold the ice."

Joseph looks at Sam, gasping and looking a wreck. Sam, not able to speak, gestures *large anything* and grabs a handful of napkins to wipe his face. Tom turns and leans against the counter, arms folded, looking toward the street where he notices a figure walking toward the entrance, a person who draws his attention. This person opens the glass door as if it would break, closing it carefully behind him, and walks to the counter while looking up at the menu.

Here is a person displaced in time, as if arriving from a prolonged absence. Elderly but fit, he wears a wide-striped zoot suit that appears to have been with him since it was in fashion. His face is gaunt, nearly concave, this aspect increased by a thick mustache, accented by a tattered but proudly worn felt hat with a brown feather tucked into the red satin band. Though at first glance he would seem pathetic, bordering on derelict, his mannerisms reveal him to carry the dignity of a man in harmony with his circumstance.

Tom is spellbound and Sam stops gulping the drink Joseph

gave him, turning to look. This man looks at Joseph and, speaking in what resembles a Dutch accent, says, "Good morning, Joseph. I would like one taco, and one bean burrito. And give me a good portion, please. I am very hungry today."

Joseph rings up the order. "Of course, Mr. Linden. That'll be a dollar eighty-six."

As Joseph prepares the food, Mr. Linden pulls a needle-point coin purse from his vest pocket and opens it, removing, one by one, the exact amount in coins, then closes the purse and replaces it. Joseph takes the change and offers the order, which Linden accepts with a slight bow and a tug on the brim of his hat. He extends the courtesy to Tom and Sam, and departs in the same meticulous manner he arrived. Once he's gone, Tom turns to Joseph.

"Who in the world was that?"

"He calls himself Robert Linden. He's been living behind the Inn over there in a cardboard box for a couple of months."

"You mean he's... homeless?"

"Well, not if you ask him. I've offered to let him stay in my garage, but he refuses. At first I thought it was pride, but I don't think that's it anymore. I can't figure him out, to tell you the truth. He said he likes it here."

Tom watches Mr. Linden cross the street as if he'd never done it before. He turns to Sam. "How much have we got with us?"

"What?"

"How much cash have we got?"

Sam reaches in his back pocket and pulls out a wad of hundreds. "Well, I've got five hundred of my own, and your usual—"

Tom gestures to hand it over. "How much?"

Sam does so reluctantly. "About two grand, I suppose."

Tom grabs the money and, without counting it, places it in Joseph's hand. "Take this and use it every time he comes in for food. If it runs out, contact Sam."

Joseph looks at Sam, who shrugs his shoulders. "That's an awful lot of tacos and burritos, Mr. Holmes. What makes you think he'll take it?"

"Just tell him... the owner died and left no will, and you have to give the food away. Tell him it's the law. He'll take it."

Skeptical, Joseph agrees. "I'll try."

Tom takes his drink and walks out. Sam and Joseph look at each other, then Sam follows.

He nearly runs over Tom, standing just outside the door. In the gas station sit six FBI vehicles, parked with doors open and agents standing, forming a Chevrolet fort. Cirrus jigs as an agent awkwardly attempts to stroke his mane, and seated on the hood of the center car is Bud. Sid, a novice hunter seeing his prey for the first time, gets out of the car slowly. Bud slides off the hood and walks toward Tom. Sam drops his cup and starts to posture himself in front, but Tom stops him. Two agents circle in behind Bud, but he likewise signals them to hold back, then approaches and stops six feet away, badge held out.

"Mr. Holmes, Bud Meyerkamp, FBI. I think we should talk."

"I'm not much of a talker."

Bud looks down at the ground, then rolls his eyes up. "I'm trying to make this as easy as possible. We'll keep this... private. For now. Just the two of us." He turns partway around, motioning toward the restrooms at the side of the service station.

"What do you say we step into my office?"

Sam forces himself in between and the two agents respond quickly, both of them formidable, but together still smaller than Sam. They're academy clones, complete with government issue dark glasses and snide expressions. Sam growls, "Wait a minute here."

One of them walks up and pokes Sam in the chest. "Hold on there, Jazbo."

Sam looks at the finger on his massive chest, then up at the agent. "*Jazbo?*"

Tom intervenes. "Meet my personal friend and attorney, Sam Brown. He's just trying to protect my interests."

Bud pushes everyone apart. "Now, now, boys, there's no need for all this. Just a little talk. Mr. Holmes and me. Is that asking so much?" The two agents and Sam stare off like alley cats. The agents, chewing gum in unison, smile sarcastically, unlike Sam. If looks could kill, they'd be dead.

"Why do I feel like I don't have a choice?" Tom asks.

"Sure you do. This time."

Tom looks around at the bizarre scene, clashing against such peaceful surroundings, and sees most of the population of mainstreet Springdale gathering. "All right. Let's go." Sam grabs his arm. "It's OK, Sam," Tom says, and hands him his cup.

"I don't like this. I'm standing right outside."

They walk toward the restrooms and the two agents follow half a step behind. Bud opens the door to the men's room, motioning for Tom to enter, but Sam steps in the way, looking straight into Bud's eyes. "I, uh, have to take a leak. Why don't you use that one?" he says, pointing to the ladies' room.

The other agent joins in. "Well, why don't you just pucker up and hold it, hot shot?"

Sam moves toward the agent, but Bud, squirming at the thought of entering a ladies' restroom, stops him. "All right, all right. That's enough." Tom opens the ladies' room door and shows Bud the way, watching Sam enter the men's room, followed by a clone.

Inside the ladies' room, Bud is blatantly distressed at being in such uncharted territory, much to the amusement of Tom, who enters the stall, then turns. "Do you think I should... sit down? Out of respect?"

"Oh for chrissake, Holmes. Knock it off." Tom urinates loudly, amplifying Bud's already frayed nerves.

In the men's room, Sam throws the cup in a trash can, pokes around at its contents, and walks into the stall. He searches around, the agent watching his every move. Sam looks inside the water tank and, finding nothing, proceeds to the urinal, pretending to relieve himself while looking up at the ceiling. The agent sniffs the air as he looks at himself in the mirror and needlessly primps his butch.

"Jesus Christ, man. You smell like a friggin' sweat horse." Sam ignores the comment, feels under the sink, and finds what he was looking for. He rips a wire loose and yanks out a microphone transmitter, which he sticks in his pocket.

Sam washes his hands and pulls a paper towel from the dispenser as the agent glares. "Yeah, well, you know why us 'Jazbos' smell, don't you?"

"Why's that?"

"So blind people can hate us, too."

The agent starts to laugh, but stops. Sam exits the men's room and, passing the door to the ladies' room, throws the microphone through the partly opened window-vent above the door.

As Tom is drying his hands, the microphone hits the floor by his feet. He and Bud look at it, then at each other. "Nice private little talk? Just you and me?" Bud stares a hole through the door. "All right, let's see it."

"Hey, I—"

Tom's expression halts him. Bud removes his coat, pulls the transmitter from his back, switches it off, and balances it on the sink edge.

"All right, you got me."

"What do you want?"

"I know what you're up to and I'm giving you a chance to call it off before you get in any deeper."

"And what is it that I'm up to?"

"Let's just say we cut the crap right here."

Bud removes an overstuffed envelope from his jacket pocket and hands it to Tom, a series of photos which Tom peruses. "What's all this?"

Bud outbursts, "You know damn well what it is. We took these this morning overhead your little 'hideaway'. Camouflage or not, my people tell me there's a launch pad under there."

Tom hands the pictures back. "I don't see any such thing."

Bud shakes his head. "Don't play games with me, Holmes. We stopped your truck last night. One thousand gallons of $N2O4$ in one tank, and seven hundred gallons of UDMH in the other. What kind of bread is it that you make with hypergolic fuel, anyway?" Tom doesn't answer. "And then there's that little fireworks display down in Mexico."

Tom is clearly caught off guard. "What are you talking about?"

Bud, a trained judge of body language, sees Tom is surprised. "The one that just happened to shoot across the top of one of your boats?"

Both men are struck awkward by this delivery of news. "If you're so sure about all this, why the choreography? Why don't you just club me over the head and drag me off?"

"A lot of important people are giving you the benefit of the doubt," Bud says, annoyed. "Why, I don't know. But I'll tell you one thing, I'll have a warrant here sooner than you think. So why don't you just cooperate and get this over with?"

"Why is this so important to you?"

Bud finds himself on the defensive and doesn't like it. "You've got to be kidding. I can see I've been giving you too much credit. Let's not mention it's plain illegal. How about all the people you might blow up?"

Tom looks at him in the mirror. "There's more to it than that. Why are you really here? I think you should be honest. Let it out."

Bud stares at him in disbelief. He reaches into his pocket, pulls out a quarter, and throws it noisily into the sink. "Here's a quarter for your advice. Now, about the crap we were cutting?"

Tom looks at the quarter. "I think it was Caesar who said a man's worst enemy is most like himself."

"I doubt it. If I have anything in common with you, I'll cut it off."

"You lost your only son in Vietnam. Since then you've been in one jam after another." Bud tenses so hard he can't move. "First the Iran scandal, then the Marcos evacuation. A few Marines get killed, it's reported as a helicopter crash on maneuvers."

"What's going on here?" Bud flares back.

"You play your game, I play mine."

"You sonofabitch, I oughta break your neck."

Tom turns around and sits on the edge of the sink. He looks down at the floor, scratching at a crack in the grimy yellow tile with his shoe. "I was out riding a few weeks ago and saw a cougar chasing down a mountain hare." Bud rolls his eyes in frustration. "One's chasing, one's trying to get away. But they're both running, driven by pain. The pain of hunger, and the pain of death. They're both just trying to survive."

"I'll tell you what my pain is."

"What's that?" Tom asks.

"You."

"Now we're getting somewhere." Tom picks up the quarter from the sink and looks it over, sobering. "1980. That was the year my son was born."

Bud looks away. "I know. I'm sorry."

Tom looks at Bud. "Do you know what your son's favorite color was?"

Bud looks back up and their eyes meet. He reels imperceptibly. At first he motions with his hand, an angry, warning reflex, but stops, confused, choked back. He begins to speak, then stops. Then, "I... don't know. I can't remember. Orange, I think. Why?"

"That's it, you see. Of all the things, all the many terrible things you miss, I've come to realize it's not just the big things, the obvious ones. It's the little ones that hurt most. How they tied their shoes, the way they held a glass. How they cried."

Bud finds his hand shaking and places it in his pocket. "And what their favorite color was."

"Yeah," Tom says. "I knew that. I knew it was silver, but I never asked him why. I didn't take the time to ask. And now I'll never know." Tom's eyes glass over, but he stops it there. "I'll never know."

Bud exhales the breath he didn't realize he'd been holding. He walks over to the door and faces it, as if he could see through the chipped paint and metal. "Rusty, my son, he liked pumpkin pie. He liked it more than anything. It started when we mashed some up on Thanksgiving when he was one. Ever since, when he got older, he made his own. He baked it from real pumpkins, had this recipe he invented with molasses and brown sugar." Bud closes his eyes. "God, was it good. I can almost smell it, the way it came hot out of the oven. That bittersweet taste. It got better every year, talk of the family. He took real pride in it."

Bud turns around and rubs his nose, as close to tears as he's ever come with a stranger, barely able to shake it off. "That was the last time I sent him anything. At Thanksgiving I sent a pumpkin over to him in Vietnam. He never got it. He was gone before it got there." The room is suddenly filled with the thick air of memories. Tom folds his arms as Bud searches for composure. "But I don't know what his first word was."

"That just cuts like a knife, doesn't it?"

"He always used to ask me, and I couldn't tell him. All the other kids knew what theirs was. I was gone, of course, whenever it was he said it. Off on another save-the-world mission. And my wife, she was there but didn't care to tell me. She didn't like me much. Hell, I didn't like me much. The thing is though, I didn't ask, before she—"

"It's OK, Bud. I know the story."

"He'd ask me, over and over. Damned if I didn't even get mad at him over it. Damn me. I'll never know. He never knew."

Bud mounts onto the defensive after a moment of silence, snapping back as if he'd been kidnapped. "I can tell this isn't getting anywhere. Maybe we'd all be better off letting you blast yourself to kingdom come." Tom stares him in the eye, puts the quarter in his pocket, turns, and departs the restroom. Bud stands there, perplexed, forcing resentment. "Fruitcake. 100% Grade A."

Tom bolts out of the restroom toward Cirrus and Sam catches up. "What's going on, Tommy?"

Tom stops. "Did you know about the probe?"

Sam gives a poor performance. "What?"

"Damnit! I thought so. It's all right, I'm sure Kirshner gagged you."

"Take it easy, now. You know he did what he thought was best."

"Best for what? I know what he's trying to do." Tom looks around at the disbanding crowd. "And it obviously worked."

"Where are you going? What about all this?"

Zion sits ready in his basket as Tom mounts Cirrus. "I'll be at the Shack. And DON'T call me."

He turns Cirrus around and looks at the circle of cars. With an angry kick of the stirrups, he charges one that has two agents sitting on the hood. They dive off as Cirrus vaults over onto the street, galloping off. The agents get up and dust off, then turn toward Sam who walks away in a hurry.

The colossal ship drifts laterally from the pier amidst fanfares of streamers, deep horn blasts, and waving passengers. Isabel and Nonna lean against the railing, looking down at whirlpools churned by the side thrusters as a stray streamer spins down and ties them together. Nonna is able to stand for short periods, even take steps occasionally, but that has been the extent of her mobility since back surgery. She runs the red, white, and blue streamer through her fingers. "You mean to tell me he didn't even tell *you* where this darned boat is going?"

"He didn't even bother telling me I was going with it until yesterday. Why should I care where it's going?"

"He's thrown just about everyone he cares about in the world on this thing."

"Obviously this has been in the works for a while. Why are we always the last to know?" Isabel asks as she picks the streamer apart.

"That's why I don't like the looks of it all. If we'd known what he was doing, we probably wouldn't have come. I tell you, this isn't right."

Isabel looks up at her. Despite Nonna's redoubt of tenacity, her love for her grandson stands above all else in her life, and this cruise to nowhere has served only to increase her distress. Isabel knows this, and her resentment at being postured so far from Tom transfers to his having left this wonderful woman behind.

"Damn him," says Isabel.

"No, darling," Nonna says, turning away from her. "Damn us, for not being able to help him." They both stare back outward as a lowering Sun casts their long shadows across the pier.

Patrick Herlihy sits still in the oak-lined chambers of a federal court justice, anticipating the arrival of one whose authority breathes from the walls and yards of books covering them. Even the Attorney General looks small in these surroundings. Tall doors open and the Honorable Shiela Bridges enters, a handsome woman of fifty, looking ten years younger and ten years wiser. She glides in wearing a black robe, which she removes and hangs on a rack, unveiling the sexy red dress lurking beneath. She walks over to a complicated desk and sits, leaning back in the leather chair.

"Good evening, Patrick."

"Your Honor."

"'My Honor' is hanging over there on the rack. Shiela, please. I've looked over the file on Holmes."

"What do you think?"

"You were right. This is shaky ground, but Meyerkamp's correct in claiming this could fall within the scope of national security. The incident with the fuel trucks will probably be reduced to an infraction, but since it crossed state lines, we'll retain jurisdiction. Some of his evidence borders on circumstantial, but there are enough points to tie a lot of this together. He's got a reasonable case for probable cause."

"Do you think we should turn him loose?"

She puts on glasses, then looks up. "I'm more concerned about your position if you don't. If this rather absurd story comes true, you could look pretty foolish considering the warning signs."

"It's Tom I'm concerned about. Perhaps we'd better talk to him."

"My sentiments exactly."

They both mull over the situation as she signs a paper on her desk. "I'm issuing a warrant. You might remind Mr. Meyerkamp this allows only a limited search and question, not an arrest. Unless, of course, he finds something to back it up."

Herlihy rises. "Understood. And I appreciate your attention to this matter. I know how full your docket is."

"No bother." She hands him the warrant. "Maybe you better sleep on this one."

He nods and exits respectfully. Shiela removes her glasses, closes her eyes, and rubs the bridge of her nose. She picks up a newspaper clipping from the file and looks at it. Silhouetted through the newsprint is the head of a little boy.

Tom rides up under a sky darkening with clouds to a small guardhouse that sits near an opening in a six-foot adobe wall trimmed by two feeble strands of barbed wire. The guard, Tall Tree, a Navajo whose size befits his name, sees Tom and opens an iron gate to let him pass.

"Good evening, Mr. Tom. I didn't expect you coming."

"I didn't expect me coming either. How's that new foal of yours?"

"Oh, he's growing much bigger today. Eats almost half a bale now."

"Bring him over to the stables and have Billy give him a nice rub and comb."

"Oh, thank you Mr. Tom. I'll do that," says Tall Tree as he closes the gate.

"And Tall Tree, nobody comes in here tonight. OK?"

"OK! Nobody comes in here. OK."

Cirrus strides in and Tom dismounts. He lets the horse walk away, then stands, looking grimly at the Shack. It's not really a shack, a name he and Francine gave it when they first moved in. It's a tiny two bedroom house, the exterior made entirely of red-brown boulders, standing exactly as it did when the newlyweds arrived. The Sun is half set behind the distant cliffs to the west and casts severe shadows off the rock house, striking the compound wall on the eastern side.

The wall is new compared to the house, making the small structure look as if it were the surviving ruin of something that was once there. Such is not the case, however. Tom created a monument, protected from the outside world, unchanging. The wall keeps out time as much as anything, for time became the enemy shortly after a happy young family started. It was here the baby was born, and everything was good. And it was here that all good began to end. This little house was both the beginning, and the end, of happiness.

Tom climbs the wooden steps to the creaking verandah, each step more difficult than the last. There he stops to watch a moth flail itself against the window toward faint light within. Then, pulling the squeaky screen door open, he walks in.

Even with all the time Tom spent here, all the days and nights of his life that seemed so normal, and those that didn't, he feels decimated every time he enters. Each article, each flower on the faded wallpaper has become something foreign, viewed through cracked eyes, something he sees for the first time, every time. He moves languidly through the room, wishing to float above the dried-out floorboards where happy people used to walk, across which final steps were taken. He settles where he always does, on a worn-out tweed couch next to a small end table on which sits a dime store lamp atop a dusty, curled doily. The soft glow from its yellowing lampshade is all that lights the room. The lamp is never turned off, not since the last night they left.

For a long time Tom could not return here, and in fact didn't until the wall was built, and then it sat alone for over a year. He picks up a package of light bulbs laying on the table next to the lamp, puts it back down, then reaches for the phone on the coffee table and places it on his lap. He dials a number on the old rotary dial, and after a few rings, the Doctor answers.

"Hello?"

"I know what you're up to. I could be really upset," Tom says.

The Doctor sits on a couch in front of a stone fireplace, the only light source in the room, with his old Dachshund Schultzie looking devotedly up from his lap. Kirshner views the flames through a glass of wine with one eye closed. "I heard about your little meeting today."

"Don't try to change the subject."

"We had an agreement, Thomas. The probe came first or nothing at all. You were just unavailable."

"How did it come off?" Tom asks.

"100%."

"Nice work."

"You expected something different?"

"No. As a matter of fact, you did me a favor."

"What's that?"

"I want this on Green tonight. No arguments."

Kirshner puts his wine down wrong, spilling it on himself and Schultzie who jumps out of his lap and runs in front of the fire looking scared. Kirshner stands, carrying the phone over to a table, and turns on the room lights.

"Hello?" says Tom.

"I don't see how we can—"

"Doc?" No answer. "It's time."

"As you wish."

"I'll be over first thing in the morning. Good night."

The Doctor puts the phone down, holds his face in his hands, then resurfaces, looking frightened. "Oh, my Lord. What have I done?" He grabs his coat and keys and hurries out, slamming the door behind him. Schultzie scurries to the door too late and looks up at the handle.

Noah's bedroom is dark but for a pale, thin slice of light coming through drawn curtains, casting a sharp line across a picture of the Man-in-the-Moon. The stillness is punctured by the sound of a turning lock. After a moment's hesitation, the door groans open, spraying light from the living room onto the opposite wall. As the door opens wider, the room unfolds. A child's room, created with the adoring hands of expectant parents, finished with the personal touches of a boy fascinated with the heavens. The walls are papered with blue sky and clouds, the ceiling a planetarium with constellations of luminous paint and a comical Moon that glows in the dark.

Tom turns on a table lamp, a hand painted ceramic of the

Owl and the Pussycat in a green boat, the lampshade poised on the tip of a guitar by which the owl serenades in silence. Tom's face shows a mixture of all he has felt since there was life here. Sorrow, fear, pity, hopelessness. And joy. No matter how deep the wounds, he cannot, and must not, forget the joy. A dull smile appears as he looks at shelves cluttered with figurines and music boxes. He picks up a rubber Goofy, Noah's first toy, then quickly replaces it as his mood convulses from tenderness to grief and back.

In a corner there's a stand-up mirror, elliptical, held in a corroded metal frame. It's tilted up just enough to catch his reflection, angled so he appears to lean backward. This disorients him as he stares at the stranger in the mirror, the person who dared remain in the world, who dared continue breathing air which should have been his son's. He looks into that traitor's eyes, then down to the bottom of the mirror where there's a piece of glass missing. And then, across the room, into his sight comes the dresser, whereupon rests the infinite weight of his world.

There he sees Theo the Bear, and the Book. Between them is a tin canister, decorated with a painting of Mickey Mouse, the Sorcerer's Apprentice, standing with one foot on the Earth and holding in one hand a crescent Moon. In the other hand is a magic wand around which Tinkerbell circles in a trail of magic dust. In front of these objects sits the photo of Noah, smiling and happy.

Tom is able to look at this for only a moment, looking into a backward sun, blinded by darkness. He turns away, his glazed scan fixing loosely on a music box, Noah's favorite, given to him by his mother on his second birthday. It's a miniature trunk exploding with animals and toy soldiers. Tom picks it up, turns the crank, and sets it back down. A tiny rocking horse tilts back and forth as it plays "You Are My Sunshine", echoing from a time when it brought smiles and delighted eyes. A grin appears, quickly replaced with pursed lips, either angry or agonized, the distinction by now useless.

Tom picks up another music box, crudely winds it to the brink of breaking and sets it down. This one, a stage of dolls, plays "It's a Small World", clashing with the other defiantly. This grating of two songs fighting against one another feeds his mood. He finds another, winds it, sets it down, and then another, and yet another until the room is filled with an intolerable cacophony of clinking little songs, deafening to his ears and his heart.

Tom falls to the floor on his knees, then folds to a seated position with his legs crossed. He covers his head with his hands, elbows propped on his knees, and closes his eyes. The sound of the music boxes drives deeper and deeper until it crosses faintly into the shadowland of terrible memories, and that is where he drifts, again.

It's night, and Tom, alone in the car, drives hell-bent down a dirt road. The headlights, beaming crazed as the car crashes in and out of potholes and skids through turns, are of little help, though Tom knows the way in his sleep. Even through the veil of tears he can see to make it back. On the front seat, clutched tightly in his whitened hand, is a paper bag. He's frantic, racing against time, exhausted. In the distance he sees flashing red lights and as he draws closer they throb against the ambulance parked in front of the Tijuana beach house. Tom turns pale as his worst fear approaches him through the dirt-streaked windshield.

Shadows flicker out the open front door, and when he turns off the engine, silence falls. The red light pulses on his expressionless face, then stops. Tom gets out of the car slowly and sees the ambulance driver standing by his vehicle. He looks at Tom, casting his eyes to the ground. Tom's movements are catatonic as he floats toward the house, staring at the driver. He turns to see people standing quietly in the living room, opens the screen door, and walks in.

Francine sits on a threadbare sofa, her face in her hands, sobbing softly. She surfaces only for a brief moment to look at Tom. On the table in front of her are two packages, gift wrapped in paper printed with faded balloons. Tom drops the bag, turns, and moves toward the black abyss that beckons, grabbing for his heart. He stops in the hallway and looks at the open door to Noah's room. There he sees one wing of the angel lamp, Theo, laying on the floor, and a small hand, still, on the edge of the bed. He drops to his knees, folds to a seated position, and puts his hands over his head. And he cries.

Tom lies on the floor asleep, his face pinched as "The Star" scratches and wavers on a child's phonograph. The first smattering of daylight breaks the darkness and he partly wakens to the song, looking over at the phonograph, wondering. Drowsy wonder turns to sudden full awakening when a helicopter roars over at low altitude. Tom stands, dazed, and hears yelling outside, then a voice shouting over a megaphone.

"Move the truck! Now! We have a federal warrant!"

Tom runs out of Noah's room up to the front window, peering through the curtains. Tall Tree has blocked the entrance with his pickup, the gate having fallen victim to federal bolt cutters, and stands on the hood, swinging a two-by-four at agents trying to dismount him. From what Tom can see, vehicles are clustered just outside the wall, some sheriffs' cars and some unmarked. Cirrus twitches in front of the verandah, Zion sitting on the saddle, facing away from the action. Tom stops to collect his thoughts, closes his eyes, and takes a breath. Looking upward, he backs toward Noah's room.

"Against the wind," he says as he turns and runs.

Tom stops in front of the dresser, his face is drawn as he gently, reverently, picks up Theo and the Book, lodging them under one arm. Finally, agonizing under all the years of heartbreak that have passed since any of this was touched, he picks up the canister, moving it toward him, clutching it to his chest. With eyes closed tight, he stands silently, then moves out the door.

Tom slips through the front door and walks up to the horse under the watchful eye of his cat. After placing the Book, Theo, and the canister in the saddlebag, and Zion in the basket, he mounts, grabbing the reins. The commotion at the gate stops as all turn to look. Bud quickly slides around the front of the truck, megaphone in hand. Tall Tree starts to lunge toward him but falls victim to the agents who wrestle him to the ground.

Bud unnecessarily barks into the megaphone. "Hold it right there, Holmes. We have a warrant. The game's over."

With a kick of the stirrups, Tom walks Cirrus toward Bud but stops thirty feet away. "Game? What game is that?"

Bud lowers the megaphone. "You know. Go directly to jail."

Tom smiles. "Oh. That game."

Cirrus blusters loud enough to edge Bud back a step. Tom reaches in his coat pocket, prompting agents to draw weapons, but Bud stops them. Tom pulls out his wallet, removes something, replaces the wallet, then throws the object at Bud who snatches it out of the air.

"The game's not over yet, Meyerkamp. It's just my move."

Tom whips his horse. Cirrus rears up, crouching Bud down, then gallops around the back of the Shack and leaps over the rear gate, leaving a dusty quiet behind. Bud erects slowly, looking at the brass-plated, engraved, "Get Out Of Jail Free" card in his hand. He throws the megaphone to the ground as all his forces stand and watch. Tall Tree nods in satisfaction, watching Tom ride over a knoll. "The Child of Skyeyes be with you!"

Bud looks at him in disbelief. "The child of what?" Tall Tree proudly crosses his arms. "Oh, horseshit." He picks up the megaphone and attempts to yell a command, but projects only a piercing squeal. All stand frozen as Bud's eyes shut, a subterranean rumble of frustration surfacing from somewhere beyond the moment. He hurls the megaphone a good twenty yards and watches with everyone else as it skids and tumbles to an angry stop against the adobe wall. The artificial calm is shattered by his bellowing, "Well don't just stand there for godssake! Let's go!" Men scramble to their vehicles, dragging Tall Tree in handcuffs with them. Bud stomps behind, joined shortly by a flustered Knowles.

Tom and Cirrus climb up onto the road from behind a grove and gallop off full speed away from Rockville. In the distance, approaching rapidly, is a battalion of cars with all manner of flashing lights and sirens, quite useless at this early hour in such a place. They serve nothing more than to draw attention as sleepy residents walk out their front doors to watch.

Just as the cars are about to catch up, Tom darts off the road, across a ditch, and out of sight back into the trees, causing the lead vehicle to screech brakes and donut to a stop facing the wrong way. The others barely manage to miss, swerving and sliding past, one ending up half in the ditch. A chopper rises from behind a wash and positions itself overhead, beaming a searchlight down in broad daylight like an alien craft and adding to the confusion by whopping dust into its light shaft. Sid and Bud jump out of the lead car and Bud looks down at the ground, then at Sid.

"Son of a BITCH!" he shouts over the noise.

"Are you thinking... what I'm thinking?" Sid asks.

Bud points his finger at Sid's face. "Don't you think that! Don't *even* think it!" He looks around and up at the chopper. "Ten million bucks worth of hardware and goons around me, and I'm chasin' a guy on a horse. Sid, I don't like horses."

"I don't think it's the horse we're worried about," Sid offers.

Bud points again. "I SAID, don't think that!" He draws a walkie-talkie off his belt, gunslinger style. Sid notices and gives him an *oh-brother* look, prompting a brief stare off. "Attention all units, we're proceeding to location Delta One. Feather Two, you head for Delta Four and hover as long as you got gas. Copy?"

"Feather Two, roger," scratches the radio.

The chopper banks sharply and angles off toward distant

yellow cliffs. Bud marches to the car, peels rubber turning it back around, then sits rumbling as Sid trots up to the passenger side, looks in, and enters. Another squeal of tires and they're off, followed by the caravan of lights.

Cirrus splashes across the river, hoofs up a bank on the other side and stops. Tom's heart races and he heaves for breath, not so much from the ride as the tumultuous parade of events. He reaches into the saddlebag and pulls out his phone. Pausing to collect his thoughts, Tom licks the sweat from his upper lip and speed dials. There's no answer. He looks at the sky in frustration and tries another number.

The blockhouse has no windows, only a narrow slot in the solid cement wall. Standing in front of the steel door, now wide open, is Marion "Butch" Lee, Butch short for "Butcher", a handle he picked up in Operation Enduring Freedom. He stands, looking straight up. Butch chews tobacco, necessitating an occasional spit, a habit that disgusts even himself as evidenced by the look on his face. Sunlight is filtered from above, casting checkered patterns across the ground, and the helicopter echoes down as a phone rings inside. Butch walks in, then comes back out holding a cordless handset. "Blockhead. Go."

"It's Tom. Where's Doc?"

Tom's voice brings him to attention. "Doc? Well, he was here all night, but he just left. What's going on around here? He's got us all on Green."

Tom drops the phone to his side and shakes his head. He brings it back up. "Listen, Butch, this is important. Did he say where he was going?"

"No, he didn't. Wait a second. He did say something about rerunning a sequence on the service module engine. Sticky valve or something. By the way, you know anything about this damn chopper? It's hovering right overhead, blowin' dust everywhere. It's pissin' me off."

Tom pauses. "I don't have time to explain. Get somebody

up on the roof and tell them to do anything short of shooting it down to get it out of there. And Butch, I want you to listen very carefully."

"I'm listening."

"It's time for Blue." Butch swallows his tobacco and drops the phone, spitting and gagging. "Butch? Butch? Hey, are you there?"

Butch picks up the phone. "You didn't say what I think you said."

"Code Blue, Butch. Now!"

"Yeah? Well what about Code Red, and White?"

Tom tries to check his ballooning frustration, holding the phone down again, then continues. "We're skipping Red and White, Butch. You see that chopper up there? Do not pass Go, do not collect two hundred dollars. Jump directly to Blue. Am I making myself clear?"

Butch's voice tightens. "Wait a second, now. We... we have a password for Blue. Yeah, how do I know it's you? What's the damn password, Tom?"

Tom looks across the valley. Of course there's a password. They set it up that way, but he hadn't expected this and can't remember right now. He searches. "Red Rock. Red Rock!"

"No way! No way, man! That was last month!"

Tom explodes. "Screw the password! Damnit Butch! Read my lips! CODE BLUE! NOW!"

Butch coughs again, then motions with his lips. *Code Blue?* "Jesus, Joseph, and Mary." He turns his head around to look at something behind him, moves his frightened gaze upward to the top of it, nearly looking at the sky, then runs full speed away.

Tom rides Cirrus back down to the river and dismounts. While Cirrus drinks, Tom splatters water on his face, looking up at a daytime Moon sitting high, ghostlike behind the winter-blue sky. From the remotest edge of his vision something glints. Tom turns to look, shielding his eyes from the morning Sun burning just above the east rim of the canyon. Off in the distance he can barely make out a man's figure standing on a massive slice of rock that tumbled from the ridge before humans were walking upright. Tom squints to see, then stills as he realizes it's transparent, glass-like. The figure turns toward him, and when he does, sunlight prisms through him and beams a rainbow shaft across Tom like a knife-edge spotlight, shocking him backward into the water. The glass man turns and disappears behind the rock.

Tom has stopped trying to make sense of these visions because somehow, in some layer of himself, he understands deeper than mere logic would permit. The one thread he feels in it all is a commonality of purpose, yet to be revealed. The first came a few months after Noah's death when he brushed against suicide and sought the counsel of Billy's father, Gabriel Graymare, a tribal elder turned pastor. Gabriel embraced Tom's grief and consoled him with tales of eternal life and heavenly reunions, none of which Tom could fathom. During that session, however, as Tom watched Gabriel talking, all sound silenced, and from Gabriel's moving lips outpoured liquid gold that ran across the floor like shining lava, turning everything it touched to gold. And then in the familiar flash of light, it went as quickly as it came, yet Tom had still heard every word. He never said anything to anyone about it. At first they came rarely, but now more frequently, almost daily.

Tom gathers up Zion and in one motion, mounts Cirrus and kicks him back into a gallop.

Robert Linden climbs down from the rock.

Billy, dressed only in fringed leather pants, sits bareback atop a stallion at the edge of a bluff. He watches Tom and Cirrus race across the flatland below, slide down an embankment, then run along a narrow dry-wash. Billy turns his horse and lopes away.

Dirt roads are not usually twenty yards wide. Kirshner's 4-wheel drive Bronco rattles down the center and the Doctor looks tired, disturbed as he drives robotically along, relying on his instincts. His trance is broken as he notices a horse and rider in the distance coming toward him. He stops the car and slowly exits, straining to see if he's imagining things in such an exhausted state. He pulls his wire-rimmed spectacles out of his pocket and applies them to his head, his heart racing when he realizes who it is. Tom pulls Cirrus to a skidding halt and gets off the horse. He takes Theo, the canister, and the Book from the saddlebag and walks toward the Doctor.

Kirshner looks down at the objects, then into Tom's eyes. The years he spent on this endeavor have been fraught with roller coasters of emotion: triumph, disappointment, challenge, guilt. The most difficult of all has been the task of striving with all his ability to accomplish a goal he desperately hoped would be abandoned. The entire effort to this point had been an extravagant catharsis, the motivation an acting out of his friend's grief. However, as evidenced by the resign in Tom's eyes, the time has come to play it out. Regardless of what motives he imagined Tom to have, seeing his armful of cargo strikes Kirshner to the core. Choked with emotion, he looks up at the sky.

"My dear boy," he says, looking back at Tom. "It has been such a long journey. You would think it was about to end, but you have such a very long way to go." He embraces Tom, and thus the objects between them, then gently releases, stroking Theo's head. "Please, come back home."

Tom grabs Kirshner's shoulder with a strong grip. "I suppose part of that depends on you, doesn't it?"

Kirshner pats Tom's hand. "Go, Thomas. God be with you."

"You ride Cirrus back and make sure Billy gets him."

The Doctor looks at the horse in fear, mounts inelegantly, and rides off on the head of a pin. Tom turns and enters the truck, leaving the door open for his cat. Zion licks a shoulder, stalling against an uneasy feeling. Against better cat judgment, he hops in and crawls under the driver's seat as Tom slams the door and, wheels spinning in the dirt, skids and slides off in the opposite direction.

Isabel stands alone at the forward most railing of the top most deck of the ship, leaning into the wind. Her hair blows back across a white-fringed shawl draped over a formal gown of lustrous silver silk, her face tilted toward the Sun with closed eyes.

Passengers linger nearby, keeping their distance. She opens her eyes slowly and looks down to the deck below, noticing a boy in a wheelchair. He is alone also, his chair aligned fore and aft, and rolls forward and back in it with the pitching of the ship. His only interaction with the chair is to apply braking to control speed and distance of glide. Isabel smiles, then returns to the confused mood she began with.

On the very bow of the ship near the loading hold is something covered by a huge tarp. This raises her curiosity, but only for a moment, roughly the extent of her attention span. Isabel takes her cane and starts to walk away, encountering the stares of those nearby, appreciative, but never comfortable with her celebrity.

Francine walks barefoot on the beach, playing driftwood-fetch with her golden retriever, Sessna, the dog's frantic enthusiasm contrasting her pedantic throwing. After a couple of rounds, Sessna is sidetracked by a small mongrel that scurries up and sniffs upward. Wet noses bump, seemingly in play until, to Sessna's surprise, the dog snarls and attacks her leg. She howls in fright, unwilling to defend herself as Francine rushes up and kicks the dog away, sending it off. Sessna looks up, humiliated and hurt, licking her chops in embarrassment, and trots off towards the house, head down, leaving Francine alone with the driftwood. She hurls it into the waves.

The mongrel jumps into the water and swims out to the wood, retrieving it to her feet. Francine crouches down, takes the stick, and can't help but pat the dog on the head while Sessna watches from a distance with a look of confused betrayal. From behind, she hears a whistle, followed by a child's voice that unnerves her more than it should.

"Sandy! Here, Sandy!"

Francine turns to see the silhouette of a boy near the water's edge, sun rays spraying behind his head. She squints, barely able to look. The dog jumps into his arms and Francine shades her eyes, looks down, then looks up again to find no one. She rises and walks quickly toward the house, her arms embracing herself against the chill of ocean air.

Billy sits cross legged in front of a morning campfire with his head bowed, chanting under his breath. He raises his face skyward, eyes closed, and throws powder into the fire, flaring it with pinpoint sparks of magnesium. Robert Linden watches from behind and walks toward Billy, but stops a few yards away. Linden says, "Sha quanna, heo matto no kita pa."

Without turning around, Billy answers, "Yototek, raxota ishne Tobats."

Kirshner trots Cirrus toward the back of the warehouse and sees the flashing caravan of vehicles racing in the direction of the front gate. He dismounts as awkwardly as he mounted and, hugging the wall, slips into a side entrance, running across the expansive floor toward the office door.

From under the hanger-like doors, long shadows of approaching cars and people spill across the concrete. One lone guard sits by the smaller door, watching the Doctor enter the offices. He turns toward the door as someone tries to open it. The guard steps back as intruders attack the metal door and finally propel it open. The FBI pours in, guns drawn, followed by their leader, Bud, entering like the conquering Caesar. After a standoff of stares, they grab the guard, overzealously containing him. Men spread across the floor looking up and around in confusion at the quiet emptiness. Bud spots the offices across the floor and motions for his men to follow.

Kirshner grabs an armful of manuals from a filing cabinet, opens the control room door and enters, closing it and testing the locks.

Tom arrives at the compound gate, a ten-foot high chain link barrier spanning the width of the dirt road as it enters the compound clearing. The left portion of the fence abuts a ravine wall that forms the east side of the compound. The right continues down to the river that parallels the road as the tributary emerges from the narrow ravine. The rock wall across the river tapers down sharply as the river passes the compound and continues northbound to join the Virgin.

The compound itself is an elliptical clearing, fifty yards wide from the east ravine wall to the outward curve of the river, a hundred yards long from the fence to the far end. The sheer wall across the river is dark and wet, nearly always in shade, thousand-year-old water trickling from a contrasting white-lime calcium layer halfway down the face. The river curves left upstream and disappears around the clearing, while the blockhouse sits just inside the fence at the edge of the river. A linear shadow lays across the river and partly up the wet wall.

Tom starts to open the gate with a garage door opener, but rethinks and stops it after a foot or so. He repositions the Bronco as a barricade, collects his precious articles, and gets out. Just as he squeezes through the gate, Butch runs up, shotgun in hand, ready for action. Realizing it's Tom, he calms slightly, still red-faced and jittery. He looks at Tom's armful, twitching one eye.

"Hot damn, Tommy. I guess this is it."

"Now or never, right?"

"I'll tell you something. You've got *some* huevos. I wish I was goin' with you."

"I'd love to have ya." He pokes Butch in the gut. "Too much specific mass."

"Up yurs, good buddy."

"How we doin'?"

"Had a failure on the cooler an hour ago. The temp's up on the A-Z. Plus the top load's shy since the truck never made it."

"How shy?"

"Maybe... fifteen percent."

Tom ponders. "Well, not much we can do now." Zion scampers up to Butch, body sweeps his leg once, then sits on his haunches and, licking a paw, passes over one ear as they watch. "You know what that means."

"Company's coming." He grabs the back of Tom's neck. "Buona fortuna, Tom."

Tom looks at the shotgun. "Hey, careful with the artillery. I don't want anybody hurt."

"Roger that," Butch pouts.

Tom looks into his eyes, then hurries away toward the far end of the clearing where there's a wide path that disappears, turning left around the ravine wall. He passes a small square building servicing two twelve-foot diameter spherical tanks, each feeding a six-inch cast iron pipe that parallels the path and disappears with it.

Butch closes the gate, takes the length of chain hanging from the latch, wraps it around both sides twice and secures it with a padlock. He walks over to an electrical box and throws a foot-long knife switch. A pulsating red light comes alive at the top of the fence next to the sign: WARNING!! HIGH VOLTAGE FENCE- KEEP OFF!!!

Inside the warehouse office, Bud and Sid each sit on a desk, puzzled as agents rifle through file drawers, turn over trash cans, and generally eyeball the room. Bud taps his nose. "I don't get it. Something's missing here."

An agent walks in. "We found his horse tied up in back."

Sid and Bud look at each other, then Bud inquires, "What about the old man? Any sign of him?"

"Not since he took off last night like a bat out of hell in that four-wheeler. At least we thought it was him. Hard to tell from that distance in the dark."

Bud looks around the room for the umpteenth time, then rests his eyes on the control room door. "Anybody try that closet?"

Another agent responds. "I did, but the door's locked."

Bud looks at him with raised eyebrow. "Oh, dear. The door was locked? Then I guess we'd better not open it."

As the agent looks away, Bud walks across the room to the door, tries to open it, then really tries, exasperating himself in the process.

Inside the control room Kirshner frantically inputs commands on a keyboard. He looks up and back at the sound of the door being assaulted, picks up the console mounted phone, and enters a number. "Any sign of him?"

Tim Goulet, a strapping young ex-Marine, black sunglasses secured by a neon pink strap around his neck, sits in a short jetway with the capsule hatch open at the end and answers over a speaker phone, having to turn down *Whose Line Is It?* on a TV monitor. "No, Doc, nothin' yet. Let me look." He stands, stretches, and walks over to a porthole to see Tom standing eleven stories down, looking up. Tim waves, and Tom waves back. "He's down at ground zero. Looks like he's comin' up."

Kirshner wipes the sweat from his forehead. "Better get him going, Tim. Someone's trying to break in here, so I'm locking out my terminal."

"Roger that, dude. I'll kick his butt as soon as it gets up here."

Kirshner hangs up. "Roger that, *dude?*" The pounding stops, freezing Kirshner as he turns to look over his shoulder. He quickens the pace in advance of the inevitable.

Up in the office, everyone stands by the door, panting, most of all Bud. "Jesus! What the hell's this made of, kryptonite?"

"Yeah, it's just a closet door," says the same agent.

Bud looks at him again, this time anger overshadowing irritation. "Jerry, you dweeb. How did you *ever* make it into the academy, much less get out? I swear—" Suddenly Jerry's comment hits him. He exits the office, Sid following.

Bud stands on the warehouse floor in line with the wall that the door opens into, assessing the next set of offices on the other side. "Now what kind of closet do you suppose is eight feet deep?" he asks no one, then yells across the floor. "Get me a crowbar! Pronto!"

Tom faces a concrete pad the size of a small house with a six-foot launch arm on top, directly above of him. As he tilts his head up, he admires, foot by foot, all 141 feet of the Noah 1, a reconstructed Titan 3c booster, its brushed aluminum gleaming in the sun. It has, mounted on each side of the first stage, solid fuel boosters, though half the size of the originals. It stands poised, aimed skyward, threatening all 1,300,000 pounds of potential thrust. A towering "N1" runs up the side of the booster, above that the same "H" which marked the stack of the cruise ship.

Perched at the pinnacle is a third stage unlike one a Titan has ever supported. The shining black capsule looks like a twenty-foot bullet, sitting atop a service module four feet wider than the launch vehicle itself. Stenciled on the capsule is a raised hand with a butterfly perched on top.

The elevator door opens and Zion darts in, followed by Tom. As the door closes, Tom stands at the back, reading the floor annunciator: G,1,2, and 11. Zion sits beside him, looking up as well. Tom looks down at him, Zion looks back, then they both return their gaze to the annunciator as Tom pushes the 11 button and the elevator moves upward. "Second floor: Lingerie. Sporting goods... Yarn." No reaction. "Catnip." Zion swishes his tail.

The elevator door opens and Zion jumps onto Tim's lap, an obvious friend. "Hey, Wildcat! Give me five!" Zion paws at his outstretched hand. "Doc's goin' ballistic. Sounds like the man's on his back." He looks at Tom's armful. "Snap!"

"You could say that." Tom places his cargo in a plastic container sitting by the open hatch, closes the lid, and sets it inside the capsule. Doing so, he notices a poster of Pink Floyd's "Dark Side of the Moon" taped to the jetway wall. He turns toward Tim.

"Cool, huh?" Tim says, tickled with himself. "It's kind of... real white in here. Needed something to send you off with."

Tom grins. "Guess we better get this show on the road."

There's a stressed silence as Tom looks at Tim holding Zion. "Don't worry, Homes. I'll take good care of him 'til you, you know, get back."

Tom nods. "Yeah, sure. I know." He walks over, strokes Zion's head, and places his hand on Tim's shoulder. "Take care of yourself while you're at it. Sam'll make sure you don't get hammered too hard."

"Wanna see a hammer?" He clenches his raised fist. "Don't

worry about it."

Tom grabs Tim's fist, turns sadly, and starts to enter the hatch, then stops. He turns back around. "Oh, hell. You don't get off this easy." Tom pulls his cat from Tim's arms and carries him into the capsule.

"It's the *Purrminator*! Meow'll be back!" Tim beams as he closes the hatch behind Tom.

The capsule's interior isn't cramped, as were the Gemini predecessors. Colors are in a spectrum of light greens and browns, most surfaces covered with molded, lightweight plastic. The Doctor felt Tom might need friendlier surfaces to encounter as he learned the business of weightlessness and the certain unplanned trajectories he would take during the course of getting his bearings.

The bottom diameter is twelve feet, the usable interior length over fifteen feet with a bulkhead separating the control area from a pressure lock, making the control area ten feet long, allowing Tom to stand. The command seat is horizontal in the launch attitude, braced against the bottom of the capsule and attached to a rail. Facing the seat is a console with a desk and in the console three flat-screen monitors. A keyboard is embedded in the desk, and that is the extent of instrumentation. No dials, no knobs, no gauges.

Tom puts the cat on the seat back, stores his cargo in a bay to the right of the console, and reaches up to the panel. He touches heat activated switches near the monitors, causing the capsule to come alive in all manner of lights and displays, similar to a state-of-the-art airliner. The center screen shows a camera view from the top of the booster looking straight down. Zion looks up at the panel as, with the push of another switch, Tom locks the interior hatch mechanism with the ominous clang of a jailhouse door.

Kirshner anxiously eyes a blank monitor, then stills as it flickers to life, showing a view of the interior of the capsule with Tom looking straight into the camera. "Anybody home?"

"Thomas, thank God. Listen—" A resounding thump from behind, followed by another, turns the Doctor around. "I'm afraid

I'm about to lose control here."

The capsule's left screen displays a Mac desktop and Tom taps a touchpad, opening up a video control menu. One more tap and the center screen presents a wide-angle shot of the control room with the Doctor in center frame. Tom hears the banging going on behind.

"That would make your location the 'out of control' room, then, wouldn't it?" He doesn't get the laugh. "You think you got problems? Take a look at this."

He changes the view on the screen to one looking straight up from the capsule. It shows camouflage netting above, with the barely discernible image of a helicopter hovering overhead.

Kirshner gasps. "Oh! That does it, Thomas. We have to scrub." The picture on his screen returns to the capsule and Tom puts his face in the camera, the wide angle lens sweeping his Cheshire Cat grin around his head.

"Who do you think will win? Him or me?"

"Neither, son. Neither."

"Wanna bet?"

Bud repeatedly applies the crowbar to the door and finally, with full body English, propels it open, nearly departing it from the hinges. He stands to catch his breath while looking at his accomplishment, the wide stairway leading downward, then scans around at his amazed cohorts, gloating.

"Let's go!"

Kirshner turns around to witness the thunder of angry footsteps clanking down the metal stairs.

Tom watches the monitor as Bud and company appear, guns drawn, stopping in a compacted group in front of the Doctor. They're momentarily idle as they look around, shocked to find what they expected all along. At a loss for words, as well as alternatives, Bud yells, "Grab him!"

Two of them rudely grab the Doctor's arms and launch him out of his chair as everyone stares, the absurdity of the action manifesting in a vacuous silence. Bud looks around the room and finally realizes Tom is present on the monitor, watching in disgust. "Well, I guess you really got me now," Tom's image reviles. Everyone else in the room is confused until they find the monitor. "Let the Doctor go."

Bud searches for any kind of comeback. "Yeah, right!" Still searching, he dribbles, "You got to be kidding." As Bud squints at the screen, he begins to make out Tom's surroundings. The reality of what's there crumples his face.

Tom leans forward. "There's nothing he can do now. Get your hands off him."

Bud rocks nervously, gnashing as he looks at the uncomfortable sight of his men restraining an old man in a purple cardigan. He motions with his gun, forgetting he's holding it. "Let him go."

As Kirshner is released, he rearranges his clothing and glares at his captors. Bud looks at his gun, slides it back in the holster, then goes nose-to-nose with him. "Listen here, Rocket Man. I don't buy that crap for a second. If you want to make things a little easier on yourself, you just... take the key out the ignition, or whatever *freakin'* thing you have to do to put an end to this adventure of yours."

Kirshner relishes a pause. "He has the master program. I can 'pull the plug' for you here, but then you'd just miss the fun of watching."

Bud turns toward the monitor and stares. As much as he hates to, he's beginning to believe them. He looks at the floor, biting his lip, then around the room, finding only more helplessness, none of which he needs to add to his own. He grabs the walkie-talkie. "Unit Three, Unit Three, this is Watchdog, over."

Three cars angle in front of the compound gate, agents wandering around in disarray. Two of them attend a compatriot who's holding his hand, his hair standing on end. Another leans into a car and pulls out a microphone. "Unit Three, go ahead."

Bud's voice screeches across the radio. "What the hell's going on out there?"

"Well, sir, we're at the entrance, but there's a real solid gate here and it's got about a million volts runnin' through it. Not to mention somebody inside's fired a warning round over our heads. Over."

Butch crouches against the blockhouse wall, shotgun over his shoulder, then scoots low to the ground back into the blockhouse.

Bud explodes into the walkie-talkie. "Well, crash the gate then! Good God! Do I have to spell *everything* out for you?"

After another pause, the agent's voice wavers back, "No sir, I don't think these men are ready for that. Not without rubber suits. Perhaps if we get some bigger equipment out here."

Bud builds up a charge and unleashes, "You'll get some bigger equipment out there all right! ME!" He walks up to the monitor and puts his face in it.

Inside the capsule, Bud's face takes up the entire screen. "You listen to me, Tommy Boy. You ain't goin' *nowhere*! If I have to personally climb up there and yank your ass out!" he yells, fogging the screen with his blast.

As his words echo off the cement walls and everyone in the control room cringes, Tom looks back calmly. Without saying a word, he taps the touchpad and the screen goes black. Bud stares at the blank screen with equal blankness, then looks down, followed by a slow scan around the room full of eyes darting everywhere. They are not surprised, but flinch nevertheless at, "GodDAMNIT!" He points his finger at the Doctor. "Keep him away from this. He touches one button and everybody gets lunch with me in HELL!" He turns the finger toward his men. "Sanderson, Albright, you come with me." Bud vaults up the steps three at a time, leaving behind a wake of shattered nerves, and welcomed silence. One agent rolls up a chair and motions to Kirshner.

"Have a seat, Doctor."

Tom watches displays on the left screen as Zion sniffs the air, unable to make sense of his surroundings. Strange smells, even to a cat: electrical wire, metallic grease, rubber. Tom reaches up to the console and unhooks his headset, a molded earpiece with a two-inch clear mic tube, and clips the wireless transmitter to his belt. After inserting the earpiece, he pushes the switch on the transmitter.

"Hey Butch, you with me?"

Butch sits in the blockhouse watching his own screens, still twitching. "Ten four. We've got company outside the gate. One got a lifetime battery charge compliments of Utah Water and Power, and the other one'll be combin' buckshot out of his doo for a while."

"Try to stay off the trigger, Butch. It'll only be harder on you later."

"The harder the better, compadre."

"I'm showing twenty-five minutes left in the sequence. We may have to abbreviate. Better get the boys out of there."

"Whatever you say." Butch picks up his radio. "Blockhead to River Rats, Blockhead to River Rats. Scramble! Repeat, scramble!"

Mr. Bullard sits on a rock, daydreaming, and responds sarcastically into his radio, "Yeah. Right."

"This is no drill! SCRAMBLE!" Butch's tone gets his attention and Bullard gets up, looking downriver.

Isabel sits in her dressing room, brushing her hair, the motion matching her mood; distant, preoccupied, melancholy. She stops, some unwelcome thought passing through, then continues.

Bud roars down the compound access road like a maniac gone wild, cohorts, Sid included, hanging onto anything in undisguised terror. Traveling too fast for the condition of the road, the car fishtails and crashes in and out of pothole after pothole. Though Bud curses out loud, they can't hear.

Tom races through checklists, inputting information as fast as the computer will respond. He looks up at one of his monitors and sees the Doctor sitting in his chair, fidgeting, guarded by his captors. Tom brings up his image on the screen in the control room again. The Doctor notices, but the others don't for a moment until they see the look on his face. They rotate around to the screen, drawing their weapons, and Tom ducks in jest.

"Whoa! Watch where you point those things."

"Knock it off, Holmes. You better get your laughs now," one sneers as they replace their weapons.

Tom ignores him. "Doc. Guess I can't count on much help from you."

"No, son. Looks like you're on your own. You know, I have a nice little tritip defrosted. I could make your favorite German potatoes. I'm sure the authorities would permit us dinner this evening."

"Nice try, but save me the leftovers. Listen, you ran the valve this morning. Everything go OK?"

An agent scrambles, running over and putting his hand over the camera. "Hold on here! You're not getting any help from this guy."

Kirshner responds through his hand. "Yes, I did. A little temperamental, but it finally worked."

The agent reels, "Jeeesus, you two! Don't do that!"

The squad at the compound gate see Bud's car approaching with its roostertail of dust and crouch behind their vehicles as he skids to a halt inches from the Bronco blocking the gate. Bud exits his car all too calmly, walking over to them. "What's the matter, boys? This naughty car in your way?" Expected silence. "Well, Uncle Bud will make it all better."

Bud gets back in the car and in a storm of spinning wheels and spraying gravel, positions in front of the blockade vehicle. He smashes into the front, pushing it over the embankment into the river, then repositions directly in front of the gate, sticking his head out the window. "And this mean old fence? Did it make an ouchy on you?"

He punches the car into reverse, shoots out fifty yards, idles, then revs the engine and crunches it into gear. As the unmarked vehicle, turned tank, roars by, Sid's face is a frightened blur. The car crashes through the gate in an explosion of sparks, bringing with it and on top of it sections of fence until it comes to a stop well inside the compound. Butch runs for the blockhouse in the distance as Bud gets out, dusty and triumphant. He gestures with both hands, ushering them inside. "Entre vous."

They scurry in, guns drawn, crouching to avoid nonexistent gunfire. Bud, standing straight up, kicks one in the behind, then struts toward the blockhouse. Overhead hovers Feather 2.

Butch runs into the blockhouse, heaves the steel door shut, secures two latches, and places a bar across, leaning his back against it. Pounding from the outside jars him off and he runs over to his bank of monitors, out of breath. He shouts into a microphone. "Mayday! Mayday! The Buzzard has landed!"

Tom switches cameras and gets a view of the blockhouse and its intruders. Then he switches to Butch's camera, seeing his sweat drenched face in full screen. "Oh boy. Looks like you're in a world of poop," Tom says.

"Looks like you're in the same world, buddy," Butch responds, power-chewing his tobacco.

"Not for long, my friend." Tom pauses. "Not for long." He opens a red guarded switch and, savoring the moment, pushes it.

Suddenly a warning siren pierces the air, jolting Bud and his men. They look around, as if the source of the siren would explain it.

The River Rats who had taken the alert so lightly jump to their feet.

On the plateau above the compound, two men who were in an underground bunker emerge, looking up at the hovering chopper and trying to wave it off, then watch in wonder as exploding charges release an acre of camouflage net, allowing it to drop away from one edge of the gorge.

The audience has taken their seats in the ship's concert hall, a three-deck, glittering wonder at sea. The last few moments of rustling gowns and clearing of throats give way to expectant silence. Poised nobly on a platform sits a full-grand Bosendorfer, lid raised. A peaceful scene of Angels Landing is projected against a screen behind and as the house lights dim, the Landing comes alive.

Inside the Earth Channel studios, a phone rings and the technical director distractedly answers as he watches a nature program. At the bottom of the screen sits the screen bug: Earth Channel.

"Hello?" He realizes who he's speaking with and sits erect. "Yes, Mr. Holmes, I'll get him. He's right here." He motions wildly to John Brandt, the program director standing across the booth, who gestures back, *what?* The TD covers the phone. "You know, the guy who signs the paycheck of the guy who signs *your* paycheck?"

Mr. Brandt walks over and snatches the phone from him. "Tom. What can I do for you?" The TD mocks with his lips, *Tom?* Brandt ignores him. "Yes, I remember our discussion. It seemed a bit far fetched." He pauses. "You mean, *now?* Full network feed?" His demeanor changes. "Yes sir, Mr. Holmes. Whatever you say."

He hangs up slowly, staring straight ahead, and says in monotone, "There's a feed on class A line two forty." He writes the number on a notepad and hands it to him. "Patch it in, bring it up network, and leave until you hear from me."

"Network? But we're in the middle of—" One look from his superior carries the same weight as the telephone conversation. The TD carries out the order.

Francine stands at the kitchen counter dunking a Chamomile bag in a rainbow mug. Behind her, the TV is on the Earth Channel, a wildlife scene suddenly replaced by a view looking down from the capsule to the ground, red light flashing off the rock walls. Francine turns and notices the screen, idle observation replaced by a whispering concern. Whatever this is, her heart says, it's not far removed from her.

* * *

Back in the control room the main monitor shows the same view. The agents hadn't noticed a display light on a panel alternating red and green. As the Doctor stares, the agents turn to it, not knowing what they're seeing.

"What the heck is that?" one of them asks the Doctor.

Bud looks up at the chopper, its loud and great churning sadly ironic to him as it hovers there, useless. Sid walks up and they look over in the direction from where the long shadow originates. Sid has to shout over the siren. "Well, Bud, whad'ya think? Should we take a look? We've come this far."

Bud tufts at the ground with his shoe. "Yeah, well, I get the feeling we've about run out of options, except to look." He walks slowly in that direction and motions toward the blockhouse behind his back, as if only half of him speaks. "Get him out of there." The men look at each other. After all, it's only a concrete blockhouse with a steel door.

Sanderson, grimacing, yells, "What about this horn?"

Bud pays no attention and keeps walking. He comes around the bend and finally is face to... face with it. Albright and two others, already there gaping, look at him, then back. He slowly lifts his head, Noah 1 towering above. "God Almighty."

Bud looks down and shakes his head as Sid and a few more agents run around the corner, stopped cold by the sight. The elevator door opens and Tim shoots out, wide-eyed, as surprised at the encounter as they. After a moment of frozen staring, Tim takes off running. They're too dazed to realize they should have detained him.

Tom has the view looking down and sees the men at the bottom, looking up.

In the control room, the agents stare at the screen and realize they're looking at their boss, looking up at them. "JEEsus. It's Bud," says one.

He looks at the Doctor, at the screen, then at the other agent who says, mouth barely moving, "He wasn't kidding after all. It's really there." He looks back at the Doctor. "You gotta do something."

Kirshner raises his hands in a display of helplessness.

Isabel enters to respectfully constrained applause, smiles courteously, and stands by the piano. The applause gives way to appropriate silence and the view of Angels Landing is replaced by the one looking down from the capsule. The audience looks at it, unsure, some pointing, some commenting, though Isabel doesn't notice.

Tom, seated in the launch position and strapped in, plants Zion on his stomach. The cat looks confused as Tom pushes his transmit button. "Attention all aircraft, remain clear of coordinates North 37-09-31, West 113-02-17. Repeat, remain clear of coordinates North 37-09-31, West 113-02-17."

In the cockpit of an F-16, a military pilot looks puzzled. He calls the controller. "Center, Neon 1. Did you copy that transmission?"

"Roger, we heard that. The coordinates are inside your corridor. Not sure what to make of it."

The pilot hesitates, then switches frequency to his military tower. "Tower, Neon 1, did you copy that?"

The Nellis Air Force Base control tower is quiet as controllers look at each other. "Roger, Neon 1, we heard it. You want to take a look? We'll scramble two for you."

"Affirmative. I think I will. See what the duty officer says." The pilot rolls his fighter toward the target area, entering the coordinates into his guidance system.

Tom looks at Bud's frozen presence on his screen, in marked contrast to the jittery troops around him. He enters a command into the computer, hesitates, and pushes one last key, putting his hands over Zion and clenching his teeth.

Suddenly the siren stops, the silence proving more frightening than the ear-splitting sound it replaced, and, taking heed from this and Tim's rapid departure, the agents run off leaving Bud and Sid alone. Sid lays a hand on Bud's shoulder, pats it sympathetically, and walks away around the bend as Bud shakes his fist at the capsule.

Bullard jumps out of his skin when a flood gate opens, diverting river water into a huge grating. On this cue, he stumbles and slips over rocks to a notch in the ravine wall.

A cascade of water gushes from under the launch pad and down a cement chute back toward the river. Bud begins walking backward and as he does so, sees sparks and flame falling from the main stage and booster nozzles. At this cue, he runs for his life.

Isabel, now seated at the piano, begins Chopin's *Nocturne in B-Major*. The launch unfolds on the screen behind her and the audience stares in varying states of confusion. Sputtering flames turn to cones of pure thrust as orange and white steam explodes and billows from the chute, filling the gorge. Isabel continues her piece.

Bud runs into the clearing, falls to the ground, and covers his head as the compound fills with steam, dust, thunder, and rocks falling from the compound walls. The blockhouse door opens and Butch emerges, fists raised in the air. "YEAH, Baby!" He's forced back in by the intensity of the launch, Tim following.

Tom grips his armrest as the capsule shakes violently. Zion's ears are flat against his head.

On the plateau, the two men stoop in reflex, the ground shaking beneath their feet, and run for their bunker.

The chopper pilots see the Titan and its blasting fire beneath. One look at each other and the chopper tilts, flying off horizontally.

Further away on the plateau, a doe looks up as smoke rises from the gorge in the distance behind her. Although she doesn't see, she runs.

Kirshner jumps from his chair when he sees the launch sequence begin. He runs over to a computer and brings up data screens. One agent starts after him, but the other holds his partner back, shaking his head.

The hydraulic launch arms fold back, releasing the Titan to inch off the pad, more and more enveloped in a rotating storm of red smoke and fire, colored further with sandstone blasted off the ravine walls.

Francine watches the Earth Channel as the view from the top of the rocket shows upward movement. She stops sipping on her tea as the implication sinks in.

Rockville's only appliance store has a few TVs for sale in the window, all displaying the Earth Channel feed. Several locals have stopped to watch, and behind them in the distance white smoke shoots up from the horizon.

Back on the plateau the men peer through the slot in the bunker, their jaws dropping in unison when they see the tip of the capsule emerge from the edge of the gorge. As the rocket materializes foot by foot, they clasp hands in congratulations.

Bud uncovers his head to look up with one eye. He sees the rocket lifting into the sky, notices a few harmless fires that started along the canyon wall, then buries his head again. Butch surfaces from the blockhouse, fearlessly determined to enjoy the event, and walks over to Bud, hovering over him, reaching out a hand. "Come on, man. You can get up now. The worst of it's over," he says as Tim watches from the blockhouse door.

Bud uncharacteristically accepts his help, then scowls. "Not for you, moron. You're under arrest." They both look up, squinting at the blazing ball of white fire. Bud slaps dirt off his pants like an old rug.

Those watching at the appliance store stare at the screen as the flickering white light rises above the horizon behind them, leaving a vertical, expanding contrail. One observer recognizes the scene and turns around, his suspicion confirmed. He taps another on the shoulder and points.

G forces manifest in Tom's elongating grimace and Zion's whiskers bend downward as he sinks into Tom's abdomen. The center console screen shows a view down the fuselage, the Earth shrinking below, and flames fanning out from the three engines.

The F-16 pilot sees Noah 1 gaining vertical velocity and tilting in the distance. "Uh, oh." He keys his mic. "Center, Neon 1, I've got a UFO. Right where he said he'd be. You guys mean to tell me you don't know about this?"

After a moment, the controller's voice asks, "UFO? You mean... the flying saucer type?"

"Negative. Looks like a ghost from the Gemini program. I'm gonna tail it as far as I can."

As the fighter prowls near Noah 1, two more approach in the distance.

Inside the Air Room of Stratcom, underneath Offutt Air Force Base in Omaha, Nebraska, an officer converses with a subordinate when an alarm shatters the silence of routine monitoring. He whips around to a wall-sized screen that shows a red target track in a westbound trajectory from southern Utah and stabs at the transmit switch on his headset cord. "Got a red arrow! Red arrow! You playin' any war games here?... You sure?" He doesn't get the answer he wanted. "Get General Noll down here. Now!" He releases the switch. "What the hell?"

Below an arcing Noah 1, the fighter hovers against a sky showing signs of space, hues of dark blue compressed against the horizon. The pilot's voice modulates across the radio waves. "I'm as high as I can go." His screen shows target acquisition on the Noah 1. "We're locked on here. Cleared to arm?"

A long silence is followed by, "Negative. Do not arm. Repeat, negative clearance to arm."

"Roger. Gonna have to break it off." The F-16 and its wingmen bank away back toward Earth.

Tom wears the uncontrollable frown of three Gs, and Zion's eyes are at half-mast as he attempts an unsuccessful meow. Monitors blink pages of parameters and a title comes up: STAGING SEQUENCE 1A.

Bud approaches Sid, who's looking through binoculars. He grabs them away and looks up, searching for the rocket.

The agents in the control room scan the maze of screens, confused, not knowing which to look at. Kirshner fixes on one that has the staging annunciation, and near that title a countdown sequence. On another screen is the view looking down the booster. Kirshner points at that monitor. "Watch! Watch! Staging." Excitement turns to worry. "Oh, God. Be with us."

Bud still searches for the target until a metallic flash appears in the sky. Through the binoculars he sees the main and side boosters drift away, followed by another flash as the second stage ignites.

The capsule jolts, then returns to the rumble of acceleration. Tom attempts a thumbs-up, as much as five Gs will allow.

On a control room monitor, Tom can be seen attempting

the gesture and Kirshner sighs with relief.

Francine stands up, putting her coffee on the table edge. It falls off from lack of aim. "Tommy. Oh, no."

The Soviet counterpart to Stratcom is similar, though more austere, darker, and less sophisticated. The reaction to the alarm, however, is identical. An officer waves over a superior, his words, Russian or not, just as disbelieving as he points to the screen.

Inside the Pentagon a red phone rings at a long conference table, stopping a heated argument. All participants turn to look at the phone, then at each other.

President Stamp watches the Earth Channel with his secretary and several others when *his* red phone rings. He picks it up while the others stare in fright. "Go ahead... Where did you say?... Have you spoken with Bud Meyerkamp?... OK, no need to panic. Get over here and I'll explain."

As soon as he hangs up, another, redder phone rings.

The strain is showing on Tom's face until, suddenly, the thunder and shaking stop as Noah 1 enters the parking orbit. Tom hyperventilates for a moment, then regains his breath, dazed by the intense quiet. Realizing he nearly suffocated Zion in his grasp, he lets go and Zion floats off his lap. Tom gently stops the motion and holds him. "Well, Astrocat, we made it," he says as he unlocks his seat and slides forward, then swivels around and pushes a button on the sidewall. Panels slide down, unveiling a picture window on each side, one full of Earth gliding below, the other of space and stars. Tom lets out a trembling sigh.

Bud bursts into the control room and stops, puffing and looking wildly around. He spots the monitor with Tom's face, walks over, and starts to point. Unbalanced, Tom reaches out and turns his camera off just as Bud is about to yell at him. He redirects the pointed finger at Kirshner. "You and me, we're going to have a talk."

A cellphone rings and an agent pulls it out of his coat pocket, answering, "He's right here." He extends the phone toward Bud.

"Well, do you think I should know who it is?" Bud asks, looking at the phone.

"White House, sir. It's the President's aide, Faith."

Bud tenses and takes the phone in two fingers, as if it were scalding hot. "Yeah, Meyerkamp here. Go ahead, put him on." He loosens his already loosened tie. "Good morning, Sir. Mr. President… Yes, it's beautiful out here… What?… The weather? Oh, it's fine. I guess it's fine." Bud closes his eyes, tortured by the bush being beaten to death. "I've been here about a day and a half."

President Stamp is flanked on either side of a long table by military brass and advisors, all sharing Bud's exasperation. "Yes, well, it seems you were right all along about Tom. I assume it was him. Am I correct?… I thought so. How about that? Good work on your part, by the way. I suppose you have things under control?… Yes, I'm sure of that. Now listen, Bud, I want you and your people to sit tight. I'm sending a team out, and I think it's best if I take a look myself, but keep that under your hat for now, OK?… Fine. That's fine. So, I'll be seeing you soon. And, for what it's worth, you should know we feel you did all that could be done. That Tom's a slippery character. Bye now." He hangs up slowly and looks around at what resembles a modern-day Last Supper. Worried faces, awaiting encouragement.

"Isn't that something? Bud knew all about this, you know. A little high strung, but a good man. Well, let's say we get to some damage control."

The silence in the room is broken by a throat-clearing cough as an Air Force Colonel stands up, notes in hand.

The Virgin River and the Watchman

Spirit Set Free

CHAPTER THREE

We sailed across the black of space,
Away, away from that dark place,
White Eagle's wing, her fiery eye,
Higher and higher, she and I.

Into our sail the Star that Runs
Caught up and swept us past the Sun.
Round Jupiter and Mars we swing,
And laughing, bounce off Saturn's ring.

As Neptune's moons wave us goodbye,
We turn to look, the Eagle and I.
Our solar system stretched afar,
Where Earth would be, a twinkling star.

Farther and farther we glided by
Past red and orange nebulae.
Bright galaxies we left behind
That softly spin to songs of time.

And when we passed the end of all,
It rolled away, a flickering ball.
We stepped outside the pea-green boat,
And watched it off to nowhere float.

The Eagle spread her wings out wide,
And in the spread said this goodbye:
"Farewell my friend, walk tall in faith."
Then faded into innerspace.

It wasn't dark, it wasn't light.
It wasn't day, it wasn't night.
There was no sound, just silent peace.
There was no sight, just blinding grace.

When God moves through His starry realm,
Does He rejoice and laugh out loud
As stars explode and planets form?
Do shining Earthsets make him proud?

If I were He, I think they would.
I'd race a comet 'round the Sun,
Then watch the Eagle's hatching brood,
And count their feathers, every one.

Melody Baxter sits listlessly in her wheelchair while Roberta watches *The Young and the Restless*. She was the only child at the Noah House who, because of her condition, couldn't go on the cruise. Bent over at the waist, she's always looking at a sideways world. Breathing is hard, but never was there a stauncher champion that everyone is normal in some way, just with different 'positions' in life, as she says anytime someone is so careless to show her pity.

Howard, the elderly groundskeeper, bursts in the room, out of breath, tugging at his overall straps. "Roberta! Did you see what happened outside? Everybody's saying it was—"

"SHHH! Howard! Can't you see my program is on?"

"But—"

A "SPECIAL REPORT" title comes on the screen. "You see? Why is it those special reports are always during my program?" Dan Rather appears.

"Good afternoon. This just in from our newsroom. Unconfirmed reports indicate that sometime around ten thirty this morning, Mountain Standard Time, what appeared to be a rocket of some kind shot into the sky in the vicinity of southwestern Utah. The Pentagon will not comment, but says only it was not a U.S.

military, nor a NASA launch. Our sources in St. George tell us what appeared to be a large rocket booster appeared from the area of Hurricane or Rockville, and disappeared in a westward trajectory. A Pentagon spokesman indicated that whatever it was poses no immediate threat, but would comment no further. We'll have more on this incredible story as it unfolds." Roberta looks at Howard as Melody rolls toward the screen.

"That's what I was trying to tell you!" exclaims Howard. "Something took off from over yonder by Rockville about twenty minutes ago, and there's all kinds of helicopters flyin' around and the like!"

"It's Mr. Holmes," Melody says.

Roberta turns to her. "What?"

"It's Mr. Holmes. I know it. Oh, my God. I hope he's all right."

"Mr. Holmes?" Howard asks. "Now why in the world? Come to think of it, it did come from over by his place." Roberta and Howard look at each other, then back at Melody.

Bud paces, not an easy task considering the size of the control room and the three other agents standing aimlessly by. He's not sure what to ask the Doctor first, but Kirshner finally speaks up, catching him off guard.

"Listen to me. There is no point in preventing me from participating in this project. I'm sure your superiors don't want to jeopardize Thomas in any way. Now, enough foolish displays of authority. You must allow me to monitor the status of the mission."

"Mission? Is that what you call it?" Against his considerable grain, he sees the point. "All right, for now. But don't you... do anything unless you check with me first. And keep me informed of everything that's going on. No funny business."

"I assure you, there is nothing 'funny' about this business." Kirshner turns to his panel and begins inputting. Screens and pages appear, all grating against Bud's nerves because he understands none of it. "Excellent. Solar power active. Profiles all perfect. Systems nominal." He turns to everyone in the room. "We have achieved an orbit as perfect as any could accomplish. Congratulations to all of us!" A smattering of applause rises, quickly extinguished by a glare from Bud.

"You're really proud of yourself, aren't you? We'll see how proud you are when the Justice Department has something to say about it." The threat sputters and falls without effect in light of the morning's events. Even Bud is sensing that the accomplishment is hard to characterize as a crime.

The tranquility of Highway 9 is ripped by a speeding car, "ACTION NEWS" painted on the door. Shortly after follows a broadcast van with a satellite dish on the roof.

Tom has fashioned a temporary restraint system for Zion using a shirt tied around his midsection, fastened to two points on the capsule wall. Zion paws the air trying to get his bearings but eventually gives up, looking around with a confused meow. Tom opens a jar of peanut butter, scoops some on his finger, and offers it to the cat who licks cautiously, then flattens his ears back, closes his eyes, and cleans the finger off.

Tom moves over to the Earth window and grabs hold of handles placed there for the purpose of steadying himself to gaze outward. The sight of Earth moving by at over four miles per second awakens the flock of butterflies in his stomach. It looks closer than he thought it would. In fact, flying over the Mediterranean, approaching Gibraltar, he can see wakes of ships converging to pass through the straits to the Atlantic. The clouds look like they're pasted to the planet, curdled sheets of white, spread across as if by a butter knife.

Looking to the curve of the horizon, the biosphere, that great expansive sky he gazed up to so many times, is pressed to the thickness of a blue coating. The thought that he could almost reach out and smear it with a finger transports him to the memory of Noah running home from the second grade, his last grade, excited, barely able to get out to his father what he learned that day. He told Tom that his teacher, Miss Warley, showed him the Earth was smoother than a billiard ball, and the atmosphere was like a piece of paper wrapped around it. Tom remembers how proud he was to learn something from his son, something he now sees from a place Noah wanted so badly to be. Indeed, it is thin as paper, fragile as tissue, just like Noah said.

As Europe passes by, no longer a consortium of countries, but a brown, wrinkled landmass on a planet spinning around a small star in the Andromeda arm of the Milky Way, Tom is struck by the shameful truth that people would exist there, specks of dust on this spectacular orb, yet be plotting each others' ruin, not even visible as life-forms from this point of view that took him eight minutes to reach.

A red light blinks on the console, accompanied by a repeating one-second tone. He hesitates, then, re-aiming the camera, turns it on. Kirshner's face appears on a console monitor. "Hello, Doctor."

"Congratulations. How's the view?"

Tom looks out the window. "Breathtaking. How's the... view down there?"

Kirshner looks around. "To tell you the truth, son, it's a bit dark here." The Doctor is shoved out of view and Bud's snarled face appears on the screen, too close for focus. "All right, Holmes, knock it off with the small talk. What the hell do you think this is? A friggin' tea party? You and your mad scientist here are in huge trouble. Everybody who even talked to you in the last six months is under arrest. And that goes for you, too."

Tom pulls the quarter out of his pocket and flips it, watching it rotate in weightlessness. Bud recognizes the coin. "Yeah, well, you're going to have a hard time takin' me in, Bud. You see, I'm going..." He brings up another page. "17,458 miles per hour."

"You're a real card, Holmes. Just never mind the comedy act. When you... if you make it back here. Let me put it this way: better get used to the 'close quarters' you got there. It'll come in handy, only you won't have quite the view. And besides—"

Once again Tom's hand reaches toward the keyboard. Bud

stops. "Damnit, Holmes, don't you—"

"You need to relax, Bud. All this animosity, it's bad for your health. Tell you what, I'm going to dedicate the first selection to you."

Tom's face disappears. "Jeeesus! I hate it when he does that!" He turns toward Kirshner. "What did he mean? What 'selection'?" Kirshner switches the monitor to the Earth Channel and its view of the Earth.

Tom opens a locker, displaying a collection of CDs, ponders, then chooses one, inserting it into a slot in a nearby electronics rack. After some paging, he types on the keyboard.

On the Earth Channel, across the bottom of the screen, marquis style, appears the following: TO BUD, WITH LOVE, TOM. He looks at Kirshner, not wanting to believe what he's seeing as Huey Lewis's *Small World* plays over the channel's soundtrack. Bud holds his forehead.

Isabel shakes hands as she leaves the concert hall following her performance. The projection screen shows the Earth view but she still hasn't noticed. People are staring, so she looks up, puzzled. Captain Wright, a devilishly handsome Englishman in his mid-fifties, meets her at the door, and after a strained smile to the passengers, ushers her away. Isabel cooperates with a look of surprise.

He takes Isabel into the radio room and motions for her to sit down. As she does so, she sees Nonna sitting in her wheelchair. Isabel turns to Captain Wright. "What's this all about, Captain?" She turns back to Nonna. "Nonna? Will somebody tell me what's going on?"

Captain Wright reaches over and turns on a TV, displaying the Earth Channel. Isabel stares a moment, searching. She looks at Nonna, at the Captain, then back at the screen. "Oh, God. He did it." She puts her hands to her face. "Is he all right?"

"Details are sketchy," Wright answers. "But, judging from

the camera feed, it seems everything is OK."

"Did you know about this?"

"I knew something about it. I was told to open this envelope when I got a call from the channel. We have special communication gear on board. I wasn't sure why until now." He walks over to the doorway. "Mr. Greer, would you come in here please?" A young man wearing horn-rimmed glasses and a suit enters. "This is Rick Greer. He's part of this... whatever it is. He's from the station."

"Miss Flore. Very pleased to meet you," he says, shaking her hand. "I saw your performance at the Forum in Rome. Consider me a true fan. It's an honor."

Isabel careens through the compliment. "What 'communication gear' is he talking about? And what does the station have to do with this?" she asks as if it were his fault.

"Basically, it's the satellite network. They're using it for communication and telemetry."

Isabel glances at Nonna, who shrugs her shoulders. "Do you mean... you can talk to him?"

"We have the capability, yes. But the authorities are all over the launch site. Mr. Holmes is maintaining silence, except with the control room. It's basically up to him who he talks to."

Isabel looks to Nonna, who sighs, "He's a pip, our Tommy. A real pip."

Bud has given the Doctor a nicotine break, forcing him upstairs. Kirshner walks a tight circle on the warehouse floor, talking to himself in Polish. Naturally, he wants to be in the control room and Bud knows it. "OK, Doc, it's time to give me the 'big picture' about this... 'mission' you're all so proud of." Kirshner doesn't answer. Getting no cooperation, Bud walks to the back door, opens it, and breathes in some crisp Utah air. "I suppose we can add obstruction of justice to the courtroom menu."

Sid enters from the other side of the floor where the receiving door has been partly opened. He runs across and up to

Bud, out of breath. "We've got *a lot* of press out here."

"I told you, there's nothing to say yet."

Sid whispers, "Washington called. They want you to make a statement, to take the edge off. They said to give out as little as possible, but—"

"I THINK I know how to handle these situations." Bud speaks to his men, but stares at the Doctor as he walks by. "You keep him right here."

Kirshner smashes his cigarette out. "Now see here. I don't see why I can't—"

Bud stops and walks back up to the Doctor, so close that Kirshner leans back. "He got himself up there. He can *damn* well get along by himself until I say so." Bud walks away, leaving Kirshner leaning.

Gathered at the warehouse entrance gate are press vehicles, cameras, and law enforcement keeping them at bay. Bud's car pulls up to the gate and he exits, swaggering defiantly toward them. Several reporters recognize him, one turning to his cameraman. "Oh, great. That's Meyerkamp. He's a real hardnose. Here goes nothing, literally."

When Bud arrives, microphones are stuck in his face, clearly irritating him, but nobody asks a question right away. Bud recognizes Noelle Crane and acknowledges her. She's a Midwestern, homespun beauty, formerly Miss Nebraska, and her emerald green eyes, sitting keenly in a charming sea of freckles, contrast her radiant auburn hair.

"Miss Crane. Go ahead."

"Noelle Crane, ABN. Agent Meyerkamp, we have no real information. Can you make a statement?"

"I'm not authorized at this point to give out any details. I can say there is no immediate threat to national security. We're still trying to put the pieces together."

"Come on now, everybody knows something took off out of here. What, or who was it? We all know this property belongs to Thomas Holmes."

Bud hesitates. "Some sort of vehicle was launched from here. That's correct. It wasn't a government operation, and Mr. Holmes was involved."

Another reporter noses in. "Well, is there somebody *in* that vehicle? What about the feed on the Earth Channel?"

"Yes. He, Mr. Holmes, is up there. And he appears to be all right." The reporters turn away and run to their cars or pull out cellphones. Bud yells at their backs. "And by the way, this was a highly illegal and dangerous stunt! A lot of people could have gotten hurt!" He kicks the dirt.

Mr. Brandt sits at his desk, unbending and rebending a paper clip when the phone rings. His secretary answers at her desk just outside and yells through the doorway, "It's for you, Mr. Brandt. Mr. Holmes."

"Mr. Holmes? Holy..." He lifts the handset carefully. "Hello?"

Tom leans back in his seat. "Hello, John. Can you hear me OK?"

"Yes, I hear you fine. Sounds like you're right next door."

"Hope I'm not catching you at a bad time."

Brandt looks at his associates who have gathered at the door. "No. No, not at all. I'm, what can I say, surprised to hear from you. Like this, at least."

"We can thank Rick Greer in telecom for that. I'm sorry I kept you out of the loop on this. Tight security, if you know what I mean."

"Yes, sir. No problem. I've spoken with Rick and he explained. He showed me the, uh, plan you gave him. I'm afraid, though, we're waiting for the other shoe to drop with the FCC."

"We anticipated that, and Rogers in legal will assist you in that area."

"Very well. I'm pleased to hear it." After a pause, he continues. "By the way, sir, I just wanted to say that, well, we're all very relieved down here that you're... safe."

"You mean, alive?"

"I guess that's the gist of it. Best of luck, from all of us. And please, come back." Brandt realizes he's wandering.

"Do me a favor. Make sure the concert comes off as planned. It means a lot to me."

"Number one priority, Mr. Holmes. You can count on us."

"Thank you, John. You take care."

Before Brandt can answer, the connection ends. As soon as he puts the phone down, the onlookers spontaneously burst out in applause.

Tom stares out the window when he notices Zion clawing the air. He locates the relief tube and with some experimentation, places it behind Zion and scratches his palm.

Marine One waits on the White House lawn, blades churning. Secret Service stand readied, watching while one of theirs chases the First Pet, a lumbering sheepdog named Kelly. President Stamp trots across the lawn and on the way steps in a First Pile. He stops, tries to scrape it off, then continues, limping on the affected foot. The pilot watches in disgust as he tries to scrape it off on a step of the helicopter. Finally, the President enters and Kelly clambers aboard with a push from behind. The co-pilot dons his oxygen mask, eyes watering, not wanting to offend either the President or Kelly, who sits innocently on his regular seat.

Bud sits at a desk in the warehouse office with his feet up, Sid in a chair across the room reading a newspaper, when agents burst through the door, ushering in a handcuffed Sam chewing bubblegum. "Counselor. Have a seat," Bud says with a superior flair.

After blowing a world-class bubble, popping it, and sucking it back, Sam says, "If it isn't Elmer Fed. 'Be vewy vewy quiet. I'm hunting Jazbos.'" He gets a good laugh out of an agent who quiets after a sharp look from Bud. Sam holds up his cuffed wrists. "Are these necessary? They aren't my size."

"Not really, I suppose. But I like the looks of them. Makes

me feel like... I'm in control. I kind of need that right now."

Bud considers, then motions for the men to remove the handcuffs. Sam rubs his wrists and pulls up a chair. "Let's get this over with nice and tidy. You ask me a question, I'll plead the Fifth, and we won't waste a lot of time."

Bud stares straight ahead. "Oh, well, if I were you, which fortunately I'm not, I wouldn't worry too much about time. You're going to have plenty of that on your hands. To waste, I mean."

"I hate to rain on your lynch party, Boss, but, trust me, our defenses were all printed out ahead of time. And they're every bit as well planned as the rest of this operation."

Bud ineffectively tries to hide the fact he suspected this. "That might very well be. But getting there, to the courtroom... you see, for now I'm in charge of you getting there. And I don't intend to make it very easy for you. Any of you."

"Why are you taking this so personally? You have some anger issues you'd like to share?"

Bud pulls a quarter out of his pocket, flips it once and almost tosses it at Sam, but replaces it instead. "Never mind the five-'n-dime analysis, Brown. You're a lawyer, not a shrink. I'll ask the questions, you either answer or not." He pauses. "Come to think of it, I get the feeling I'm barkin' up the wrong suspect. The best thing I can do is keep you away from the others. This Fifth Amendment stuff is kind of like a virus. I don't want you spreadin' it around."

Bud motions to Sid. "Get ahold of the Rockville authorities. We need a place to put people."

"There are no Rockville authorities," Sid responds.

"Well, where's the nearest government facility?"

"There's the Town Hall in Springdale. Or St. George."

"St. George is too far. All right, take him, them, to Springdale for now, and tell the people there to hold on until I sort this out. We'll set up shop in Springdale," he says, grasping for any sense of order.

Sam smiles as he's led out of the room, and Bud stares back out the window, watching them walk Sam across the empty floor. The fight is starting to go out of him, but he regroups and follows.

Tom is in the process of changing clothes, having trouble with the simple task of pulling on a pair of sweatpants. Attempts to insert a leg cause him to propel away, pranging his head on the corner of the console as he rotates. He anchors himself by holding the seatback, and pulls his way into the seat where he sees Zion fast asleep in his newly fashioned retainer of netting and straps, upside down, tail floating peacefully in space. Tom sits at the console and surfs TV channels, stopping at a special report prompt, underneath which scrolls: The Last Frontier: Civilians in Space. Connie Chung appears.

"Good afternoon, from ABN. As the incredible story of a private citizen in space unfolds, we've learned that Marshall Thomas Holmes, a wealthy U.S. businessman known by most Americans, has successfully launched himself into Earth orbit, much to the amazement and apparent indignation of authorities. We join Lance Renfro from our Las Vegas affiliate. Lance?" Tom looks out the window, disturbed. Though he fully expected this, he's uncomfortable watching it.

Renfro speaks into the camera. "Yes, Connie. I'm standing outside the bakery owned by Holmes, which apparently is some kind of control center for this operation. Activity is increasing here and statements by those in charge are sparse to say the least."

"Has anything been said about the international reaction to this unauthorized launch? After all, a rocket shooting up into space has got to cause some concern when no one knows why it's there."

"Yes, of course. Although the people in charge here haven't been willing to comment, our sources in Washington confirm that there were some tense moments on the 'hot line', so to speak, but that everyone concerned is satisfied there's no immediate threat. Even though we're not clear on the reason for this... operation, no one seems to think it means any harm to anyone."

"And what about the potential danger to those underneath

the launch path? Has there been comment by anyone about that aspect of this operation? Weren't there pieces of that rocket falling out of the sky? I understand most of the launch occurred over land, unlike the NASA launches that go out over water.

"Well, Connie, there have been absolutely no comments by anyone associated with this mission. We do know that a Dr. Werner Kirshner was the brains behind the whole operation. Our sources in the FAA and the military say that they have in fact located the spent first stage booster in a remote part of the California desert within a restricted military area. The impression by those who seem to know about these things is that the launch path was deliberately set up to be over areas were there was no, or at almost no possibility of things falling on people. The comment has been made, however, that this is true only because the launch seems to have gone off as planned. It might have been a whole different story if something went wrong. Connie?"

"I see. That's very good information, Lance. We're all relieved that no one was hurt as a result of this daring act by Mr. Holmes, including himself."

A convoy of helicopters appears from nowhere, causing Renfro to stoop, their wake kicking up a dust cloud. "Whoa! Like I said, things are getting busy here real fast!"

"I see that. We'll be back with you soon, Lance. Thank you." She turns to the camera. "Next, we have a report from Noelle Crane who's been covering the local issues in Springdale, the small town nearest these events where Mr. Holmes has close ties. Noelle, can you hear me? We seem to be having trouble with communications. Noelle?"

Noelle's crew stands in front of the Noah House and catches sight of their reporter exiting the front, cajoling Melody along, pushed by a guarded Roberta. Howard trails behind trying to lend support, as uncomfortable as any local with all the commotion. Noelle has sincerely but shrewdly found these willing characters for her piece. She straightens Melody's hair and whispers words of encouragement as the camera crew tactfully tries to find a way to bring the camera down to Melody's level while keeping Noelle, who kneels beside her, in frame. Roberta is worried, but knows better than to try to stop Melody when she's determined. "Are you sure you want to do this? Are you OK?" Roberta asks.

"Yes, I really want to," Melody assures her.

Noelle realizes the crew is motioning that network is waiting as an assistant hands her a mic. "Hello, Connie?"

"Yes, Noelle. We've had some problems getting through."

"Good afternoon. In the midst of all this confusion, I've come across a remarkable young lady who knows something about Mr. Holmes and insists on telling us. I'd like to introduce Miss Melody Baxter. Melody is one of the special children here at the Noah House, a children's hospice built by Thomas Holmes in tribute to the son he lost. Melody, what is it you'd like us to know?"

Tom sobers as he hears this, turns toward the screen, and comes across Melody's face.

"Thank you, Miss Crane. I just wanted everybody to know that Mr. Holmes is one of the best people in the world, and if it wasn't for him, all of us here at the House wouldn't have such a wonderful life. We all love him very much, and I'm not sure why he went up in space, but I think it's because he's still real sad about his little boy. No one must think bad about him, and we all want him to come back safe."

Noelle stares at Melody as an unfamiliar current runs through her. She gropes for words. "I understand you're the only child left here. Can you tell me where all the other children are?"

"Yes, Mr. Holmes was very nice and he gave them all a special trip on one of his big boats."

"And why aren't you there with them?"

"Well, I wanted to go, but the doctor said it would be better if I stayed here. Because of my condition." Melody strains to look up at Noelle and their eyes meet. Noelle is flushed and her eyes fill, overcome by a troubling mixture of pity and admiration for this afflicted girl, rising from part of her held prisoner.

Noelle looks into the camera and as she attempts to speak, the same convoy of helicopters roars over, giving her a moment to collect her emotions. After they pass, Noelle looks back into the camera.

"Whatever the motivation behind this operation by Thomas Holmes, as you can see, there are those here in Springdale who care very much about him, as he does about them. And I think we can all join with Melody in hoping that he's able to return here, to this special place, safe and sound." Noelle drops the mic down to her side. A phone rings inside the House and a woman sticks her head out the door, calling to Howard.

Connie sits quietly for a moment, then speaks to her monitor. "Thank you, Noelle, and thank you too, Melody. I'm sure we all feel the same." She turns back to camera. "We'll return after a short break." When the camera light goes out, Connie grabs a tissue, gets up, and rushes off the set as the crew watches.

Inside Noah House, Howard picks up the phone. "Hello?... Yes, hello Mr. Holmes. How are you?" He suddenly remembers the situation. "Oh, my stars. Mr. Holmes! Is that really you?... Yes, I'm OK, I guess... Oh, you did? No kidding, you watch TV way up there?" Howard straightens up. "Yes sir, she's quite a brave girl. We just couldn't stop her. She wanted to tell everybody about you... I understand. I'll talk to Mr. Brown right away, and you can be sure we'll stay real close to Melody... Yes, I'll tell her... Thank you, and a good day to you, too, sir."

Howard hangs up slowly. "My stars." He hurries out the door.

Tom leans toward the window and looks up at the Earth moving above him. As he turns his gaze to the other window, he's struck by the vision of the Moon against the blackness of space. He clicks through a few screens to the path projector page, showing computer models of the Earth, Moon, and his current orbital path. Flowing from the Earth to the Moon is another projected path, yellow in color, tracing around the Moon and back to Earth in a figure eight.

Springdale's Town Hall, seat of government for the town of two hundred-plus inhabitants, isn't much larger than a doublewide mobile home and sits next to the town baseball field. Any man-made structure looks small when this far into Zion Canyon, but when Bud roars into the gravel parking lot and gets out of his car, he's disappointed that his "command post" looks more like a one-room schoolhouse. Sid is there to greet him as he walks toward the entrance, the exhaustion showing on both of them. Bud wipes the sweat from his forehead. "This is it?"

"'Fraid so."

"Well, let's try to..." Bud is starting to fade. "Let's just go inside. I got word Stamp is on his way, and we need to have things in hand." Doesn't make much sense to either of them.

The Town Hall consists only of a City Manager's office, the "administrative" section, really a few file cabinets and a computer, and the meeting hall for the Town Council, the size of a large living room. Sue Bently, a portly woman in her thirties, really runs the town, though her official title is Assistant to the Manager. When Bud and Sid walk into the narrow waiting area in front of the counter that separates her desk from the door, they run right into the back of an agent, one of five, all standing in the already crowded area. They shuffle around to make room for Bud, and when he's finally in far enough to see around them, encounters Sue, glaring at him while bouncing her ten-month-old in her arms. It's obvious this commandeering of her domain has not set well at all.

"Are you this 'Meyerkamp' they've been whining about?" Suddenly there's silence from the troops. Bud bites his lip. "This may be a one horse town to you, Mister, but even one horse can leave a pretty good pile, and you're steppin' in it big time. Now, I've got a town to run, small as it is, and I can't do it with all your 'Men in Black' marching in and out of here. Good Lord, man, you'd think the Martians had landed."

Sue's astute and perfectly delivered observation leaves an arid silence, interrupted only by a wet sneeze from her daughter, spraying a fine mist onto Bud's battle-worn suit. He gestures for all but Sid to go outside. "I apologize, ma'am, but this is all happening pretty fast and we're doing the best we can. I do appreciate your cooperation in letting us use your facility. We'll be out of here as soon as we set up a proper command post."

Sue pats her baby's back, with success as she offers up a belch even Bud would be proud to own up to. Sid and Bud look at each other. "Oh! Sweetie sweets! What a nice burper for Mommy!" Her pride quickly reverts to the awaiting scowl. "Who said I ever cooperated? Let me see... how'd they put it? 'We're taking over your building.'"

"I'm very sorry. I'll have a talk with my men about that." Didn't help. "I need to see the prisoners. Can you show me where the cells are?"

Sue, raising an eyebrow, looks at Sid, who grimaces. He hadn't gotten around to telling Bud yet. "Oh, sure." She points toward the hall. "In there." At that moment a child's squeal of laughter comes from the other room. Bud cranes his neck that way, then advances toward the "jail".

Bud walks into the empty hall and looks around as if he'd gone into the wrong room, noticing an open door at the far end from which light and long moving shadows spill across the floor. He looks at Sid, who looks away. Bud walks toward the light.

As Bud approaches the door, he hears the voice of a little boy, Anthony, and every step reveals more and more of what's going on inside. "All right you! Stop that right now or I'll shoot you, you filthy animal!"

The crack of a cap gun startles Bud and he puts his hand on his holster, coming into full view of the scene. Anthony, three years old, wearing a police badge loaned by one of Bud's own agents and a cowboy sheriff's hat, holds his prisoners, Sam and Tall Tree, at bay in the end of a deep closet piled high with everything from mops to city records. The "cell" is secured by a two-foot-high infant gate wedged in the doorway. Anthony turns around and sees Bud, and then Sid's head, which peers around the doorjamb.

Anthony frowns. "Hold it right there!"

He shoots the cap gun at Bud, who flinches even though he tried not to. Sid sticks his tongue out at Anthony and withdraws as Anthony squints, then gives Bud the evil eye. "You're a bad man! You're a *very* bad man! I'm sending you to the cornfield."

Bud looks at Sam, who nods in full agreement with Anthony's plan. Tall Tree, his hands tied with yarn, shoots at Anthony with a toy bow and rubber tipped arrow, knocking the sheriff's hat forward on his head. Anthony spins around and pumps another round into Tall Tree, slumping him over dead once more.

Bud groans. "Oh, my God. I really *have* lost control."

Anthony turns back around. "You shut up, you! These are my prisoners and you're not takin' 'em!" After one more glance at Sam and his broad smile, Bud turns toward Sid and starts to get in his face, but before he can say anything, notices movement in the office area and hears the screen door slam. He run-walks in that direction.

Bud sees President Stamp standing there and drops his head in defeat. Sue holds her baby, speechless, her mouth hanging open. Secret Service slither in and secure the Town Hall as the President smiles at Sue. "Hello, I'm Jonathan. And you are?"

While Sue is trying to squeeze out some form of reply, Stamp takes her baby and holds her. "I'm, I'm,… Susan Bently. I'm the Assistant Town Manager."

"And this is?"

Sue tries to remember her baby's name. "This is... oh. This is Kiki. I mean, actually, it's Kirsten. My little boy, Anthony, can't say Kirsten, so he calls her Kiki."

Stamp scratches Kiki's chin. She giggles. "Hi, Kiki! I'm Johnny."

"Shawny!" Kiki gurgles proudly.

"That's right!" He turns to Sue. "Nice to meet you, Sue. I'm looking for Bud Meyerkamp. Is he around here?" Sue, unable to take her eyes off the President, motions toward the hall with her head. Stamp turns in that direction to see Bud standing in the doorway, an odd shade of pale. "Ah. There you are." Stamp walks into the hall before Bud can stop him. The President looks around and starts toward the closet, curiously, as he speaks. "Well, I guess Springdale's on the map now. It'll be a household name by tomorrow." Secret Service take positions in each corner of the hall while Bud makes a futile attempt to head him off.

"Uh, Sir..." He looks at the Secret Service. "Perhaps we should find a more secure location for a briefing."

The President suddenly appears in the closet doorway. A Secret Service agent is in there as well, standing still as Anthony repeatedly kicks his leg. The agent flinches not, having endured similar torture training at the academy. Anthony looks up and Sam bolts to his feet, declaring, "Anthony! This is the President!"

"No he's not! *I'm* the President!" Anthony insists as he throws a rubber arrow at Jonathan. The agent imperceptibly watches its flight, having already checked out the weapon.

Kiki points at Anthony. "Buzzer!"

"She calls me Buzzer 'cause she can't say 'brother'. She's just a baby," Anthony explains.

"You must be Anthony. I'd like you to meet somebody." Stamp motions for Bud to come over, who does so reluctantly. "This is Bud. We call him that 'cause nobody can say 'Norbert'. He's a policeman, too."

"Norbert? He's a bad man! He's a *very* bad man!"

Anthony tries to shoot Bud again, but there's no ammo, the agent having secured the caps, turning them over in his hand. Stamp removes the gate. "You did a real good job with these prisoners, Anthony, a *real* good job. And now these other policemen and I are going to talk to them. OK?"

"OK," Anthony agrees sadly. The President leads his party into the hall and shakes Sam's hand after turning Kiki around so she's facing over his shoulder.

"Mr. President," Sam says.

"I don't think I've seen you since the ceremony at the White House, after you won the Super Bowl."

Sam is surprised he remembered. "That's right, Sir. One of the best days of my life. The ceremony, I mean."

"One of mine too, actually. The Super Bowl, I mean. I won a bundle." Several eyebrows rise. "From my wife. That's legal, isn't it, counselor?"

"Depends what you won, I guess." This gets a laugh from Stamp. Bud scowls at Sam. Joking with a President while a prisoner is patently unacceptable. Sam ignores him. "Oh, and I'd like you to meet Tall Tree. His family goes back several hundred years around here. Tall Tree, this is your President."

"Last Chief here was Sunman Whitewater. Your soldiers took our land, scattered our herds," says Tall Tree.

Everybody cringes except the President. "Tall Tree, it's an honor to meet you. Actually it wasn't *my* soldiers who took your land, but I'll take responsibility. We did a great dishonor to your people, and I've been trying to help take away that dishonor."

Sam turns to Tall Tree. "President Stamp's program helped your sister, Steps in Streams, make that rug factory you like so much, Tall Tree."

Tall Tree ponders, then reaches his hand out to the President. "Steps in Streams is very happy, and not so mad at the human beings now. You and I, we will sit and smoke the pipe under the full Moon."

Stamp accepts a firm handshake. "I'd like that."

Bud can't resist. "Seems to me, smokin' some kind of pipe about lost you the election there, Mr. President." Sid throws his arms up in disbelief, walking away.

"I just won't INHALE!" Stamp retorts. He'd been patting Kiki, and she responds by barfing her milk down his back. Though the agents rally quickly, as if they could do anything, Sue wedges between them and reaches out as Stamp, having experienced this many times as a father, hands Kiki over and removes his coat.

"I'm so *sorry*, Mr. President."

"Nonsense. I was getting hot in this anyway. She can tell her grandkids about this one!" He hands the coat to the Secret Service who converge on it, pulling out handkerchiefs as if a national tragedy occurred. He points to Sam and Tall Tree and turns to Bud. "Let these men go."

"With all due respect, Sir, I've arrested them under a valid federal warrant. I don't think—"

The President loses his patience. "Would you rather I pardoned them, Norbert? I can do that, you know. It says so in the Constitution. What is it you think they're guilty of?"

"Well, I... conspiracy to commit..."

"What, Bud? What? Conspiracy to help some poor 'sonofa-bitch' almost blow himself up? For heaven's sake, let them go. We've got bigger issues to deal with right now. And I seriously doubt they'll skip town. Don't you?" Bud nods to them and they both respect-fully depart. As Sam walks by Bud, he hands him another "Get Out of Jail Free" card.

Stamp points at Bud. "Briefing at the bakery. One hour," he says, then walks away. Bud stands conquered, looking at Sid, who stares him down.

"What?"

Dusk is a magical time when the air flows out of the canyon, bringing with it the close to another day of daunting stillness, another contribution to eons of dependable, gradual change. Intricate sandstones and streaks of colors so vivid during the day, ever changing and reshadowing with each inching movement of the Earth, blend into shades of browns and rusts as the glow from the setting Sun bathes the canyon walls. Branches rustle and leaves whirl in the wind, and the gentle roar of the Virgin fills the background of majestic silence that is Zion Canyon.

The Driftwood Lodge sits at the outskirts of Springdale and consists of three buildings. Two are older motel types, one with a second story facing down the heart of the canyon, the other, perpendicular, flanks the Virgin River. Across the swimming pool is a newer building, more modern, yet still detailed with verandahs and natural cedar. That building has been cordoned off for the Presidential party, and the Secret Service stand guard.

The parking lot of the Driftwood never looked like this. Dozens of vehicles are parked askew, half of them broadcast vans with satellite dishes pointing in unison toward their orbiting targets. Camera crews mill around in groups, laughing and carrying on like a tailgate party.

Room 211 is on the second story of the building facing the canyon. The room is small, barely fitting a bed, desk and TV. A picture window views the canyon through the verandah, separated from neighboring verandahs by wooden trellises. Noelle Crane has checked into 211, unpacked, and is into her jeans and a sweatshirt that displays the ornate emblem of a university: Screw U. She sits in a chair on the verandah, her feet propped up on the redwood railing, sipping a long overdue glass of wine, further mellowed by the mooing of a cow that grazes in a pasture below. The TV mumbles in the background and there's a knock at the door.

"It's open!"

In comes her cameraman, Scott Johnson, always in a good mood, carrying a cold beer and a bag of chips. He walks out to the verandah and plops down in the chair next to her. They sit parallel, facing the canyon as Scott crunches chips, offering the bag to Noelle. "Man, oh, man. What a place. Un friggin' believable."

Noelle waves off the bag. "I am such a pea brain. I've been working in Vegas for ten years, only two and a half hours away, and not *once* have I ever been here."

"Well, we're two pea brains in a pod then, 'cause I grew up in Provo, and I didn't even know it existed. Un friggin' believable." They stare quietly, then he reaches out his hand and she takes it. After a few moments she stands and leans against the railing, savoring breaths of canyon air while closing her eyes.

"I don't know, Scotty. I came here to cover a story. An unbelievable story." She looks up at the first twinkling star. "But there's something happening inside me I don't understand."

"What are you saying?"

"That little girl, Melody. At first I felt such pity for her. Until I realized she's twice the person I am. What is it about children? Where do they get that kind of strength?"

"They're born with it. They're born with hope, faith. Belief that anything's possible."

"Then they grow into... us. What a joke. We get more and more scared, more and more hateful."

"No kidding. We don't just grow older and die. We grow

old inside. Look at what 'adults' have done to this world. Too bad we can't be born grown up and get younger every year, and end up as babies. Then just... fade away."

"*Curious Case of Benjamin Button.*"

"What?"

"You just told the story of Benjamin Button. It's a short story by F. Scott Fitzgerald. I always knew there was something magical about it, but I didn't really understand until now."

Scott takes the last slug of his beer and sets the empty on the railing. "I find it hard to believe someone as fine as you isn't married with children. You seem like you'd be a natural."

At this, Noelle eclipses, glancing off some hard memory. Scott stills, sensing her mood shift. "I bought that idiotic theory that I 'didn't want to bring children into this screwed up world.' How dare I? Children are the hope of this screwed up world. If only I could be born again, and start all over."

Scott stands and embraces her, cradling her head on his shoulder. "That's quite enough Crane-bashing for one day. For better or worse, we've got the story of the century to cover here, and I tell ya, I'm really jazzed about it. I don't know what this Holmes character is up to, but there's more to it than just some poor wretch who lost his kid, trying to kill himself."

"He took part of all of us up there."

He lifts her face. "Uh-huh. Now let's enjoy the ride."

She manages a wry little smile, resting her forehead on his chest. "I hate you."

"I hate you more. Now, I say we go pork out on some Mexican at that Bit 'n' Spur down the road."

She nods, and after an awkward stillness, they regroup and head into the room. As they glance at the TV they see Bonnie Mattista fumbling cross-eyed through her broadcast. She's on a split screen, the right half a view of the Earth from Noah 1. Across the top is captioned: LIVE FROM THE HOLMES CAPSULE, COURTESY OF THE EARTH CHANNEL. Although she doesn't notice, and neither do Noelle and Scott as they snicker at her, typed words are appearing across the bottom.

"Oh, wow, it's the 'real' news. We better watch," Scott snips.

Mattista stumbles on. "As we follow this incredible story of the first civil... rather, civilian space launch by a private... person, we all wonder why, why would a private... person risk his life, and possibly lives of others, on such a dangerous act?"

Noelle and Scott both cross their eyes and look at each other, mocking together, "I don't know, Bonnie, WHY?" They break into laughter, then bump hips.

"Ooooh! Good one!" Noelle boasts.

Scott punches the TV off.

Tom is typing, transcribing from a coffee table book suspended in front of him, *The Home Planet*, a collection of Earth photographs from space, each page captioned with a quote from an astronaut. He looks out at the Earth passing beneath, Zion lying on his lap, though every time Tom takes his hand away, the cat rises and Tom gently pushes him back down.

The Holmes living room, an expansive sea of terra cotta tile with islands of comfortable furniture, occupies the entire point of the home, rendering a 270-degree view of the canyon narrowing in the distance. Rosalee sits on one of those islands across from a TV and watches as the last words appear. She reads, barely aloud, "In space one has the inescapable impression that here is a virgin area of the universe in which civilized man, for the first time, has the opportunity to learn and grow without the influence of ancient pressures. Like the mind of a child, it is yet untainted with acquired fears, hate, greed, or prejudice. John Glenn Jr."

The empty warehouse floor has been transformed into a briefing venue furnished with a podium, a projection screen, and folding chairs facing them. Some fifty people are seated or milling about as Kirshner stands by the podium, talking vigorously to a few others. Washington County Sheriffs are stationed strategically, along with FBI and other authorities; Bud and Sid stand by themselves at the side, Sid intrigued by it all while Bud is bending under the growing chip on his shoulder. "Good God. Have you ever seen a dog and pony show like this?"

"I don't know, Bud, I'm kind of getting caught up in all this. There's something really exciting about it."

Bud starts to raise his dander but is halted by movement at the smaller entrance door. In flows a string of Secret Service, followed by President Stamp. The warehouse grows quiet as he makes his way to the podium and directly up to Kirshner, taking his hand firmly.

"Werner!"

"Mr. President. An honor, as always."

"Last time we saw each other I was trying to talk you into staying with NASA. Now I really wish I'd been more persuasive." Stamp pulls forward the person he brought with him. "You know Dr. Cole, of course."

Kirshner shakes his hand. "Terry, it's been too long."

Stamp puts his hand over their clasp. "We'll talk later. Right now, let's get this thing underway." He signals to an aide who steps to the podium, raising a hand to get everyone's attention, as if they weren't staring anyway.

"Ladies and gentlemen, the President of the United States." Stamp quickly quells the applause with a gesture for everyone to sit down.

"Four score and seven years ago... oops, sorry. Someone said, 'what's *he* here for,' and I thought he said 'we won the Civil War.'" Only a smattering of polite laughter. "I see, well, I'll have to place your senses of humor on the most wanted list." This time a better laugh.

"Actually, I want all you people in the scientific and law enforcement communities to set your minds at ease about a couple of things. There's been understandable concern about national security. Yes, there were a few difficult moments, but rest assured that everyone who needed to know has been told exactly what this is, and all panic buttons are up and locked. Secretary of Defense Corollo assures me that everybody's at ease. The reason I came out here was to let the people of this somewhat surprised country know that things are under control, and I'll have a short press conference about it tonight."

He pauses, looking around. "You all know Tom Holmes was, is, an old friend of mine from college, back when almost anybody could get in." Now an honest laugh. "The worst thing Tom's done here is put some people at risk, not the least of which was himself, in preparing and pulling off this... mission. To be sure, he'll have to answer to me, as well as others, when we get him back down here. But the matter at hand right now is just that. Getting him back. And to this end I've committed, as much as reasonably appropriate, our resources at NASA, including," as he points, "Dr. Terry Cole, who most of you know, and many others of you that have been kind enough to come here to volunteer your help. So let's get down to the business of finding out what the heck happened."

Stamp motions to Kirshner, puts his arm around the Doctor's shoulders, and feigns hitting him on the jaw. "This is Dr. Werner Kirshner, who directed project development at NASA when I was just a little President bouncing on my daddy's knee. He left NASA when I took office, which I took personally. Doctor?"

Stamp withdraws, leaving Kirshner uncomfortably quiet at the podium. A short round of applause rises until everyone realizes that perhaps it's not warranted under the circumstances. The Doctor pushes keys on a laptop computer next to the podium and a photo of Noah 1 sitting on its pad projects onto the screen behind him.

Bud shakes his head in disgust. "For chrissake, they're makin' a hero out of the old buzzard."

Sid whispers a hint of rebellion. "There's a lot of people out there who think he is." Bud scowls at him, the disapproval becoming more and more strained.

"Thank you, Mr. President, for allowing me this opportunity. I realize I could be in quite a different place." A prickly quiet settles in the room. "Although at this point the launch vehicle is not of that much consequence, this was a conventional Titan platform, resembling the 3c model, with smaller solid propellant boosters, though they were not zero stage engines. They fired simultaneously with the main engine, expiring at approximately ninety percent of the first stage sequence, and remaining attached to that stage throughout separation. Minor modifications to the center nozzle assembly provided more efficiency, and therefore greater payload capability. The two main stages were powered by standard hypergolic fuels used in the Titan programs, UDMH and nitrogen tetroxide. For those of you unfamiliar, these fuels ignite on contact and need no cryogenic temperature environments. Although they render lower specific impulse, and are therefore less efficient, it was necessary that we retain on-demand launch capability, in the manner of strategic warhead delivery systems." This analogy, alluding to the clandestine events of Tom's departure, makes both the Doctor and the crowd uneasy.

He changes slides, showing a view of the capsule being lowered by crane onto the booster. "The payload module, however, is entirely original in design. You will note that there was no escape tower assembly. Mr. Holmes did not feel the option for escape was... feasible for him." Kirshner pulls a handkerchief from his pocket and dabs his forehead to the accompaniment of a few mumblings from the audience.

"The capsule is made of advanced grade metals and synthetic polymers, giving it a high degree of strength at reduced mass. For this reason..." The next slide is a computer graphic of the Earth. With the punch of a key, a caricature of the Noah 1 is seen launching from the area of Utah and traced behind it a representation of its path. "...we were able to achieve a retrograde orbit, which, as many of you know, requires considerable more energy."

With another keystroke comes a similar rendition, this a live portrayal of the capsule's present path. "Here is our current position in the parking orbit." The next slide is a blueprint cross section of the capsule. "The computer system on board is extremely sophisticated and entirely self contained, more powerful, in terms of navigational programs and systems management, than the Space Shuttle. The electrical system is supplemented by a retractable solar array, capable of sustaining the ship, for practical purposes, considering life support constraints, indefinitely. There is oxygen and food to sustain one person for approximately three weeks."

The next slide is an artist's rendering of the Earth, surrounded by satellites. "Communication is maintained directly through the system of satellite transponders which are part of the Holmes cosponsored telecommunications array placed in orbit over the last decade. As for reentry..." The Doctor's next slide shows the Earth and Moon with a figure eight path drawn around them. Flustered, he quickly moves through this, past several similar pictures, until he gets to one that shows a reentry path. "...we have the same solid propellant deceleration package used in the Gemini missions, utilized for reentry from Earth orbit. The heat tiles, however, are a derivative of Carborundum, similar to those of the Space Shuttle. Reentry will be accomplished, as it was in other missions, by rotation about the capsule's displaced center of gravity, concluding with a similar parachute drogue system as was used on the Apollo vehicles." After a few moments of silence, the crowd begins talking among themselves. "Now, I'm sure you all have questions."

Nearly everyone raises their hand. Kirshner takes a strategic breath, choosing a woman. "Yes, Dr. Reynolds."

"What system are you using for position updating on the spacecraft, and for navigating?"

"We do have transponders on board, although we used them primarily to warn the ATC system during the launch, since we don't have ground based tracking. We are primarily inertial, with triple laser gyros, coupled with redundant flight management computers updating continuously from the same global positioning system in general use by commercial aviation. Finally, however, the computers contain an extremely aggressive three-dimensional model of cardinal celestial navigation points as well as Earth, Sun, and lunar positioning models. The craft can navigate extremely accurately, in other words, entirely on the position of the stars and our own solar system. All three of these position fixing systems are resolved by the computers to a final coordinate that should be true within one meter." Next hand. "Dr. Geckler?"

"You mentioned a three week supply of life support, but

you haven't told us the plans for this... mission. How long are you going to keep him up there?"

This makes the Doctor visibly uneasy. "I must say first, that when I said the computer system was self contained, I meant that literally. Mr. Holmes has complete control over the mission from his capsule. I can do nothing from down here at this point. There is a function that will allow reversion to ground based command, but only if there are no inputs from the capsule for an extended period, some sixteen hours, in case of incapacitation. As for what his plans are, that is entirely up to him."

This invokes a hush. Another hand goes up and Kirshner fields the question.

Kirshner sits on his desk, tapping a pencil, watching through the window as the audience disperses in pockets of con-versation. An FBI agent stands guard at the closed control room door and Bud sits at another desk, defiantly in control of the situation. The door to the office opens, President Stamp walks in, and Bud dutifully stands. Stamp looks at the agent, then at Bud.

"OK, Meyerkamp, the standoff's over. I want your men out of here. We need to stop interfering with the Doctor's work."

"Oh, I see. It's *work*, now. At what point did we skip from the conspiracy stage, hurdling over federal offenses, directly to 'work' without passing Go?" He glares at the Doctor. "And don't bother with the Get Out of Jail Free card."

"I beg your pardon?" asks Kirshner.

"What are you talking about?" asks Stamp.

"Never mind. I'm just kind of confused about the chain of command here. I realize you're the President and all, but I wasn't under the impression I took orders *directly* from you. I've got a crime scene here."

Stamp walks over to Bud, puts his arm around his shoul-ders, and leads them both over to the door. He speaks quietly, be-tween them. "Commander in Chief, Bud. That's another name for my job. I send armies out all over the world and do really big things.

Somehow I think I can tell you to knock off this pit bull mentality you've gotten over all this, and 'sit down, shut up, and take it ease,' as my Italian grandmother used to say. You've done your work, and you were right all along. Now, I'm ordering you, as your beloved President, to take a few days off. Besides, I talked to Herlihy and he said we're not pressing any charges, against anybody. Yet."

He slaps Bud on the back and walks toward Kirshner. Bud looks at the both of them, then motions for his man to follow, their exit punctuated by an exclamatory slamming of the door. Stamp breathes a sigh of relief. "Boy. Who needs a few good men when you have just one of those? Now, let's go downstairs and have a little talk."

Kirshner and the President enter the control room to find a Secret Service agent who stands to attention. With a gesture from Stamp, he leaves without a word. Kirshner falls into his chair and pushes another toward Stamp. On the screen is the view of Earth, the soundtrack now faintly playing *Come Together*.

Stamp listens. "Is he playing that from up there?"

"He insisted on it being a, how shall I say... business venture, on paper. A remote broadcast booth, so to speak."

Stamp nods in admiration. "I see. Sort of a world crisis and tax deduction, all wrapped up in one. Yes siree, that's Tommy for you."

"I think it had more to do with giving something back to his viewers. He always believed that the common man, the citizen who paid for the space program, never got enough back from it. Personally, that is. Never really was able to enjoy it."

"Uh-huh. Well, I'll buy about one tenth of that. Not that that tenth isn't... commendable." He leans forward. "But let's 'cut the crap,' as our dear friend Meyerkamp likes to say ad nauseam. What's really going on here?"

Kirshner purses his lips, pondering. He reaches up to the keyboard and with a few entries brings up the images he rushed through during the briefing: the model of the Earth showing the figure eight trajectory to the Moon, around the back, and returning. Stamp stares at it, then looks back, pursing his lips as well.

"I see. And when is this going to happen?"

"Actually, it was programmed as an option. An option, I'm afraid, he's likely to take. As you probably know, there are certain windows for translunar injection, having to do with the relative positions of the Earth, Moon, and vehicle. In terms of energy management and life support envelopes—"

Stamp holds his hand up. "Please, Doctor. The *Apollo for Dummies* version."

"Two hours."

Kirshner opens his desk drawer and pulls out an ashtray and cigarettes, offering one to Stamp who hesitates, looking up at the stairs and back. The President takes one cautiously as Kirshner reassures him with a raised hand, lighting them both up. "Don't worry, no one will come down here."

Stamp takes a drag. "I only do this when I'm feeling helpless. Not very often. Elaine would have a fit, not to mention the Surgeon General. It would cost me poll points."

"Your secret is safe with me."

Stamp relishes another drag, with guilt. "I take it you can talk to him whenever you want?"

"I can ring him. Whether he answers or not is up to him."

"Are the lines secure?"

"Three lines, all encrypted to RS level four military."

Stamp blows a soft, rolling smoke ring. "Beam me up, Wernie."

Kirshner reaches over to his panel and punches a console mounted phone pad.

Tom is torturing Zion with a rubber ball he keeps suspended just out of pawing range, the cat tethered to the overhead panels by thin ropes attached to a makeshift harness around his midsection, secured by a velcro strap. Tom sips on a container with a straw and squirts some into Zion's mouth, the cat licking at suspended water droplets. The buzzer startles both of them and Tom answers by activating the speaker phone.

"Crew lounge."

"Good evening, Tom. At least it's evening here. How's it going?"

"Actually, it was evening for a little while, now it's dawn again. This retrograde orbit really makes things seem like they come around in a hurry."

"I envy you, my boy. I envy you. Listen, there's someone here, an old friend of yours. He'd like a few words."

"Not the Budman, I hope. I think we're all talked out."

"This fellow carries a little more weight, and a lot less aggravation."

Stamp's voice comes across with a reasonable Bones impression. "Aye, Captain, the phasers are locked! We'll never make warp speed before the Klingons catch us!" Tom winces. He grabs Zion and fastens him to an overhead velcro parking strip, fashioned for the very purpose of cat stowage, then switches to the feed from the control room and activates his camera. Tom's face appears on the screen. "Holy smoke, Tom. We were the Top Trekkies at MIT, but don't you think you've taken it a little far?"

"Mr. President. I saw on the news you were headed out there. Are you that bored, or are we in that much trouble?"

"The last time you called me 'Mr. President' I recall losing six electoral votes. Something about reservation land in New Mexico."

"I warned you not to mess with sacred ground. Bad medicine."

"Yeah, well, I made a mistake. Now, let's be sure we keep you from making a bigger one." No response. "I know all about your little 'side trip'. Don't worry, it's just between the Doctor and me. But really, you've done quite a thing here already. You're a goshdarned working man's hero. Now don't be a fool. What would it prove?"

"This is personal. You don't understand."

The President looks at Kirshner, takes another helpless drag, then puts the cigarette out in the ashtray. "Listen, we had quite a NASA party out there. Kirshner put on a real show for them. Never saw so many pencil-necked geeks in one place. I had to wear a pocket protector just to fit in." Kirshner looks down at his pocket protector. "I've assembled a team to help get you down, against some pretty strong objections, I might add. In fact, it seems there's quite a rally in the international space community offering to lend a hand. Kind of a 'brotherhood of man', touchy-feely sort of thing. Whad'ya say you go ahead and spin around up there for a while, then we'll get you home so I can personally take a big bite out of your ass. Make me look good."

Tom leans back in his seat, putting his hands behind his head, and looks out the window. "I can't promise anything. Thanks for the help, though." Stamp looks at the Doctor again, in resignation. As they both look back at the screen, Zion's tail sweeps down. Kirshner lurches forward in his seat, dropping the cigarette from his mouth.

"Oh, no! This can't be true! You got that damned cat up there?"

Stamp shoots a look of humorous pity toward the Doctor. "Oh boy. You've *really* got your hands full." He turns toward the monitor. "Godspeed, Tommy. Elaine and I will be prayin' for you." He pats Kirshner on the shoulder and leaves.

The Doctor struggles unsuccessfully to contain his temper. "Christ, Thomas! We put in all this effort, and now we've got a one hundred million dollar litter box? Are you out of your mind? Let me rephrase that. You *are* out of your mind!"

Tom pulls the cat down and scratches his neck. "Take it easy, dear. Everything's under control." He takes a gallon-size Ziplock, puts it over the cat's rear end, and clamps it with two chip clips, making the scratching sign on his palm at the camera. "Remember?" Kirshner looks away in disgust. "Besides, if I didn't take him, I would've given him to you."

Tom takes Zion and puts his face in the camera, filling the screen with a pink nose and whiskers. Kirshner sneezes and waves at the sight in frustration as the screen goes dark and Tom signs off, laughing in the background. Kirshner takes a pile of papers and throws them in the air.

Watchman Lookout rests on an eroded foothill just northeast of and under the Watchman, a humbling monument that stands guard over the entrance to the canyon. From the west, the Watchman looks like a giant chiseled crown, from the east, a rock castle. The trail to the lookout takes a considerable, though not strenuous hike, tracing outcrops of sandstone that formed the plateau over millennia. Darkness is fleeting as the Moon, now waning, threatens to rise over the East Temple, and a meteor shower streaks across the night sky in a dazzling display of celestial fireworks.

Tall Tree stands silhouetted, westward, against the faint appearance of the widening canyon, the town of Springdale twinkling its few lights several hundred feet below. On that spot have stood generations of his people with the stars shining on their backs, at times when their destinies were about to metamorphose. Tall Tree raises his arms straight to the heavens, arcing them slowly back down to his side.

Inside one of the cruise ship's lounges, the troops from Noah House have assembled in various states ranging from out of control to bouncing off walls, according to their mobility. Isabel enters the lounge, pushing Nonna in her wheelchair, and after a few moments of observation, sticks her fingers in her mouth and whistles loud enough to turn everyone. The crowd comes to attention and moves in her direction as she motions. Once they've settled down, Isabel addresses them.

"Hello, children."

"Hello, Miss Isabel," they chant in unison.

"There's something I have to tell you, and it's about Mr. Holmes. I don't know any easy way to put it, so here it is. This morning he launched himself into space in a rocket he and his friend made. Right now he's all right and he's orbiting the Earth."

They all look at each other in excited surprise. Roger, a leukemia victim with only a few scattered crops of hair, raises his hand. "You mean like the Space Shuttle? I didn't know he was an astronaut."

Isabel looks at Nonna, then back. "Well, honey, he wasn't, really."

Roger beams. "I guess he is now, isn't he?" This gets a laugh from the kids.

Lacy, a five-year-old with Shirley Temple ringlets, limps forward on her artificial leg. "Is he coming back?"

Isabel wells up. "I think so. I really hope so."

Walter-the-leaf-raker jumps up. "He *is* coming back! Mr. Holmes told me that when I got on the boat, he might come out of the sky to see me!"

All the children exclaim, "Wow!"

Captain Wright hurries in and turns on a wall mounted TV, switching channels until it reaches an "ABN Special Report" graphic. He motions them over.

Wiley's has become a public meeting place of Springdale, much as taverns have for centuries when events brought citizens together, for better or worse. This time it's a little of both: concern over the plight of their controversial neighbor, and confused elation over their proximity to the historic adventure. There are no shortage of "spirits", either, to go with the continuum of emotions. Butch and Tim are unabashedly raucous over the feat of their employer, and rebelliously proud of their participation in it. Seated at the bar, they, for the umpteenth time, clasp hands in a high five that turns into a mock arm-wrestling match. This causes the beers in their other hands to overflow onto the bar. Wiley wipes it up, again.

Tim brags, "Dude! We did it, didn't we?"

"We beat it! We sure did! God Almighty, when that sucker shot off like that, it damn near rattled the fillings right out of my head!"

"Fillings, hell. The only thing that rattles in a jarhead like that is the ball bearing you call a brain," Tim says.

"Oh, yeah? Bite me."

"First there's gotta be something to bite."

Butch takes his beer and attempts to throw it on Tim who

sways to the side, diverting the beer to paint the back of Sam, sitting next to him, facing the other way. Sam barely flinches, his flinching mode toned down by his own celebrating. He slowly turns around and locks both of them in his cross hairs. Above them the TV shows the "Special Report" graphic which dissolves to Connie Chung. Before Sam can retaliate, the tavern door swings open and Sid walks in, looking like he's ready to let go, followed by Bud. Butch is facing in that direction and his face manifests his astonishment.

"No way."

Sam turns to look. "Way."

Sid and Bud spot them staring and Butch raises his empty mug with a smile as Sid walks toward them. Bud grabs his arm but it's apparent Sid's had enough as he pulls away, takes off his coat, and continues toward the bar. Bud hesitates, then follows.

Butch shouts over the noise, "Wiley, two beers, on my card."

"Thanks. Appreciate it," says Sid.

Bud surrenders. "Why not."

Tim looks at Bud's back. "Your suit looks a little... scorched there, Meyerkamp." Tim and Butch aren't trying very hard not to laugh. Sam doesn't try at all, bursting out a mouthful of beer.

"Ouch! Fried Fed!" says Butch. Sid looks at him, laughing.

"You three musketeers are really proud of yourselves, aren't you?" Bud says, almost sad.

"Damn straight!" the two exclaim. Yet another high five clasp. "HOOOAH!"

Tim holds his mug up. "TOMMMeeee! The TOMmeister! Makin' ROCKets!"

Sam looks at them, then at Bud as Sid downs the entire beer in one shot and produces a belch so deep only a dog, or other beer drinker, could hear. Sam raises a fist. "Yes! Our tax dollars at work! Finally."

Bud, trying not to participate, looks up at the TV to see an empty podium with the Presidential Seal, flanked by aides. He flails a finger toward the TV, getting Wiley's attention. Wiley looks up and raises the volume, herding the crowd toward the bar.

* * *

Reporters are camped outside Francine's home, getting no response to repeated efforts at the doorbell. One reporter stands on the small patch of front lawn, smoking. A voice calls from inside the broadcast van. "Come on! He's walking out now." The reporter drops his smoldering butt on the grass and his cameraman huffs, picks up the butt, and throws it in a garbage can after putting it out for him.

Francine sits on a kitchen stool with a glass of wine, waiting for the press conference. President Stamp walks toward the podium.

Tom spins the clear cup as he listens to a CD of Native American flute music. He glides over to the window to look out, another "night" nearly over, the nights lasting less than forty-five minutes. Tom stills as he sees green pillars of light spraying up from the Earth, as if there were a giant crack and its inner glow was escaping. He realizes he's passing through the Northern Lights. Then, at the edge of the Earth, defined on the darkside as the razor-edge where stars stop, another sunrise erupts; first a luminescence, then a rapid-fire rainbow, changing colors like a rotating prism powered by white-hot light as the Sun burns through the thin atmosphere and sears his vision. Tom looks back down to the darkness and sees a shooting star streak beneath him. Thus another flood of realization washes over him, another touch upon the unfathomable truth of where he is.

Tom notices Stamp on his monitor and turns up the volume.

"Good evening, ladies and gentlemen, fellow citizens. Generally, the Office of the President does not respond to the activities of private citizens. However, as most everyone knows, an American, Thomas Holmes, has launched himself into Earth orbit in a vehicle he assembled with the assistance of Dr. Werner Kirshner, a former NASA scientist and eminent father of rocketry in this country."

* * *

In the cruise ship lounge, all sit transfixed.

"I address you tonight because many of you are understandably concerned about national security issues, specifically certain super powers that would be alarmed by an unscheduled launch such as this. Rest assured I've spoken to all necessary leaders and explained the nature of this phenomenon. In fact, they've expressed concern and kindly offered any assistance necessary in helping to resolve this to a favorable conclusion.

"As for the issue of someone launching a vehicle through our own airspace, you can imagine the criticism I, as well as other entities in our strategic defense and law enforcement communities, have taken. Frankly, fellow Americans, we were caught flat footed. For this I personally apologize, an apology to be outmatched, I trust, only by that of Mr. Holmes. In my, our, defense, I should add, however, that we were aware of some of the activities surrounding this... mission, and in the process of investigating them, obviously not in time. Our intelligence assets, correctly, did not profile Mr. Holmes to be the type of threat that would warrant scrutiny better applied to activities of terrorists and other malignant forces which threaten the security of our nation. This is a large country, and we simply cannot monitor every square foot of it for the movements of our own citizens. This... accomplishment, for lack of a better word, by Mr. Holmes and Dr. Kirshner, was a fantastically elaborate display of ingenuity and deception, one nearly deserving of recognition as good 'ole American cunning and determination, were I not so disturbed at the degree to which they embarrassed my administration."

The crowd at Wiley's has become silent.

"I am well aware of the mixed emotions many of you have over this surprising act of daring on the part of Mr. Holmes, and I would be blind if I didn't acknowledge that to many this is seen as some great human triumph. It is true, history was made. Perhaps not good history, but history nonetheless. To those of you that cheer Tom on, I must say one thing. Don't try this at home!"

* * *

Inside a department store in Tokyo, a crowd has gathered around a wall of TVs, the speech translated into subtitles as on-lookers whisper.

"I have spoken to Tom, and it's no secret he and I have known each other many years. He's doing fine, and I've encouraged him to take all measures necessary to return back to Earth safely. His vehicle, I've been assured by Dr. Kirshner, has the capability to do just that. However, Tom is in control of his own fate up there, and I can't tell you what he has in mind. We will do everything within our power here, with the assistance of NASA, to help him, to ensure his safety, and to ensure as well that he does not become a hazard to the rest of us down here."

Francine downs her wine.

"Why he has done this is a question only he can answer. Certainly, he has personal reasons, and we that know him are confident he meant no harm to anyone, despite the dangerous nature of such an act. He apparently took all possible precautions and was effective at not posing a critical danger to any persons not associated with his mission. Nevertheless, when he returns, and I certainly hope he does, he will have to answer to me and others for certain infractions, and what some are calling reckless behavior."

Melody watches on a TV that was laid on its side for her in the Starbridge.

"However, that is not our concern at this time. He is an American citizen, he is a citizen of our planet, and a fellow human being. Tom, in a certain way, represents all of us, as have astronauts of all nations before him. I, for one, welcome the opportunity for the people of this planet to focus on the well-being of one person, even if only for this brief interlude in the daily travails of our world, instead of on the demise of those with whom they continually quarrel. For these reasons, we all, I trust, wish him well, and he is certainly in my prayers, and I hope yours. Many shared his grief, as I did, when he and his wife, Francine, lost their boy, Noah, many years ago. And if I were a betting man, I would bet little Noah is praying, wherever he is, for the safe return of his father. Thank you, and good night."

Melody wipes a tear from her cheek.

Isabel stands, barely able to excuse herself, and hurries out of the room. Nonna chases her the best she can.

Isabel leans over the railing, sobbing, as Nonna finally catches up. She waits, then places her hand on Isabel's back. "I know, honey. I believe in my heart he's going to come back, safe and sound. And after that, I'll hold him down, and you whack him a good one. Or would you rather hold him down? Your choice."

Isabel turns, wiping her face. "I guess I can't compete with the President, can I? I wonder who else he talked to. For God's sake, I would think at least he'd call *you*!"

"I think he's calling people in order of the least hell he'll catch. That puts me pretty far down the list. I'm even below the President, and damn proud of it." Isabel works up a near smile as she embraces Nonna, who assures her, "You know Tommy will call you when he figures out what to say."

"I just don't understand how he can do this to so many people who care about him. Doesn't he know how scared we are?"

Nonna holds her at arm's length. "Listen to me. Nobody knows the man better than I do. When that child died, so did something inside his father. There's somewhere between life and death people go. Tom's gone somewhere, to do something neither of us can understand, and I don't think he does either. But I have faith that wherever he's going, he'll come back to us, and he will have paid whatever price he has to pay, whatever cross he has to bear, and will be a better person. A new person. Have faith."

Isabel bows her head.

Watchman Trail appears in the distance as a faint line scratched into an escarpment. Moonlight casts pale shadows across the landscape from the jagged canyon skyline far above as an unlikely train of hikers, darting flashlights ahead, makes its way toward the lookout led by Sam, followed by Butch and Tim, Sid and Bud lagging behind.

Bud is complaining between labored gasps for air. "I can't believe you talked me into this. I should have my head examined."

"You *are* having your head examined. Now shut up and don't waste your breath," says Sid, not quite as winded.

The party turns the last climbing bend and emerges onto the edge of the plateau, gazing around while refilling lungs from the gusting night air. Asymmetrical trees silhouette all around, still guardians of the lookout. Bud is spooked. Sid's heart races as he closes his eyes, turns his face up, and is buffeted. Suddenly Sam spins around.

"What was that?"

Tim looks around. "Cripes, I don't know!"

"Take it easy. Turn off your flashlights," Butch says. They comply, bringing darkness upon them. Bud shines his at them.

"What? What's going on?" Bud asks.

The three whisper-shout in unison: "Turn it off!"

Bud fumbles, then finally gets it off, also whisper shouting, "What?"

"SHHHH!"

Out of nowhere, going as swiftly as it came, is the shadow of a man running by so close his heat brushes them. Bud jumps back a foot into a thorny bush. The figure, Tall Tree, disappears down the trail they just negotiated.

"Holy... What was *that!*" exclaims Bud, no longer whispering.

"Tall Tree," Sam answers calmly. Bud rests his face in his hands.

Sid never moved his closed-eyes gaze from the heavens. "This is amazing. I can see the stars with my eyes closed." Bud looks at him, speechless.

Kirshner paces the control room. He stops again, presses the phone pad, and awaits a response. One of the monitors shows a graphic representation of the capsule moving in orbital flight toward a point where the projected path diverges, tracing a trans-lunar segment. At the point of divergence there's a red flashing circle, and in the corner of the screen, a clock labeled "TRANS-LUNAR INJECTION" rapidly counts down, just past the two minute mark. Under it, "DISARMED" flashes in green.

"Thomas. Don't you do it."

As the capsule falls through space, the Sun is preparing to set behind the Earth. Bursts from two control jets start the capsule rotating.

On another monitor, a graphic of the capsule is accordingly rotating. Kirshner catches it out of the corner of his eye, looks up at the TV feed, and sees the Earth shift.

"Oh, dear God. No."

He resumes punching the phone pad as he watches the "DISARMED" annunciator turn to a red flashing "ARMED".

Inside the capsule, the same annunciation is on the monitor. Tom, Zion in arm, is strapped in for the burn as the clock ticks off to zero. A glow appears outside the window along with flecks of debris, the capsule vibrates, and the engine accelerates them on their journey out of Earth orbit.

Kirshner watches his monitor. As he switches pages, a window comes up on the screen blinking: WARNING. He clicks on the window and the engine parameter screen appears with a red box around the fuel-flow annunciator. He mutters, "What's this now? That damn valve," holding his finger down on the phone button.

Tom is looking out the window. The persistent phone forces him to turn and notice the same warning. He turns on the speaker. "What's going on?"

"We're getting a low fuel-flow. My guess is the valve didn't open full." His flight path screen shows the projected path bending slightly, tracing a segment past the Moon and arcing around it and off the edge of the screen. "I told you that valve wasn't—"

"Don't start, Doc. What do you want to do about it?" As soon as he speaks, there's a stronger vibration and the warning message disappears, followed by a flashing caution box. "Now what?" He returns to the engine page.

"Looks like the valve went full open. We've got normal thrust," Kirshner says as he scans parameters.

"Except that we've got an energy problem now."

"I realize that, Thomas. The computer's asking if we want a modified burn."

"And?"

Kirshner rubs his chin, runs through more pages, then taps the screen. "I don't think it's a good idea right now. We're better off letting the burn run its time out as programmed. That way we can get an accurate path vector. Make sure the valve closes."

"Just fix it during the correction burn?"

"Yes, I think that's best."

The clock is running down from one minute. They both watch, each second throbbing the Doctor's nerves until it reaches zero. The engine shuts down and the capsule returns to its serene glide. "Well, looks like a good shutdown," Tom says.

Kirshner returns to the path screen. The projected path now figure-eights around the Moon, back to Earth, but in an exaggerated swing, elongated past the Moon. The path is green to where it curves halfway around the Moon, then red the rest of the way back. He props his elbows on the desk and lays his face in his hands. "I'll get to work on this."

"Anything I can do?"

"No. Nothing. Let me take care of it."

"How's it going down there, anyway?"

Kirshner contemplates. "Nobody's in jail, yet. But I have to say, there are a few people very unhappy with you about now. And I don't mean the authorities. I suggest you reach out and touch someone. And let's do the rest of this together."

"Understood."

The Doctor clicks off-line, thinks, then dials a phone number.

A woman's voice answers. "Cardona residence."

"Cindy? It's Werner Kirshner. I'm sorry to call so late. Is Louis in?"

The five hikers stand silhouetted on Watchman Plateau against the lights of Springdale and the faint canyon in the distance.

Aboard Air Force One, Stamp reviews papers in the airborne Oval Office when there's a knock at the door. An aide walks in and hands him a slip of paper, then walks out. After reading it, he shakes his head, leaning back in his chair.

Tom unstraps himself, swings the seat around, and looks out the window. The Earth already appears to be smaller, if only due to the angle of the capsule away from it. He puts Zion's face up to the window to look out.

From outside, Zion's face gazes toward Earth. He paws at the glass and meows in silence.

Inside room 211, Noelle sleeps restlessly, popping up at the bleating of the phone. She answers in a stupor, listens, then reaches for the remote and turns on CNN.

A news anchor announces, "This report now from the Johnson Space Center in Houston, Texas. Rob Fanghella has the story. Rob?" The shot switches to a Saturn 5 booster laying on its side like a fallen giant, illuminated by rows of floodlights. This serves as the backdrop for Fanghella, the CNN correspondent.

"Yes, Roger, at 1202 this morning we were advised by Dr. Cole, the designated NASA coordinator assigned to the Holmes case here at the Space Center, that the capsule carrying Holmes has initiated a transition from Earth orbit toward the Moon. Here's an excerpt from the impromptu news conference we managed to catch."

Dr. Cole appears on the screen, uneasy, flanked by colleagues. "About one hour ago, our tracking system monitoring the status of the Holmes vehicle detected a change in flight path consistent with a translunar trajectory. This was confirmed by Dr. Kirshner, the operative manager of the Holmes expedition. NASA has no official comment since this is not a mission in any way connected with NASA. There is nothing we can do for Mr. Holmes at this point, although the President has requested we lend our assistance in providing data and path calculations which might be of use to Dr. Kirshner. For now, that's all the information I have."

A reporter's distant voice asks off-camera, "Do you have any opinion about the future of Mr. Holmes' flight?"

"I can only say that his team has shown extraordinary resourcefulness in what they accomplished to this point. As I was led to understand by Dr. Kirshner, they had, or have, at least theoretically, the capability for reentry and recovery. However, I must say that the complexities of attempting a lunar mission on such limited resources is troublesome, to put it mildly. I don't have enough information about the depth of their mission architecture to comment any further on their chances of success. I will only say that they'll need all the help they can get." Dr. Cole walks away, a flurry of questions striking his back. Fanghella stares at his monitor until he realizes he's looking at himself, then turns toward the camera.

Noelle stares at Fanghella's face on the screen. "Come on, Robby, you can do it. Open your mouth. Speak."

Fanghella recovers. "All of us following this story are having a hard time keeping up with events as they... weave in and out through the night."

"'Weave in and out?'" Noelle says, squinting one eye.

"I guess what I'm trying to say is, we're all caught up in this... adventure. This idea that a regular person, an individual, can chase such a dream. A dream that many of us have had, I know I have, wondering what it would be like to feel the power of a rocket underneath, to feel the dangerous vacuum of space a few inches away, to look down at Earth from a distance." He pauses. "And we've all hoped Tom Holmes would come back safely. Now, things have changed. Now he's headed toward the Moon. It sounds both exhilarating and fearful, two emotions I'm sure Mr. Holmes shares with us. Rob Fanghella for CNN."

"Nice save." Noelle returns to the phone. "Oh boy. Well, I'm going to get some sleep. This is going to be a long one. Good night." She hangs up the phone, turns off the TV and lays down, eyes wide open.

Cole hurries down a hallway, his assistant trying to keep up. "Doctor, what about the numbers? Something's not right. I thought we talked about that."

He stops and turns toward her. "I spoke to Kirshner and he said it's nothing they can't adjust during a TLC burn. It's not our position to create any hysteria or speculation. He asked that we say nothing, so we won't. Is that clear?"

"Yes sir." Cole walks away. "Yes *sir*," she repeats, no more comfortable with the implication than he.

In front of the ship's bridge is a narrow balcony just outside the expansive glass windows. Isabel stands alone, facing the bow, the wind blowing through her hair. Mr. Greer enters the bridge and exchanges words with Captain Wright, handing him a message. The Captain takes the paper and walks out to the balcony. He approaches Isabel, hands her the paper, says something, and walks away. She stares at the paper, then crumples it in her hand and turns back into the wind, this time leaning into it with her eyes tightly shut, and her heart breaking.

The Moon sets in Zion Canyon over the Court of the Patriarchs, only a wobbling sliver remaining. It slips away, darkening the night.

Constellations rotate in a dizzying, streaking disc around the North Star.

The El Rio Lodge is one of Springdale's older motels, set slightly off and parallel to the highway, closer to the center of town than the Driftwood. Flanked by souvenir shops, it retains the 50's flavor when round, heavy cars of bright colors and hood ornaments parked in front of the sliding glass doors of the street level rooms. The gray FBI vehicle looks out of place in front of room number 3.

Bud tosses in bed, jostled into the day by pounding on his glass door, and lifts himself under the weight of a hangover. The pounding persists, increasing in deliberation. "All right! All right! Hold your freakin' horses."

He rises out of bed, stumbling side to side like a newborn bull, gropes for the door and slides it open a few inches. A piercing slash of sunlight cuts across his face and grimace turns to wince. Even less welcome is Sid's all too eager nose poking in. "What the hell time is it?" Bud rasps.

Sid pushes a cup of coffee at him. "It's time to start the first day of the rest of your life. Now get your flabby butt out here and let's take a hike."

Bud is taken back by this stranger in Sid's voice. He peers back out. "I feel like I'm on the last day of my *first* life. How did I let you talk me into that last night? My hair hurts."

"Listen, Buddy Boy, last night was the first time I've ever seen you... not act like yourself. And that's a real big improvement. See you in the coffee shop." He starts to leave, then stops. "Oh, by the way. Holmes shot himself to the Moon last night."

Sid walks away. It takes a moment to sink in, then Bud calls out through the door. "What?"

Sid sits in a booth at the Bumbleberry Coffee Shop reading a paper, headline facing away: HOLMES MOON BOUND. Bud, covered in a wrinkled suit, shuffles up, each footstep turning up volume on the throbbing. He sees the headline as he sets his suitcase down. Sid lowers the paper. "Good morning, Sunshine."

Sid, dressed in jeans and a denim shirt, isn't looking like he's about to head out of town. "What the heck are you doing? We've got a plane to catch in Vegas in four hours," Bud whines.

Sid turns a page. "I'm not going."

"Not going?"

"That's right. Is it the 'not' or the 'going' that's throwing you?"

Bud is yet more disturbed. Sid is not himself. But then again, neither is Bud. "Time out here. We're supposed to be back in Washington today."

Sid says, from behind the paper, "Wrong. *You're* supposed to be back in Washington today. I called in and took... well, I took some time off. I'm staying here for a while."

"A while?"

"Yes. Is it the 'A' or the—"

"OK, OK. Put a sock in it. I get your point. I don't know what's going on with you, but I'm getting as far away from this place as I can."

"Sit down, have some coffee," Sid says without looking at him.

"Not a chance. I'm out of here." There's an interval between them neither is used to. "Yeah, well, I'll see you in... 'a while'."

Sid salutes him goodbye as Bud stands puzzled, looks askance, and walks away, turning back for another look as he opens the glass door. Sid continues with his paper.

The "Welcome to Springdale" monument, made of blocks of local sandstone, stands quietly until Bud's car roars by.

Bud looks in his rearview mirror and sees the monument shrinking in the distance.

The Driftwood serves continental breakfast from a small self-serve kitchenette, attached to the sundry shop on one side and lobby on the other. The lobby gift shop opens into a lounge furnished with tables and sofas. Views of the hotel buildings, nearby pasture, and canyon are framed through three walls of picture windows. News teams have taken over all of it, and ABN has commandeered the majority of the sitting area as an operations base. Reporters and techs crowd in and out of the kitchenette, bumping into each other, getting their claim on coffee, rolls, juice, and cereal. From the lounge, a determined voice turns heads like a bugle call.

"Come on, gang, let's settle down here! We've got a lot to do." Jeff Nauman is the site manager for ABN and motions his people into the room as they gather and the chatter dwindles to whispers. Noelle stands with Scott at the back, sipping coffee. Scott stuffs a whole sweet roll in his mouth, earning a disapproving nose wrinkle from her.

"As all of you know, or at least you better know by now, our space traveler has left the 'surly bonds of Earth' and is on his way to the Moon. I don't have to tell you this is the story of the decade, or the century, or millennium, or whatever else you want to call it, and we need to be on top of it. Right now we've got three correspondent teams and about ten leads to cover. Most important, I need a crew out at the bakery to try to get a one-on-one with Kirshner. We need some real info on whether this guy has a chance in hell of ever making it back. Any volunteers? Noelle, you want to take this one?"

"Actually, Jeff, I was going to take a chance at another interview with the girl, Melody. At the Noah House."

Nauman frowns. "I thought that was already covered. Didn't you already do her? We need input here. Information."

"I realize that, but there's more to this story than rockets and orbits. I think the heart of it is in the why, not the how. There's something about her that... I don't know. I just know I have to talk to her again." She looks around the room. "Maybe Warren can do the factory."

"I see. I'll buy that." He doesn't look like he buys it. "Warren, are you up for the bakery spot?" Warren tugs the brim of his golf cap, deferring to Crane, the senior correspondent. "This better be good, Noelle. Let's not get accused of going for the soft spot. Might take the edge off."

Noelle stares at him, then walks away, dragging Scott by the arm. Nauman cringes at his own remark.

She storms out of the lobby, flailing the glass door ahead of her, and nearly knocks Sid over. Noelle stops, then recognizes him. He looks different though. Perhaps the clothes. "Oh. Agent... Knowles. Wasn't it?"

"That's right. Miss... Crane. Wasn't it?"

"Yeah. Sorry. Are you all right?"

He waits for her to pass, holding the door open, and starts to enter, staring. "I'm just fine. Real fine, thanks," Sid says as their eyes meet before the door closes. Noelle doesn't like that she liked him. Scott notices, makes a face, and she belts him on the arm, then continues the storming.

Bud stands in a crowded D concourse boarding line at Las Vegas's McCarren Airport, out of sorts and annoyed by the slow movement.

Finally aboard National Airlines Flight 711, Bud finds his row and stuffs his bag into the overhead. He crashes into his window seat after struggling by the elderly lady sitting at the aisle. Settling in, he looks up at the TV monitor, finding, to his dismay, the feed from the capsule, the Earth now a complete sphere. The caption reads: "From space I saw Earth—indescribably beautiful with the scars of national boundaries gone... Ahmad Faris."

At 37,000, feet Bud stares blankly out the window.

"Good morning folks, this is your Captain speaking. Welcome aboard National 711, nonstop service from Las Vegas to Baltimore. Flying time today is three hours and fifty-six minutes at an altitude of thirty-seven thousand feet. Weather out there is snow showers, temperature twenty-four degrees Fahrenheit. I'd like to point out on the left side of the aircraft, almost straight down, probably the most famous place on Earth these days. That's Zion National Park, one of the most beautiful spots on Earth, but you may know it better as the launch site for the first civilian manned mission into space."

Bud looks out, then, irritated, pulls the window shade closed. The lady reaches over and shoves it back up, craning to see. He scowls at her and rests his head back, closing his eyes. After a few moments, he reopens them and looks back outside and down.

Not the typical cruise ship cabin, Isabel's three room suite perches on the top passenger deck, directly over the bridge. She's just taken a shower and, bundled in a white terry robe, stands on her balcony, impatiently brushing out a knot at the end of her hair. Isabel stops, unsure why, to look out at the stark ocean horizon. Her phone rings and she walks back into the cabin, answering on the third ring.

"Hello?"

There's an unsteady silence, punctuated by hissing static. Tom's voice wavers through eighty thousand miles of space.

"Isabel?"

She drops the brush to the ground. Her eyes fill, but she fights it off, her hand covering her mouth as she catches her breath. "Oh, God. Tommy?"

"How are you?"

"But, you sound so close."

"About a third of the way."

She walks back outside with the phone, looking at the morning Moon, disbelieveing that she's speaking to an invisible speck racing toward it. "Are you OK?"

"I'm doing great, actually. Pretty much right on course."

"How is it that you know exactly where you are, and I have no idea where I am? You and your 'Mystery Cruise'. What's this all about, anyway?"

Tom has Zion on his back in midair, lightly scratching his belly so as not to launch him. "You wouldn't want me to ruin the surprise, would you?"

"Nothing would surprise me anymore, Tommy. I'm worried sick about you. Are you going to make it back? Or did you ever want to?"

"If I'd intended to kill myself, I could have done it a little cheaper, you know."

"Remember the definition of 'intention' from law school? Wasn't it was 'a desire, or substantial certainty?'" As soon as she says it, she wishes she hadn't, shaking her fist at herself.

"Isabel, I didn't want to—"

"No, no. I'm sorry. I just don't know... I don't know how to handle this. I'm scared. Really scared. And I miss you."

"I miss you too."

"You know, when you were here, I was upset I had so little of you. And now, I'd give anything to have whatever it was I had of you... here. Not flying away from me at 17,000 miles an hour. I feel you slipping away." She starts to cry.

"4,832, actually. Earth's gravity's slowed me down a bit, but the Moon'll pick it up."

Isabel wipes her face with her sleeve. "Damnit, Tommy! Stop it!"

"I'm sorry. I just wish you'd quit writing me off. Give us some credit. I do plan to make it back. I swear."

"Really? And when you come back, who will you be?"

Tom looks out the window. "I don't know, Isabel. Sometimes we have to lose ourselves, just to find ourselves."

Isabel laughs through her tears. "Jesus, Tommy. Couldn't

you just walk around the block a few times, like the rest of us?"

"This is just a bigger block, honey. A longer walk, that's all."

She dabs her eyes with a tissue pulled from her bathrobe pocket. "Right. Next time I tell you to go take a hike, I'll think twice."

"Listen, I've got to keep the phone bill down. These long distance calls are killin' me." Now it's his turn to wish he hadn't said that. She closes her eyes.

"Goodbye, Tommy. I love you."

"Take care of yourself, Isabel."

A cruel blast of white noise drives the phone from her ear. She slams it down and starts to cry again as she stomps her bad foot and falls backward onto the couch.

The ABN news van pulls up in front of Noah House and Noelle and Scott get out. Scott opens the rear doors, lifts out a broadcast video camera, and starts for the building, but Noelle stops him. "I want to talk to her first. I'm not sure if we're going to shoot her."

"Are you serious? Nauman's going to flip if we don't come back with something."

"Well, Jeff doesn't understand that reporting isn't all production. This is about people. Sometimes what you don't report is more important than what you do."

"Huh?"

"Go get some... establishing shots. Whatever. I don't care right now. Let's just put some heart into this."

The *huh?* lingers on his face as Noelle enters the House. He walks over to a playground populated with pieces of rockets and other space program leftovers. There's a first stage Atlas booster laying on its side that children can run through, and a Gemini capsule propped up with its hatches open and a slide coming out the back. He aims the camera in that direction.

Noelle enters into the stillness of the empty House and

continues down the hall looking for Melody. As she approaches the double doors to the Starbridge, she looks through the window and stops. Inside, Melody sits in the center holding a dustpan, watching through her sideways world as Roberta sweeps the floor, the view of the Earth keeping them company on a TV in the corner. Noelle pushes the door open. When she enters, Roberta stops her work and looks up. Melody, seeing Roberta's reaction, turns her wheelchair as Roberta walks quickly toward Noelle.

"Can I help you?" she asks defensively.

"I was hoping I could talk with Melody for a few minutes."

"No reporters. No more interviews for Melody. You already got your story."

Roberta opens one of the doors and gestures for her to leave, but Melody intervenes. "It's OK, Roberta, I want to talk to her. I like Miss Crane."

Roberta looks at both of them with a frown in her eyes. "All right. But keep it short."

She walks out, taking one last look through the window as the door closes, leaving a gentle silence. Noelle draws a guarded breath and walks over to Melody, unsure how to position herself. Finally, she grabs a chair and pulls it over, sitting down and leaning forward where she can see Melody's face. "So, Melody, how are you holding up under all this? You look fine."

"Oh, I'm OK. It's kind of lonely here without the other kids. But I have Roberta, and sometimes other people come by to visit me."

"Honey, I'm not here to interview you or anything like that. I was hoping maybe we could be friends."

"I'd really like that. All my other friends are gone. The kids, I mean."

"I guess you know Mr. Holmes is going to the Moon now."

Melody strikes a thoughtful pause. "I know. It sort of bothers me because I'm afraid for him. But I'm... I don't know, I'm excited for him. I know it's what he wants."

"What do you think he wants?"

"I'm not sure, but I think he wants to stop hurting."

"Do you think he's trying to run away?"

"I don't think so. I think he's trying to run *to* something. I know how he feels. I hurt a lot, too, but I don't want to run away from anything. That would be too lonely."

Melody moves her wheelchair over to a picture window that looks out toward the canyon, framed by a weeping willow waving in the breeze. Noelle stays where she is, needing the distance. "You know, Melody, I didn't come here to talk about Mr. Holmes. When we met the other day, afterwards, I couldn't stop thinking about you." Noelle's heart doubles over. She wipes a tear, trying to catch her breath. "I just think you're the bravest little girl, the bravest person I've ever met. You were so cheerful, and positive. It made me feel very ashamed about some things. I wanted to know more about you. I wanted to know you."

"I'm not so special, Miss Crane. Sometimes I get mad because I'm not like other kids. But then I feel bad about it."

Noelle is struck a chisel blow. Such pure creations, children. They wear raiments of humility and candor with a simple grace which calls down those who would label such qualities as "grown up". She bolsters in this revelation. "What about your family, Melody? Do your Mom and Dad visit you? Do they help you?"

"My parents had me when they were older. When I was little, they called me their 'lucky accident'. Then when I got sick it was real hard on them. Daddy died right after that, and Mommy got sick too. She's in the hospital in St. George, and sometimes they bring her to visit me. Once, when I felt real strong on her birthday, Roberta and Dr. Bitner brought me there. We had a party in her room with cake and everything. I haven't seen her in a while, though. I miss her."

Noelle walks to the window and sits on a bookshelf. She strokes Melody's hair. "I'm sorry about your daddy. It sounds like your mommy has helped you a lot. She must be a wonderful lady. I can see her peace in you. And her strength. The way you're so good about your challenges."

"Mommy made me understand about being sick. When I was little I would ask her why God made me hurt so much. It's like

I was resentful toward Him. I thought He didn't care about me. But Mommy said He was full of mercy. She told me a famous writer said that mercy fell like a gentle rain from heaven, and I just ended up between the drops. But sooner or later it will rain all over me, and I'll be all brand new, because God loves me."

Noelle grabs a tissue from a box on the bookshelf, dabbing her eyes. "Oh, Melody. God bless you. He does love you, and He has blessed me to know you."

Melody strains to look up at her. "Don't feel bad, Miss Crane. I'm very proud to know you. I've seen you on TV and I feel important since I met you."

Noelle bends down and kisses her on the head with more love than she's ever felt for another human being. "No, Melody, it's me that's important now, because I know you." She stands. "I'll be back very soon to see you. Please take care, sweetheart."

"Goodbye, Miss Crane."

Noelle gathers herself and walks out of the room with fire burning her heart, encountering Roberta outside the Starbridge. Roberta is moved by what she sees, aware of a transformation. In this realization, she lays a healing hand on Noelle's shoulder.

Noelle bursts into tears. "Roberta, my heart is breaking. How can something so precious, so innocent, be afflicted like that?"

Roberta embraces her. "Remember, Miss Crane, our Lord said Melody is blessed, and that she will inherit the Earth."

"But must she suffer so?" she angers.

"The doctors say she hasn't much time left. Her heart is enlarged and she has very serious kidney trouble. I pray she will meet Him soon, and her suffering will end." This is too much for Noelle. She runs out.

Noelle opens the van door and jumps in, startling Scott who was staring out the window. "What's wrong?"

She cries hard for a moment. "Let's go."

"Go? Where?"

"Never mind that," gesturing with her hand. "Just go."

Scott complies, pulling out onto the highway. They're no more than a few seconds down the road when she spots something. "Pull in there." He has to hit the brakes to make it into the driveway.

Emmanuel Church looks like it was transplanted from 18th century Boston. Its white exterior contrasts sharply with the colors of the canyon, a steepled, one room sanctuary nestled among pepper trees that grew around it like gentle green angels. Noelle gets out of the van, looks it over, and firmly walks in. Scott steps out as well and scratches his head. He walks toward the church, up the wooden steps, and quietly opens the tall white doors.

Scott enters, moved by the simplicity. It looks bigger inside than he thought from the exterior. Simple wooden pews face an altar spanning the width of the chapel, softly lit in canyon light cast through a glass wall at the rear that frames the majestic sheer cliff of Mt. Kinesava. Three stained-glass windows on each side of the church bathe the walls in fragile colored figures. Noelle sits in the front pew, her head bowed in prayer. Scott sits in the back pew.

From the departure end of Runway 15 at Baltimore International, looking toward the approach through a snow shower, the landing lights of National 711 grow to two white beams. The 757 takes form like a metallic ghost, flares, and lands, blowing snow flurries upward as the engines spool to full reverse thrust.

Bud's home is small, furnished in early divorced working-man. It is functional, plain, and tired. The clicks of a lock turning are followed by the creaking open of the front door and a bitter blast of wind. Bud enters, throwing his bag on the floor, shivering through the shock from desert to blizzard. He kicks the door shut behind him, brushes snow from his coat, and hangs it on a coat tree near the entrance. Bud looks at his surroundings as if he'd walked into someone else's house. He moves over to the fireplace, lights a Duraflame log on the gas burner and squats in front of it, rubbing his hands, then stands and stares at himself in the mirror over the mantle, fixing his thinning hair. There he encounters the portrait of his son and picks it up.

Rusty smiles the guarded smile of a Marine boot camp graduate in full dress. Tucked in the lower right corner of the frame is a smaller picture. There, Rusty stands in front of a burned-out hut, his face smoke-stained, holding a Vietnamese baby in one arm, his rifle in the other. This moment of silence is broken when Igloo, a blinding white Husky, scurries in, nails clicking frantically on the hardwood floor. As Huskies tend to do, he's so excited with anticipation at the impending hug he has to run circles around the room to keep from exploding. Bud replaces the picture and finally gets hold of him and scoops him up, kicking, whining, and licking. He puts Igloo down and watches as the dog darts in and out of every room of the house. A voice comes from the hallway.

"Buddy? Is that you?"

Harriet Meyerkamp is Bud's mother, a frail but healthy eighty-five-year-old wearing a fluorescent red, green, and blue muu muu, covered above the waist by a gray pullover, further accented with bright-pink fuzzy slippers. She peers around the corner and when she sees her son, extends her arms. "You're home! I'm so glad to see you!"

Bud walks over and hugs her warmly. "Hi, Ma. It's been a long trip." He walks over to his coat, pulls out a wrinkled brown bag, and hands it to her, his face twisting at the sight of her outfit. "Here. I picked up some rolls from Charlie's. But just one tonight. You know what Doctor Rummel said."

"Oh, bless you, son. You are a thoughtful boy." She kisses him on the cheek after pulling him down toward her. Bud is always uncomfortable with affection. "I saw you on TV! You looked so... intense. Isn't it all so exciting, what's going on? Did you get to meet Mr. Holmes?"

Bud bristles. "Meet him? I came this close to locking him up before he pulled this... stunt of his. It's a damn foolish thing he did. He put a lot of people in danger, and got a lot of people in trouble." Bud has an out-of-attitude experience, hearing himself bark out a point of view that sounds distant, from a part of him fading away.

"Oh, phooey. You sound like the old farts down at the

Center. I swear, if I hear the word 'irresponsible' one more time, I'm going to whack somebody." She whacks him on the arm, smartly. "Get the point, Buckaroo?"

Bud rubs his arm. "Geez, Ma. What's *your* malfunction?"

"Oh, I think it's just grand what that boy did. For heaven's sake, you'd think he killed somebody the way people are carrying on. He just did what men have been doing for thousands of years. He went exploring, and people should just leave him in peace. By golly, there've been enough times in my life I wished I could shoot myself into orbit, or else a few other people I don't care to mention." Bud looks her over, then snickers. "What are you laughing at?"

"Nice outfit, ma. You look like a barker at a Hawaiian circus."

She hits him again, causing him to rub his arm again in earnest. "Well, somebody needs to bring some color into this... mausoleum. Sometimes I think you're colorblind, or else I was struck colorblind when I moved in here. Now, go sit down. I'll fix you something to eat."

"No, I'll get something. You sit down."

"Nonsense. I've been going batty around here. I need to do something useful."

Bud gives in, kicking his shoes off and settling in front of the TV. He picks up the remote and shoots it at the wide screen. The set glows on to CNN where there's a full screen of Tom's picture, dissolving to a shot of the seared launch site. Bud punches at the remote, finally stopping on *Home Improvement*, feeling momentarily at home as Tim grunts triumphantly over his hot rod. This is only fleeting, however, as he drifts away and recalls Watchman Lookout, the Moon, a running Indian, and the canyon. The uneasy daydream snaps him back to the present, and he doesn't really feel so much at home. Igloo sits at his feet, looking up at him with his head cocked. Bud gives him the same look back.

"What're you lookin' at?"

The news van pulls into the parking lot of St. George's Mountain Vista Convalescent Home. Noelle gets out and hurries toward the front doors, Scott trying to keep up. He grabs her arm, bringing her to an annoyed halt. She won't look at him.

"Whoa, Noellie. Help me out here. We've been running around all day. You won't talk to me. What's going on? What does this have to do with our story?"

"Scotty, I'm not really sure. Probably nothing. But I'm not reporting right now. I'm just... following my heart." She looks into his eyes. "Somewhere along the line, I learned that's where journalism lives. The story finds you. You don't find it." He pushes her toward the door.

Noelle enters and walks up to the receptionist. "Excuse me," showing her ID, "I'm Noelle Crane, ABN news. I was wondering if I could have a few words with Mrs. Baxter. If she's up to it, that is. I'm not here to interview her."

The receptionist stares at her. "Just a moment." She picks up the phone, dials an extension, whispers, then hangs up slowly. "Someone will be right with you." Noelle looks around at the waiting area, unkept, stark, colorless. A few beat-up folding chairs angle at each other, one with a torn magazine on its seat.

From down the corridor, an elderly man with a kind face appears and recognizes her. "Hello, I'm Dr. Holly." He shakes their hands. "You were inquiring about Esther Baxter?"

"Yes. I don't mean to disturb her, but I've gotten to know her daughter, Melody, and I was so touched by some of the things she said about her mother, I felt like I wanted to speak with her."

Dr. Holly looks at the receptionist, then back at Noelle. "Please, come with me."

Noelle glances at Scott. "Sure. Of course." Doctor Holly walks her down the white hallway. As they pass a rec room, Noelle stops and peers in. It's empty but for a woman sitting at a table alone in front of a checkerboard. She's dressed in a hospital gown, her white hair tossed across her left shoulder. She makes a move, then turns and looks at Noelle.

"Miss Crane?" says Dr. Holly. Noelle sees he's down the

hall, standing in front of his office. She looks back into the room and the woman is no longer there. Noelle walks toward him, then looks back. "Please," he says, pointing to the open door.

He ushers her into his small, chaotic office, closes the door quietly behind them, moves a stack of files from a chair and offers it to her as he sits behind his cluttered desk. "Please, sit down." She sits on the edge, as if bracing herself. "Can I trust your confidence?" he asks.

"Of course. I'm sincerely not here to interview her."

Dr. Holly pauses. "Mrs. Baxter passed away a month ago."

Noelle stares at him as her eyes well up once again. "But I—" Her heart clenches, taking her breath. "I don't understand. I just spoke with Melody an hour ago."

"I consulted with Dr. Bitner when this happened, and frankly, he felt it best not to tell her. I'm not sure if you know how ill Melody is, but in light of the fact she's not expected to last much longer, Dr. Bitner saw no point in burdening that little girl with any more sorrow, at least for now."

Noelle stands and walks toward the door, stopping in front of it. She stares at the frosted glass and at Dr. Holly's backward name. Half angry, half devastated for Melody, she turns around. "You people underestimate the strength of that girl. I know I did."

Dr. Holly sees the tears threatening in her eyes. "You're right. Melody is a survivor. None of us ever thought she would live this long, but that was her doctor's opinion and since there's no more family, he has presumed to take that position. And I assure you he loves Melody, and has her best interests at heart. In any event, it's his decision, and—"

Noelle motions *stop* with her hand. "I told you I would keep your confidence, and I will, but I disagree with both of you. A person's pain is their pain. No one has a right to take it away or dole it out at their discretion."

"I respect your opinion, Miss Crane."

"Doctor, let's just all pray for that little girl. I've never felt more like taking on someone else's burden than since I met her. I'm not sure who I am anymore, but I know I'm a better person because of her."

"Melody does that to people."

She extends her hand. "Goodbye, Doctor."

"Goodbye," he says with a caring handshake, covering her hand with his other. Noelle walks out, leaving him with a pang of concern.

Soft shades of sunset filter down upon the minibutte of the Cantina as Kirshner and Sam savor an aperitif, each in quiet solitude. The door opens and Rosalee enters. "Doctor, there's a call for you on line two. Do you want to take it?"

"Do you know who it is?"

"It's the President."

"Yes, dear, I'll take it." He picks up the phone. "This is Werner. How are you?"

Heavy snow drifts across the White House lawn. Stamp holds the cellphone with one hand to his ear and with the other chips one-armed at orange golf balls toward an invisible target. Kelly lopes after each and brings it back. Nearby, Secret Service stand guard, despite their freezing disbelief.

"Oh, I'm fine, considering. Sure wish I was back in the canyon, though. It's a bit much out here."

"I understand. What can I do for you?"

"How are we doing so far? Since our friend decided to go against our advice."

"Actually, everything is nominal. We have a translunar correction coming up in a couple of hours. But that is fairly routine. If any of this can be routine."

"Terry tells me it's not quite so nominal. Never really understood that word. Is it a cross between normal and, what, terminal?"

Kirshner smiles. "It means things are within parameters. Yes, we had a small... malfunction, but it's fixable." Sam freezes and darts the Doctor a look of one betrayed by silence. Kirshner pretends not to notice.

"Roger that. Well, keep me informed, will you?"

"Mr. President, somehow I think you are already informed."

"Even so, I prefer to hear from you directly, if you don't mind."

"I understand."

"Goodbye, Werner, and God be with you, and with Tom."

"Thank you, Sir."

Stamp closes the phone, throws it to a waiting aide and, exercising his authority, takes a full swing, driving a ball up into the falling snow and out of sight. He looks proudly at the aides who dutifully confirm his pride. In the distance, the crash of the ball hitting something sends a Secret Service agent into the snow drift, Kelly close behind.

Sam starts to open his mouth but the Doctor waves a finger back and forth as he sips his Grand Marnier.

At the Driftwood lounge, the same group has gathered, this time the mood more restrained. Noelle and Scott are at the back, the only ones standing as a disapproving silence hangs after Nauman's last words.

"Now, let me get this straight. We got the piece from the bakery, thanks to Warren's crew. Jerry shot stock footage. And you got... nothing all day? Noelle, you were supposed to be the lead story. What happened?"

"Like I said, I was doing... research. I'm working on the... Honestly, Jeff, I'm not sure what I'm doing."

"You hit a dead end?"

"No. Not at all. There's just a few things to sort out. Some unexpected things."

"Can you share them with us?"

"No."

Jeff holds his face in his hands. Slowly his eyes emerge. "Do we have an ETA on this unexpected... thing?"

Noelle hesitates. "No."

"Do you have any idea the heat I'm going to take from the Tower over the coverage tonight?"

"I'm sorry." Noelle turns away and leaves, Scott following.

Jeff is dumbstruck. "OK, people. Warren, you're taking the lead tomorrow. Meeting at 6:00 A.M. sharp. Lance, give me a brief on your story line."

Out in the parking lot Scott is once more trying to keep up, his frustration outmatched only by hers. "Noelle! Noelle! Wait up!" She stops, shaking in the night air. The wind circles around them and high cirrus blanket the sky as the last moments of fading dusk portend a change in the weather.

"Scotty, please. Don't start on me."

"Hey." He turns her toward him, grabbing both shoulders. "It's me, Scott. Remember? What can we do for you right now? What do you want?"

"Right now? I could use a stiff one." He raises an eyebrow and she belts him on the arm. "A drink, you moron!"

At least he got a smile out of her. He points to the van. "Get in."

Inside Wiley's there's a buzzing crowd of locals, Noelle and Scott's entrance causing only a momentary lull. The residents of the canyon are getting used to celebrities in their midst, and a few *hello* nods break the ice as everyone goes about their business. Scott leads her to the bar and waves his member card at Wiley.

"Hey, folks. What can I get you?" Wiley asks with a smile.

"The lady here said she wants a stiff one." Before either can even think of cracking a smile, she flashes them both a dangerous *don't-you-dare* look. "Any suggestions?"

Wiley leans forward and half whispers, "I tell you what. I've got some tequila, or at least that's what they say it's like. Made by a local Indian tribe around these parts. 'Big medicine'."

Noelle looks at Scott and declares, "Go for it."

Wiley lifts a one-sided smile as he sets two shot glasses on the bar and pours from a bottle with a stark label, nothing on it but something resembling a petroglyph. Scott and Noelle pick up the glasses, look at each other in fear, and down them simultaneously. Scott, after a beat, cocks his head to one side as his eyes roll back in his head. Noelle bends straight over at the waist and, while in that position, stomps her leg twice, hard, on the floor. She comes up for air, glassy eyed, not noticing the bar got real quiet. They look at each other, then around at the crowd which bursts out in applause. She manages an autonomic outburst, "My GOD!"

A voice comes from behind. "Rocket fuel!" Noelle turns around to see Sid, shaking his head. "I know how you feel. That was me last night."

Noelle wipes her mouth with her sleeve. "Why, Mr. Secret Agent Man. I'm surprised."

He looks at her, then at Scott. "Come on, let me join you guys in another round. The second one's easier. Trust me."

Noelle stands, almost nose to nose with Sid. "What the hell. Why not." Sid leads them toward his table and drags a chair over for her while waving Wiley down for another round, but Noelle drops into one before Sid has a chance to offer his. Wiley walks over and puts down three shot glasses, three glasses of ice water, and a bottle of Big Medicine. Sid fills the shots, clinks glasses, and pours his down his throat. Though he's tamed the body reaction, they can see the rocket fuel light off in his face. He slams the glass down. "Cheers!"

The other two brace themselves and try again. This time Noelle does the head cock, and Scott just shudders top to bottom. "I recommend you stop at three," advises Sid.

Scott gets his focus back. "I think I'll take your advice."

"So, Agent Knowles," Noelle says with an adorable pre-slur.

"Sid, please. I don't think we've been properly introduced." He offers his hand. "I'm Sid."

Noelle takes his hand. "Noelle."

Scott follows. "Scott Johnson. My pleasure."

Scott looks at Noelle, and she purposely doesn't look back. Instead she turns to Sid. "So, mixing a little pleasure with business, Sid? I didn't think you guys did this."

"Actually, I'm trying to find that place that isn't business *or* pleasure.

"And is there such a place?"

"I'll let you know if I find it."

"Please do, 'cause neither one's working for me."

"Bad day?"

"I wouldn't say that. Just a 'big medicine' day. Very big."

Sid pours three more shots, puts the cork back in the bottle and pounds it down. They toast again, bravely shoot them back, and set the glasses upside down on the table, each closing their eyes as they lean back in their chairs. Noelle opens an eye to half-mast and sneaks a look at Sid.

Kirshner pages through screens on the monitor, stopping on the flight path annunciator when his phone rings. "Hello," he snips, punching the speaker phone on.

"Werner," Dr. Cole says. "Are you OK?"

"My apologies, Terry. I'm worried about this procedure."

"Did you come up with anything?"

"Unfortunately not. I spoke with Cardona and he said the tolerances were a little close on the valve bushing. He thinks the temperature may have tightened it up a little. We pulled it from him before he was able to run the proving cycles."

"Well, it did open, after all. That's a good sign. There's no working that valve a few times to free it up?"

Kirshner pauses. "I'm afraid this is a design flaw on my part. We elected... I elected not to install dedicated shut-off valves on the fuel tanks. We went ahead with this integrated shut-off, flow-control for simplicity. So much for simplicity."

"I see. So you can't cycle it without lighting off the fuel."

"That's correct."

"I know you're coming up on this burn, so I'll let you go. I just wanted to wish you my best. And by the way, we re-ran the numbers and came up with the same values for your correction. If everything goes right, you should be dead on."

"Thank you again, Terry. Goodbye." Kirshner hangs up and returns to the path page. Directly ahead of the capsule's image there's a red flashing circle, in the corner an annunciation: TRANSLUNAR

CORRECTION, with a clock counting down in green from two minutes. He picks up the phone and tries again to reach the capsule, slamming the handset down in frustration. "Damnit, Thomas. Answer." Just then the phone buzzes and he turns on the speaker. "Well, it's about time."

Tom's voice has a slight response delay. "Sorry, Werner. Just stepped outside."

"Very funny. Now can we please coordinate this burn?"

"Of course. Should be routine though, right?"

"I certainly hope so. It's just that confounded valve."

"What are you worried about? It opened, didn't it?"

"I worry. It's my nature. Now just unlock the override for my computer. Can you do that?"

"I don't see why not." Tom has mastered, or at least managed, the business of floating inverted. He pulls up menus on his monitor and releases the override, allowing the control room access to capsule systems. "Just to confirm. I show a one minute, twenty-four second burn with a delta correction of .051 xy by .994 yz."

"Confirmed. Minus one minute, forty-five seconds, counting. Mark. I show fuel remaining at two hundred five kilos, estimated burn of forty-seven kilos. That's awfully close. I wish you hadn't done this with the fuel you had."

"Wishing backwards doesn't work too well, Doc."

"You knew you launched short of service module fuel. You should never have risked this foolish trip around the Moon."

"Hey, so far so good. Now stop bellyaching. It's bad enough I can't do a parking orbit because of fuel, but we've got enough for the transearth burns and some left over. OK, Mom?"

"It's too close for me. I don't like it."

"There's that positive attitude!"

Kirshner has nothing to say, watching the clock ticking down through one minute. He lights a shaky cigarette as he pages through screens of system and engine parameters.

From outside, the capsule approaches an ever closer blinding half-moon, craters and geology clearly visible. Attitude jets ignite on one side, then stop. Another set of jets do the same and extinguish, and after a few seconds, the main engine ignites in a barely visible shock cone.

Tom is strapped in his seat with Zion on his lap, watching his monitor. "Light off."

Kirshner watches the engine page. "Roger, I confirm. All parameters nominal... normal."

"Valve's full open. I told you not to worry. It's bad for your complexion."

Kirshner frets under his breath, his sense of humor on hold. "Come on. Come on." The flight path screen shows the projected path arcing, tracing a more symmetrical loop around the Moon.

Inside the Johnson Space Center a flight follower watches a screen, not as sophisticated visually, displaying only rolling data. He motions to someone near him. "Hey, look here. There's a change in velocity and a little in path, too. Here comes the correction."

"Think there's a problem?"

"No, he said he'd call us if there was anything unusual. Do you think we should tell Cole?"

"I guess not. Not if there's nothing unusual. Let's see how it pans out."

Kirshner stands, squints at the screen as if it were threatening him, and watches the burn timer count down from 20 seconds. Pacing, he takes in nearly the whole cigarette in one drag and coughs it violently back out.

Tom has the same annunciator, counting through 15 seconds, down through 5 seconds, 4, 3, 2, 1, 0...

Outside the capsule, the engine still burns.

Kirshner stares at the screen, eyes still watering, and suddenly an "ERROR" box flashes next to the clock, its numbers now red and counting up from zero. He presses the transmit switch. "Tom? What's going on up there?"

Tom likewise stares at the screen in disbelief. "Hell. It didn't shut down. It didn't shut down!"

Kirshner's voice shouts through space. "For God's sake, go to manual! Shut it down!"

"Manual. Roger." Tom stumbles through menus, getting confused. "Wait, here it is, manual systems." He bogs down through more menus. "Hydraulics. Life support. Engine. Here it is. I got it." He punches the *enter* key and waits. "Oh boy. It didn't help. It's still burning."

Kirshner drops the cigarette from his mouth, already gaping open. "Let's not panic. I tell you what, you locate the emergency override switch on the rear accessory panel while I try manual down here." He scrolls through pages on his computer, more deftly than Tom, and enters his shut down command. "Mary, Mother of God. Tom! Did you locate the switch?"

Tom, having left Zion suspended in midair, is upside down, feeling along a panel by the pressure lock. "Yeah, here it is. I found it." He pushes the toggle switch but can tell it did no good. "No joy, Doctor. It didn't shut down." The transmission delays aggravate already frayed nerves.

Kirshner covers his face, then grabs a manual, rapidly flipping pages. "All right, Thomas, listen to me. Find the circuit breaker for the valve. It's on the P42 panel, and the position is..." straining to see the numbers, "Christ!" He finds his glasses in his pocket and half puts them on. "It's position L13. L13. Did you copy?"

Tom voice is faint, distant, as small as the speaker from which it vibrates. "L13. Roger."

"Right, L13. You reset it, and if that doesn't work, try it a few times to shock it. That valve is fail-safe closed. Maybe we can shock it loose. Meanwhile, I'm going to look at the damage down here. Got it?"

Tom's voice is even smaller, compressed. "Got it."

The Doctor takes a moment to collect his thoughts. He switches to the flight path page, the projected path now arcing into the lunar surface. Kirshner's lips barely move, as if he were afraid Tom could read them. "Oh no. We've got to change trajectory. Otherwise, oh my God, no." He feverishly enters numbers into the computer.

Tom has located the circuit breaker panel and, using a flashlight, searches for the breaker, running his hands along each row. Zion floats by and meows, struggling to maneuver as the acceleration parks him into the window. Finally Tom finds the breaker and, closing his eyes, pulls it. Nothing. He rests his head on the panel, then tries again, and again, and once more, this time leaving it out. Fear crystallizes on his face.

As Kirshner pounds away on the keyboard, Tom's weary voice asks, "Doc?"

Absorbed in concentration, he barely answers. "Yes? What is it?"

"It didn't work."

Kirshner stops. After an agonizing pause, he says, "I see." He hits the *enter* key. "Well, I've worked out some numbers. Take a look at the flight path."

Tom, moving in slow motion as the weight of the situation bears down, brings up the page and sees he's on a collision course with the Moon. "Looks like this flight's going to... end a little early."

Kirshner stares at the burn time, now up to six minutes and thirty-four seconds. "Listen to me, that's not going to happen. I think it's fairly certain we can't stop that engine, so it's just going to run out of fuel. But the trajectory can be altered so as to avoid impact with the lunar surface."

There's a gravid silence. "Yeah? And then what? Out toward... Mars?"

"Well, at least then there's time."

"Time for what? Maybe the first alternative is the best. It's closer to why... never mind. I think we should just leave it."

"No way. You forced me to go this far with you, and I'm not going to let you just crash into the godforsaken Moon. Besides, I already programmed it in, and you can't stop it."

The capsule's attitude jets ignite. Tom can tell what happened. "Kirshner, this is *my* flight! You give it back to me!"

This time Kirshner's voice is distant, but not small. "Not any more it isn't, son. I don't think it's in your hands anymore." Tom watches the screen as the projected path moves toward the edge of the Moon.

At the Space Center, the flight follower watches his monitor, this time his eyes open wide. "Hey, George?"

"Yeah?"

"You better call Cole down here."

"He's home asleep, for heaven's sake."

He continues to stare, parameters rolling green across his face. "Yeah, well, get him down here."

Kirshner watches the projected path approach the edge of the Moon, then jump along the edge and arc outward around the Moon to the left edge of the screen, into space. He looks down in a pitiful combination of anguish and relief.

Tom, cradling Zion in his arms, sees the same thing and shakes his head. The vibration in the capsule stops. "Shut down."

Kirshner lays his forehead on the desk.

The Earth is a blue-white globe in the distance as the capsule approaches and disappears past.

The Narrows

Child of Skyeyes

CHAPTER FOUR

I brushed the stardust from my eyes.
"Keep them closed," a soft voice sighed.
Two kisses touched them, one on each.
My spirit stilled, I could not breathe.

I found myself just sitting there
Atop a crystal-rainbow stair.
And as I turned, there by my side
A girl stood tall, with jeweled eyes.

Her face gazed up and smiled at light
That came from nowhere, pure and bright.
Her arms and hands raised up in praise,
Her cream-white dress danced round her legs.

"What is your name?" I thought to her.
Her heart spoke back, "I'm Diamond Girl.
I'm everyone who's ever loved,
Who's ever seen the pure white dove."

"Please help me, Diamond Girl," I cried.
With feathered brush, my cheek she dried.
"Don't be afraid, my precious one,
I'm yours until forever's gone.

Come walk with me and hold my hand,
I'll take you to Forever Land.
We'll play where every story's told,
Where rainbows meet and turn to gold."

A step of red, then one of blue,
Each color brought us closer to
Where rainbow stairs curve down and down
Through orange cotton candy clouds.

Were God a child in such a place
And sat on rainbow stairs alone,
Would He create with all His grace
A Diamond Girl to share His home?

Would He hold out His hand to her
And walk through clouds down colored steps?
Could such a touch upon His cheek
Bring joy so great, to steal His breath?

On the east-facing flank of the mansion, glass walls of the living room open onto a vast expanse of cedar terrace. Sam leans with his elbows on the railing, alone, having just finished a heart-wrenching cry. From inside, Rosalee's mournful weeping drifts through the open door. The Sun hasn't broken the canyon rim yet, but even if it had, only a lighter shade of pale would cast itself upon Sam's stricken figure.

A storm lets its approaching presence known by a foreboding swash of dark clouds. Patches of morning sky occasionally peer through weak spots in the closing layer of stratus, but not for long as thunder calls in the distance. Wind swirls around Sam, still half dressed, awakened early for the sad news of the night's cruel events.

Of all the ponderous thoughts that trample across his bruised heart, he's particularly wrenched by the emptiness the loss of a loved one leaves in the world; how the departure of a cherished soul from life can make that world such a lesser place, can reduce the essence of every particle of matter, living or not, turning what used to be mere existence into an aching burden. This, Sam realizes, is but a fraction of what Tom suffered, and through his own demise finally imparts to Sam the sorrow he could not express. He dolefully raises himself and walks into the living room.

Rosalee sits on the couch, her face buried in a pillow. Dr. Kirshner sits near her with his hand on her back, and a few feet away, Matt, wishing he could cry, stares out the glass in bound up anger. Sam enters near him, stops, and their eyes meet. Matt looks back out, unable to speak.

After a few moments the phone rings. No one wants to answer, but Sam finally picks it up. "Hello... Yeah, he's here. Who's calling?... Hold on. Doc, it's for you. Terry Cole."

Kirshner stands, touching Rosalee's head, then walks around and takes the phone, clearing his throat. "Yes, Terry. Thank you for calling... I'm afraid that's exactly correct. It was a malfunction of that valve. We couldn't stop it... I appreciate that, and I'm sure Tom does as well, but there's nothing to be done at this point. I'll be making a statement this morning, and I very much appreciate your discretion in this matter... There's really no need for you to come out here... Very well, I understand. You're welcome, of course. Goodbye." He hangs up, turning to Sam. "The President asked him to come out. To help."

Sam snaps. "Help what? What can he possibly do? What the hell can he do?"

"Nothing, of course. But he means well."

"Right."

Kirshner puts his arm around him as Sam looks away. "We need to get going."

"When can I talk to him? You said I could talk to him."

"Soon. He just wanted... he wanted some time alone."

"Alone? How much more alone can he get? For godssake, wanting to be so stinking alone is what got him into this whole.... this... damnit. I tried so hard to reach him. Why couldn't I just reach him?"

"None of us could, my friend. It wasn't anybody's fault. Come, let's go. We'll talk more later." He turns to Matt. "You'll watch after Rosalee?"

Matt never turns around. "Sure, no problem. I'll stay here with her. You go on ahead."

Kirshner motions for Sam to follow.

Noelle tosses in her sleep, fighting her pillow until the phone rings, scaring her into the day again. She reaches for the phone and knocks it off the nightstand. Finally finding the handset, she groans, "Hello?... Yes, Jeff." She fumbles for her watch. "What time is it?... A press conference? Now? What's going on?... All right, I'll be ready as soon as I can." She gets up and walks over to the balcony door, opens it, and is caught by a knifing gust of wind, recoiling her back. After closing the door she peers through the curtains and the darkness of the morning settles upon her. Something is wrong.

Inside the Driftwood lounge everyone quickly gets coffee, trying to organize. Noelle, bundled in a thick sweater, walks in, her overcast mood matched by that of everyone else, as if they all had the same bad dream. Scott is there to greet her and Nauman walks up from behind. Noelle shudders. "What's this all about?"

Nauman sips his coffee. "I honestly don't know. Kirshner called a press conference for seven thirty this morning. He phoned the front desk at six and asked them to tell us."

"Why so early? Do we have any idea?"

"He didn't say, but I tell you, this isn't right. I can feel it."

"Oh, God. You don't suppose—"

"Let's not speculate. Let's just not do that."

On the upper deck of the ship there's commotion in the hallway outside the luxury suites. Though it's still dark, the light from an open door casts crossing shadows from movement within. Captain Wright exits, stopping to look back. He sees Nonna sitting on the edge of a couch in her bathrobe, covering her eyes with a handkerchief. Isabel appears as a blur walking past and out of view, then reappears, her face washed in tears. She walks up the entry passage and slams the door shut.

Bud stands at his front window staring out at the snowfall,

blowing on a cup of tea and fogging the pane in front of him. He takes a quarter out of his pocket, flips it once, then puts it back.

Harriet's voice echoes from the kitchen. "Buddy, are you sure I can't fix you something? You've got to eat something." She enters the room whisking eggs in a bowl, wearing the same muu muu, or a duplicate of it, this time covered by an even louder apron. She stops to look at him.

"Son, what's wrong?"

"I don't know. I couldn't sleep last night."

She walks back into the kitchen and proclaims, "Oh, dear. Bud? You better come in here."

There's a small TV on the kitchen counter, and on it a view of the warehouse, reporters milling around. Noelle converses with a colleague, then, getting her cue, addresses the camera as Bud walks into the kitchen.

"Good morning, from Rockville, Utah, this is Noelle Crane for ABN news. We've been called here early this morning for a press conference by Dr. Werner Kirshner, who most of you are aware by now has been the person technically responsible for launching Thomas Holmes into space a few days ago. We don't know the nature of this—," listening to her earpiece, "I understand Dr. Kirshner is arriving, so we'll switch to his position now."

Bud runs into the living room and turns on the big TV. The scene at the warehouse is still as it was when the last conference was held, though now there are TV cameras and the accompanying blaring lights. Kirshner approaches the podium, Sam standing grimly by his side. The crowd grows quiet.

"Ladies and gentleman, I want to thank you for assembling here on such short notice. I will get directly to the point. The news I have to report regarding Mr. Holmes is not good news, I'm sorry to say. Last night, at approximately midnight, we commenced a planned burn of the service module engine to make a correction in trajectory. The valve on that engine failed to close. In spite of our efforts, the engine could not be shut down and eventually ran out of fuel. As a result, the trajectory and velocity of the capsule placed it into an interplanetary flight path which will render it unable to return to Earth."

A moan rises from the audience. Kirshner waits for quiet. "Through some adjustments in the direction of the vehicle, I was able to prevent the flight path from impacting the lunar surface. Unfortunately, however, the result is that it will reach the Moon, and the gravity of the Moon will cause the capsule to come within six miles of the surface, then continue on a path which will take it away from both the Moon and the Earth."

He dabs his forehead with a tissue. "Mr. Holmes is still in good health, and his spirits, well, as you can imagine, he is disappointed. However, he asked me to convey to all of you who have been kind enough to wish him well, that he understood the risks involved in this mission, and does not regret having done what he has done. That is all I have to say. I will be available now to answer a few questions."

A pall hangs over the room and sniffles travel through the crowd as a reporter raises his hand. Kirshner acknowledges.

"Thank you, Dr. Kirshner. I'd like to express, I'm sure on behalf of all of us, our sadness at this news." Kirshner nods. "What is going to happen to Mr. Holmes?"

Francine sits on the couch, watching in horror, her hand over her mouth. Kirshner's image falters, flickers, then returns.

"After passing the Moon, his life support systems will last anywhere from two to three weeks, depending on the strenuousness of his activities. He will feel no pain, I can tell you that much. As the oxygen depletes, he will eventually grow tired, and in effect, fall asleep."

Another reporter raises his hand. "You've said there's nothing that can be done. I thought there was some kind of retro rocket system, to slow him down so he could come back to Earth."

"That is true, in the sense that there's a conventional retro system, similar to the ones used on the Gemini missions. However, it is a solid propellant system, designed to be deployed only for reentry deceleration from Earth orbit. It would be of no use in slowing the capsule in this condition." Noelle raises her hand. "Yes,

Miss Crane."

Bud watches, inexplicably shaken.

"Then, there is no hope for Mr. Holmes."

"From this world, I'm afraid there is none," Kirshner says while looking down. Only a cough intrudes on the silence. "Thank you all." Kirshner walks away with Sam and the crowd sits fixed, Noelle standing.

Bud turns the TV off and looks at Harriet, a tear glistening on her weathered cheek. "That poor boy. How he suffered in his life. And now, now it's over." She looks at Bud, seeing in him something she hasn't in many years. It disturbs her, yet stirs her heart. Bud, too, has suffered, and like Holmes, his own heart had turned cold. But in this look Harriet sees a glint of life, even if only anguish or confusion, both of which can be signs of a spirit reawakening. Bud walks down the hall and she follows.

He enters his bedroom, takes the suitcase he hadn't unpacked yet and opens it, pulling out dirty laundry, then gathers clothing from his drawers and closet, stuffs them in and slams it shut. "Buddy?"

"Don't ask me why, Ma, but I'm going back out there. I'm not sure I know myself."

"You go, son. You go out there. Whatever it is that's there for you, I think you need it."

Bud looks into her loving eyes, then hugs her tight. "Will you be all right? I'm sorry to leave you here again."

"I'll be fine. I'll miss you, though. Just hurry back." She holds him at arm's length. "Or send for me! I could use a change of weather." He kisses her, then rushes out, unaware that her hand reaches toward him.

Back at the Driftwood the crowd has returned. Nauman stands looking out the window when he sees Noelle coming down the walk. As she enters and encounters him standing there, her eyes pierce him. "Your story got enough 'edge' in it now?" He has nothing to say as she leaves him in a frost and walks to the kitchenette.

Scott has fixed a hot chocolate and when he sees Noelle, offers it to her. She takes it, but sets it down and falls into his arms. He embraces her and closes his eyes as she stares unfocused, her head resting on his shoulder. The Driftwood receptionist approaches cautiously with a drawn face.

"Miss Crane?" Noelle turns the unfocused gaze toward her. "There's a call for you."

"Please, take a message for me."

"It's Melody. She sounds very upset." Noelle follows to the phone, closes her eyes, and grabs hold of her wounded spirit. "Hello? Melody?... Yes, honey, I know... I'm so sorry." Noelle bites her lip. "What is it? What is it that I said? Tell me." Noelle opens her eyes. "What can I do to help you?... Are you sure? Is that what you really want?... All right. I'll see what I can do. But you have to promise me something. Promise you'll try to not be too upset. Try to get some rest, and be strong. OK?... OK, then. I'll talk to you real soon. And I love you... Goodbye, Melody."

She puts the phone down. The receptionist is struck by the resolve in Noelle's eyes, eyes that walk away on a mission.

Noelle enters where the news crowd is standing in sad confusion and pans the room until Nauman appears in her sights. He looks directly back, as if he felt her stare cut through him, and is drawn toward her. When he arrives, she puts her arm around his shoulders, firmly escorting him out the side door. Through the window, Scott watches him shudder in the cold of the weather, and the moment. Noelle is speaking at him, not to him, and he nods, as much in survival as agreement.

Kirshner bounces a tennis ball off a small section of the control room wall between two equipment racks, irritated at the lack of anything to do. He scans a page on a monitor, only fueling the frustration. The phone rings and he answers curtly. "Hello."

"Hello. Who is this?" a woman's stern voice asks.

"Who is *this*?"

Nonna sits in her suite, the connecting door to Isabel's

open. "This is Juanita Holmes."

"Mrs. Holmes, I'm so sorry. I didn't recognize your voice. This is Dr. Kirshner."

"Oh, it's you, Doctor. I have to say, I'm not very happy with you right now. I'm not blaming you. I just wish you'd never met my grandson."

"I'm very sorry, Mrs. Holmes. I do blame myself. I should have stopped him."

"You know as well as I do no one can stop that boy when he sets his mind to something. Now, I'd like to talk to him. Can you arrange that?"

"I'll certainly try." He puts her on hold, looking at the phone, then buzzes the capsule.

Tom gazes out the window. He has a paddle board and taps the rubber ball toward Zion, who patiently waits as the ball wobbles toward him, making a clumsy, zero-G swat at it. The buzzing phone is ignored at first, then he answers with the handset.

"Yeah, what is it?" He stiffens up. "Yes, of course, put her through." Tom winces, as he always does when she calls to scold him for not calling. Especially this time. He turns on the speaker phone.

"Hi, you. I swear I was going to call."

"Uh-huh. So, do you have any idea how pissed off we are at you down here?"

"Let me guess. Very pissed off?"

"Well, just a little less than we are heartbroken."

"I'm sorry. Truly, I didn't want this to happen."

"Really, now. You could have fooled me."

"There's a difference between wanting something and not caring if it happens," Tom says.

"Never mind what everyone else around you cares about." No response. "Why, Tommy?"

"This was for Noah."

"And you think this is what he would have wanted for you? To end up like this? I don't think so." Again silence. "Something's missing here. I can't put my finger on it, but I know there's more to it. Anyway, I didn't call to scold you. I just wanted to tell you that I love you, and my prayers are with you."

Tom searches. "I love you too, Nonna. And I'm sorry if I've hurt you, or anyone else. Just understand I don't regret this, and I'm OK with it. I'll be OK. Try to let Isabel know that somehow."

"I'll do what I can. Will I speak to you again, before—"

"I'll call. I promise."

"Peace be with you, Tommy."

"And also with you." After a pause, the line disconnects. Nonna hangs up and buries her face back in her wash rag.

A heavy downpour has unloaded on McCarren from a foreboding thunderhead that parked itself over the airport. Bud runs out of the terminal holding a newspaper over his head and dodges creeping traffic into the middle island where the rental car vans stop. He sees the Alamo van start to pull away and runs faster, a considerable effort carrying his bag and wearing his overcoat. When he catches up, pounding on the door, the driver opens and tries not to laugh while helping a drenched Bud aboard. Bud falls into a seat and, exhausted, stares out the window as sheets of rain batter millimeters away. He barely hears the driver's babbling over the PA.

"Hello, folks, my name is Reggie, and I'd like to welcome you to Las Vegas. Sorry about this weather! I know it isn't what you came to Vegas for, and we don't get it that often, but when we do, it's like everything else around here. Big, bright, noisy, and non-stop!" The PA drifts away as Bud slips into his thoughts.

The rental car wipers strain to fend off torrents of rain as Bud squints through them, leaning forward to read a road sign: ENTERING VIRGIN RIVER GORGE; CAUTION- WINDING ROAD, TRUCKS USE LOW GEAR. The Virgin River sliced its way through a mountain range some eighty miles downstream of Zion, exposing tilted gray and light-yellow strata that angle nearly straight up in a

Narrows of their own. His car enters the curving descent into the gorge to the accompaniment of a flash of lightning followed abruptly by a clap of thunder.

Every piece of news equipment in Springdale has assembled in front of Noah House, satellite dishes pointing up at a menacing sky, cables snaking, and cameras lined up in a bank in front of the statue of Noah. News vans display logos of each major network and microphones point at waist level as reporters mill around, not sure what they're waiting for.

Noelle pushes Melody's wheelchair down the corridor to the front doors where they see the activity outside. As they reach the door, she stops.

"Are you ready, Melody?"

"Yes, Miss Crane. I'm ready."

Noelle opens the glass doors, pushing Melody through as the throng gathers. She positions Melody a few feet from the microphones and Scott cues her.

"Good afternoon, from Springdale, Utah. My name is Noelle Crane. As I've been covering the Thomas Holmes story, I've gotten to know a very wonderful young lady, and I'm proud to say she has become my friend." She looks at Melody, thunder rolling in the distance. "Melody is very special to everyone in Springdale, and she's been left alone here at the Noah House while the rest of the children went on a cruise provided for them by Mr. Holmes, before he left."

Noelle turns back to the cameras. "You may have seen my interview with Melody a couple of days ago when she expressed her feelings and concern for Mr. Holmes. Since then, we all know what happened, and Melody was watching the news conference given by Dr. Kirshner, explaining Mr. Holmes' situation. She heard me say something that hurt her. I indicated to Dr. Kirshner that there was no hope left for Mr. Holmes, and it upset Melody very much. So she asked me to arrange for her to say something about it, and that's why we're here today. So, here's Melody, and I ask all of you, from my heart, to listen to what she has to say." Noelle walks over to her and positions the wheelchair by the microphones.

Inside the capsule Tom watches his monitor.

"OK, Melody, you're all set." Noelle backs away, crouching down so Melody can see her, and the crowd stills.

Melody looks at Noelle. "Thank you, Miss Crane. Thank you for letting me talk to everyone here, and out on TV." She turns to the camera. "Miss Crane told me that Mr. Holmes might be watching. If you're watching, Mr. Holmes, I hope you're feeling all right. I'm really sorry about what happened to your spaceship, and I'm very sad about it. I want you to know I'm praying for you, and how grateful I am for all the things you did for me, and for all the other kids. I know they're praying for you, too. I don't know if they're watching, but if they are, I wanted to say that I miss them and I hope they're having lots of fun."

Tom closes his eyes, overcome with the conviction that he had not spent more time with her. The magnitude with which he allowed his pain to diminish his life looms before him, casting blackness across his heart. In running from the pain of his loss, he avoided the very things his son would have had him embrace: children, afflicted or otherwise. He built hospitals and showered them with generosity, yet withheld the most precious gift he could have given. Himself. And still she is grateful to him.

The Noah House children have gathered around the TV by the ship's pool and watch Melody, pointing at the screen in excitement at seeing their friend.

Melody wipes her mouth with the scratchy sleeve of her sweater. "Even though I want to say this to everybody, I especially want to say it to all the children in the world who are listening."

A family in India, gathered around the TV, reads Melody's words, translated into subtitles.

"Mr. Holmes has done a lot of things for children all around the world who are sick, or hurt, or hungry. He lost his son, and it hurt him very bad, and I think he's tried to help us because he couldn't help Noah anymore."

Another family watches in Mexico.

"I think it's time we tried to help him, all together. Mr. Holmes, I made a picture for you." Melody raises up a few inches and pulls a paper from her lap, displaying it to the camera. It's a drawing of the solar system with a big orange Sun and planets around it, each with its orbital path. Where the Earth would be, however, she drew a bright yellow star.

"The Indians who used to live here a long time ago believed stars were living things that traveled through the sky and hunted and had a happy life. One of them was a mountain sheep named Na-gah. He climbed the highest mountain. It was very hard for him and he almost died trying, but his father was so proud, he made him into a star that would never move, to help other stars find their way. That was why the North Star stands still."

Camera flashes strike the picture as photographers position for a better shot. "I've always felt people were like stars, shining bright from inside and helping other people find their way. I think when all of us shine real bright together, we're like one big star, and maybe we can help you find your way back home." She strains to look at Noelle, who moves more into her view.

"Miss Crane said something on TV that really bothered me. She's a wonderful lady and didn't mean anything by it, but when she said there was no hope left, it made me very sad, and I got a little mad. I don't want to be disrespectful to Miss Crane, or other grown-ups, but I don't think they should say there's no hope. My Mommy told me that when children pray, God listens real hard to hear us because we're little, and He treats our prayers like they were special."

Back at the Noah House, camera crews let their equipment run and stand frozen.

"I learned in church that when more people pray about something, the louder God hears it. So what I wanted to say was, tomorrow night at eight o'clock, which is my bedtime, I'm going to say a special prayer to help Mr. Holmes, and I'm going to shine as bright as I can. And I'd like all the children in the world to do the same thing at the same time. Maybe it will help. Maybe God will hear us, and do something for Mr. Holmes. And for all of us."

She looks at Noelle and at all those staring in heavy silence. Noelle walks over and crouches down beside her, placing her hand on Melody's shoulder.

"Thank you, Melody. I'm sure everyone who heard what you said will try to help you and Mr. Holmes. I know I will." She turns back to the cameras. "Melody is right. It's not my place, or anybody's place, to give up hope for someone else no matter how hopeless it seems. I, too, believe the prayers of children are special, and I also believe that children are the hope of this world, and of our future. I think we can all agree that the grown-ups of this fragile planet have done enough damage, and have not preserved or made a better world to pass on to Melody and all the children like her. We all owe it to them, and ourselves, to let their prayers, and their hopes, and their shining, guide our way." She looks at the crews, then back at the camera. "Noelle Crane, Springdale, Utah."

Noelle rises as it starts to rain, turns Melody's wheelchair, and pushes her back into the House. After the doors close, everyone stands still.

Tom watches this strange scene. The cameras still live, pointed to where Melody was. The screen dissolves to a CNN anchor, who turns solemnly toward the camera. Tom reaches over and turns off the monitor, looking outside at the Earth, now visible as a globe through the window. He picks up the phone and enters a number.

Inside Noah House, Noelle shakes the rain off her jacket, her hair drooping from the downpour. A phone rings in the background and she looks at Melody, feeling something's different, though she can't quite put her finger on it. Until she realizes Melody is completely dry. Roberta leans out of a door with the phone in her hand, a surprised look on her face.

"Melody, there's a phone call for you."

Noelle wheels her over as she looks at Roberta, and Melody takes the phone. "Hello?" Her face lights up. "Oh my gosh! I can't believe you called! Did you see me on TV?"

The Noah House kids are beside themselves about seeing Melody. Isabel and Nonna, standing on the deck just outside the lounge, watch through the glass in dazed uncertainty at the transpiring events as Walter runs up to them. "Did you see? Did you see that? Melody was on TV! I know Melody! I met her once!" Isabel touches his shoulder, unable to respond.

He runs off and Nonna looks up at Isabel, who looks away and says, "What's going on here? It just all seems so... out of control. How are those kids going to feel when nothing happens?"

"Careful, darling," says Nonna. "Your lack of faith is showing." Isabel walks over to the railing. The Sun prepares to set on the sea as it hides behind a cloud bank, darting shimmering rays of pink and red on the water, a glowing ring of fire in the center of peaceful stratus. She puts on her sunglasses, awaiting the sun's blinding farewell yet to come in the sliver of sky just above the horizon.

Sid, Scott, and Noelle sit in the churning water of the Driftwood's poolside jacuzzi as a light rain falls, spattering into the bubbles. Noelle sips a glass of wine, Scott a beer, and Sid keeps trying to light a damp cigar, his Bic on empty. The sound of a wrought iron gate opening and rattling shut doesn't even evoke a glance. A pair of crooked, hairy legs come into view, a bathrobe is thrown on a lounge chair, and the arrival steps in. As he lowers into the water, Bud brings with him a pipe and settles in without saying a word. Sid stops trying to light for a moment as he looks, barely believing his eyes, then continues his futile effort. Noelle takes another sip.

"Bud," remarks Sid.

"Light?" Bud offers, flicking his silver lighter and easily producing a vigorous flame.

Scott laughs out loud, and Noelle looks up to where the Moon sits brightly in a break in the clouds, but only for a moment as lightning flashes and the growing storm retakes the sky.

It's a cold, clear, blustery morning at Rockefeller Center, the familiar street corner outside NBC's Today Show studios. Katie Couric stands on the sidewalk, wrapped in a full-length black wool coat. When the camera light comes on, the crowd cheers, waving the usual array of signs. She's sequestered a man wearing a T-shirt with Melody's drawing silkscreened across the front. Under the picture is an 800 phone number.

"Matt, I've got a fellow here, Dan, Graffet was it?"

Graffet, long gray hair and beard, responds confidently. "Yes, ma'am, that's right."

"I see you've got a shirt on that has the picture Melody Baxter showed us in her press conference yesterday. What's going on here, Dan?"

"Katie, I own a business where I make and sell T-shirts, a silkscreening business, and when I saw that wonderful little girl, I decided to print these up. There's a toll free number here, as you can see, and I'm giving all the profits to a fund for her so she can donate it to whatever children's charity she wants. Anyone can just call this number, and we'll send them one for eight dollars. Six of it will go to the fund."

"I see. And how many of these did you make up?"

"As many as people want. God's been very kind to me, and I'm happy to give some of it back. That's got to be the bravest little girl I've ever seen."

"I have to agree with you on that. And you can count me in for one." She presses her earpiece. "And Matt says he'll take one too." She turns to the camera. "Well, as you can see, the story just keeps right on going," she says, holding up the T-shirt. "Any of you who want one of these just call Dan here at 800 555 5263. And Melody, if you're watching, I think I can get one for you."

Graffet leans into the shot. "I already sent her a case."

"I see. OK, back to you, Matt."

Noelle, wrapped in a towel and untangling her wet hair, is frozen in mid-brush, caught when she began watching the piece with Couric. The shot shifts back to Matt in the studio and she resumes brushing, shaking her head as she walks back toward the mirror.

A substantial part of the Virgin runs through the Holmes property and, having left the canyon, meanders in gradual loops through the parunuweap. The storm has subsided, but the sky is still dark and rain will begin again soon. Sam, sitting by a small rapid, throws stones into the water, plopping them into pools formed by tree trunks and boulders. Matt appears on the opposite side but says nothing, joining in with the target practice. They hear splashing downstream where the river turns a bend out of sight and look in that direction as Billy approaches on Cirrus, maneuvering upstream through the water's edge. Cirrus makes his way between them and stops, bowing to drink.

"Good morning," Billy says.

Sam only nods.

"Hey, Billy."

No one feels like talking. Billy looks up at the clouds. "We haven't seen the last of this one yet. Tall Tree says it's a warrior storm." Matt looks up. "Pow wow tonight on the Watchman. You should come."

"Maybe we will, if it don't rain," Matt replies, still looking up.

"It won't. Tall Tree wouldn't call it if it was." Billy continues upstream as Sam and Matt look at each other, then resume the stone throwing.

Bud pumps a cup of coffee from the dispenser at the Driftwood kitchenette. Sid enters, bundled up and chilled from the wind outside. He pulls the stocking cap off his head and ruffles his hair. Bud looks different, dressed in jeans and a thick brown corduroy shirt, in fact almost identical to what Sid is wearing. They look each other over, obvious patrons of the same souvenir shop clothing rack.

"Hey, good morning," says Sid.

"Morning."

Sid fixes another coffee. "Boy, that wind cuts right through, doesn't it?"

"No kidding."

"You never said what brought you back here. I was really surprised to see you."

"Yeah, well, not as surprised as I am. I just... I had a few things to take care of."

"What things?"

Bud takes a sip. "It's personal, actually. Nothing to do with Holmes, or any of that."

Sid stares at him. "No?"

"No. Not directly."

Sid lays a hand on his shoulder. "I know. I'm not here for that reason either."

Bud stares straight ahead as Sid walks away. That's surely the most personal they've ever been, and that thought alone bothers him, as does nearly everything else lately.

The Shack compound is still manned by federal agents. Bud pulls his car into the entrance and is blocked until the guard recognizes him and lets him through. He gets out of the car and stands, looking at the small building. The last time he was there he never entered, giving chase to Holmes. Still unsure of his reason for coming, he walks up the creaky wooden steps and opens the screen door. Before he enters, he looks in.

Bud crosses the threshold and closes the door so it doesn't make any noise, then looks at the faded room. A gray overcast finds its way in through yellowed sheers and partially closed shutters, the glow from the table lamp standing as a sentinel to a life that once existed, memories not his. Even the sound of his breath intrudes on the etherial silence. Bud knows the details about the Holmes family, but they've always been parts of a dossier, profiles of people, backgrounds. For the first time he feels something of what happened. He senses the warmth from a young family, the beginnings of a life, and the end of it all. Each artifact, each momento, a picture on a shelf, old magazines in a rack, whisper of the people who lived there. Real people.

Bud walks to the kitchen doorway and stops. The kitchen is small, barely enough room for a table up against a peeling wall with three wooden chairs, one still turned out. On the windowsill there's a dried-out mason jar with skeletons of wild flowers drooping over the edge, the wrinkled petals laying where they fell long ago. Bud stands there and looks at it all, piece by piece.

The door to Noah's room is ajar and Bud presses it open, stepping in. A frigid wind passes through his heart as the sorrow of a little boy leaving his room for the last time envelopes him. Now he understands what Holmes was running from. Here in this room, Bud is a father again, the father of another lost son. He backs out quickly, sensing he's trespassing on another's grief.

Bud walks back into the living room and after looking around again, sits on the couch. He closes his eyes, drifting back to a distant life.

The vision is yellow-hazy, a backyard with grass, trees and sunshine. A swingset squeaks in the distance and a little boy leaps off and runs to Bud, who scoops him up, holding him over his head as the boy giggles and pulls on his nose. Bud hugs him, puts him down, and watches as Rusty runs back over to the swings, motioning for his daddy to come push.

Bud lowers his head and weeps quietly.

Noelle walks down the corridor with a brown paper bag in her hand and turns into the Starbridge, expecting to find Melody, but sees only Roberta who looks at her with frightened eyes. "She's out on the patio. I'm worried. She's not herself."

Noelle hugs her. "We have to be strong. We have to, for her."

Roberta wipes a tear. "Please, you go to her."

The patio opens onto a grassy field with the aged willow hovering over. Melody stares out toward the field, watching as a man in a brown suit with a felt hat walks away. Noelle stops, wondering, then tightens as Melody starts coughing. Noelle rushes up. "Melody, honey, are you OK?"

Melody tries to catch her breath. "Could you get me a tissue? They're over there on the table." Noelle hurries and pulls the last few tissues from a box sitting on a picnic table and gives them to her. Melody dabs her mouth. "I'll be all right."

Noelle hands her the bag. "I brought you some cinnamon toast. Mike over at the Bumbleberry said it's your favorite when you go there."

"Thank you, Miss Crane. I really do love it, but I'm not hungry right now. I'll have it later."

"Sure, honey." Noelle takes the bag and sets it on the picnic table. A dark fear rises as she blinks back another flood of desolation. "Are you sure you're OK? How do you feel?"

Melody looks back across the field, pausing to notice empty corn stalks bobbing in the gusty breeze. "Actually, I'm kind of happy."

"That's nice. Any particular reason?"

"Mommy came to visit me last night."

Noelle's grabs the edge of the table, her knees buckling. "Your Mommy? What do you mean?"

"She came to see me in my room last night. It was kind of late, but I didn't mind."

"But your Mommy, she doesn't usually come to see you at night, does she? Maybe you dreamed it," Noelle says in hidden panic.

"No, I wasn't dreaming at all. I was very much awake. In fact it was right while I was saying my good night prayers. She was looking really well, better than I've seen her in a long time. But she didn't stay long."

Noelle covers her eyes. "What did she say?"

"She told me she was going away for a while, and that she loved me very much."

"Is that all she said?"

"No, she told me it was my time. That soon I wouldn't be hurting anymore, and to get ready for that. Then she just went away." Melody contemplates her mother's quiet arrival and departure. "I was really happy to see her." Noelle fights back yet again the sting of tears and begins to shake, looking around. "So, I want to be all ready. And I was hoping you could do me a favor."

Noelle tries to mask the muted terror of it all, dabbing her eyes with the napkin from the bag. "What is it, honey? What do you want?"

"I was wondering if you would go buy me a new dress. There was a really special one in the window of the store next to the market. I saw it again a few weeks ago when Roberta let me go with her. It's all white, with red lace along the bottom, and Indian beads around the collar. I have some money saved."

Noelle looks to the sky for strength, then back to Melody. "Of course, Melody. I'll get you the dress. And don't worry about paying for it. It's my present to you. I want to give it to you. Is that all right?"

"That's very generous. Thank you. I'd like that."

Noelle stands up, leans over, and kisses Melody on the head, closing her eyes. "I'll go get it and bring it to you. But you eat something for me. Promise?"

Melody tries to look up at her. "I will. I promise."

Noelle walks away, tight lipped, driven by a cyclone of love, fear, anger, and confusion.

Tom sits in thought, staring at his monitor. It shows a close-up of the lunar surface in vivid detail, shining so brightly he has to squint. He relocates Zion by ripping the cat's velcro belt from the mating pad attached to his leg and reapplying him to the one on the wall, evidence that the logistics of cats in space have been evolving. Zion has become accustomed to the absurdity of his various positions, as cats tend to do.

Tom drifts over to the window and stares at the growing Moon. In spite of the disaster that befell him, he's still overwhelmed at this accomplishment, and humbled, having dreamt of it all his life, as did Noah. He draws back, moves over to a locker, and opens it, pulling out a small backpack covered with Jetson characters, and revealing behind it the canister and the Book. He reaches out and touches them, then closes the locker.

From the backpack, Tom pulls out several objects. First, a Pez dispenser with Speedy Gonzales's head. He pulls the head back, launching a Pez slowly toward him and catching it in his mouth. Pez in space. Truly a first, he thinks as he takes out a cassette tape, looks it over, sticks it into a cassette bay and pushes *play*.

All the games are played and the songs are sung,
Dinner's over and I'm in the tub.
I better hurry and get one more hug,
Before it's time to sleep.

Sleep, gonna close my eyes and sleep,
Until it's morning time.
Sleep... before it's time to sleep.

Tom remembers this was Noah's favorite bedtime song.

He floats through the open bulkhead door into the pressure lock, a narrow corridor spanning the width of the capsule, opens a locker, and carefully pulls out a spacesuit, gold-faced visor and all. The only act Kirshner performed that could be considered criminal was to use his access to the Smithsonian vaults to "borrow" a training suit from the Gemini 4 mission. After positioning it to one side, he reaches further in and extracts a coil of umbilical cable, then looks the suit over, unfolding the arms and making it presentable.

> I've had a drink of water and a story told,
> I've got my blanket to keep me from the cold.
> The light is out and the curtain's pulled,
> It'll soon be time to sleep.
>
> Sleep, gonna close my eyes and sleep,
> Until it's morning time.
> Sleep... it'll soon be time to sleep.

Tom enters the flight deck, reopens the locker, and reaches in. This time he pulls out Theo the bear, turns him around a couple of times and lets him go. Tom taps one leg, rotating Theo slowly, and it occurs to him how happy Noah would have been to see his best friend as a space traveler, spinning like that.

This thought draws him back again to the days of his family, he and Noah, and Francine, when life was so simple and so full. No longer able to put off what he knows he must do, Tom reaches in and takes out the canister, holding it in both hands. He moves over to the console and lets it go, watching as it floats in front of him, then picks up the phone and enters a number.

> My mama loves me, that is plain to see,
> My Daddy loves me sittin' on his knee.
> Their love grew and it created me.
> Now it's time to sleep.
> Sleep, gonna close my eyes and sleep,
> Until it's morning time.

Sleep... now it's time to sleep.
Now it's time to sleep.

Francine is picking at a salad when the phone rings. She looks over at the answering machine and lets it answer, her outgoing message short and detached. After the tone there's silence, followed by, "Hey Francie, it's Tom. I guess I missed you."

She lunges for the phone, knocking the handset to the floor. Finally getting hold of it, she answers, "Tommy? Is this really you?"

"How are you?"

"How am I? How are *you*? That's the question."

"I've been worse. A lot worse."

"Where are you?" she asks.

"Where am I?"

Francine rolls her eyes. "I know, blonde question. Remember those people that went around saying there was never an Apollo mission? That it was all a big hoax, done in a TV studio? This time I wish it were true."

"I need you to know I didn't want it to end up like this. I knew it might though, and, well, that's the way it goes."

"You know, Tommy, I'm heartbroken. Of course I am. But there's part of me that knows you did something you really needed to do. And I know you well enough to know you're at peace with it. I can't say I understand why you did this, but I'm proud of you."

"Thank you. Of all the people in the world, I knew you would understand."

"Don't get me wrong. I miss you, and I can't imagine this world without you in it. But then again, there are other worlds, aren't there?"

"You bet there are." Tom looks out the window, then back at the canister rotating slowly in front of him. "There's something I have to tell you."

"Go ahead."

Tom pauses. "I've got Noah here with me."

Francine covers her mouth. For a moment she can't speak. "Oh, Tommy."

"I know. I'm sorry. I had no right."

"No. No! Don't say that." She reels from the shock of it, from the thought of her son's remains racing toward the Moon. "Now I understand. Now I know what you've done. I know what you're doing. Excuse me for a moment."

Francine drops the phone down on the counter and doubles over, then takes a tissue from a box and wipes her eyes and face. She recovers enough to pick up the phone. "You really did it. You made his dream come true."

Tom chokes back a flood. "I don't know, Francine. I don't know where his dreams are. But I do know that what's left, what we have left of him, will finally rest where he always wanted to be. At least I can give him that much."

"Tommy, you must know we have more of him than that. You have to believe he's still with us. It's the only thing that's kept me alive."

"I wish I could. I'd give anything to feel him, to see him, to sense him near me. But the only thing I've felt for all these years is the emptiness of a world without him. There's nothing of me left here. Wherever he is, I can't find it, no matter where I go."

"Just look in your heart, Tommy. That's where you'll find him."

Tom stares at the canister, then looks out the window at the edge of the Moon and into space. "If I knew where my heart was. But he took it with him, Francie. He took it someplace with him."

Francine's voice breaks like glass. "I pray for you. I pray you find that place. And when you do, say hello for me."

"Goodbye, Francine. I love you."

"Goodbye, Tommy. I love you too."

The phone disconnects and Francine walks out onto the balcony, slumps into a chair, and lets her own flood go.

Noelle stands in front of the shop Melody described to her, looking at the dress. Of all the shops in Springdale, Barry's sits back behind an ancient oak, the frontage visible to those who know to walk up the crooked stone path. It's a Victorian home, the living room converted to a simple but warm establishment for purchasing handmade clothing. Helen Barry, an elderly woman with a smile of ages, approaches Noelle from around the verandah.

"Oh! Miss Crane! What an honor. I've been watching your stories on television. You were so sweet to our little Melody."

Noelle extends her hand. "Please, my name is Noelle. The honor is mine. And your name?"

"My goodness, how impolite of me. I'm Helen Barry. I've lived in Springdale all my life, and my grandparents before that. They were one of the original settling families here," she says with a soft glow of pride.

"What a wonderful life you must have had, growing up in this beautiful, peaceful place."

"Wouldn't trade it for the world. Although, I must say it hasn't been too peaceful around here lately."

"I know. And let me personally apologize for all of us who've invaded your life."

"Not at all. We're only sorry it ended up so badly. Tommy Holmes is a wonderful man. He and his family used to come into my store when they were, well, when they had nothing. But, oh were they happy. And that darling little boy. Such a tragedy."

"I can't imagine what it must be like to lose a child," Noelle says from a place hidden in a corner of her.

"I lost my daughter when she was fifteen to polio. My God, if I could have shot myself to the Moon, I'd have done the same thing. But, what can we do? We have to keep going, somehow. That's how we keep them alive. In our memories."

"I'm terribly sorry."

"No, please. I'm sorry for going on about it. Is there anything I can help you with?"

"Yes, actually. I came to get that dress in the window."

"That's Melody's dress," Helen says gravely.

"She asked me to get it for her."

Mrs. Barry looks at her, and the unspoken truth of what

that dress represents passes between them. She enters the shop, reverently takes it from the window display, and looks at it, stroking the coarse white material. She disappears, then walks back out with a plastic bag in her hand.

"She always comes to visit it. I've had many offers to sell this dress but I always kept it for her, bless her little heart. How that poor thing has suffered." She looks at Noelle. "We've all prayed for the day when her suffering would end."

"She seems to think that day is near." Noelle reaches into her purse, but Helen stops her hand.

"No, please. I would never take money for this. I always wanted her to have it. As many times as I've offered to give it to her, she would never take it." She folds the dress with loving kindness and slides it into the bag. "Somehow she thought she'd be able to save enough to buy it. I guess she finally did."

"Actually, she agreed to let me get it for her."

Helen stops. "Then she must care a great deal for you." She extends the bag to Noelle. "Give her my love."

Noelle takes it, touching her hand. "I will. And thank you, from Melody." She walks out, and Helen clenches her fists over her heart.

President Stamp sits at his desk, looking over one of Graffet's T-shirts taken from an open case on his desk. The intercom buzzes. "Mr. President, Dr. Cole is here."

"Send him in, and have Faith come in also."

The door opens and Margaret ushers in Dr. Cole as the President stands to greet him. He puts the T-shirt on over his long sleeve shirt, then pulls two more shirts out of the box and hands one to each, decreeing to Margaret, "Go ahead, put it on."

"Now?"

"Why not?"

Margaret pulls it over her dress, messing her hair in the process, curtsies and leaves the room. Stamp shakes Cole's hand, and Cole makes a sheepish query with the shirt. "Not necessary. I only have executive authority to make fools of my immediate staff. And myself, of course." He picks up a few more shirts. "Amazing. A real tribute to free enterprise, don't you think?"

Cole agrees out of courtesy. "I suppose. Either that or crass opportunism."

"Now, now, Terry. I had a conversation with Mr. Graffet myself. This is truly for charity and we're glad to help here at the White House." The door on the other side of the office opens and Faith Neumann enters, a statuesque thirty-year-old with long, straight, fire-red hair, also wearing a T-shirt. "Doctor, Faith Neumann, one of my public affairs liaisons. Faith, meet Dr. Cole."

"Of course, Dr. Cole. I'm a great admirer."

"No, please, let me do the admiring."

Stamp wags his finger. "You better watch this old fox. He thinks women are impressed by his huge brain." Cole is embarrassed as Faith smiles at him. "Well, down to business. I asked Faith to give me a briefing on the public reaction to this Holmes business, and I wanted to get it straight from you what's going on with the technical end."

"Well, Sir, I'm afraid there's no hope for Mr. Holmes."

"So I've heard. But I wanted to be prepared for how this is all going to end."

"My understanding is that with the solar power array he has, the capsule will remain functionally habitable for years, with the exception of the oxygen supply. He'll have about another eighteen days of that remaining."

"When it runs out, will he suffer at all?" Faith inquires.

"No. Actually, he'll gradually get very tired and fall asleep. That's about all there will be to it."

The President walks around his desk. "Will anybody know when that happens? Aren't there usually monitors?"

"Usually, yes, but not on this mission. He wanted none of that."

"I see. Truly, no hope at all."

"No, Sir."

"Well, I'd like you to work with Faith here and formulate

some appropriate way to handle this, from the viewpoint of NASA and the White House. I'll have to make a statement, eventually. Somehow, I'd like something positive to come out of all this." Stamp turns to Faith. "Faith, you know I was concerned over Melody's statement to the press. It was very touching, naturally, but her cry for help was disturbing. What can you tell me about public reaction?"

"Well, Mr. President, I brought a videotape the communications staff put together of TV news broadcasts around the world. If you were disturbed before, I'm not sure how you'll feel now." She walks over to the VCR and inserts it.

"The world media jumped all over this, as you would expect." The tape begins playing, muted, showing a news broadcast from Russia. Though the commentator's words can't be heard, Melody's picture appears. This cuts to an interview with a little Russian girl. "This girl in Moscow says her mother is going to set the alarm clock for three in the morning so she can get up and say the prayer."

Next, a scene at a school in Africa where a class of fifth-graders are painting a wall-sized mural of Melody's drawing, followed by an interview with a man in a business suit. Faith turns the sound on with the remote. "Jack Wilson. Fortune 500 top ten."

Wilson speaks. "Last night when I heard Melody Baxter's request for prayers, I put out a statement that I'd donate one dollar to the Unicef fund for every prayer a child wrote. I've gotten thirty-eight hundred letters already in twenty-four hours. I'd like to encourage children all over the world to do this. My offer stands." Faith fast forwards the tape and they watch scenes of children and newscasts hurry by. She resumes *play* on what appears to be a computer screen.

"This was to be expected. An Internet site was anonymously set up: www.melodybaxter.com. It already received forty-six thousand hits in less than a day from all over the world. There's a directory with thousands of prayer letters they're undoubtedly forwarding to Wilson. I think he's in for more than he imagined."

Jonathan smiles. "Jack can handle it. He's worth more than

most third-world countries."

"My Lord. The Superhighway. Little Melody's on it, and she doesn't even know," Dr. Cole says.

"Do you want to see more, Mr. President?"

"No, I think I get the picture. Let's just hope she doesn't decide to run for President. Then again, maybe we'd all be better off." Laughter escapes from his guests, followed by eyes darting away.

Noelle's car pulls in front of the Noah House and she gets out with the dress bag and a bouquet of flowers. The weather is moving in again and wind gusts around her, buffeting her hair and clothes. She stops a moment to stare at the statue of Noah.

Inside the Starbridge, Melody sits quietly reading a book propped on a music stand when Noelle enters. She lights up. "Hi, Miss Crane. Did you get it?"

"Yes, I surely did, right here."

"Oh my gosh! You did?" Noelle pulls the dress out of the bag and delicately extends it out. Melody touches the material as if it were made of spun gold. "I've never seen anything more beautiful in my life. Thank you so much."

"You can thank Mrs. Barry. It's a gift from her."

"Mrs. Barry. She's always been so kind to me. She promised she'd save it, but I didn't think she would actually give it to me. What a big present to give somebody."

One would think she'd been given the royal gown of a princess instead of a simple, inexpensive cotton dress made for a pittance by Native Americans on a reservation. To Melody, this is indeed a royal gown, and once again Noelle is convicted of her own perceptions, centering in the depth of that conviction.

"You're right. And how beautiful it will look on you. Oh, and I brought you these." Noelle produces the bouquet, withered and drooping, composed of tiny wildflowers gathered around a few miniature sunflowers, all surrounding one tired red rose. "They're not doing too well, but it's all the market had this late. I hope you like them."

This time Melody is overcome and speaks in a trembling voice. "Oh, Miss Crane." She reaches for the flowers. "They're beautiful. No one's ever brought me flowers. You'd think it was my birthday."

"We'll just call it your... unbirthday."

"Like Alice! It's my very merry unbirthday! Maybe I'll get to go through the looking glass and come out in Wonderland!"

"If anyone deserves to be in Wonderland, sweetie, it's you. Would you like to try the dress on? I can help you."

Melody ponders. "I don't think so. I'm not quite ready yet. Maybe tomorrow."

"Whatever you want, angel. I've got a dinner date. Would you like to come with me?"

"No, thank you. Roberta made me some spaghetti already. It's my favorite. Next to the cinnamon toast, I mean. But you have fun. Will you come see me tomorrow?"

"Of course I will. I'm thinking of going to that nice little church tomorrow morning, but then I'll come over."

Melody moves her wheelchair toward the window. "Maybe I'll see you at church. I go sometimes, if I feel good enough. Right now I don't feel very good. Mommy told me she'd see me there, so I think I'll probably try."

Noelle looks down in fear. "That would be nice. Goodbye then, Melody. I love you very much." She takes Melody's hand and kisses it.

"Thank you so much for everything."

Noelle walks out, once more having to bolster herself. This foreboding wellspring of choking emotion that began when she met Melody has come to the point that the slightest encounter engages her heart in a battle between weeping and unexplainable joy. She walks out of the House and stops again in front of the statue, looking up at it and the boiling sky behind Noah's outstretched hand. Another wave crashes over her as she suddenly senses his presence where she hadn't before. She looks down, her emotions manifesting in an eddy of swirling leaves, and a short outburst of tears cleanses her as it passes through.

Looking westward from Watchman plateau, the few scattered lights of Springdale reflect off a low overcast that filled the canyon halfway up the cliffs. Lightning radiates in random spots, faint explosions from above, glowing through the clouds. Thunder echoes off the canyon walls, but rain is still not there.

Noelle and Sid approach the door to 211, laughing at something said during dinner. They stop at her door and a sweet quiet fills the moment. Noelle takes his hand. "Dinner was very nice, thank you. I needed that. It's been a long time since I was out with anybody."

Sid lifts her chin with his other hand. "You know, if a girl thanked you after the first date in high school, that was the kiss of death."

Noelle leans up, kisses him softly on the lips, and ends the kiss with a stroke of his cheek, looking him in the eyes. "Was that the kiss of death?"

"More like the breath of life," Sid says, light-headed from her touch. He kisses her back and they melt away, then return as their lips part in warm billows of breath. "Want to call it a night?" he asks, hoping not.

"Not really. I kind of get room fever here after dark. I sit in the room and look out the window, and it's just black. But I feel this enormous, majestic canyon towering outside, as if I can feel the shadows of those huge walls weighing down on me. Sound a little looney?"

"I know exactly what you mean. Last night I woke up at three in the morning and sat straight up in bed. I don't know what woke me, but I had this urge to step outside, so I did. I just stared at these giants all around and suddenly I could breath easier. I swear, I almost heard them whispering."

"The Paiutes who lived here believed everything had life. Rocks, mountains, everything. Legend has it each of these great mountains was once a brave warrior in heaven their God Tobats placed here when he made the Earth. They called the Earth Tu-weap."

"How do you know all this stuff?"

"I was just reading about it. Melody gave me a book."

Sid hesitates. "Listen, want to go on a little... adventure?"

Noelle makes a half-scared, half-smiling face. "Adventure? I don't know, Agent Knowles."

"Come on. You're an investigative reporter. I'm an investigating officer. Let's do some—"

"Let me guess. Investigating?"

He pulls her by the arm. At first she's barely moveable, then tilts and allows herself to be dragged off.

Watchman Trail is black-dark but for the flickering ray of a police-grade Maglight from behind a bend, becoming a hand-held light shaft as it turns the corner. Noelle fusses, pointing her own Barbie flashlight, a pencil beam compared to his. "Now *this* is looney. I'm not so sure—"

"Shhh! Shush now, Miss Crane. You'll wake up the rocks." She glowers at him, pushing him forward.

They negotiate a steep little switchback and come upon a flat stretch of trail that passes under an outcrop of deep red rock, cracked in large, checkered patterns. It forms a natural shelter, imposing in its stillness. Sid moves his flashlight up the rock face, inspecting the fissures. "Moenkapi formation."

"What?" Noelle asks, staring at him.

"I bought this great book today. It's called *Sculpting Zion*. If you look across the canyon during the day, you'll see this layer. It sticks out, different from what's above and below. It's dark red and has this pattern. Look."

She contemplates his observation, following the beam of his light, then looks back at him. "Well, I'm pleasantly surprised."

"If I remember right, it's about two hundred fifty million years old. Used to be mud at the bottom of some sea." He stops to look back at her and aims the light in her face, his heart blinded by the flash of green from her eyes. "Surprised? Why?"

"I mean, surprised in a good way. I didn't think you were into… appreciated this kind of thing. This is coming out all wrong."

"I'm listening."

She scratches her nose. "It's just that, I've been trying to figure you out. In the time we've spent together, I'm seeing a side of you that doesn't fit the… It's you and that Meyerkamp. The two of you seem like—"

Sid touches her lips. "Let me take it from here. Seem like… Laurel and Hardy?" She spits out a laugh through his fingers, which he wipes on his coat.

"I'm sorry. I'm embarrassed," she says, trying not to laugh.

"Mutt and Jeff?" Laugh turns to giggle. "Dumb and Dumber?"

This time she snort-laughs. "What the heck was that?" he says, imitating her snort.

Noelle belts him on the arm. "Stop it!" She fumbles her flashlight and traps it with her arm, causing it to shine straight up her chin, making the campfire monster-face.

"Oh!" Sid exclaims.

"What?"

"It's the campfire monster-face. You're really scary. Yikes."

Noelle crinkles her forehead at him, still shining the light up. "Campfire monster-face? What are you talking about?"

"Come on. Are you trying to tell me you didn't do that on campouts?"

"I never camped out. Where do you camp out in Nebraska? Let me see... the *flat place?*"

"Well, what about sleepovers? You know, the fuzzy slipper, up-all-night, hair-in-curlers, giggle fests with your girlfriends? No sleepover monster-faces?"

"Who are you, and what have you done with Sid?"

Sid stares at her. "Here, watch." He shines the light up his chin and makes a ridiculous face, more like he's about to throw up than any monster.

Noelle stares, blinks a few times, then comes out with a halfhearted, "Aaaaa."

"Pretty scary, huh?"

"No, not really. Unless you call seeing your nose hairs scary. I guess that's pretty scary." This time he belts *her* arm. "HEY!" she protests with a startled laugh, rubbing her arm. "Are you just a little psycho?" She walks under the overhang and sits on the ground with her back up against the rock wall. "Sit down here before we start throwing punches."

He complies, snuggling up next to her, to her pleasant surprise though she's trying not to show it. Noelle reaches in her purse and pulls out a small candle in a glass holder and lights it with a match from the restaurant. Sid's eyes get big. "That's the candle from the restaurant table," he accuses.

She looks at him, leaning slightly away, shrinking. "I'm going to bring it back. I swear! I just wanted it for tonight. I love candles and the one I bought broke." He looks at her with a one-eyed squint. "It's not stealing if you're going to bring it back. Is it?"

"Larceny. It's a misdemeanor. The wrongful trespass of another's property without consent. It doesn't matter if you intend to bring it back. You've committed a crime, Miss Crane." He rubs his chin. "Won't that look great? 'ABN anchor-princess jailed for heist at local restaurant. News at eleven.'"

Noelle looks at him like he's lost his mind, or she's losing hers. Same look either way. "Well, gee. Are you going to arrest me then?" He reaches behind his back and produces his handcuffs. She looks at them, then back at his impish grin. "You're going to *handcuff* me?"

"Why? You like being handcuffed?" This time she really hauls off and thumps his arm. "OK, OK. Truce. I might actually need this arm tomorrow. Good grief. You've got quite a right hook there, Missy," Sid complains, rubbing.

They sit quietly for a moment, watching the flickering candlelight dance off their rock shelter. Noelle asks softly, "So, really now. What got you paired up with Meyerkamp? Why are you still out here? Why are you a cop?"

"Agent. Please."

"Sorry, Agent... Mutt."

Sid smiles, but gets a little serious. "Actually, I'd been behind a desk too many years. Right out of the academy, I got recruited into forensics, mainly because I got a Ph.D. in microbiology. DNA research was my specialty in grad school."

Noelle is truly amazed. "Are you serious? A Ph.D.? I'm impressed. I'm... Wow."

"Oh, don't be too impressed. Ph.D. stands for 'piled higher and deeper.' I know a lot about every cell in your body, but I spent too much book-time, missed out on a lot. I don't know much about people. It was time to get out in the world, be a real... 'cop'.

"Agent."

"Right. So, Meyerkamp needed a partner. He goes through them pretty fast."

"I can imagine."

"He'd rather work alone, but they force people on him. Try to keep him... tamed a little. So, I volunteered. Bud's actually a pretty good guy when he lets his guard down, which is almost never. He's been through a lot, and he's got a good heart in there. Reminds me of Dad some. Anyway, I heard he was working on something out here and I wanted to see this place. It's hard to explain. I knew I had to come here. I didn't even know why. Now I understand why."

"Why?" Noelle asks, really looking at him.

He scratches at the dirt with the handcuffs. "I lost my dad last year. He went into congestive heart failure and I realized how much I'd taken him for granted. We never got along very well, all the typical things between an overbearing father and a perfect son," Sid says, shaking his head. "But we had time to start all over again, at least for a few weeks."

"I'm so sorry, Sid," she says, taking his hand. "My brother had the same thing going with my father. Daddy passed away before Jimmy, my brother, made it back from overseas. I never saw Jimmy cry until then. Always the tough guy. He still hasn't gotten over it, the regret, what he wanted to say. People wait until it's too late. Nobody comes and knocks on the door and says, 'Hey, it was all just an act. It didn't really happen. Now you get to do it right.'"

"No kidding. I got lucky. My dad and I became friends. He's the one who told me about this place. He always loved it here and I never listened to him. Now, I do. I feel like he's here with me, and I decided life's too short to sit behind a desk. So, here I am. Sitting with a sexy criminal under a rock. Isn't life great?"

"And here I was really getting to like you. Now I'm not so sure."

"Hmm," Sid contemplates. He shines the flashlight back up his nose. "She likes me..." He feigns pulling a hair out of his nose, flinch and all. "She likes me not." Noelle looks at him in utter astonishment. He pretends to pull another. "Ow! She likes me."

"Yuk! Stop that!" she demands, laughing against her will. He does it again, to accompaniment of another blow to the arm. "Dork!"

He looks at her like *she's* the psycho. "Brat!"

She gets an *oh-yeah*? look on her face, glancing sideways. "Creep."

"Goof."

"Butthead."

"Supergoof."

"Peabrain."

"Nobrain."

She barely falters. "…Pizzaface."

He looks truly insulted. "Skank."

"*Skank*?" she horrifies.

Sid rethinks. "Sorry. Withdraw skank. Replace with… perfect angel," he says, really meaning it.

She smiles.

They finally reach the top and walk onto level ground of the plateau. "Look at this view," he says, pointing to the widening canyon and the lights of Springdale below. The clouds have parted in places and the moon's glow feathers them. Where the night sky is visible, stars shine brilliantly in patches.

"That's the most beautiful sight I've ever seen," Noelle says as a burst of wind nearly pushes her over.

"Dad used to do this to us when we were driving at night. It scared the daylights out of us, pardon the pun."

"More flashlight games?"

"Watch." He holds the flashlight out in front of them like a headlight, then turns it off. Darkness falls from the sky and Noelle shrinks into his arms.

"Now that's scary. In an awesome way." Sid turns her toward him and they drift into a passionate kiss. Still in the kiss, Noelle opens her eyes to half-mast and notices a faint glow from behind a knoll on the trail ahead. It takes a moment to sink in, especially since her mind, and lips, are elsewhere. When it does, half-mast goes to full wide-eyed stare. She pushes off the kiss, leaving Sid in tranced confusion.

"Sid?"

"What?"

"Over there. What is that? That light."

He's forced back to the world, unwillingly. "Light? What light?"

Noelle grabs his shoulders and turns him around, pointing. "That. Over there."

He scans, then sees what she's talking about. "You're right.

It looks like a campfire. Let's go check it out."

As he starts to walk, she grabs him. "Sid! What are you doing? I don't think we should go over there. We don't know who it is."

He looks at her with a pout, tapping his side. "Did you forget? You were just necking with an Officer of the United States, and he's packing. Now, come on." Once again he drags her along, giving her the *shhh* sign.

They walk half hunched-over to a boulder that sits on top of the knoll, around which the trail continues toward the sight of the glow, Sid sliding to the edge. What appears to him when he pokes his head around is indeed a campfire, bordering on a bon-fire. The most striking figure is Tall Tree standing across the flames, wearing only deerskin pants and war paint. He stands with his arms folded, staring up at the sky. Four others sit around the fire with their legs crossed and blankets around their shoulders. Sid strains to see who they are, finally recognizing Matt, and then Sam. He turns to Noelle.

"It's Brown and Clifton. Holmes' people. And that Indian from the rock house. Take a look."

Noelle creeps around the boulder, surveys, and returns. "That's Tall Tree. Scott was telling me about him. He's a Navajo, not like most of the Native Americans around here. Scott ran into him taping some footage of that house. Tall Tree stopped him, some-thing about stealing the spirit of the house with pictures."

"I heard they don't like cameras."

"He got talking to him and found out he was adopted by Paiutes because they killed his father by accident. I think Tall Tree said when you kill somebody, other than war, you owe their family an honor. You have to take some honor from your own family and give it to the son. So they made him some kind of priest, or medi-cine man. Whatever it is they are."

Sid takes her hand and leads them toward the fire, ap-proaching slowly. Billy sees them and rises, at first suspicious, then realizing who they are. He taps Sam, pointing, and Sam spots them and stands also. Matt notices and turns to look, but doesn't bother, turning back. When they're within a few yards, Billy gestures. "Welcome. Come, join us."

Throughout all this, Tall Tree hasn't moved, still staring up. The fourth figure, Robert Linden, stands and walks toward them, extending his hand. "Good evening. My name is Robert Linden." He shakes Noelle's, then Sid's hand.

"Noelle Crane."

"Sid Knowles."

"I am very honored to make your acquaintance." He points to his spot. "Please. The two of you share my blanket. I have another for myself. Please."

Sid and Noelle sit down with the others, wrapping themselves in the blanket. Linden gets another, sits a few feet away, and silence resumes as all stare at the buffeting flames. Sid and Noelle look up at Tall Tree, then rest their heads together, feeling the warmth from the fire, and the warmth from each other.

Zion floats serenely, tethered to the ceiling and looking through the passage to the pressure lock. An arm appears, an arm enclosed in a spacesuit, then a leg, and finally Tom, missing only the helmet. Zion arches his back, not an easy maneuver in weightlessness. Once he realizes it's Tom, he looks curiously at this strange sight. Tom moves himself over to the console, enters commands, checks parameters on the screen, then looks at the cat, reaching out a gloved hand which Zion paws at. Tom floats back into the pressure lock and out of sight. A vault-like door slides across the opening, clunks shut, and on the face of the door, symmetric stainless steel arms connected to a wheel turn and snap overcenter, sealing off the control deck.

All sit quietly looking at the fire, listening to the crackling of burning brush until, without warning, Tall Tree raises his arms straight up, then arcs them down to his sides. Tall Tree turns his back to the fire and Billy stands and walks up behind him, facing the rest. He touches his back to that of Tall Tree, who raises his arms waist-high, palms up. Tall Tree speaks in Navajo as Billy translates.

"Narrogwenap, the storyteller, died, and his spirit blew into the rocks. Ioogoone, the Canyon, speaks."

Noelle and Sid look sideways at each other.

"In the long time ago, the people before our people, who were the Anasasi people, lived in Tavi Maus Wintook, the Land of the Setting Sun. There was no food, or animals to hunt, or skins to wear. After many times, they left the caves to search for a new land, the land of Tavi Maus, where the Sun rises.

"Four hundred plus twice forty moons they traveled, and Tobats, the Ancient of Days, appeared many times, once as a rabbit, sometimes as a bullfrog, in many living things. He told the people of our people that in Tavi Maus all things would be theirs, the food, the animals, and skins. But the people did not believe and they complained.

"Then Shinoh, the son of Tobats, also spoke to the people saying that Tobats was tired of their complaining, and that he had given them everything. All once was rock, but he had put in the fire and the water so that things would live, and things would die, and there would be food to eat and water to drink.

"But the people would not stop, and they traded with Unnupit, the fallen warrior, and Unnupit Ruan, his demon warriors, and many died and fell to the ground. The land turned dark with blood and sorrows made Tavi, the Sun, hide. So Shinoh told the Great Warrior Tureris to shoot from his magic bow an arrow of fire into the sky. Through the canyons and mountains and rivers of the sky they would follow the arrow to the Land of the Rising Sun.

"The people followed the arrow and they came to Ioogoone, this canyon. But they complained again, and after they had the annual cry for the dead, Unnupit told them Tobats had lied and closed the canyon so they could not find Tavi Maus. Then Unnupit became a coyote and howled, laughing at them for believing Tobats.

"When Shinoh heard all of this, he came to Ioogoone as a wolf and chased Unnupit away. But Shinoh was angry with the people. So he took the son of Tureris, whose name was Tu weap-Toatsen, Son of the Earth, cast all the stars into his eyes, and called him the Child of Skyeyes. Without the old stars, the people could not find the Land of the Rising Sun.

"So Shinoh the Wolf told our people that from that time on, he would keep the Child of Skyeyes with him. And that Tureris would paint this story on the skin of a white deer, and when he was an old one, he would give the skin to a new child, the flesh of his flesh. That child would look for a sign in the sky, and if he found a sign, he would take the skin of a white deer, and all his life think of how to show the Wolf his people were sorry. He would put on the skin the story of what his people had done to show Shinoh they found the Truth of Life, and bring the skin to the burning trees at the end of his days, and the Wolf would see the story.

"If it was the Truth, the Wolf would give the Child of Skyeyes to the people, the old stars would return to the sky, and they would find their way to the Land of the Rising Sun. If it was not, then the next child would take the skins and do the same, until the Truth was told.

"So it has been for many people of our people. The stories have been told, but the Child of Skyeyes has never been seen. Chief Sunman Whitewater gave the Book to the flesh of his flesh, Little Spirit Set Free. But Little Spirit was taken away before his time.

"Our people are scattered with the wind. Like the wind, no one knows where they have gone." Tall Tree's arms raise up again, then come straight down to his chest, across his heart, and he bows his head.

"It is finished."

Tall Tree walks away into the darkness, firelight painting his back until he disappears, as if flickering out. Billy does the same in the opposite direction, leaving the others to stare into the fire. Their minds wonder what has been said, and their spirits wonder what has been felt. And what is it, that is finished? Matt and Sam stand and walk away. Noelle and Sid remain huddled under the blanket.

Noelle stares into the fire, transported by the legend into

constellations of her memory, the firmament of her life. Patterns formed by events, choices made and not made in the vacuum of self, that place where all ultimately confront their decisions. Her heart draws cold as she's struck by a falling star from her past.

Sid doesn't notice, trying to make sense of magic arrows through the sky and a talking wolf. Robert Linden stands, walks over to Noelle, and bends to one knee. She turns to him, her eyes glassed over with regret too deep to allow tears to pass. She looks into his eyes and everything stops; her heart, her breath, the universe. Sid looks at him, still not knowing where Noelle has gone.

Robert Linden speaks softly as he touches her hand. "You are forgiven. She sends you love, and sends you peace." He stands and walks away.

Sid remains lost, confused by Linden's words as he watches him disappear into the cavernous night. He turns to Noelle, about to ask what Linden meant, when he sees she's collapsing inward. Fear strikes at him, somewhere new, that place she has taken in his heart. A place he just found.

Sid reaches toward her, feeling himself pulled into the black hole of torment that has enveloped her, but she stands and runs over to the edge of the plateau, and there bends over and leans with her hand on a boulder ten times her size. Sid runs after her and stops a few feet away.

"Noelle?"

She shakes, nearly convulses. "Oh my God. Oh..."

Sid pales. "What? What is it?"

"My God. Sid." She struggles for breath. "He knew. He knew what I was thinking. He knew I was thinking about her."

Sid walks a step closer. "What? What did he know? I'm getting scared."

Noelle turns and Sid nearly folds at the sight of her, a fusion of terror and revelation looking out at him. The three feet between them is the span of creation, and the silent moment, eternity. Noelle glazes over. "I knew all along, it was a girl," she groans as the tears finally find their way. "She was a girl... and she sends me peace. She forgives me." Noelle runs to him, falling into his arms, crying so hard she brings him to the verge of his own tears. "Noelle... tell me. Who forgives you?"

She breathes in long, gulping breaths, lifts her head, and looks into his trembling eyes.

"My daughter."

"Your daughter? You have... you had a daughter?"

Noelle looks up at the patches of stars, only blurred streaks through the tears. "Yes, I did." She grabs her hair, grimacing. "I aborted her at four months."

Sid closes his eyes and for the first time in his life, feels the true pain of another person. He rests his chin on her head. "Oh, Noelle. I'm so sorry." She backs up, wiping her face, and puts her hands in the pockets of her jeans.

"Do you know what it's like to secretly hate yourself, every day of your life? To spend every day of your life in regret? Fighting off the urge to justify something so terrible that the thought of it blacks out the Sun?"

Sid turns away, then turns back. "But... you must have had a reason, Noelle."

She marches up to him. "It doesn't matter if I had a reason!" Noelle shouts, beating her fist on his chest. "It doesn't matter what reason!" Another fist to the chest. "I did it! That's what matters! I killed my daughter!" She turns away. "My sweet angel. My ballerina... My best friend. The most precious gift God ever gave me."

Noelle drops to her knees, then all fours, crushed down. "Oh. Oh, Jesus, it hurts so bad." She falls to her side, then rolls onto her back. Sid kneels beside her, taking her hand as a tear falls from him. "Noelle—"

"This world I didn't want to bring her into is a paradise, because love lives here. And I took that from her. I deprived her of my love, a love God gave me, to give to her." She covers her eyes with her arm, afraid to look at the stars, each one an eye of the Almighty. "All these years one thing has tortured me more than anything else. I didn't even give her a name. I didn't even do that. The ultimate betrayal. I took her life, and didn't even give her the dignity of a name. God help me," she cries.

Sid is swept over by an anger he can't explain, a searing white-hot dagger through his heart. He grabs her by the arms and sits her up. "Right now. You name her right now."

Noelle, lost in her agony, tries to focus on him. "What? I,—"

"Now. Do it. Just like those Indians you admire so much. Look around at this world, and give her the name she's always had."

Noelle shifts her startled gaze upward, and blurred stars sharpen as she blinks tears from her eyes. "Celeste. Her name is Celeste."

"Celeste. That's wonderful. It means Heavenly. It was my grandmother's name."

Sid looks around at the plateau, a barren landscape on a planet of grief. The trees, the rocks, all wait for his response, demanding he listen, and understand, and rescue her. In their stillness, he does. In their silence he hears her message. He rises and lifts her to her feet.

"Noelle, listen to me. I can't say I understand what happened here, but you have to listen. He said she sends you peace. That means she's alive. Celeste lives. Somewhere, she sees you, she loves you. Just because you can't see her dance, doesn't mean she doesn't dance for you, in your heart. She's still your best friend, because she knows how much you love her, how much you've always loved her." He lays his hand on her tear soaked cheek. "She did what friends do. She forgave you. Now, honor her. Forgive yourself, and take the peace she sent you."

Noelle looks up at him, embraces him, and they cry it out together.

In the Starbridge, Melody has made a small altar on top of a wooden crate and placed there a candle, a vase with the flowers Noelle brought her, and her Bible, which lays open on the music stand. She lights the candle with a weathered book of matches, stops to stare into the flame, then glances over to the clock on the wall, seeing it's a few minutes before 8:00 P.M. She wheels herself over toward the light switch by the door, but stops halfway and covers her mouth, coughing so hard her eyes water. Melody regains her breath, continues over to the switch, and turns out the lights, leaving only the glow of her sanctuary across the room. Melody is shaken by the violence of that coughing spell, and on her way back erupts into another, this more frightening than the first.

Roberta is watching television when she's struck still by the sound of the coughing, something she's not heard from Melody for a long while, something that brings a choking fear to her. She runs toward the sound.

Roberta arrives outside the Starbridge, but before pushing the door open, looks through the glass and sees Melody arriving at her altar. She looks at the wall clock, realizing the time for Melody's prayer has come. Not wanting to disturb the moment for her, Roberta retreats back down the hall, takes a chair, and places it outside the door, sitting secret watch over her frail charge. She pulls a string of worn pearls from her sweater pocket and closes her eyes.

Outside, a deluge drops from a microburst, plummeting torrents of rain that strike the patio so hard, they bounce up a layer of splattering water a foot high. Lightning flashes the Starbridge every few seconds, one clap of thunder on the heels of the next.

Melody touches the pages of her Bible, then presses her hands together, putting the tips of her fingers to her lips, and also closes her eyes.

Tom is in the pressure lock, closed off from the control cabin by the bulkhead door. He has the helmet on, his face barely visible through the gold shield, and has locked his umbilical into the receptacle. Tom turns toward a switchbay shielded by a plexiglas panel and slides the panel clear, revealing a guarded button. He lifts the guard and pushes it, causing a red light to flash. In the pulsating glow, the words "Pressure Release" appear on a placard, and "Armed" flashes in the button next to it. He presses that button and a muffled hiss accompanies bits of debris dancing around him.

When the hissing stops, he shuffles sideways and looks directly above where he reaches up and slides open a panel labeled "Hatch Release". A T-handle appears which he pulls until a green light illuminates next to the hatch. Tom reaches up to the round hatch with both hands and grabs the wheel. He hesitates, but finally turns it, and along with the turning a series of levered arms move inward, releasing the door latching pins. At the end of the wheel's travel, the hatch springs downward. He pushes another button in the overhead panel and the hatch drops down a few more inches, moving along its track and unfolding a sweeping blanket of stars. Tom hovers motionless as the hatch reaches its limit and stops. He is struck both by the vision, and the fact he survived depressurization. He shuffles down the narrow passageway back to a locker, removes the canister, placing it in a mesh bag attached to his suit, then moves back to the hatch and looks up again.

Children on the ship have gathered, including those from the Noah House, and formed a circle, holding hands around the ship's minister. Heads bow, and shortly after, Isabel enters from a side door. When she sees the circle in prayer, she stands behind Walter and places her hand on his back. He turns partly around and half opens his eyes, smiling when he sees her.

The first light of day arrives in a children's bedroom in Africa where several sleep together. Mother enters the room, waking them gently, pointing at the clock. They sit up in bed and clasp hands, the youngest unable to stay awake, flopping back down on his pillow, though his hands stay clasped.

A one-room schoolhouse in India bustles with activity, children of all ages working projects or playing. The teacher reminds them of the time and they return to their seats and also pray as silence falls over the room.

Most of the Maui Village Elementary School students have

gathered in the auditorium after school. Melody's drawing is projected onto a large screen.

The capsule appears larger than Earth, about to set behind the lunar surface that now passes ever swiftly by. The hatch is open and Tom's helmet appears as he pulls his way up the ladder. He continues until he's halfway out, then stops. At the position he came through the hatch he was facing Earth. He feels, however, an intimidating presence behind him, and turns around to see the Moon, so close he feels he could touch it, even reaching his hand toward it.

Tom and the capsule are dwarfed by a lunar sea directly above. At fifty thousand feet, rilles and mountains and craters are daunting geological formations. Stark, knifing shadows cut across landscapes of devastation, the gray, gritty world of extremes, no compromise between light and dark; where the Sun strikes and where it doesn't, the difference between melting heat and shattering cold. Only the matter of rock and dust survive. Yet, it is elegant chaos. There is majesty in the boulder-strewn battlefields of time, symphony in ejecta fanning downstream of ancient impacts, momentary catastrophes with no one there to marvel in the silence of eternity. Such thoughts, without words, pass through Tom, the language of awe.

With the Moon gliding by, Tom pulls himself all the way out and floats, facing the surface. There he is, Earth's first civilian to reach this frontier, a common explorer across a sea of empty space, his ship offshore of uncharted land. And how lucky, and thankful, he feels. Tom knows in his heart that someway, somehow, he shares this unspeakable moment with Noah.

Dr. Kirshner pets his dog as he stares at the overhead monitor, showing a view from the capsule toward the lunar surface. In the foreground, the umbilical floats in and out of view. The intercom buzzer sounds. "Yes?"

Sam's voice answers, "It's me, Doc."

"Hold on."

Kirshner pushes the lock release, the sound of the door opening followed by Sam's heavy footsteps coming down the stairs. He appears with a quizzical look on his face, lighting up when he sees the dog. "Hey! Schultzie!" He lifts Schultzie from Kirshner's lap and strokes his head. The Doctor looks at this pair, a small dog dwarfed by a gigantic man, and manages a smile. "So, what was it you wanted to tell me?"

Kirshner points to the screen. Sam looks, unsure what he's supposed to see, then notices the cord. "No way. That's not what I think it is. Tell me it's not."

"I'm afraid so."

Sam shakes his head. "I can't believe he really did this. And everything's OK?"

"So far."

"Is he plugged in? Can you talk to him?"

"Do you mean, can *you* talk to him?"

"Me? Well, yeah. That would be incredible."

"I think he can hear me, but he hasn't responded. In a few minutes he'll be on the other side and we'll be in signal loss."

The Doctor points to the push-to-talk switch on the console and gestures for Sam to try. Sam, still unsure, starts to reach, but stops. "Wait. Is all this going... out?"

"No, we cut off the network feed before he went EVA. Go ahead, give it a try."

Sam cautiously pushes the button. "Hey, buddy, it's me, Sam. Can you hear me?" There's only silence. Then, Tom's voice.

"Hey, Sam. I hear you. What's up?" Tom's helmet comes into view, upside down, as he maneuvers himself in front of the camera.

"What's up? You, brother. You're up. *Waaay* up."

"Boy, tell you what. You should see this. I wish you were here."

"They don't make space suits that big. If I were up there, they'd have to classify me as a heavenly body."

"I'm sure there are a few young ladies down on Mother Earth that would agree with that."

Sam smiles a smile as wide as his heart. "I've got to say, Tom, except for this one major disaster, you've really done it this time. I still can't believe you're not..." Sam can't bring himself to say it.

Tom's transmission is fading. "I can barely hear you. I think we're about to go black. Just hold your thought until I come out the other side."

"Hey, brother, I've been black all my life, and I know how it affects communication." Tom's voice is but crackling static as the picture on the monitor turns to snow. "I guess that's it."

"For thirty-eight minutes and twenty-four seconds. Normally it would be shorter, but because of his trajectory, he'll be in the shadow longer."

"What's he going to do back there, anyway?"

Kirshner hesitates, looking at Sam. "A funeral."

"What did you say? A funeral?"

The Doctor puts his hand on Sam's great shoulder and leads him toward the stairs. "Come, let's get a cup of coffee and I'll tell you about it." As they climb the stairs, Sam looks back and up to the monitor, staring at the snow as he leaves.

The Moon draws closer, blanking out the heavens, itself a gray-brown sky as the capsule races toward its point of maximum gravitational encounter. Tom, using handles positioned on the exterior, pulls himself to a compartment door, four-feet by three-feet. He removes a tool from a pocket of his suit, secured with a tether, and inserts it into a recess in the service module near a corner of the door, then turns it one revolution and does the same in a recess at the opposite corner. After replacing the tool in its pocket, he grabs hold of a handle and turns it until it unlocks, opening the door. He reaches in and slides out a platform holding a scale model of the Apollo Lunar Excursion Module, the Spider, as its original designers affectionately called it; a clumsy, boxy contraption, functionality at its homeliest, and here true to smallest detail, gold foil-wrapped landing struts included. Releasing latches secured to each landing strut, he frees the LEM, also attached to the capsule with an umbilical, and allows it to float off the platform. Inside the compartment door there's a control panel he activates with a master arming switch, illuminating a green light near a key pad. Using a pencil-like object attached to it, he enters commands into the system. The LEM's position lights come on as well as a tiny floodlight that illuminates the top section. Tom pulls the LEM closer and rotates it so the top faces him, exposing a cylindrical cavity.

Francine sits at the edge of her bed and holds in her hands her favorite photo of Noah, the one where he sits joyfully in a supermarket coin-operated spaceship, squealing as it rocks him. In the photo, Tom crouches behind the little astronaut, his hand on his back for safety and support, looking at him with adoration. As she does nearly every night, Francine wipes her eye, then reaches to put the picture back on the nightstand, but stops as something stirs. Instead, she places the picture under her pillow and lays her head on it while looking out the glass doors to the moonlit ocean outside. Francine closes her eyes, searching for what peace sleep occasionally gives her.

Tom has taken the canister from the mesh bag and stills over his son's remains, trying his best to say a final goodbye. Though very little has made sense since Noah passed, this moment, to which the entire effort was directed, makes the most. How one agonizes over the death of a child, agony that writhes and swirls around unanswered questions, unfulfilled dreams, feelings of failure, the abyss of never-ending loss. All the things Tom was never able to give his boy. Well, here, now, in this great adventure, one simple dream of a little son is to be made true. In such a sad way, Noah made it to the Moon.

Tom clutches the canister to his chest, then slides it into the fitted cavity of the LEM, pushing it down until a spring locks it in place. He rotates the LEM, removes the umbilical, plugs it into the control panel, and pushes the LEM away. Tom enters commands into the panel that bring up "LEM SYNC" on a digital display. A few more entries flash "ATTITUDE ALIGN".

The LEM has drifted some 30 yards, the capsule shrinking against a canvas of stars. Tiny bursts of air from control jets erect the LEM parallel to the lunar surface.

Tom makes another entry, this time annunciating "DE-SCENT ALIGN". He turns to see the LEM against its backdrop of passing craters, rotating to a deceleration attitude, its engine facing the capsule and angling the LEM downward. The final command: DESCENT BURN.

The LEM's engine ignites, and it shrinks slowly in the distance.

Tom closes his eyes as the LEM disappears to a pinpoint, and he drifts away to images of Noah, Francine, and himself during their times as a family, some individual portraits, some together; Noah's birthdays and other precious moments of his short life, and the brief but treasured memories they shared. Tom remembers a song he heard after Noah died.

> I think I'll go to Heaven,
> There I will lay me down.
> Leave all the pain behind me,
> Bury it in the ground.
> Maybe they'll talk about me,
> I pray it won't be lies.
> Tell them I went to Heaven.
> Heaven is in your eyes.

When the LEM reaches a few hundred feet above the surface, the canister ejects and tumbles in partial-gravity slow motion, end over end. It hits the surface, spraying a cloud of moondust, bouncing back up with it.

> I think I'll go to Heaven,
> I heard it's peaceful there.
> They don't allow your troubles.
> Everyone's had their share.
> When I can be someone who,

Never needs a disguise.
Then I will be in Heaven.
Heaven is in your eyes.

As the canister tumbles, the top opens and Noah's ashes fling into a rotating pinwheel, mixing his remains with lunar dust raised by the impact, and they slowly settle back down, forever.

People in Heaven,
Never look back.
Higher and higher,
The past fades to black.
I think I'll go to Heaven,
Sail on into the night.
Watch as He sets my spirit free.
Watch as my heart takes flight.

Maybe I am too simple,
Maybe I am too wise.
Maybe I'll go to Heaven.
Heaven is in your eyes.

Tom finds himself standing on Main Street in Disneyland. Looking down, he sees he's dressed as he was before he donned the spacesuit, but the suit is gone. It is night; no one else is there. The streets are wet, the glow of lampposts reflected in the shining pavement, but there's no rain. He stands still, not understanding.

Tom looks around, then down the street toward Main Street Plaza. This place is so familiar to him. The times he came with his son flood back to him, the joy on the little boy's face, the spinning frenzy of the crowds, the parades. But none of that is here now.

A dream? No, he knows dreams all too well. Hardly asleep, he feels more alive than life itself; all at once there is no boundary to him. He is everywhere, and nowhere. He is.

Has he passed, he wonders? Oh, God! There's no breath in him! He's not breathing! There is no air, yet he's still alive, beyond alive. There is no breath, yet he smells cotton candy and popcorn, but there is none.

Tom notices movement in the Plaza and begins walking toward it, hardly moving at first, barely able to feel his body, but then walking quickly, finally running. As he reaches the Plaza he stops, seeing what before was only a shadow. In front of him stands

Pluto, as he'd seen him other times, eight feet tall, walking among the crowd, but now he is different. The costume looks the same, but he's not smiling. Nor is he frowning, simply expressionless. Pluto looks at him, then turns and continues walking slowly toward Tomorrow Land.

Tom closes his eyes, wondering if when he opens them this will all go away. But he doesn't want it to go away. *Where in God's name am I?* He opens his eyes again, finding nothing changed, weakly backs up to a bench, and supports himself as he sits down, laying his face in his hands. Then in the faint distance he hears something that grabs at his heart, as if to make it burst. It's the voice of a little boy.

"Daddy! Come on! Over here!"

Tom freezes. It's the voice of a little boy, certainly. A voice that has haunted his mind and his soul in a wasteland where it's absence has become an intolerable, aching silence. It is Noah's voice.

"Daddy! Over here!"

Tom forces himself to stand, and he looks toward Tomorrow Land where the voice echoes. He begins walking, faster.

"Noah?"

Now he's running again, straining, dragging behind him years and years of heartbreak, and as he enters Tomorrow Land he sees another figure standing half in light, half in dark near a lamppost. This time it's Pinocchio, with the same expressionless face. Pinocchio looks at him, then turns his head toward Tomorrow Land. Tom stops again, watching, then looks where Pinocchio is looking, and sees in the distance something that has never been in Tomorrow Land.

True, there was a Rocket to Mars, ages ago when he was a child, long since gone before Noah was born. Now there's a different kind of rocket. It looks familiar, and yes, it comes to him. It's the rocket ship Noah drew for him so many times, now bathed in colored floodlights, standing a hundred feet high. But this one is real. Or is it? There's a crooked white picket fence around it, and inside the fence cartoon trees and flowers and fluorescent green grass, just like in the drawing. But that's not all. Standing in the narrow gateway of the fence, is Noah.

Noah waves. "Daddy! It's me!"

"Noah?" he asks. " Honey, is that you?"

Tom walks toward him in disbelief, not caring because if it isn't real, it surely feels that way, and that's good enough. He runs toward his son, who also runs toward him until they meet and Tom scoops him in his arms and embraces him tight, closing his eyes, though the tears pour out. Noah hugs his father's neck and as Tom kisses his cheek, he cries, "Oh, Noah. Oh, my God. I've missed you so much."

"I love you, Daddy."

"And I love you, son. I love you more than you'll ever know."

"I do know, Daddy. I do."

Tom puts him down and looks at him, seeing he's dressed in a shiny jumper with rockets and planets and stars all over it. The thought by now occurs, as inconceivable as it all is, that he's wearing his favorite one-piece pajamas, transformed into a little boy's spacesuit, a transformation which surely took place many times in Noah's dreams. Tom looks around, reeling in confusion. He sees, rising from the vibrant green grass, a flagpole. Waving briskly at its top is a flag of Melody's drawing, this impossibly wonderful touch charged further by the fact he feels no wind at all. He stares at his boy, not knowing what to say.

"I... I'm so confused. I don't understand."

"I know, Daddy. Don't try to. Not right now."

"But I—"

"Daddy, I came to tell you I don't want you to be sad anymore." He leads his father over to a bench. "Here, sit down."

Tom sits and looks into his son's eyes, searching as Noah sits next to him. "I want to believe this is really happening. But, lately—"

"You're wondering about the things you've been seeing. Like the boy in Grandpa's shop."

If there were air, Tom would gasp. "You know about that? But, how—"

"It's inscape. That's what the poet Hopkins called it."

"Inscape?"

"Julia told me about it, near the end when she was teaching me how to write poems. It's being able to see what something really is. The true nature of it."

Tom stands and walks a few feet away. He leans forward, his hand on one hip, then turns around. "Why?"

"After, I saw how you and Mama were, and I asked him to help you. He gave you that."

"Who did?"

Noah doesn't answer. Instead he looks over at the rocket. "It's time for you to go on with your life now."

Tom walks back and sits again, placing his hand on Noah's leg. "Son, how can I go on? How can I?" Anger wells up in him. "You died the day before your ninth birthday."

"No, Daddy. I was born again on that day." Noah looks through Tom's eyes, beyond. "I died on September eleventh. I died on November twenty-second. I died on December seventh and October first and August sixth and August ninth and July twenty-seventh, and a thousand times thousands of times."

Tom closes his eyes, not knowing, yet somehow understanding, somewhere new. Noah reaches up with one hand and touches Tom's face with the other, and Tom is shot through with a flash of light, unlike any light he's ever seen, this from inside. The light explodes into a spectrum of colors, spreading like glowing rivers through the veins of his soul.

Noah stands and faces him as Tom opens his eyes. "Things are different here, and someday you'll know. We pray in colors, we hear in wonderful dreams, we see in love, we feel in music."

"Noah, my precious son. Help me. Help me understand."

"You wanted to know about silver."

"Yes. Yes I did."

Noah smiles a bright smile, sparkling. "Remember when I was four? I asked you how a mirror worked, how I could see myself in it?"

"Of course, honey. It was in the basement. It was that old

stand-up mirror. You kept walking around the back, expecting to find yourself on the other side."

"Yeah, and there was a crack at the bottom. So you took a screwdriver and pulled off the glass and showed me it was just silver. It was the silver, like magic. Ever since then it was my favorite color, because it's like both black and white at the same time. It's a color, but really it's all colors because everything's reflected in it. It becomes whatever is in front, and makes a whole new world behind. It makes us see ourselves, our world, in a different way. I saw you and me standing there that day, and for the first time I saw how much you loved me. I saw it in the mirror. It was in the silver."

Tom closes his eyes. "Thank you, Noah." He hugs his son again. "What do I do now?"

"You'll know what to do, Daddy."

"But, I can't get back, I—"

"You'll know."

Tom spins inside, falling. "What about Mama?"

"Mama knows."

"What do I say about this? Am I supposed to tell anybody?" he asks, falling faster.

Noah looks into his eyes, and there Tom sees a righteous anger coming through from somewhere, from someone. An anger infused with love, an anger so dark and at the same time so full of light that Tom grips the bench as if he'd be blown off to oblivion.

"Tell them to stop it. Stop the killing. Stop the hurting. Tell them to wake up and treasure every moment, before it's too late." Noah looks up at the rocket and then down to two characters standing on each side of the gate; one, the Sorcerer's Apprentice, the other, Tinkerbell. Mickey motions with his wand. "I have to go now."

Tom panics, getting on his knees. "No! I can't let you go again! I can't!"

Noah looks back at his father. "Remember when I used to ask you what heaven was like?"

"I would say it has to be perfect. Whatever anyone would want it to be, then that's what God would give them."

"You said it was different in each person's eyes. I always remembered that." He looks back at the rocket, and once more at Tom. "Don't forget, I'm part of your heaven, too." Noah strokes his father's hair. "Live every day like it was your first, and your last. And realize that the measure of your life isn't how many breaths you take, but how many times your breath is taken away. Please, be happy. For me."

Tom embraces Noah one last time. "I promise I will be. For you. And for me, too."

"I love you, Daddy."

"And how I love you, Noah."

Tom lays his forehead on the little boy's chest and lets the tears flow, then pulls back and sees them running silver, like liquid mercury, laying on Noah's suit. In them he sees reflected his sorrows, all the sorrows of men, and shining back, the exaltation of rebirth and of reconciliation. And in them, he sees himself reflected. He is a child.

Noah takes Tom's face in both hands. As Tom looks up, he sees sky in Noah's eyes. Bright blue sky with perfect clouds. Noah lets go and walks over to the fence where his two companions gently touch his shoulders, then turns back. "Tell Mr. Meyerkamp that it was 'Yagi'."

"Yagi?" Tom responds, wiping the silver tears from his eyes with the back of his hand.

"Rusty's first word. It was their Siamese cat, Mr. Miyagi. He saw him jump on the couch and pointed at him." Noah is escorted to the door of the rocket. He enters, stands in the doorway, and looks back. With a cheerful wave he says,

"I'll see ya later, Daddy."

Tom waves back and watches as a hand, then forearm, appear from inside the door, those of a young girl. Dancing in and out of the doorway is the hem of a cream-white dress. Noah looks up at a face that Tom can't see, takes the hand, and disappears as the doorway dissolves into the side of the ship. Tom stares, unable to move. After a moment, streaks of colored laser light blast out from under the ship, bouncing in all directions, followed by a spectral burst of steam and sparks that blind him as he partly covers his eyes with his arm. The ship appears to lift off, but really becomes engulfed in the blaze of surrealistic light. Tom buries his head in his arm.

Francine sits on the edge of her bed, eyes closed, sobbing, the picture clutched to her chest. Her tears, however, evidenced by the brilliant smile on her face, are tears of joy and gratitude.

Roberta has fallen into a deep sleep in the chair outside the Starbridge. She's suddenly awakened and looks around, then hears a bloodcurdling sound, that of bones snapping, as if some giant were cracking his knuckles, and it's coming from the Starbridge. In fear, she rises, moves to the door, and slowly opens it. When her eyes adjust to the dark, they fill, and her mouth drops as she covers it, motioning the sign of the cross with her other hand.

"Oh, dear Jesus! Melody!"

Tom floats outside the capsule, back in his suit, his eyes closed as if in sleep. He slowly opens them and as he regains his bearings, turns himself around and faces the capsule, cast against the Moon. Around the moon's approaching edge is a glow, one he knows to be an impending Earthrise. Tranquility has overtaken his sorrow as Noah's works drift through him, washing it with the first peace he has felt since his son died.

As he watches transfixed, the Earth breaks the lunar horizon with a flash of earthlight that sweeps across him and the capsule. He pulls himself to the LEM compartment, closes it, locks it, and continues to the hatch, going in head first.

Zion hears noise coming from the other side of the door which opens with a hiss. Tom, his suit floating in the pressure lock behind, gropes in and pulls himself over to the chair as Zion watches suspiciously. He looks out the window at the bright Earth, and then, from the corner of his eye, catches something on the monitor. It's a flashing red annunciator: ERROR.

Inside Johnson Space Center, only a few engineers man screens at this hour. One of them looks puzzled and waves his colleague over. "Would you take a look at this?"

"What's going on?"

"It the Holmes vehicle. We just regained tracking on him."

"So? What is it?"

"Look," he says, tapping the screen with his pen.

The other looks intently at the screen, inputs a few key-strokes, and raises first one, then the other eyebrow. "This can't be right. Not from what they've told us." He motions to another. "Hey, Elmer. Come over here a minute."

Sam is slumped over in a chair, asleep, as the Doctor, his own eyes at half-mast, stares at his panel monitor. The path projection screen, showing the unfortunate trajectory toward the void of space, is frozen with a title underneath stating "LOSS OF SIGNAL" and a clock beneath it counting down from five minutes. As he watches, that statement flashes. The Doctor looks up at the TV monitor and sees it change from snow to a forming image of the Earth, static-riddled at first, then rendering into a clearer image. The panel monitor annunciates "SIGNAL REACQUISITION", and as it does so, the path projection begins bending.

"That's early," he whispers, feeling disoriented. With this, Kirshner's eyes widen. In the corner of the screen appears the same error message present in the capsule. As he watches in astonishment, the path projection bends until it reaches the figure-eight shape, stopping tangent with the Earth's edge. Kirshner sits straight up in his chair, then reaches for and pushes the transmit switch.

"Thomas, this is Werner, do you copy my transmission?"

After a few seconds, a ragged but intelligible response breaks through. "Yes Doctor, I hear you. About four by three. How me?"

"About the same, but it's resolving. How are you doing up there?"

The question has in its tone more than mere inquiry. Tom senses this. "Suppose you tell me?"

Kirshner hesitates. "I'm... not sure. Do you see what I see?"

Tom's voice also hesitates. "Are you getting an error message?"

"Yes, I am. Must have something to do with that path projector. Did you check it out yet?" Kirshner asks.

"No, not yet. Let's do that now. Let me know what you come up with."

"Roger that. Hold on."

Tom punches entries into the keyboard, and the "ERROR" is supplemented by "CODE 36". He pulls up another page displaying "MASTER ERROR CODES" with a numbered list he scrolls down until he reaches 36, titled "TIME SYNC". He highlights this, hits *enter*, and another screen appears titled "TIME SYNC DATA", also with an "ERROR" message flashing. The page shows two lines of running clock times, each out to 1\1000th of a second, the top labeled "Ground Elapsed Time", the one below "Capsule Sync". The capsule time is running some six minutes behind that of Earth. In fact, under the two clocks is annunciated: Minus 00:06:36.363.

"Doc, you still there?"

"Yes, Tom, go ahead."

"I've got a clock error here."

"I've got the same down here. I show your time base behind six minutes plus. How could that have happened?"

Tom thinks a moment. "I really can't say. I've had a pretty—" In mid-sentence he looks at his Marvin-the-Martian wristwatch and stills. There's liquid silver across his hand.

Kirshner's voice brings him back. "Yes? Tom? What is it? Are you still there?" Kirshner looks puzzled.

Sam has finally come around, bleary from a deep sleep. He rises from the chair and walks over beside the Doctor, stretching. With his lips he asks silently, *Is Tom back?* and receives a nod. Sam feels pleasantly surprised, though not sure why.

"I'm still here. If you can hear me, I guess I'm still... 'here!'" Tom says.

"What's the matter?"

"I'm not sure if you'll believe this."

"Try me."

"It's my wristwatch. It's six minutes behind your clock, too."

"You mean it matches the clock up there?"

A wave of static hisses through, then, "Bingo."

Kirshner looks at Sam. "It's that silly watch I gave him. I only paid nineteen bucks at Target for it," Sam explains, not understanding the look on Kirshner's face.

Kirshner's look doesn't change. In fact, he never takes his eyes off Sam. "I tell you what, Thomas. Let me think about this. I'll get back to you."

"Fine with me. I'm not going anywhere."

Kirshner lets go of the transmit switch. "I don't believe you are, my boy. I don't believe you are."

Sam stares the Doctor down. "What?"

"Sit down, Samuel." Kirshner moves the chair toward him as Sam looks anxiously at the monitor. "Please. Sit down."

The capsule streaks by, headed toward Earth.

Eden Cove

Star That Runs

CHAPTER FIVE

And when the rainbow steps emerged
Through clouds into Forever Land,
My Diamond Girl took both my hands
To bless my spirit with these words:

"The skies of all the days of men
Have gathered in your gentle eyes
To show us nothing ever dies
Where children's smiles and love have been."

A street of gold stretched out a path.
We walked along, each step a dream,
Along a singing silver stream,
Through fields of bright green Easter grass.

It took us through a yellow wood
Of chocolate trees and candy ferns,
Then 'round an ice cream hill we turned,
Before the Lake of Joy we stood.

Reflected in its golden shine
Forever City shimmered bright,
And from its gates a ray of light
Flowed rainbows from her eyes to mine.

I woke then to a gentle rain,
Back in my quiet room alone.
I looked around, I felt my home,
The Moon beamed through my windowpane.

Up above, the cartoon stars
Shined through a patch in painted clouds.
The pea-green boat lamp softly glowed
Upon the owl's still guitar.

God is a child, I realize.
He is like me, with sky for eyes;
His smile the light we travel by,
His love the wing that makes us fly.

He laughs, He cries, He runs, He plays,
His tears have washed our pain away.
He brought me Diamond Girl to say,
He'll see us on Forever Day.

Noah Holmes, Age 8

oelle is again in restless sleep when the faint glow of dawn invades the room. The phone rings, jolting her into the day yet again. She looks around, disoriented as the persistent ring grows louder with each burst, rubs her eyes, and sits up on the side of the bed. "This is getting to be a frigging routine. Who needs an alarm clock?" Noelle snatches up the phone. "Who is it, and what is it?"

"Miss Crane, it's Werner. I was wondering if you could come to my home as soon as possible."

She pulls her hair back, trying to wake up. "Is there something happening?"

"I'd prefer not to discuss it over the phone. Could you come?"

"I take it you mean... right now."

"If you don't mind. And please, no cameras."

"I see. As you wish. I'll be there as soon as I get dressed." Noelle hangs up with her finger, thinks, then enters a number.

After a couple of rings, Nauman groans, "Hello?" He looks like a hybrid of Nicolas Cage and Stan Laurel in the morning.

"Jeff, it's me. Is there anything going on, with Kirshner, or Holmes, or anything like that?"

"Not that I've heard. The capsule should be back in contact, but nobody's called me. Why? What is it?"

"Nothing. Never mind. I'll call you later."

"I don't get it. What—"

She hangs up, leaving him with his mouth open. He sits up and enters a number of his own.

Noelle's car pulls up in front of Kirshner's house to find a CNN van in front with an impatient reporter pacing, camera ready. She gets out of her car and walks toward the front door like she didn't see him. He heads her off at the front porch. "Never mind, he's not answering," he snipes.

"What are you doing here?"

"You haven't heard?"

"Heard what?"

"Oh, I see. It's not out yet."

Noelle takes off her sunglasses. "What's not out yet?"

The reporter gloats, "Our sources at NASA got the information for us. Must still be 'in house'. Just watch CNN if you get a chance. Isn't that where you get most of your story line anyway?"

She's tempted to strike back, but restrains herself. Instead, she walks up to the front door and rings the bell. The curtains protecting the picture window part, then the door opens to let her in. The reporter rushes up. "Dr. Kirshner, do you have any comment about this so-called hoax regarding the Holmes expedition?"

Noelle turns around sharply, indignant and confused by the question. Kirshner grabs her arm and pulls her in, glaring at the reporter as he slams the door shut. The reporter looks at his cameraman in frustration.

Thirty minutes later the front door opens and the crew outside, joined by several others, scurries to attention, cameras pointed. Noelle accepts a warm hug from Kirshner, who quickly withdraws, walks forward, and stops at the position for her statement as if it were marked. As soon as the first question flies, she holds up her hand.

"There are no statements to be made at this time. Dr. Kirshner will not have anything to say until a press conference to be held later today." She looks directly at the reporter. "Check your local ABN station for details." At this, she marches to her car, gets in, and speeds away.

Sid is watching CNN at the El Rio when there's a knock on the glass door. He moves over and opens it without taking his eyes off the screen until he realizes it's Noelle. She embraces him and doesn't release at the normal rhythm. When she finally lets go he sees something in her eyes, some giant, amazing secret. "Noelle, I don't know what's going on, but I'm liking it better every second. You feel like letting me in on it?"

They both turn toward the TV to see footage of Noelle walking away from the reporters at Kirshner's house. Sid senses the triumph in that walk and turns to her. "What are you up to, Supergirl?" They turn back toward the screen as the CNN anchor appears.

"To reiterate, there are unconfirmed, yet reliable reports from NASA that the Holmes capsule is in fact returning toward Earth, contrary to the scenario laid out by Dr. Werner Kirshner. As the entire world knows, he stated that Holmes was doomed on a trajectory toward outer space due to a malfunction of the capsule's rocket engine. This development has led to speculation that the entire story was some kind of hoax, a cruel one if true, considering the reaction by children around the world and their prayers for help. We are told by Noelle Crane of ABN, the only person Kirshner would speak to, that a press conference will be held sometime later today."

Sid turns to Noelle with a look of wonder. "No way."

"Very big way. Very big, and very real."

"But I don't—"

Noelle takes his hand in hers, tightly. "I'll explain in the car. Right now, we're going to church."

"Church?"

"Church. Don't worry, no lightning bolts for unattendance. A few *en*lightening ones, maybe. Come on." She leads him out as he scrambles for his key and barely slides the door shut.

Though the storm has passed on, left behind are billowing, threatening thunderheads, contrasted against a brilliant blue sky, trailing centurions heeding the land not to forget what has moved on. Rays of light streaking through the canyon from the rising Sun illuminate them and cast dark shadows beneath, shadows that crawl down the canyon and over Springdale like reverse spotlights.

Much of Springdale's population filters into Emmanuel Church as Sid parks the car. He gets out and runs around to open her door, helping her out. A frigid blast of wind cuts through as a shadow overtakes them, casting darkness over the church. Noelle pulls her sweater tighter and Sid puts his arm around her, both of them looking up toward the foreboding sky. "It's not over yet," Sid remarks.

She looks over at a canyon wall and the shadow that cuts across it. "'Even the darkness is not dark to thee, the night is bright as the day; for darkness is as light.'"

All he can say is, "Wow."

"They were my Dad's last words to me. It was his favorite Psalm. He was a pastor." Sid strokes her hair, looks into her eyes, and in that moment, falls in love with her.

The congregation doesn't notice Noelle and Sid take seats next to the aisle in the back pew. A frightening flash of lightning strikes, followed by thunder that rattles the stained-glass windows as rain begins spattering on the roof.

Pastor Neal stands in front. "Let's pray. Heavenly Father, as we gather before you today and hear outside this church the might of your power, we're reminded of the magnificent way you care for us. Even as the thunder and lightning frighten us, yet are followed by falling rain which cleanses and nourishes us, so it is, Father, that your great love and power bring to us righteous and reverent fear, followed by your gentle healing hand. Be with us today, Lord, and nourish us with the flood of your Spirit, that we might understand how much you love us. Amen." Neal addresses the congregation. "Won't you all please stand as we begin our worship today in song?"

As everyone stands, Patricia, sitting at the organ, begins the hymn and sings as the rest join.

My life goes on in endless song,
Above Earth's lamentations,
I hear the real, though far-off hymn
That hails a new creation.

Through all the tumult and the strife,
I hear it's music ringing.
It sounds an echo in my soul.
How can I keep from singing?

The rain builds to a crescendo, running down the windows in sheets. The double doors of the church blow open, though the music still plays and most continue to sing. As the congregation turns around, they are struck still. Standing in the doorway, silhouetted by the light from outside, is the figure of a girl. Because of the backlight, her features are not visible, but it's clear she's soaked head to foot, her white dress with the red trim dripping on the floor.

While though the tempest loudly roars,
I hear the truth, it liveth.
And though the darkness 'round me close,
Songs in the night it giveth.

No storm can shake my inmost calm,
While to that rock I'm clinging.
Since love is Lord of Heaven and Earth,
How can I keep from singing?

Gradually, she takes a step at a time until a collective gasp arises. Noelle steps into the aisle as Melody walks toward her.

Melody approaches, stops, and gazes into her eyes. Noelle strokes her cheek, as if to see if she's real, and Melody gently touches her hand, then looks toward the altar and walks further. As she continues up the aisle, awe, tears, and joy spread down each pew. In one row, standing in a line, are Tall Tree, Sam, and Matt. Mrs. Barry swoons, catching herself on the back of the pew.

> When tyrants tremble in their fear,
> And hear their death knell ringing,
> When friends rejoice, both far and near,
> How can I keep from singing?

> In prison cell and dungeon vile,
> Our thoughts to them are winging,
> When friends by shame are undefiled,
> How can I keep from singing?

Melody stands in front of the altar, staring up at Pastor Neal as the hymn ends. She walks up the two steps to the open sanctuary, bathed in sunlight that cascades through the glass wall, and looks out at the monumental view of Kinesava. The light, reflected off the orange-white cliff and cast through the waving angel tree, sprays flickering iridescent rays into the sanctuary and upon her. Neal walks up to her, puts his hand on her shoulder, and leads her as she sits in the front pew for the first time.

Several parishioners rise and run out the doors as Pastor Neal stares at Melody, his eyes glazed over. He looks down at the podium, smiles, and tosses the notes of his sermon over his shoulder, bringing on a relief of laughter that spreads through the church. After looking everyone in the eye, he turns to Melody again, contemplating. "Join me, please. Psalm 139, verses 14 through 16." He waits as the shuffling of thin scripture pages, decorated with an occasional sniffle, adorns the spiritual silence that fell upon Emmanuel. Neal recites from memory and the congregation joins:

"'I praise thee, for thou art fearful and wonderful.

Wonderful are thy works!
Though knowest me right well;
My frame was not hidden from thee,
When I was being made in secret,
intricately wrought in the depths of the Earth.
Thine eyes beheld my unformed substance;
In thy book were written, every one of them, the days
that were formed for me, when as yet there were none of
them.'"

He pauses. "'Thine eyes beheld my unformed substance.'
You know, I saw Melody on TV, as I'm sure you all did, when she so
boldly announced to the world that it had no business telling her,
or anybody else who has faith, that there was no hope. Because,
where is the source of hope? It is surely from He who can behold
who we are, who we will be, and who we were, when we were not
even formed yet. Those who were dead rose, those who were blind
saw. Those who were lame walked. But you know, they walked,
and they rose, and they saw, while they were still 'unformed substance'. We go through every day living a grand illusion, thinking
we know what's going on around us because of what we think we
see, what we think we know, when in fact it's what we *can't* see,
what we *fail* to know, that is most important. Things are not what
they appear to be. Ever. Because only He knows 'the days that were
formed when as yet there was none of them.' And today, Melody,
whom we all knew to be afflicted, is not what she appeared to be."

Neal contemplates as he searches for a passage. "Let me
just read this to you. It was a guiding passage to my seminary group.
Proverbs 8:23:

'Ages ago I was set up, at the first, before the beginning
of the Earth.
When there were no depths I was brought forth, when
there were no springs abounding with water.
Before the mountains had been shaped, before the hills,
I was brought forth;

Before he had made the Earth with its fields, or the first of the dust of the world.
When he established the heavens, I was there, when he drew a circle on the face of the deep,
When he made firm the skies above, when he established the fountains of the deep, when he assigned to the sea its limit, so that the waters might not transgress his command,
When he marked out the foundations of the Earth.
Then I was before him, like a little child.'"

He turns toward Francisco, seated at a grand piano near the right side of the sanctuary, and Francisco performs *Children of the Living God*. Melody stands, eyes closed, head bowed, and hands clasped. She begins rocking to the music and the congregation stands with her.

Children of the living God,
Come and sing, sing out loud.
Children of the living God,
Sing to the living God.

Sing of the wonders He has made,
Bird in flight, falling rain,
Sing of the wonders He has made,
Sing to the living God.

On the forward deck of the ship, the wheelchair is in the same place where Isabel watched the child in it the day before. Now, however, the wheelchair is empty as it rolls forward and back with the pitching of the ship. The boy stands at the bowsprit, leaning forward into the wind.

How He loves us with great love,
He who sits enthroned above.
For our lives He spilled His blood,

Sent His spirit like a flood.

Children of the living God,
Sing to the living God.
Children of the living God,
Sing to the living God.

In a one-room shack in an Ecuadorian ghetto, a mother calls for her child, looking for her frantically in the small room, then notices the open door slamming in the wind. As she walks toward it she sees wooden crutches lying in the doorway and looks outside, her expression turning from worry to astonishment.

Sing of His gentle healing hands,
How they found the lowliest man.
Sing of His gentle healing hands,
Sing to the living God.

Sing of the mercy that He gives,
Though we sin, He forgives.
Sing of the mercy that He gives,
Sing to the living God.

In a hospital room, a nurse enters to find an empty bed with wires dangling from a monitor. Over at the window, a child stands on a chair, straining to see outside, the Sun shining on her face.

How He loves us with great love,
He who sits enthroned above.
For our lives He spilled his blood,
Sent His spirit like a flood.

Children of the living God,
Sing to the living God.
Sing for the morning when He comes,

In the clouds, glorious Son.
Sing for the morning when He comes,
Sing to the living God.

Isabel sleeps soundly until awakened by the ringing of the phone. She squints at the clock, realizes how late it is, rubs her eyes, and answers. "Hello?... Yeah, Nonna, I know. I can't believe I slept this late. I never... What?... He's what?... But that's impossible, isn't it?" She sits up on the edge of the bed, looking around, lost. "OK, OK. The Captain's cabin... Yes, I'll hurry."

Isabel wonders if she's still asleep. Some kind of cruel dream, Tom coming home. A few more moments of looking around convince her that it isn't a dream. Instead, perhaps, a dream come true.

Out in the hallway, the door to Isabel's suite flies open and she bolts out, barely thrown together. She makes her way down the narrow hallway to an intersection where she's nearly bowled over by Walter, who stops just short of impact and looks at her. Instantly she sees something in his eyes. The clouded look that accompanied his condition is gone.

"Walter?"

"Hi, Miss Isabel. How are you this morning?"

Isabel looks at him sideways. "Never better, Walter. How about you?"

"Same here." As he walks away their eyes remain fixed until he turns and runs off.

Captain Wright stands by his window, staring at the rolling sea outside while Nonna sits in her wheelchair, eyes closed. A forceful knock shakes the door and he walks over and opens it. Isabel stands there, then enters the room. Nonna watches her enter, looking into her eyes. The Captain lets the door close and as they both turn toward him, purses his lips at the lack of explanation for any of it.

Inside the warehouse, equipment still stands from the last press conference and the same crowd has gathered. Only the mood has changed. Small groups talk in whispers of skepticism, bordering on impatience. Kirshner appears from the offices accompanied by Sam, Noelle, and Sid, all sensing the tension as the crowd silences and moves toward the chairs. Kirshner approaches the podium with his supporters on each side, and Noelle walks to the microphone.

"Please, be seated. I realize that my presence up here is a bit unorthodox, but I want you all to know I'm here today as Dr. Kirshner's friend, not as a journalist. We're aware of the questions most of you have in regard to the events of last night, and I'll let the Doctor explain. But I want to tell you that I stand behind him, and I put my professional reputation on anything he says here today." This meets with muted glances among the audience, now faced with the testimonial of one of their own.

Kirshner walks to the podium. "Before you ask any questions, I would like to make a statement." He reaches over to the laptop and brings up the path projector on the screen behind him, showing the capsule on its way to Earth. Then he turns on an overhead projector sitting next to it on the table, slightly washing out the screen, takes a grease pencil, and writes on the projector in large letters the formula: $E=MC^2$.

"I am fully aware that most of you look upon the events of last night with great confusion, skepticism, and even distrust, and I understand. I am here to tell you today that what has happened is as unexplainable to me as it is to you, although I have come up with a modest theory which, I'm afraid, will further subject me to criticism from the scientific community, and from the public as well. But frankly, it's the best I can do.

"To begin with, I will state categorically that any allegations of fraud, deception, or manipulation are unfounded, and I will not stand here and defend myself or anyone else as to those accusations. As Almighty God is my witness, what I have said in the past regarding this mission and the events that transpired are absolutely true." He turns to Noelle. "Miss Crane and others have been kind enough to stand up for me, and I assure you I would not allow them to do so if this were not the case."

A hush comes upon the warehouse. "When Mr. Holmes' vehicle transitioned behind the Moon, it indeed had no fuel for any kind of deceleration burn, other than the single burn, solid fuel retro engine designed solely for the purpose of deceleration into an Earth recovery path at the end of the mission, had we remained in, or returned to, Earth orbit. It would have been useless to utilize that engine, and in fact it remains unused. The projected path was as we described it, into an interplanetary trajectory with no hope, or I should say now, no apparent hope for recovery due to the increased kinetic energy caused by the uncontrolled trans-lunar correction. And, by the way, all the flight path data as I described it was independently verified by Dr. Terry Cole at NASA."

He dabs his forehead with his handkerchief. "When the capsule reappeared from loss of signal, it was on a perfect, and I mean that literally, perfect flight path that will return it precisely to the originally intended point of Earth gravitational capture and recovery. This data is also confirmed by NASA. What of course remains unanswered, is an explanation of this... change in events."

Kirshner looks to his silent audience. "In the most simple terms, the only method of obtaining desired flight path is, always has been, and always will be, simple energy management by use of engines, either to accelerate or decelerate the vehicle. Along with trajectory corrections, of course. What was required to obtain the desired result in this case was deceleration, or a removal of kinetic energy, or force if you will, from Mr. Holmes' capsule. This was conventionally unavailable, as I have said, because there was no fuel for the main engine to decelerate the capsule. So, energy had to have been dissipated in some other manner."

Kirshner stops to take a sip of water. The CNN correspondent can't contain himself any longer. "This is all a bit much. If this is what you say it is, it seems impossible. What are you getting at?"

"Please, bear with me. I'm now going to give you the only explanation I can. When the capsule regained communication with our systems, the only noticeably unusual data, other than the 'impossible' change in flight path, was a discrepancy in the clocks between the capsule and the time base here on Earth. Further, as incredible as it may seem, Mr. Holmes' wristwatch matched that of the capsule."

With this information, the entire audience catches its breath. Kirshner takes a laser pointer and points to the formula behind him, each letter in turn as he refers to it. "'$E=MC^2$.' Energy equals mass times speed of light, squared, one of the most basic concepts of physics. In order to decrease the energy, mathematically, either the mass of the vehicle or the speed of light must decrease. The mass of the capsule has not changed, and the speed of light is thought to be a constant. However, that factor itself contains a time element: feet per second, miles per hour, et cetera. Somehow stop time, and that factor would equal zero, for whatever duration time stopped, and consequently decrease the energy factor. There is also the theory, which has gone around for decades, that when one reaches the speed of light, time... stops."

Kirshner pauses and another reporter stands, looks at Noelle, then up at the screen. "Are you trying to say, with this business of the clocks, that time stopped?"

"If it did, in the exact amount, then the capsule could have lost the energy necessary to return to Earth, using the gravitational fields of both the Earth and Moon."

"If I understand you correctly, not only would time have to stop, but stop exactly the right amount to achieve what you say has happened."

"Precisely. And when I say precisely, again, I mean that literally. Even if we had been able to execute our own deceleration burn, never could we have done it with the precision that has occurred here. This vehicle appears to be returning to the Earth recovery window without need for a correction. The retro rocket package will not be used, and the traditional double-skip maneuver will be accomplished directly from the transearth segment into the atmosphere. This was accomplished with... unfathomable exactitude." With this, a mixture of amazement and agitation passes through the crowd, emotions that often accompany exposure to the unexplainable.

"You expect us to believe, then, that time stopped up there, exactly to the bizillionth of a second, so that Holmes will return to Earth on a dime? Sounds like some kind of cosmic circus act, doesn't it?"

"Quite a concept, isn't it? That of time 'stopping' for a measurable amount of time? In any event, I can't expect you to believe anything. No person can understand what another thinks or believes. But I will tell you this. In my journey through science, the most grandiose, the most moving concepts, were always those that appeared unbelievable when contemplated. I've told you all that I know, and tried, in the most human, and therefore fallible way, to explain what I can't even comprehend myself."

Another reporter stands. "Has Mr. Holmes said anything about what happened back there? Is there any clue to what caused this?"

At this, Kirshner looks at Noelle, then back at the reporter. "He has said only that something happened, but will not discuss the details."

"What's going on here? Did he have a 'close encounter' or something?" the reporter snorts sarcastically.

A nervous, almost giddy laugh goes through the crowd. Kirshner turns serious. "Whatever happened appears to be of a highly personal nature, and it will be his business to reveal it, if and when he so wishes."

"Well, is he ever going to make a statement? He's refused to appear to the public since this whole thing started. Don't you think he owes it to all of us down here to say something? Honestly, you're asking us to swallow a lot with not much explanation."

Before Kirshner can respond, a female reporter stands up and turns aggressively. "You know, why is something like this so hard for everybody to accept? Surely you've heard all this stuff coming across the wires about kids getting healed. And then there's Melody here in Springdale. I saw that little girl with my own eyes, before and after, and I tell you what, I don't know what happened, but whatever it is, I believe it, and I thank God for helping her.

Maybe we should all start believing what we see, instead of what we think we should see." She turns back to the podium. "Doctor, what are Mr. Holmes' chances of returning home safely?"

"Naturally, any sort of reentry maneuver is fraught with danger, particularly in an untested system. However, I must say that considering what has happened so far, I am of the feeling that things are... destined to turn out in our favor. Thank you for your patience."

Despite the flurry of questions, Kirshner walks away with Sam. The audience turns toward Noelle, who walks over to the female reporter and hugs her as the crowd forms around them.

The waning light of day casts a warm glow of earthen colors across the canyon as Bud sits in an old rocking chair on the porch of the Shack, reading a newspaper. On the front page in expanded headlines sprawls: SPECIAL EDITION: WORLDWIDE HEALINGS. HOLMES' MIRACLE TRIP BACK. WHAT NEXT? A picture of Melody walking away from church takes up the entire front page. Bud hears commotion from the front gate, lowers the paper, and squints to see what's going on. A woman sits in her car, arguing with the agent manning the gate. Reporters snap pictures as Bud hurries down from the verandah and walks toward the activity. When he arrives, he intervenes.

"What the heck's going on here?" He looks at the woman. "Is there something I can—" He realizes it's Francine, recognizing her from his files, and turns to the agent who intercepted her. "Let her through. I'll handle this."

She offers her hand out the window. "Thanks. Francine Holmes." Bud stares at it, then takes it as if he'd never touched a woman's hand before. She surprises him with a hearty grasp.

"Yes, ma'am. I know who you are and I apologize for the misunderstanding. Just drive your car on in here." The handshake continues a few cycles too long, only because Bud's been unable to unlock his stare upon her. She breaks it by letting the car roll forward. Bud follows on foot, opens the car door, and helps her out. She pops the trunk open and takes out a small suitcase, which Bud eyes as Francine closes the trunk, climbs the steps to the verandah, and stops. She gazes around, taking in the Shack, it's walled-in world, and the afterglow of all it has witnessed. Then she turns to Bud, looking him over.

"And who exactly are you?"

"Bud Meyerkamp. Agent Meyerkamp, actually." He walks up to the verandah and extends his hand. Francine looks at it and smiles, taking it once more. "I'm sorry about the business at the gate, but my men are under orders to keep everyone out. It's more for the protection of the property than anything else, what with all the press and public coming in." Realizing he hadn't let go of her hand, he withdraws the handshake. They lock eyes for a moment until she looks back at the gate.

"And you're the last line of defense, I suppose."

"No, actually. I'm not even on duty. To tell you the truth, I'm sort of on vacation, or leave. Or something. I really don't know what I'm doing, exactly," Bud fumbles.

She senses his trepidation and lowers her guard an inch, looking back into his eyes. There she sees something. Something unexpectedly comforting. "I know what you mean. I'm not sure what I'm doing, exactly, either. I haven't been here in a long time."

"I know."

"You know?"

"Well, I know from... I know a lot about you, from when I was working this case. I know you haven't been here." An odd silence comes upon them. "I'm sorry about everything that happened. I'm sure it's been difficult."

Francine ponders. "Thank you. It has been. I've not been able to deal with any of it. Until last night."

"Last night?"

"For a long time, I didn't even know what questions to ask. And last night, I got the answers. The answers to questions I couldn't even ask. Something told me I had to come back here. So, here I am."

"Are you sure you want to go in there? Can I help somehow?" Bud offers.

"I need to do this alone. I might even take a nap, but thanks for asking."

Francine walks toward the screen door, which Bud rushes to open for her. She looks inside, takes a breath for courage, and steps into the doorway as Bud carefully closes the door behind her. After hesitating, she looks back at Bud through the screen.

"Will you be here when I come back out?"

"You bet I will." After a moment, he asks, "Did I just shake your hand twice?"

"Uh-huh." She smiles, closing the front door. He walks back over to the chair and sits down, out of sorts. He looks back at the door, then stares out across the canyon and watches the last slice of Sun disappear behind Mount Kinesava.

Charles Grodin sits at his desk on the set while a makeup artist dabs the last few spots of reflection from his face and backs away. The floor director signals him, counts down, and points as the light comes on the camera.

"Good evening. There have been a lot of things going on during the last week, and especially the last day or two. You all know what I'm talking about, this Thomas Holmes story and all its twists and turns. First he goes up there, then he's never coming back, then he's coming back, and nobody knows how. And I'll tell you right now, no one's more confused about it all than me. I've gone back and forth, from one side to the other. I thought it was interesting at first, then I thought it was all a bit much. Then I felt bad when he... blew off his rocket or whatever happened when he was doomed to float off into space. Finally, last night, there's this business of him on his way home, and I thought, like a lot of other people, it was starting to smell like some giant hoax or something. I watched that press conference by Dr. Kirshner, and I didn't know what to think after that.

"But guess what? There are some other things, some miraculous things, that all seem to have happened at the same time. Not the least of which has to do with a girl named Melody Baxter. That name had already become a household word, what with her pleas for help and the big prayer she arranged all over the world. But what's happened to her since yesterday... well how else can we say it? She was healed. Instantly. And she wasn't the only one. Nobody can accuse that little girl, no matter what you think of Holmes or all his rockets or money or whatever, of anything but being honest. She spent most of her life bent over in a wheelchair. She had all kinds of other problems, and to be frank, a lot of people thought she wouldn't live very long. Until yesterday. Yesterday, she walked into her church. That's right, she walked.

"Tonight, I've arranged to talk to Melody through a satellite link, and also with Noelle Crane, the ABN reporter who most of you will recognize. Noelle seems to have taken Melody under her wing, and from what I can tell, has her best interests at heart. We'll be talking to them in just a couple of minutes, so don't go away. I can promise you, this is a child you're going to want to listen to. If anybody has answers to all this, I'll bet it's her. We'll be right back."

Parked in front of Noah House is a broadcast van with a transmission station extended and cables running into the main doors. Down the hall, the doors to the Starbridge are open and bright light pours into the hallway.

In the middle of the room, two chairs angle at each other. Melody sits in one, Noelle in the other, both wearing the T-shirts. Television spots are arranged for the interview with two cameras in waiting and cable bundles winding across the floor and out the door. A monitor sits directly across from them, and on it Grodin prepares for return from commercial. The location director stands near them wearing headphones, listening. He turns to them.

"OK, we're on in 10 seconds."

"Well, honey, here we go." Noelle says.

"I'm ready, Miss Crane."

The director counts them down, Grodin getting the same on the monitor. "For those of you who just joined us, we have with us live via satellite, Melody Baxter and her friend, Noelle Crane of ABN. Good evening, ladies. How's our connection out there?"

"Five by five, Charles," Noelle says. "You look great. It seems this talk show business agrees with you."

"It agrees with me just fine, Noelle, although I suppose there are those who wish I'd go back to acting. So, Melody, how are you doing? You look wonderful."

"I'm feeling wonderful, Mr. Grodin. I'm a little nervous though. I always loved your *Beethoven* movies so much. I never thought I'd ever actually get to talk to you."

"That's really sweet of you, and I'm glad you liked those movies. They were a lot of fun to make. So, what do you think about all this?"

"I'm so excited that this happened to me. But I'm just as excited for all my friends, and all the other people in the world, too."

"You know, Noelle, you've made friends with Melody and gotten to know her. It strikes me I've never seen a person so concerned with others, in spite of her own problems."

Noelle touches Melody's shoulder. "It's extraordinary, Charles. If there's anything we can learn from this child and all that she's said, it's about caring for another person without that caring being... clouded or conditioned on what our own lives are about. Unconditional love. It's what we all need, and what so few of us can give."

"Melody, you must know that so many people out in the world don't understand what happened to you, or to all these other children. Is there anything you can say to them about what you think happened? Is there some kind of pattern or something?"

"I'm not sure exactly, but I'll bet that everyone who was helped said that prayer with me that night, or somebody they knew said it for them."

"So you think that the prayer caused all this? But the prayer was for Mr. Holmes, wasn't it? Something very... unusual happened to him. He was helped, and no one can explain why or how, and a lot of people think, well, you know, they think he faked his problem. How does this all make sense to you?"

"First of all, I'm not sure what you mean by making sense. It seems to me that most people in the world don't make much sense, with the things they do and say."

Grodin's signature smile appears. "Melody, I'll tell you what, if anything makes any sense, it's what you just said, don't you think, Noelle?"

"Charles, I've learned more about myself in the few days I've known Melody than in fifteen years of therapy. In fact, it seems to me none of us listen to children nearly enough. We tend to dismiss what they say as... childish. Now there's a term that applies more to us than them."

"How true. So, Melody, you have no trouble in believing in these miracles. Well, how silly of me. How could you? Look what happened to you."

"I don't get it why people find it so hard to believe in miracles. My Mommy told me I was the greatest miracle in the world to her. She said every time a child is born, it's a miracle, but nobody pays attention to it that way."

"I can see why Miss Crane made such good friends with you. I'm sure if I were out there, I'd want to be your friend too. You're a very special child. No, let me take that back, you're a very special person. So, you feel that the prayer made all this happen. But don't people pray for help all the time? Why do you think all this happened the way it did?"

"We can't figure out what God does, or why, and that's what makes Him God. But I do believe some things about the way He works. I believe that when we pray, we're like mirrors. I got that idea once when I was trying to send a message to the kids in the treehouse outside. They couldn't hear me, so I tried to get their attention by reflecting the Sun in a mirror at them. I thought later that when we're trying to get God's attention to something, it's like we're trying to shine His light there with our prayers. And the better people we are, the better the mirrors we are, and the more of

His light goes there."

"I think I'm getting the picture. So this time there were a lot of mirrors, weren't there?"

"That's what I think. And kids are really good mirrors, because they're clean, and bright. I think most people, when they get older, they get dark. They don't reflect much of anything."

"And why do you think all these wonderful things happened to you and the others if you were asking for help for somebody else?"

Melody pauses. "Well, I suppose somehow all that light got reflected back at us. We got our prayers sent back to us. When I was healed, I remember a big light. It was inside me, like a rainbow. That must be what happened. Whatever it was, I just thank Him so much for everything, and I hope and pray that everyone in the world can be a better person, and help shine His light back."

"Well, God bless you, Melody, and thank you. You know, Mr. Holmes has a TV up there, and I hope he watches me sometimes. In case he's watching right now, is there anything you'd like to say to him?"

Melody pauses again. "Yes, I think so." She looks directly into the camera. "If you're listening, Mr. Holmes, I'm just so happy that you're coming home, and I know you'll be happy about my being able to walk. I can't wait to see you and give you a big hug. I also hope you feel like saying something to all of us down here, because we prayed so hard for you."

Tom is watching, Zion sleeping on his lap. Melody stares directly at him.

"I don't know what happened to you up there behind the Moon, but I hope it helped you, and you won't have to be sad about Noah anymore. I know he loves you, and he wants you to be happy. And we all love you down here, too." Melody ends her message with a smile, and Tom blinks to see it. Grodin comes back on the screen.

"What else can I say, except that maybe we should think about lowering the age for elected office in this country. I mean *really* lowering it. We'll be back after this."

As the show goes to commercial, Tom switches it off, the path projection returning to the screen, his capsule now more than halfway to Earth. He looks out the window and sees the Earth coming closer, the South Pacific a lustrous shade of blue, embellished with golden glints from the deepening angle of the Sun. Tom moves closer to the window and as he does so, puts his hand in his pants pocket and finds the rock, the one Billy handed him. He takes it out, looks it over, and again the flooding sensation comes upon him, the oddness of unexplainable familiarity.

He looks closer at the rock, noticing its strange shape, like an eight, as if worn in the middle, or as if two rocks had joined. On one end there's an unnatural scar, chipped off, revealing unlikely strata. Tom holds the rock at arm's length toward the earth, thinking it odd that this specimen made the journey with him, older than man himself, once a part of that magnificent planet, gone, and now returning by the hand of a man. As he holds it over the Pacific, a flash of light comes off the water and illuminates the rock.

And then another vision, this more intense than any, this full of mandate as he's drawn toward the rock at a speed greater than light. And when it's over, he knows it's the last, the final inscape. This time he's not confused, but enlightened, and though he doesn't understand the meaning yet, knows it is to come and give purpose to all the engulfing mysteries of the previous visions. He puts the rock back in his pocket.

Isabel leans against the stern railing, watching the ship's broad wake churn the deep blue water to fluorescent aqua. From the ship's PA system comes:

"OK, fans, this is your cruise director, Debra, and it's time to reveal the destination of our Mystery Cruise. For all of you that entered the contest, here are the totals: one hundred fifty-seven of you thought we were going to Alaska. I guess you can tell by the temperature you lost. Three hundred sixty-nine thought it was

Mexico. One hundred eighty-seven guessed the Panama Canal. One hundred five thought we were coming back to Los Angeles. Nice try, but no dice. Right now, I'd like all of you to take a look off the port side of the ship. That's the left side for you landlubbers."

There's a stampede over to that side. Since Isabel's already at the stern, all she has to do is turn in that direction. "If you look off to the horizon you'll see a large island that looks like a volcano. That's right! Two hundred twenty-five of you smart cruisers guessed Hawaii. Congratulations! That's the beautiful island of Maui, and we'll be making our way off shore of Lahaina in an hour. Each one of you lucky winners gets a free T-shirt from Hilo Hatties!" There's a great shout of joy, especially from the children.

A ship's tender bumps the dock in Lahaina and the crew jumps off, lines in hand, Noah 5 anchored in the distance. The crew can barely get secured before a herd of squealing children pour out and run in all directions, followed by frantic chaperones. Once they've disembarked, Isabel pushes Nonna's wheelchair down the gangplank and they face up toward the steaming Sun.

Isabel and Nonna enter the bar at the Hard Rock Cafe, taking a small table. The waiter, a striking, tanned figure in shorts, approaches and lays down cocktail napkins. Nonna looks up and smiles.

"What can I get for you two beauties?" he asks.

"Oh, how about a room?"

"Nonna!" Isabel exclaims.

The waiter winks. "I don't know if I could handle all that… experience."

Nonna looks at Isabel. "Oh for heaven's sake, girl, I was just joking." Isabel looks away, pretending embarrassment. "We'll take two of anything with an umbrella."

"Gotcha," he says as he walks away. They both can't help but watch. Nonna looks at Isabel watching, who looks at Nonna to find a *caught-yeah-lookin'* look. Isabel pokes her in the arm, then looks up at a projection TV.

An NFL playoff game is in progress, just coming back from commercial, and John Madden stands with Al Michaels in the booth. Madden holds the microphone like an ice cream cone. "Al, this game has been a giant track meet from the beginning. We got over two hundred yards rushing by both teams in the first half, with only four completed passes for San Francisco, and five for Dallas. Who would have thought?"

"Well, we said at the beginning that with Steele still injured and Grant running on a bad ankle, the 49ers' ground game would have to come alive. As for the Cowboys, it all goes to the credit of the 49ers' corners. What can you say about Bradbury and Swenson? They've completely frustrated the wide receivers, and Caldwell can't seem to find anything open in the secondary."

"He couldn't find the Goodyear Blimp if it was in the secondary the way he's throwing today," adds Madden.

Michaels cringes. "Anyway, we'll see if the strategy changes for the Cowboys here in the second half. By the way, folks, we'd like to remind you all that following the second playoff game, HTV will be carrying, live, the *Cruisin' for Kids* benefit concert broadcast from a ship, I guess we found out this morning is in Hawaii. It was some kind of mystery cruise where nobody knew where they were going until they got there. And somehow it's all connected with this unbelievable space adventure with Thomas Holmes, isn't it John?"

"That's right, Al. He owns that ship, and he arranged for all those kids to go on it before he went up in his rocket. I don't know about you, but that whole story has really got me thinkin' about a lot of stuff. Whatever happens, I know they've already raised something like over two million dollars just with those T-shirts, and a lot more on the Internet for children's charities."

"And this concert stands to raise even more, especially considering all the incredible things that have happened. Many of the kids on that ship were sick or crippled, and suddenly they aren't. None of us understands what's happened, but it doesn't matter. We're just thankful for all of it," says Michaels.

"You got that right. Plus, they're going to have Marcy Marxer and Cathy Fink, and a bunch of other people."

"I'd guess you don't go to Hawaii much since you don't like to fly."

"Yeah. Maybe I should put some pontoons, or whatever they are, on my bus. I could even get some of those slacker linemen down there to, you know, row with those big oars. Kind of like one of those Viking ships? A little trip to Hawaii, I'll bet they'd be movin' a little faster."

Al looks at him in wonder. "I'll be sure to tell them you said that." He turns back to the camera. "We'll be back with the halftime stats after this message."

When the camera light goes off he looks back at Madden who motions, *what?*

☀

Night has fallen upon the Shack, softened by an unexpected Indian summer brought by the tropical wave that passed through, inducing Bud to drift asleep like a faithful watchdog. Francine comes out stretching and yawning, letting the screen door slam and waking Bud, who sits up in a stupor. She looks at him and starts to laugh until she realizes she woke him.

"I'm sorry. I didn't realize you'd be sleeping out here. How long was I out?"

Bud stands up and nearly falls over, a failed attempt at nonchalance. "I wasn't sleeping, actually. Well, maybe just dozing."

"There's a difference?"

"About three hours."

"What?"

"You were asleep about three hours."

"I see."

Bud rubs his face. "Oh, you meant the difference between, dozing and sleeping. I thought..."

Both realize the futility of continuing and look away. Francine is still trying not to laugh. "Should we start over?"

"I think maybe we should." She walks back in and he sits back down. Then she walks out, stretching and yawning again, not very convincingly.

"Hello. How was your nap?" he asks artificially.

"Oh, fine. How long was I out?"

As Bud answers, she lip syncs. "About three hours."

"I see. Would you like to take a walk?"

"I'd love to. You lead the way."

Francine walks down the steps and he follows as she takes the path toward the back of the Shack. Bud walks a few steps behind, content with the view. "It's how tight your eyes are shut."

"What's that?" she asks.

"The difference between dozing and sleeping."

"Ah, ha. OK."

He catches up, and after a few more steps, she takes his arm. He looks down at that arm, around which her hand is gently draped, then straight ahead.

Tom sits at the console, his chin cradled in his hands, looking out the window. It's still sinking in that the Earth is growing larger instead of smaller. Of all the miracles that happened back home, none is more elegant than his return when he had accepted the end of his life in the blackness of space. He was saved, and can hardly believe it, by the generous farewell of his son. Even if he'd been destined to float off to his death alone, he would have done so content with having been with Noah once again. Yet, still this humbling gift he received, and from his son, or through his son. He takes a remote and points at a Tivo player, running the Grodin interview on his screen in rewind scan. He stops and selects *play*.

"I can't wait to see you and give you a big hug. I also hope you feel like saying something to all of us down here because we prayed so hard for you," Melody says again.

He pushes *pause* and her face freezes on the screen. Certainly he must honor that request, but has no idea what to say, much less how to say it. Unable to resolve what to do, he looks at the locker where he stored Theo and the Book. He glides over and takes the Book out, returns to the seat, and places it on his lap, laying his hand on the cover. He hasn't opened the Book since just after Noah's memorial service. Of course, he knows its contents by heart, having listened to Sunman tell the legend to Noah so many times, as was the tradition. And Noah knew it to the minutest detail, knowing as well, even at that young age, the onerous duty that was his to draw a page when the time came. But as much as he wanted to, he hadn't come to the point before he passed away that he was prepared to tell his story, and that hurt him more than his own fatal suffering.

Tom opens the cover as if it would disintegrate in his hand. It's an ancient book, compiled over generations by ancestors using deerskin and leather string, replaced occasionally, but not for over two hundred years. He stares at the first page, then turns to the next, revealing simple drawings on each. As the pages turn, the stories revive in his mind, each the culmination of an old life, an attempt to make sense of that life, and to offer an answer.

As he reaches the last page on the right side of the Book, he stops, knowing that on the other side Noah was to have drawn his own answers. His hand rests on it as if trying to feel through to that other side, and, considering what happened hours before, senses the emptiness of what should have been, what story should have been told there by his son.

But in that moment Tom is charged with the revelation that Noah's life was completed before his very eyes. How could he betray what his son had done with thoughts of emptiness and untold stories? With this thought he turns that last page, and as it comes into his view, his face draws, and his eyes fill.

A brilliant three-quarter Moon illuminates a tight bend of the Virgin River a mile or so behind the Shack. Moonlight glitters off the water as it cascades down a small patch of rapids at the center of the bend, continuing to a pool where glitter turns to wavering reflection. In the peninsula formed by the bend is a small wood, centered on an expansive skeleton oak.

Bud and Francine approach the river, still arm in arm, and walk up to the water's edge. She looks up at the Moon, then at the oak, its universe of branches quivering in the wind, amplifying the twinkling of the stars. "It's been twelve years since I've been here. Nothing's changed. Not one rock, not one twig. Nothing. Where does time go?"

Bud still can't take his eyes off her, and hardly tries. "Who says it goes anywhere? It's us that come and go. That's why it feels the same when you come back. Nothing changes, not really. It was here all the time, waiting. Waiting for you to come back."

Francine turns to his stare, holding it in her own for a moment. Then she walks a few steps upriver and stops, facing toward the oak. "And was it waiting for you?"

"I'm here, aren't I?"

Francine walks into the middle of the river just upstream of the rapid. She ends up in just above her knees and wobbles to maintain balance against the current and the stones. Bud lurches forward a step. "What are you doing? Are you nuts?"

"I haven't been river walking since…" Francine looks up at the Moon.

"Since?"

"Since, a long time."

"Jesus, do you have to do it *now*? That water's got to be freezing! And it's dark."

"It's OK. You get used to it. Come on."

Bud steps back, not believing his ears. "What? Come out of there. You're going to get sick."

She flicks water at him. "Oh, stop that."

Bud flinches at the freezing drops and looks at her like she's the Mad Hatter. He glances back longingly at the trail, then at her, shaking his head. "If you weren't so… I'd…" He walks into the river and wrenches. "Oh. Oh, God." He sploshes up to her and gives her a stare as icy as the water. "Ju *shitsu*, that's cold."

"Ju *shitsu*? Is that what you said?"

"Never mind. You proved your point. Now let's get out and head straight for the hospital. Or funny farm, better idea."

"Take it easy, you'll survive." Francine grabs his hand and leads him a step at a time upriver. Bud teeters one side to the other, stepping on the slick round stones. She slips a few times also, both using the handhold for support, one nearly pulling the other in.

"Francine, Whitewater, Holmes, whoever you are, where are we going? And why?"

"It's just a little farther." Both banks of the river are blocked with bare thickets, but up a few more yards there's an opening to the right leading to a clearing by the oak. Once they arrive abeam the clearing, she stops and looks toward it. "This was our favorite place to camp, the three of us. It was so perfect, especially in the fall when things were starting to cool off and the leaves were turning colors. We'd build a fire out of the oak branches. It would burn all night."

Bud feels like he's trespassing on her private remembrance. "You know, we could have just walked along the bank and crossed here."

Francine lingers in the memory, hearing his comment from it, distant and echoing as the river pushes against them. She looks upriver. "My son, Noah, he loved to river walk with his Daddy. He always wanted me to go up the Narrows with them, but I never would." She looks down at the water. "Oh, how I've despised myself for that."

"Were you afraid?"

"I suppose, a little. All the talk about flash floods. But that's too convenient. Since when does a mother not do something with her child out of fear? The more fear, the more reason to go. That's what we do. Protect."

"But Tom was there to protect him."

"And who was there to protect Tom? No, I didn't go because I stopped cherishing the moments. It was easier not to go than it was to go. That's before I learned that the hard things are the ones that make you grow." She bends down and reaches into the water past her elbow, coming up with a gray speckled rock. "I finally did go up the Narrows, too late."

"Why too late?"

Francine pauses to stare at the rock, wiping the water off to feel its slippery moss, glowing green in the moonlight. "Noah's last wish. After he died we found an envelope he left us, to be opened when he was gone."

"Francine, are you sure you want to—"

"Yes, please. I need to." He puts his arm around her and she lays the side of her face against his flannel jacket, looking back upriver. Her voice quivers through restrained tears. "He wrote a poem about a dream he had, and he wanted Julia to read it at his memorial. That's all he wanted. He was very specific about it. He didn't want anything said but the poem."

"Julia was his 'life partner'. I saw that in the file, but I didn't understand what it meant."

"A life partner is someone who helps terminal patients experience the most they can with the time they have left. With children, they teach them things, different things that help them learn. It's hard to describe."

"I get the idea," Bud says, solemnly.

"She taught Noah about philosophy, about botany, astronomy, about God, about life. And death. And poetry. We didn't know he wrote the poem until after he was gone."

"So she read it for him. Where?"

"That's the thing. Noah never stopped amazing everyone. He isn't like other people. He's from a different place. I understand now."

"Is?"

"Yes, is." Bud strokes her hair, a reflex also from a different place. "Noah said in the letter he left that he wanted his memorial at a place he called Eden Cove. It's a spot on the river, up the Narrows, his favorite place. He finally got me there."

"How many people were there?"

"There were only thirty-two. He made a list. Of course, a hundred or so followed anyway, but they stood back. The Cove is at a bend in the river, like this one, only the canyon walls tower up, straight up. It's not far up the Narrows, but most of the time you're in the river, against the current, sometimes up to your waist. When you come around that bend, though, you find yourself facing... Eden. Noah said it was the closest thing to heaven on Earth. It's a giant hollowed out part of the rock wall, and the river turns away at that spot so there's a beautiful slope going up into the shelter, with rocks and trees and flowers, and ferns, all protected. He and Tom would go up there in the rain and watch it fall.

"The walk up the river that day... every step was work. Nobody spoke. I cried all the way. That was the only sound you heard, besides the river. The weeping whispered off the walls, the rocks, like the wind. At first I could barely stand, but with each step I learned how to walk the river. I learned not to look down, but to feel my way across the stones, to use the current to keep my balance. I learned to trust myself, and by the time I got to the Cove, I realized I could sense each stone before I stepped on it. I felt him helping me with each step. I felt him there."

Francine leads Bud by the hand out of the river, up the bank, and under the oak. There he sees this was somebody's place; a fire pit, a bench hollowed out of a fallen tree, a swing moving in the breeze from a low branch. He sits her on the bench and kneels before her. "So that day, he was *your* life partner. He brought you up there. He taught you to walk."

A tear traces her soft cheek, reflecting the silvery light from above. "He did. He taught me to walk in faith." She touches his face. "I never told anyone this before, but when Julia read the poem, I heard his voice. It wasn't hers. It was his. I thought I was losing my mind."

"But it was his voice, in the poem, coming through her."

"No, it really was his voice. And now I understand why, since..."

"What?"

"Someday, maybe I'll tell you."

Bud stares into her crystal-blue eyes, then starts unlacing her boots. "Let's get these off before you catch pneumonia." He takes off both boots and peels off her wet socks. "Oh, my gosh," he marvels. "Those are the most perfect little feet I've ever seen. Look at them."

"Aren't they, though? I've always been proud of them."
Francine smiles. "So. You're a 'foot-man', are you?"

If it's possible for Bud to be embarrassed, he is. "No, actually. I've always thought feet were terrible things, so... awful most of the time. But look at these. They're... just perfect." He rubs them to warm them up.

"What about yours?"

"Oh. I have Fred Flintstone feet."

"Hmm," she purrs. "I always thought Fred Flintstone was... sexy."

Bud starts to say something, then stops. Instead, he puts her socks and shoes in her lap, picks her up in his arms, and carries her down the bank and across the river, almost falling in once.

A helicopter skims across the ocean at whitecap level toward the cruise ship in the distance. Inside, Marcy Marxer and Cathy Fink sit wide-eyed, the wind lashing from an open door.

The chopper roars up and over the ship, then sweeps a wide circle around it. All over the ship, passengers, led by children, wave. Banners hang shipwide, announcing the concert as TV cameras record the arrival. The chopper tilts onto its pad at the bow where earlier it had hidden under the tarp, and as the blades circle down, Marcy and Cathy step out, waving back, then walk along the cordoned-off pathway, shaking hands and patting heads, the children beside themselves at seeing these two in person.

They enter a dressing room with a small entourage of lucky kids who won a contest to be behind stage. Captain Wright is there to greet them, shaking both Marcy's hands. "Hello, Miss Marxer, Cathy. Captain Wright. Welcome aboard."

"Thank you," Marcy says. "I can't believe this reception. We were just saying this has got to be the most excited group of kids we've ever seen."

"There's been a lot of excitement around here for the last few days. You're jumping on just 'turns up the volume' if you know what I mean."

Cathy shakes his hand. "Well, nobody's more ready for this than we are. I hope we didn't keep you waiting."

"Not at all. It's a little tight, but we're still on schedule."

Cathy reaches out and snatches one of the children who'd been staring, giving her a squeezing hug, the others looking at each other in disbelief. Marcy kneels down and reaches out a hand to each as the Captain watches with a big British grin. "I hate to break this up, but I need to talk to Cathy and Marcy for a minute. Would you mind stepping in here?" They follow into the sound booth and Captain Wright closes the door. "There's something I need you to know, but this is in confidence."

"Is something wrong?" Marcy asks, concerned.

"No, nothing like that. We received a call from Mr. Holmes. He's going to make an appearance at the end of the show, but he didn't want it to be announced because he didn't want to upstage the performances. He prefers it that way, if you don't mind."

"I don't mind," Marcy replies, turning to Cathy. "Do you?"

"Of course not."

Captain Wright lays one hand on each's shoulder. "After Sonya's dance, we'll just cut to the feed from the capsule. Remember…" He makes the *shhh* sign and they do the same. Marcy opens the door to find little fans crowded in front of it.

Dad, a Latin American, sits in his chair peacefully watching the closing credits of the playoff game on a faded but functional TV. His surroundings are poor but he leads a happy family. The peace is shattered by a herd of kids, some his, some not, some Latin American, some not, all huffing from playing outside. Dad watches as they take over the room, his daughter jumping onto his lap. She squeals, "It's starting! It's going to start right now!"

Mom walks in with bowls of popcorn on a tray and he looks at her for help, but she just smiles. On the TV, the concert opens with a replay of the chopper arriving, background music an instrumental of Marcy's *January, February, March*. Colorful credits appear: "'Cruisin' For Kids' Benefit Concert for Children's Charities." The shot cuts to Marcy and Cathy stepping from the chopper, signing autographs as they make their way into the ship, then leaving the dressing room.

The stage is set with a twelve piece band. Colored spots sweep across, balloons spread everywhere, and a full array of broadcast cameras and personnel await. Hanging TV monitors and a big screen projection behind the stage show the opening sequences on the air. Captain Wright stands stage-right talking to the floor director who backs away, counting down. A prompter signals the packed audience, mostly children, who thunder applause, whistling and screaming.

Over the PA comes, "Boys and Girls, Ladies and Gentlemen, all around the world, live from the S.S. Noah 5 in the waters off the Hawaiian islands, HTV is proud to present the 'Cruisin' for Kids' Children's Charities Concert, starring Marcy Marxer and Cathy Fink…" Big cheer. "Isabel Flores…" Another big cheer. "Our own star studded children's talent show…" Biggest cheer. "And all kinds of other cool stuff including a magic show. But right now, I'd like to introduce the host of our show, let's give a huge Cruisin' welcome for Captain Michael Wright, Commander of the Noah 5!" A boisterous ovation greets Captain Wright as he runs onto the stage and, after a few exaggerated bows, brings the ovation to a close.

"We here on the Noah 5 have had an unbelievable week, as all of you are certainly aware. Although this concert was arranged many months ago by Mr. Holmes, none of us could have imagined the events that have occurred, not just here, but all over the world. I guess what I'm trying to say is that even though this started as a fundraising event for worldwide children's charities, it's now also a celebration, a celebration for many things. I urge everyone watching to call the toll free numbers that will appear on the screen and help children everywhere, and at the same time say thanks for all the wonderful things that have happened. Let's all make a real difference to the precious children of this planet who need our help, to be fed, and to be cared for. I think now more than ever we understand that we owe them everything we have." This inspires a round of applause.

"Also, we have a very special surprise at the end of the show, so stay with us. On that note, it's time to get started. Boys and girls, ladies and gentlemen everywhere, it's my great pleasure to introduce the stars of our show, Cathy Fink and Marcy Marxer!"

The kids jump to their feet as the band opens an extended intro to *Ride 'Em High*. Marcy and Cathy run on stage, waving and blowing kisses, and motion for the group of contest winners to take their place on the side of the stage to participate in the play-along song. At the opposite corner of the stage, a teenage girl signs the words of the concert. Marcy sings,

> Ride 'em high, ride 'em low!
> Holler "Yippie-ti-i-o!"
> Spur 'em, fan 'em, let 'em know,
> You're the champ of the rodeo!

> I'm all dressed up and rarin' to go,
> Rarin' to go to the rodeo.
> You'll be there, you buckaroo,
> Oh my gosh, how I love you!

> Ride 'em high, ride 'em low!
> Holler "Yippie-ti-i-o!"
> Spur 'em, fan 'em, let 'em know,
> You're the champ of the rodeo!

In the barrio living room, the kids are jumping up and down as Dad finally lets go of a smile. They all holler, "Yippie-ti-i-o!"

> Well, cowpokes come and cowpokes go,
> It's one dern thing I very well know,
> To you, cowpoke, I'll e'er be true,
> Gosh, oh gosh, how I love you.

> Ride 'em high, ride 'em low!
> Holler "Yippie-ti-i-o!"

Spur 'em, fan 'em, let 'em know,
You're the champ of the rodeo!

The children of a Moscow tenement gather around an antique black and white TV. They also holler, "Yippie-ti-i-o," colored
with a Russian accent.

Clap three times!
Tap three times!
Snap three times!
Reach right over and touch your toes!

Everybody listening here,
Put your elbows in the air.
Put your hands up over your head.
Shake your hands then shake your head.

Shake 'em high! Shake 'em low!
Shake 'em to the rodeo!
Put your fingers on your knees
And smile so I can see your teeth!

President Stamp watches in the Oval Office with his five
and three-year-old girls, trying to keep up as they raise elbows, shake
hands, and shake heads. He's finally able to put his fingers on his
knees and show his teeth, as they do back.

Clap three times!
Tap three times!
Snap three times!
Reach right over and touch your toes!

Put your left foot in the air,
And wave to your right foot a-way down there.
Left foot forward, left foot back,
Tap your left toe, clickety-clack!

Hop on your right foot! Hop, hop, hop!
Hop and hop and hop and stop.
Move your feet from side to side,
Now you're doin' the pony ride.

In the Townhall, Sue holds Kiki in her arms while Anthony insists she follow with him. She teeters with her left foot in the air, trying to wave at her right foot. Anthony helps by waving at it for her. Sue refuses to hop, however.

Clap three times!
Tap three times!
Snap three times!
Reach right over and touch your toes!

After the group yodel is over and the song ends, applause and cheering erupt, as much for the audience's participation as for Marcy, who applauds back. From this she goes right into *Rock-a-Bye Boogie* and the applause turns to clapping as children in the audience stand and dance to it in the charming free-form natural to little ones.

Tom watches on his monitor as events take place during the concert:

Walter is in the usual magician's box with swords being plunged into him, some by his friends who squeamishly push them through and scream as he pretends to be impaled.

Captain Wright is put into a curtained glass closet and made to disappear, reappearing from backstage to the pretended surprise of most.

Isabel sits at the piano playing a children's medley with a child sitting on each side of her on the bench, staring up at her.

A clown administers balloon hats of every variety, the most

ridiculous, some bloated pink farm animal, placed on the head of Nonna.

A ventriloquist has a dummy on one leg and Angela in a red tutu on the other. He tries to make her act like a dummy, unsuccessfully since she, and everyone else, can't stop laughing. The real dummy, of course, takes full advantage.

The children's talent show features: two Elvis imitations; a gut bucket duet; a six-year-old Britney Spears; a poetry reading by Maria, something having to do with a hamster that saved the world; an exchange between lovers from Act Two, Scene Two, of Romeo and Juliet, wherein Juliet is a clam and Romeo a lobster, reading catatonically from cue cards while wielding foot-long pinchers, "It is my soul that calls my name!" (this the idea of the children's cruise director, inflicted on two ten-year-olds who got the most detentions); a karate demonstration to the accompaniment of MC Hammer; and a very respectable accordion recital presented by the boy who left his wheelchair on deck.

Marcy stands at center stage with the curtains closed behind her. Three microphones hang from above, just over her head, spread five feet apart and aligned with the front edge of the elevated stage. Twenty-four children from the audience rise and walk toward the stage down the auditorium aisles. As she speaks, half of them sit on the edge of the stage and the rest stand behind them.
"Even though grown-ups in the world have differences and problems, there's one thing that's really obvious, and it's something everyone needs to think more about. We are all one people, and children all over the world are the same beautiful people, no matter where they are. During the last week, here on the ship, these twenty-four wonderful kids have been rehearsing in secret for a very special gift to all of us. There's nothing sweeter in this world than the voice of a child, and when children sing, even the songbirds stop to listen. Ladies and gentlemen, boys and girls everywhere, we present the Cruisin' for Kids Choir."

Marcy walks down the steps to the floor and kneels in front, facing them as the choir director does the same. The projection screen lowers, and as the children sing *All Around the World*, an a capella round, portraits of children from countries around the world appear behind them.

All around the world there are children like me
Across the continents, across the sea.
When I wake up they say goodnight to the Sun
And when I sleep their day's begun.

Good night, Bonne nuit
Buenas noches, Laila tov
Guten nacht, Spokonia nochee,
Oyasuminasai.

All around the world there are children like me
Across the continents, across the sea.
All around the world there are children like me
When I wake up they say good night to the Sun
Across the continents, across the sea.
And when I sleep their day's begun.
When I wake up they say good night to the Sun

Good night, Bonne nuit,
And when I sleep their day's begun.
Buenas noches, Laila tov
Good night, Bonne nuit,
Guten nacht, Spokonia nochee
Buenas noches, Laila tov,
Oyasuminasai.
Guten nacht, Spokonia nochee,
[BOTH:] **Oyasuminasai.**

All around the world there are children like me

Across the continents, across the sea.
All around the world there are children like me
When I wake up they say good night to the Sun
Across the continents, across the sea.
All around the world there are children like me
And when I sleep their day's begun.
When I wake up they say good night to the Sun
Across the continents, across the sea.

Good night, Bonne nuit,
And when I sleep their day's begun.
When I wake up they say good night to the Sun
Buenas noches, Laila tov,
Good night, Bonne nuit,
And when I sleep their day's begun.
Guten nacht, Spokonia nochee,
Buenas noches, Laila tov,
Good night, Bonne nuit,
Oyasuminasai.
Guten nacht, Spokonia nochee,
Buenas noches, Laila tov,
Oyasuminasai.
Guten nacht, Spokonia nochee
(ALL) **Oyasuminasai.**

When the song ends, the choir bows as Marcy presents them and applauds with the crowd. The rest of the concert's performers appear in line to bow as well, all to standing ovations. The house lights dim to near darkness, and thus the chatter of the audience. Everyone leaves the stage but Cathy.

"We've saved something very special for our last performance. Miss Sonya Temple is the winner of the talent show and her story is like many of the stories that happened this week. Just a few days ago, she was crippled, and now, you'll see, she dances. That's a miracle, of course, but not a greater miracle than the smile of any child, or as the love that children bring to this world. Sonya celebrates her life, and the lives of all children, no matter what their condition. And we, the adults of the world, must celebrate them, always, every day, every minute, in everything we do, and everything we say. They are the light of this world. They are God's light, shining upon us all. As Gibran said, 'They are the sons and daughters of Life's longing for itself... For their souls dwell in the house of tomorrow...'" Cathy leaves the stage.

The burgundy and black swirled curtains slowly part, revealing a dark stage. A spotlight glows upon Sonya to the left, a ballerina sitting in seiza position, head bowed, her right hand touching the floor, her left arm reaching for the sky. She remains there, still. Another spot glows upon the center of the stage, illuminating one of her leg braces, standing straight up as if suspended. Placed in the top of it is a bouquet of pink roses. A third, dimmer spot comes upon Cathy and Marcy seated at the right edge of the stage, Cathy with a baritone guitar. They perform *Save One Wish for You* to Sonya's dance.

> If I could fly I would,
> Spread my wings and soar across
> The mountains and the sea.
> All the birds would look at me
> And I'd be flying free.

Sonya rises, both arms floating in the air, her face raised to the heavens, radiant, and she begins twirling slowly, like a gentle breeze. She wears a flowing silk dress, mother of pearl in its luminescence, with blue and green and purple brush strokes top to bottom as if a rainbow spilled upon her dance. She spins, a graceful, small eddy, and in the movement circles the brace.

> If I could jump so high
> As the cow I saw above the Moon,
> Chasing stars and spoons,
> Make the children laugh and play
> And have a happy day.

Melody and Noelle run waist high in green spring grass, the Virgin flowing nearby. A bright, warm Sun shines upon them and they shine back, joy and celebration pouring from their laughter.

> One wish, two, I have for you,
> Wish number three is just for me.
> Wish number four for my friends next door,
> Wishes left over when you need some more.

Sonya kneels before the brace and bows, then rises and takes one rose from it. With that pink flowered wand, she dances free, touching every other rose with it, each in turn.

> If I could paint the sky,
> Hold my brushes in my hand,
> Once again I'd fly,
> Paint the wishes I could see
> Swirling in the breeze.

Noelle takes Melody's hand as they run, and swings her in a wide circle of freedom. Melody takes her other hand and they lean back as they circle, beaming smiles toward the hidden stars.

> If I could close my eyes,
> Drift into the colors
> That I painted once before,
> Know that wishes do come true,
> And I'd save one for you.

Sonya takes her rose and throws it to the audience, and in her dance returns to the brace and takes one rose at a time, throwing each to outstretched hands.

> One wish, two, I have for you,
> Wish number three is just for me.

Wish number four for my friends next door,
Wishes left over when you need some more.

One wish, two, I have for you,
Wish number three is just for me.
Wish number four for my friends next door,
Wishes left over when you need some more.

Sonya finishes by returning to where she started, her arms and face again raised high, and like a bloom closing in the night, folds down to her starting pose.

The lights go dark as the song ends, and the screen illuminates behind, displaying a view from the capsule toward Earth, now too large to be seen entirely, and bringing a sigh from the audience. The Earth dissolves to a shot, from inside the capsule, of the cover of the Book. The cover takes up the entire screen, Tom's hand resting upon it.

On the face of the Book are simple drawings of constellations with a warrior standing amidst them, shooting an arrow upward. The colors are muted, made from berries and leaves and dirt, faded over generations.

Tom's voice wavers through space and atmosphere. "This is the Legend of Skyeyes."

Tom's hand carefully turns the cover to reveal a page of weathered deerskin with faded figures: two mountains, each with a sun in different positions. Between them are people, above them the figure of a child with stars for eyes, and beside him a wolf with his mouth open, as if speaking.

"In the time of the ancestors of the Anasasi, God, who was called Tobats, was angry with his people because they did not believe he would give them what they needed as they traveled from the Land of the Setting Sun to the Land of the Rising Sun. He sent Shinoh, his son, to them, and Shinoh took the stars from the night, the stars that guided the ancestors in their journey, and threw them into the eyes of the Son of Tureris, who he named the Child of Skyeyes. Tureris had shot the Arrow of Fire into the Land of the

Stars to lead the way, but now the old stars were hidden, and the people did not know where to go, because they did not know the new stars. So Shinoh became a wolf, and he took the Child of Skyeyes to himself, and said to the people that when they found how to save the Child, they would have him, and the stars in his eyes would guide them to the Land of the Rising Sun. But he said also that only the very old or the very young could speak to him, for only they could know the truth. 'When you are ready to speak,' said Shinoh, 'walk toward the setting Sun, and I will set a tree afire to purify your heart.' So it was that the Book began, and the people would look for a sign in the stars, and then talk to the Wolf in the hope of freeing the Child."

Tom turns the skin over to reveal on its back another drawing. It also has similar figures of the lands, and of the Child and Wolf, with the Wolf's paw across the Child. Also in the drawing are many warriors fighting, many warriors dead, and blood running. At the top of the page is a large star in the center of a constellation.

"The first sign came after many flesh of the flesh, and it came upon an old man named Eagle's Nest who saw in the new stars the shape of an Eagle, and in it, a bright star that had never been seen before. So he gave the Book to his son, Parunuweap, and told him to please the Wolf. His son became a great warrior and fought all the tribes in the lands, and he killed many and took all the lands. At the end of his days, he went to the burning trees and brought to the Wolf the beads of many dead warriors, and also many treasures from all the lands he had taken. 'All this I have done to show how mighty my people are, and to give you all the lands, and the treasures of all the people,' said Parunuweap. But the Wolf spoke and said, 'I am not pleased, old one. Not all the lands or all the treasures will save the Child of Skyeyes, for he has no need of them.' So Parunuweap left without the Child."

Tom moves the Book to the opposite page. There, in the center, people hold hands and exchange baskets. At the top there is a figure of a black Sun, and next to it a star.

"Again many people of the people passed, many generations, until a great chief, Red Bird, had a son, and on the day the boy was born, the Sun in the sky turned black, and when the blackness came, Red Bird saw stars in the daytime, so he called his child Star of Day. And he gave the Book to Star of Day, who made peace with all the tribes and became their leader. All the tribes lived in peace during his lifetime and multiplied greatly. They hunted well and had much corn. And at the end of his days, he went to the burning trees, and to the Wolf he brought branches of peace, and a basket of corn and a basket of meat. 'I have made peace in all the land, and all the tribes are my brothers. I bring to you the peace of my people,' said Star of Day. But the Wolf said, 'I am not pleased, old one. This peace is only among your people. It is not the peace of the People of the Stars, and your tribes will war again. This peace will not save the Child.' So Star of Day left without the Child of Skyeyes."

Tom turns the page over. This one has at the top a rock on fire, great pueblos, and in the center of the largest pueblo, an image of the Wolf with people kneeling before it. At the bottom, the Wolf holds back the Child.

"This time was the longest time between people with no sign, until the fifth passing of the children of Star of Day when there was born one called Snake of Fire. When he was born, a snake crawled into the fire that heated the knife his mother used to cut him from her, and the snake watched her as it burned. Her husband, a great warrior, had died of fire, and told her before his spirit left that his son would be born of fire. Because of this, she knew her son would speak to the Wolf. When Snake of Fire grew, a flaming star fell to the Earth and the Earth shook, and the pueblos they had built fell to the ground, and many died. So Snake of Fire had the people build a great pueblo to honor the Wolf, and for many years they built it, with much hardship. When it was finished, Snake of Fire made from stone an image of the Wolf and placed it in the center, and all the people came and laid on the ground to the Wolf's image, and before it burned a fire that never went out. At the end of his days, Snake of Fire went to the burning trees, carrying a torch from the eternal fire, and laid it under the burning trees. He told the Wolf of the great pueblo, and brought a likeness of the wolf that everyone worshipped. 'All the people of the lands, from the edge of the world to the canyons of the sky, worship Shinoh, and sacrifice the white deer to honor him,' said Snake of Fire. But the Wolf said, 'I am not pleased, old one. The wolf of stone has no heart, and without a heart, there is no spirit. The pueblo shall fall, and the fire shall burn out, and they will not save the Child of Skyeyes.' So Snake of Fire went away."

Children around the world watch the Book, hearing the stories. Mothers and fathers, grandparents and great-grandparents, old and young, watch and listen as pages turn and strange figures appear.

Tom moves one more time to a page on the right. At the top are figures of clouds, lightning, and rain, but in the center of the clouds is a hole, and in the hole, stars. At the bottom is the Wolf again, this time with a river curving by him, with people digging near it building dams and levees.

"And in the time of the people just before our people, there lived an old woman whose husband had died, a woman who had no children. Her husband left her the Book, but there was no child for her to pass it to. She cried every day and every night, and she cried so much that tears began to fall from the sky. It rained every day and every night, and the land was flooded with tears from the sky. She prayed that God would stop the tears because she thought he was crying for her. Then one night as she was about to throw the Book into the waters, a break appeared in the clouds above, and in it she saw the new stars that had been called Tureris, because they looked like a bow and an arrow of fire. At that moment, she heard a baby cry, and when she went to it, found it alone in a tree, because its mother had put it there before she drowned in the waters of tears. So she called the baby Crying Rain, and when he grew up, Crying Rain said that he would bring the waters to the Wolf, so that he could drink forever of the tears of God. Many years all the people used their tools and their great knowledge, and they turned the river, and changed its course until it flowed by the burning trees. At the end of his days, Crying Rain came to the Wolf and showed him what they had done. 'We have conquered the land, and changed the course of the great river. We have brought you the Tears of God, for you to drink of forever,' he said. But the Wolf said, 'I am not pleased, Crying Rain. Your people have done great works, but the Wolf does not drink of the water of this river, but drinks of the Water of the Spirit. This will not save the Child of Skyeyes. But I tell you this. I have grown weary, and will wait not much longer. Your people will be scattered across the Four Winds. The end is coming, and the Book will be closed.'"

At this, Tom takes hold of the page, but hesitates in turning it, his hand trembling. Finally, he does turn it, and on the back appear similar drawings, more like that of a child. It is not old like the others and the figures are in crayon color. Although many of the figures are the same, at the top is a star with a trail behind it. In the center is a flaming arrow and a rocket that points to a red butterfly. From underneath stream many colors. Beside it is a drawing of the Moon, and just above it sits a constellation whose stars form a wolf looking down. At the bottom is a child's eye with blue sky and clouds inside.

Melody kneels before the TV, only a few feet away. As the glow from the picture bathes her face, she reaches out and touches the screen.

"The people were scattered across the winds, but the great-great-grandchild of Crying Rain, Sunman Whitewater, kept the Book. One night, as he was very old and lay dying, he looked up at the night sky in his beloved land, Ioogoone. His daughter was there, and his little grandson who was also dying. Sunman was heartbroken because his grandson had not been given a name of his people. The grandson looked up at the heavens and saw a bright star with a long trail of stardust flying behind it, and he pointed to it and said, 'Grandfather, look!' Just then a butterfly landed on his outstretched hand. Butterflies, in the language of the ancestors, are called Spirit Set Free. So he said to his grandson, 'You shall be called Little Spirit Set Free."

Francine and Bud watch. She dabs her eyes with a tissue.

"'This is my sign. It is the Star That Runs. You shall go to the stars and bring the Book to the Wolf, Shinoh, and the Child of Skyeyes will be free.' After he said this, Sunman died. And not long after, Little Spirit Set Free died also. Little Spirit took the Book and he went to the Wolf, but he said nothing. The Wolf looked at him and said, 'Little Spirit, I am pleased, for it has always been known that only a child can save a child. Only those things pure of spirit can save the pure spirit. That which is the Ancient of Days is just born, and that which is just born, has always been. You are the Child of Skyeyes. It is your true spirit I have kept for you, all the years gone by.'

"So the Wolf went into the sky, and when he did the new stars passed away, and he became a new constellation in the old heavens. Little Spirit became one with his true spirit, then went into the sky, and his eyes became stars in the old sky. And when Little Spirit went up, he took the stardust from the Star That Runs, and sprinkled it down upon the people. All the people saw that the stars they knew had returned, but they also saw the Wolf and Skyeyes, so they followed them, and found the Land of the Rising Sun."

With this, Tom closes the Book. On the back cover is a drawing of the Star That Runs.

The Sun is about to rise as Isabel stands at the stern, watching the wake when there's a shipwide announcement. "Attention ladies, gentlemen, and children. This is Captain Wright. Sorry to wake you so early, but your presence is requested as soon as possible on the starboard side, above decks.

Isabel looks around, as do a few other early risers who turn to stare at the speakers, then off the starboard side.

The Earth looms ahead of the capsule, the deep blue of the Pacific sparkling against the Western coast of Mexico. Explosive bolts discharge at points around the perimeter, and the service module jettisons, drifting away as the capsule rotates.

Melody is sleeping, but not for long as Noelle bursts in the room, barely put together, waking her up. Melody looks at her smiling face.

Tom straps himself into the seat and plants Zion forcefully into his lap. The cat looks up, worried.

Passengers are appearing on the starboard deck, looking

confused.

The unused retro package is jettisoned, exposing the heat shield. After a moment, the capsule angles to reentry alignment.

Bud is sleeping on the couch when the phone rings. Not sure whether to answer, he looks toward the bedroom and Francine appears in her Pepe Le Pew pj's.

The capsule jolts as it encounters the Earth's atmosphere and shakes as G forces build.

Those toward the bow notice the helicopter has fired up and lifts off the deck, heading out to sea. Hanging outside the open door are flippered legs in wetsuits.

Flames coming off the heat shield lick the rim of the capsule. G forces bury Tom into the seat, and Zion into him. The capsule vibrates as a profuse sweat runs down Tom's pressed face, Zion's eyes shut tight and his ears flat against his head.

Kirshner stands in the control room watching the path projector as it bends toward a spot in the Pacific Ocean. After checking data, he looks up at his monitor, showing a hand-held camera image of the skies above the ship.

Passengers on the ship stand next to the cameraman, looking in the direction he's scanning. Suddenly they point wildly toward the sky and he, after looking in that direction, aims the camera. First a colored pinpoint, the capsule appears with its triple array of striped parachutes.

Noelle and Melody watch. Noelle claps and Melody stands as they watch the capsule swing peacefully down.

Francine and Bud watch the image of the capsule splashing into the water. The chopper arrives, hovering over it, and the capsule hatch pops open. Tears of relief stream down Francine's face. Bud raises his fist. "Yes!"

The helicopter lands on the ship's bow and Tom jumps out with Zion in his arms, Isabel standing close by. She walks up and throws her arms around his neck as a formation of military jets performs a low pass across the ship.

Melody sits in a chair on Driftwood Beach, a small sandy bank a few feet from the Virgin River. It's a secluded shelter, accessible through a wooden gate in a split-rail fence behind the motel. A grand tree frames the river, two trunks diverging from a single root, one blossoming a canopy of leafy branches over the beach, the other boldly arching over the river, a rustic bridge for those who float under on slowly spinning tubes.

Melody looks across the river, blinking at sunlight that flickers through branches as they wave in the breeze. And she sings, in the solitude of her thoughts, the song she heard in Noah's room the day Mr. Holmes brought her there.

She remembers it was a mild afternoon, a light wind flowing from the canyon in spring. The Sun weighed low on the horizon, large and orange, and spread a gossamer glow over the Shack. Marcy was there with her guitar and the Noah House children, standing outside the window of Noah's room.

Mr. Holmes held Theo and the Book, and he led Melody up the stairs to the verandah. They stopped there to admire the distant canyon skyline, then entered and went to Noah's room. The door was still open from the time he left to fly to the Moon, and they walked quietly into the darkness, but this was no longer a tomb of sorrows. Noah's father went to the window, parted the starry curtains, and opened it, letting in the light of the fading world, and bathing the room in the velvet radiance of sunset.

He walked over to the dresser as Marcy and the children sang the song outside, the words drifting into the open window with the breeze, the song about wishes for tomorrow and the dreams of those who've passed this way. Mr. Holmes stopped, looked at Melody, and with certain peace, placed Theo and the Book back on the dresser. Then Melody, with the grateful heart of a healed child, touched her lips, and placed the kiss upon Noah's smile, shining at her from the picture.

Melody dwells upon this memory and tenderly turns the pages of a picture album laying on her lap. She touches each of her three favorite pictures as she admires them, the song in her thoughts warming her recollections:

> As the shadows fall, and the daylight fades,
> And the Moon rises high in the blue,
> When the night rolls over the misty glade
> It's a wish for tomorrow and you.

Tom and Zion sit on the ship's deck alone, facing outward to a setting Sun.

> Here's a wish for tomorrow, with the hope of today,
> And the dreams of the past ones who've walked this way.
> We will sing each new day's awakening,
> And we'll see what tomorrow brings.

Francine and Bud sit on the porch at the Shack, smiling. Harriet stands behind, her hand on Igloo's head, watching them with a smile also.

> As the Sun draws near from its hideaway
> And the silver begins to shine through,
> When the songbirds carry the night away,

It's a wish for tomorrow and you.

Noelle and Sid stand at the altar, with Melody as Maid of Honor, and adopted daughter.

Here's a wish for tomorrow, with the hope of today,
And the dreams of the past ones who've walked this way.
We will sing each new day's awakening,
And we'll see what tomorrow brings.

We will sing each new day's awakening,
And we'll see what tomorrow brings.

And he shall go to the stars

www.SkyeyesNovel.com

Earthset Press is committed to donating a portion of each copy of Skyeyes purchased online from www.SkyeyesNovel.com to children's charities.

We encourage and are grateful for any personal donations by readers to these organizations, or to any other that dedicates itself to the furthurance of children's rights around the world, and to providing them care, food and guidance.

ACKNOWLEDGMENTS

Every writer has his or her "scripture" of inspiration and guidance, mine being Rebecca McClanahan's *Word Painting*. (Writer's Digest Books.) Her insight into the art of description brought me to the threshold of storytelling's kingdom, and through her magic eyes I learned my voice, I learned what to say, and, of course, what not to say. The extent to which I followed her guidance is the extent to which I produced effective prose. It is no coincidence that within her wonderful book, most of the examples she presents of truly gifted word painting come from the pens, pencils, and crayons, of child authors and poets.

To Grammy nominees Marcy and Cathy, thank you for lending the poetry of your lyrics to this story, as well as your personas. Your tireless endeavors toward bringing joy to children and fostering their growth through song are a tribute to the essence of what this tale professes. Your music brought that joy to my children since they were born, and to me as well. It's my sincerest hope that this book affords you increased success, exposure, and notoriety, all of which you deserve.

My gratitude to Scott Penza and his team at The Creative Hive for their encouragement, support and enthusiasm for both the message of this story, and its development, without which an endeavor such as this would approach the impossible.

Thank you to Jessica Keets, the "Proofreader's Proofreader", for sparing me from pitfalls and potholes through your keen eyes and sharp red pen, and also to Jim Devney for your astute edit and kind words.

Marv Walsh and Arnold Scmidt of Arvato Services have displayed the collective patience of saints in dealing with the minute and tiresome details involved with printing this product. Through their efforts, Skyeyes was born to the world in a form I believe to be as significant as its content. This is a presentation for which I am not only grateful, but, as an aficionado of book packaging myself, enthralled. They represent the highest pinnacle of professionalism available in the book printing business, as does their firm. Beyond that, Marv's enthusiasm for Skyeyes has meant the world to me.

I am grateful as well to Mike Gentry at the Johnson Space Center for his assistance, and to Mary Ann Hager at the Lunar Planetary Institute for her generous help in obtaining the spectacular images placed on the cover of this book.

The Paiute legends in Skyeyes were derived from several existing legends. *Why the North Star Stands Still, and Other Indian Legends* by William R. Palmer, a Zion Natural History Association publication, was most helpful in researching the rich folklore of our Native Americans.

Finally, above all, to my three children, who taught me the joy of being a father, without which I could never have breached the subject of Tom Holmes' loss. Their shining has illuminated my life and shown me the essence of my short mission on this fragile planet. They taught me what love means through their innocence and their faith, and inspired me to fashion this story of hope, of miracles, and most importantly, of divine hands upon my own life. God bless you, forever.

ABOUT THE AUTHOR

Edward Es is a commercial airline Captain. He graduated from UCLA in Motion Pictures with a writing specialization, and obtained his Juris Doctor in 1996. Edward was an operative assistant to the President of the Warner\Columbia motion picture facility for seven years, and from there became a recording engineer. In 1985, he pursued his lifetime ambition to fly airliners, and here, with Skyeyes, has manifested what he always believed to be his true calling.

CREDITS

Lyrics included in this novel by title, writer and publisher:

Beautiful Day: Gary Rosen; Tiny Toes Music
Time to Sleep: Marcy Marxer; 2 Spoons Music
Heaven: Julie Gold; Cherry Lane Music
How Can I Keep from Singing: Traditional; Public domain
Children of the Living God: Fernando Ortega; Izzy Sol Songs
Ride 'em High: Marcy Marxer; 2 Spoons Music
All Around the World: Cathy Fink; 2 Spoons Music
Save One Wish for You: Cathy Fink; 2 Spoons Music
Wish For Tomorrow: Marcy Marxer; 2 Spoons Music
Where applicable, all rights reserved; reprinted by permission of the publishers.

Cover Art:
Moon Image: Alfred Worden; Apollo 15
Earth Image: Apollo 13
Author's photo: Noel Schwab
Additional photography: Audrey Dempsey
Graphics: Bob Dempsey, Dempsey Graphics; Edward Es
Cover design: Edward Es

Interior:
Poetry:
Page 3; Emily Dickinson
Page 381: Edward Lear (Drawings by Edward Lear)
Photos:
Chapter 1-Chapter 4: Andrei Belogortseff
www.amber-inn.com
Chapter 5: Michael Reichmann
www.luminous-landscape.com

TO PURCHASE MUSIC INCLUDED IN SKYEYES, VISIT THESE WEBSITES:

http://www.cathymarcy.com/catelog/index.html

http://www.fernandoortega.com/

THE OWL AND THE PUSSYCAT

I

The Owl and the Pussy-cat went to sea
  In a beautiful pea green boat,
They took some honey, and plenty of
money,
  Wrapped up in a five pound note.
The Owl looked up to the stars above,
  And sang to a small guitar,
'O lovely Pussy! O Pussy my love,
  What a beautiful Pussy you are,
    You are,
    You are!
What a beautiful Pussy you are!'

II
Pussy said to the Owl, 'You elegant fowl!
    How charmingly sweet you sing!
O let us be married! Too long we have tarried:
    But what shall we do for a ring?'
They sailed away, for a year and a day,
    To the land where the Bong-tree grows
And there in a wood a Piggy-wig stood
    With a ring at the end of his nose,
        His nose,
        His nose,
With a ring at the end of his nose.

III

'Dear pig, are you willing to sell for one shilling
  Your ring?' Said the Piggy, 'I will.'
So they took it away, and were married next day
  By the Turkey who lives on the hill.
They dined on mince, and slices of quince,
  Which they ate with a runcible spoon;
And hand in hand, on the edge of the sand,
  They danced by the light of the moon,
    The moon,
    The moon,
They danced by the light of the moon.

Edward Lear
The Complete Book of Nonsense